Justin D. Fulton

Rome in America

Justin D. Fulton

Rome in America

ISBN/EAN: 9783337383466

Printed in Europe, USA, Canada, Australia, Japan

Cover: Foto ©Andreas Hilbeck / pixelio.de

More available books at **www.hansebooks.com**

ROME IN AMERICA.

BY

JUSTIN D. FULTON, D.D.

WITH A SKETCH OF THE AUTHOR

BY

REV. R. S. MACARTHUR, D.D.,

PASTOR OF THE CALVARY BAPTIST CHURCH, N. Y.

*" The only country in the world to-day where I am really Pope is the
United States of America."*—PIUS IX.

THE PAULINE PROPAGANDA:

HOWARD GANNETT, SECRETARY,

TREMONT TEMPLE, BOSTON.

1887.

TO

THE LOVERS AND DEFENDERS

OF EDUCATION, OF LIBERTY, AND OF TRUTH,

WHO BELIEVE IN THE CHAMPIONSHIP

OF AN OPEN BIBLE,

AND IN FIGHTING THE GOOD FIGHT OF FAITH,

UNTIL VICTORY PERCHES UPON THE BANNERS OF IMMANUEL,

THIS BOOK IS RESPECTFULLY DEDICATED.

PREFACE.

In Motley's History of the United Netherlands there is a picture which Americans should study.

William the Silent, Prince of Orange, had been murdered on the 10th of July, 1584. The disaster was apparently universal. " Habit, necessity, and the natural gifts of the man had combined to invest him at last with an authority which seemed more than human. There was such general confidence in his sagacity, courage, and purity, that the nation had come to think with his brain and to act with his hand !" He was dead. The cause remained.

Under the rule of his enemy, Philip II., a small, dull, elderly, imperfectly educated, patient, plodding invalid, with white hair and protruding under-jaw and dreary visage, were America, the East Indies, the whole Spanish Peninsula, the better portion of Italy, the seventeen Netherlands, and many other possessions, far and near, and he contemplated annexing to this extensive property the kingdoms of France, of England and Ireland. There was a country which believed in the absolute power of the Church to dictate the relations between man and his Maker, and to utterly exterminate all who disputed that position. There was another country which protested against that doctrine, and claimed theoretically or practically liberty of conscience. Three centuries have nearly passed since this memorable epoch, and the world knows the fate of the states which accepted the dogma which it was Philip's life-work to enforce, and of those who protested against the system.

France, Prussia, the Dutch Commonwealth, the British Empire, and the United States of America are the foremost nations of the world ; the nations cursed by Romanism are among the weakest.

It is ours to save America to the future, and as a means, however small, this book is sent forth.

J. D. F.

CONTENTS.

SKETCH OF THE AUTHOR'S LIFE.

BY

Rev. Robert S. MacArthur, D.D.

Pastor of Calvary Baptist Church, New York.

Almost at the hour of this writing, great meetings are holding in several languages and countries to commemorate the wonderful life and work of Martin Luther. Again the story is told of "the lone monk who shook the world," and the hearts of Protestants the world over are catching the inspiration of the hour. The story cannot be told too often. It is well that the brave man of the sixteenth century be brought out of the gathering mists of the past, into the clear light of this busy and practical nineteenth century. Luther is entitled to all the honor which the celebration of the four hundredth anniversary of his birth may bestow. Great nations will join hands across the seas as they gather about Luther's cradle. Luther was not the great theologian of the Reformation; Calvin was that. Luther was not even the great theologian of Germany; Melanchthon was that. Zwingli also has his place among the great thinkers and writers of that period. Luther understood most thoroughly his own place and work in that great movement. He described his work when he said he was " born to tear up the stumps and dead roots, to cut away the thorns, and to act as a rough forester and pioneer." One of our religious newspapers quotes Dr. Julius Köstlin's interpretation of Luther's name; it is claimed that originally it was Luder, also Ludher and Leuder. "The present form we first find proceeding from Luther himself, after he had become a professor at Wittenberg, before he

entered on his Reformation controversies, and from him
first the other branches of the family adopted it. The
name is equivalent to Lothar, which, according to its
etymology, means one who is distinguished as a
leader." Luther was worthy of his name. He was
the great popular leader of that great movement.
Neither Melanchthon, Calvin, Zwingli, nor any other
man of that day could have filled that place. Without
him there might never have been a Reformation. In
him was a wonderful combination of great qualities.
His task was gigantic ; he was a giant. For this leader
of men the world does well to-day to thank God.

But Luther carried with him into Protestantism too
much of Romanism. Perhaps this was inevitable ; it
is, however, none the less hurtful. The old conflict
rages still. If ever a series of sermons against Romanism was opportune, this series by Dr. Fulton seems
to be. Not all men can serve the truth in this way.
For many reasons this writer could not. Therefore he
ought not to make the attempt. God gives " to every
man his work." One fells the trees ; another sows
the seed ; a third reaps the golden grain. Martin
Luther had his work ; Erasmus, Calvin, no one else,
could do it. Justin D. Fulton feels himself called to
this form of defending the truth. " To every man
his work." In his broad sympathy, tireless energy,
tender affection, rich humor, sometimes severe fidelity,
intense convictions and brave, bold utterance, Dr.
Fulton is not unlike Luther. Like the great leader,
Dr. Fulton kindles other souls with the flame of his
burning zeal ; like him he considers that he cannot
remain silent, but must speak and act, because moved
upon by a divine energy. Out of these convictions has
come this volume. Into the glowing enthusiasm of
this Lutheran anniversary period it enters, telling again
of the old enemy, and suggesting, as the means of
victory, the word and Christ of God.

Another influence prepares for the reception of this
volume. Rome has recently sent among us at least two

able, artful, and insinuating men, to win Americans to
the dogmas of the Romish Church. Rome has always
shown wisdom in the choice she makes of the men who
do her work. One of these men, at least, was chosen,
doubtless, with much deliberation. He came here
confessedly to make converts to his Church. His plans
were carefully devised. His approach was industriously
heralded. His addresses were skilfully prepared, carefully delivered, and widely reported. Dr. Fulton
boldly confronted this man. Many of us doubted his
wisdom, even though we admired his bravery. It is
claimed, however, that numerous and important results justify the course he pursued. Of that this writer
need not speak. To his own Master, Dr. Fulton
standeth or falleth. Certain it is that the influence of
this foreigner, from whatever cause, is much less than
Protestants feared, and than Romanists hoped. Let us
march into the coming conflict, as Luther went to the
diet at Worms, singing, "Ein feste burg ist unser
Gott." Let us stand beside him, as he stood there,
while each with him shall say : " I neither can nor dare
retract anything, unless convinced by reason and
Scripture; my conscience is captive to God's word.
There I take my stand. I cannot do otherwise. So
help me, God. Amen !"

Readers to-day, more than in any former time, desire
to know something of the personal life of the authors
whose books they read. In harmony with that desire,
this sketch is prepared.

BIRTH AND YOUTH.*

The Rev. Justin D. Fulton, D.D., was born in
Earlville, Madison County, N. Y., March 1st, 1828.
His father, Rev. John J. Fulton, was descended from
North of Ireland stock, and his mother, Clarissa

* For some of the following facts I am indebted to the sketch in
the "Contemporary Biography," New York, but many other
facts appear for the first time.—R. S. M.

Dewey Fulton, found a birthplace in Great Barring-
ton, Berkshire County, Massachusetts, and was heir to
many of the shining qualities of the Puritan element.
In 1836 he removed with his parents to Brooklyn,
Michigan, and at the age of eleven united with the
Baptist Church.

Ministers in Michigan, as a rule, were poor, and the
father of the subject of this sketch was not an exception. He offered his son his time, but could not
promise him other help. When eighteen years of
age, the son, who up to this time had studied as best
he could when not employed on the farm, hung up
the harness one night, and on not taking it down next
morning was asked the reason why. " Am going to
college !" " How ?" " Don't know, but I start this
morning.'' At once he began preparations, and in
the fall of 1847 entered the University of Michigan
and remained there three years, paying his way by
working for his board during term-time and by selling
books in vacation. At once he took a foremost position. In his Junior year he was elected president of
the college literary society, an honor generally reserved
for students of the Senior Class. In his fourth year
he entered the University of Rochester, that he might
take Hebrew and be ready to enter the Theological
Seminary in advance. He was graduated from the
University of Rochester in 1851, and, entering the
Theological Seminary, he remained through a part of
the second year, when, urged by the Rev. Spencer H.
Cone, D.D., and William H. Wyckoff, LL.D., to
take charge of a Bible Union paper in St. Louis, Mo.,
he went there in December, 1853. The paper sprang
into a large circulation.

Then he began the publication in the paper of the
" Roman Catholic Element in American History.''
His attention had been called to the fearful character
of the Papacy by reading, when a young man, John
Dowling's " History of Romanism.'' In 1852 the
terrible persecution of the Madiai family in Italy

arrested public attention. A public meeting had been called in New York to sympathize with the persecuted and oppressed of Italy. The eloquent Drs. Bethune, Hague, and others had spoken in such a marvellous way and with such burning words of sympathy for the oppressed that the heart of the student caught fire.

Kossuth had swept through the land like a blazing meteor. The downtrodden were described by him; their woes were painted in colors of living light. All this inflamed the heart of the young student. He spoke in the Literary Society in such a way that general attention was attracted to him, and when Archbishop Hughes defended persecution, the students framed a paper asking him to read in public a reply to the lecture of John Hughes, Archbishop of New York. This started him on the investigations which resulted in the book already mentioned. In St. Louis he found a city given up to the idolatry of Rome. A description of its condition is given in "The Way Out," a book published by The American Baptist Publication Society, descriptive of the life he led, and of some of the work achieved while in the great Western gateway. In the introduction to that book he avows his faith in this strong language :

"This is God's world, and they are cowards who sit idly by and refuse to work, under the conviction that Satan is to have it and that Rome is to rule it. It is needful that the people of our land pluck up courage and be faithful to the trust reposed in them, their liberties to defend, and their Bibles to preserve, that their children may be saved from the degrading influences of supersition and converted to the service of God and made useful to their country."

The city of St. Louis, he saw, was a Romish town. The press, the wealth, the social power, all sided with Rome. It was profitable in a business point of view to bow the knee to Baal. It was hazardous to stand up for God. It is not difficult to see in the Edward Hervey of the book the Justin D. Fulton of the world.

His "Roman Catholic Element in American History" at once arrested attention and excited opposition. Its ringing words called attention to the man, and twenty-four men and women meeting in Biddle Market Hall, having had their attention directed to him, invited him to preach for them.

It was to him a providential call. Up to this time as a preacher he had never been a success. In college and in the Theological Seminary he was seldom asked to supply a pulpit, and when he did so his efforts gave little promise of his subsequent career. He loved to preach. He tried to preach, but the characteristics which made him a success as an editor interfered with his success as a minister. He was bold, radical, and outspoken. The young editor had given himself to the ministry years before, providing God opened the way. Now that the door was opened he entered it with avidity. The committee in charge of the paper objected to the arrangement. The editor replied, "I believe that I am called to preach the Gospel. If editing your paper interferes with this duty, I can give up the paper, but I will not give up the ministry." He began to preach with great acceptance to the people and with unalloyed pleasure for himself. At once he struck Romanism hard blows in the pulpit. It cost him dear. In 1854 the Know-Nothing riot came. His life was threatened. His position on Romanism, which he pictured as an intolerable despotism, gave him the sympathy of very many of the people. The true and the tried stood together in the town. In 1855 the church became so large and the paper so important that Rev. James Inglis, of Detroit, came and took the pastorate of the church, becoming assistant editor of the paper, while the editor of the paper remained associate pastor of the church. This was in April. In May, at Palmyra, Missouri, the stockholders of the paper met, and it was resolved "that it is not enough that the editor of the *Gospel Banner* be a gentleman and a Christian ; he must be-

lieve that slavery is right *per se*, and defend 1.." One
man, born in New Hampshire, voted for the resolution ; no one voted against it, and the resignation of
the editor was offered and accepted. The committee
in charge of the paper lived in St. Louis. The editor-
elect, in his first issue, made an attack upon the man
who built up the paper ; the committee saw it, stopped
the press, confiscated all published, and never permitted an issue of the *Gospel Banner* under the new
régime. The turning point in the life of the editor
was reached. Years before he had vowed that he
would preach if God would open the way. Now in-
vitations to enter one of the most successful law firms
of St. Louis, and to become the literary editor of one
of the brightest daily papers in the city, were received.
For six hours, while stripped of property, this young
man kept in his room questioning what he should do.
The vow made years before under the shade of an oak
tree came to his memory. He declined the offers, and,
almost penniless, turned his back on this city of his
love, accepted the invitation of his brother, Dr. S. J.
Fulton, then residing in Toledo, Ohio, to make his
house his home until he had prepared for the press
"The Roman Catholic Element in American Ilis-
tory," and while engaged in this work received an invitation to supply the pulpit in Sandusky, Ohio. The
result was a call to the church and the securing of a
helpmeet in the person of Miss Sarah E. Norcross, who
for twenty-seven years was the companion of his life
and the mother of his four children. In Ohio he
worked like a Titan ; six churches in the Huron
Association were revived under his leadership, and the
church in Sandusky passed from feebleness to
strength. Because of the lake winds he lost his voice,
and this compelled his removal to Albany, N. Y.,
where in 1859 he became pastor of the Tabernacle
Church and spent the ensuing four years in a very
successful ministry. In December, 1863, he was for
the third time invited to the charge of the Tremont

Temple congregation in Boston, Mass., and the church
having complied with his conditions, he accepted their
invitation, and labored in this field nearly ten years.
His success in Boston was immediate and its results
wonderful. The Union Temple Church was formed
by selecting twenty-five members from the Union and
Tremont Temple churches. The union was blessed of
God. During his ministry the membership increased
to upward of a thousand, and the income reached
twenty-three thousand dollars. He was a universally
recognized force in the ministry. He always felt and
acknowledged that he was under great obligations to
the brethren of large plan, fervid piety, and devoted
zeal, who labored instant in season and out of season to
make the enterprise a success. The Temple, where
the services were held, is centrally located, and is one
of the best known buildings, as it is one of the most
popular places of resort in the city. Its Sunday
services drew crowds anxious to hear Dr. Fulton's
fervid utterances, and the fame of the pastor as an
eloquent and stirring preacher of the Gospel to the
people extended far and wide. Few strangers ever
remained any length of time in Boston without paying
at least a single visit to the Temple.

Here, as in Sandusky and as in Albany, he took a
prominent position in exposing the errors of Romanism, and in striving to bring Romanists to accept of
the offer of salvation. His success deserves to be
studied. There are those who seem afraid to agitate
this question of Romanism lest in some way an unpleasant feeling be engendered in the community.
Dr. Fulton's experience is the reverse of this. Father
Hecker, the Paulist priest, came to Boston and lectured before large audiences, claiming that this country
was soon to be under the rule of Rome. His figures
and his presumption made a strong impression upon
the community. Dr. Fulton preached the sermon,
"Romanism a Plague, if not a Peril." The effect
was instantaneous. The boasted pretensions of the

priest were exploded, and it became one of the sayings of the town, heard on horse-cars, in hotels, everywhere : " Bah ! *Romanism is a plague, not a peril.*" The sermon was printed by the American Tract Society, and very large editions were scattered broadcast over the land. Ten or twelve sermons followed. Priests and their followers came to curse, and some of them went away to pray. As a result, many of his warmest friends in Boston are Roman Catholics.

In 1873 Dr. Fulton came to Brooklyn, N. Y., to build a People's Church, and after many years of toil enjoys the support and confidence of a church where to the fullest extent it is possible to carry out the beneficent scheme he has always cherished in his heart, of preaching the Gospel to the people without regard to class or condition. Brooklyn, with its population of nearly six hundred thousand souls, is essentially a city of the people, and in it is an admirable opportunity for doing this work. Dr. Fulton brought to the undertaking a ripe experience and a settled purpose. He entered upon it with all the force and vigor of a healthy manhood, a strong will, and a heart warmly responding to the popular need. Had he been a weaker man physically he might have found it an arduous labor. As it was, possessing a magnificent physique, it afforded him delightful exercise in which the yearnings of his heart found the happiest realization. The movement bore the stamp of the man from the outset.

It partook, in a degree, of the magnetism of its originator, and evinced a vitality which showed it was destined to wrestle successfully with all obstacles, and live, increasing in usefulness with time, and honestly and ably aiding in religion's holy work. The Brooklyn Temple, a fine brick structure two hundred feet in length and one hundred and thirty-two feet in width, originally built at a cost of one hundred and twenty-seven thousand dollars, is the home of this now flourishing congregation. All classes are welcome to its

spacious audience-room. It is well lighted and venti-
lated, and in every way admirably arranged for the
purposes to which it is devoted, having, beside the
main audience-room, Sunday-school, vestry, and com-
mittee-rooms. Into the work of founding this People's Church Dr. Fulton threw his whole soul. It
was with him a labor of love in the highest, purest
sense ; his sympathy, always with the people, found a
delightful exercise in providing for their spiritual needs,
and in furnishing them an ideal Christian church—one
to which the humblest might come, "without money
and without price," and learn the beautiful truths of
the Gospel. It may be said of Dr. Fulton that in the
few years he has been in Brooklyn he has actually
created a church second in the value of its importance
in Christian work to no other in the city of Brooklyn
—a city which has earned the sobriquet of "the City
of Churches," by reason of the number, grandeur, and
importance of its sacred edifices. The Centennial Baptist Church is in full sympathy with its honored pastor
in purpose and in plan ; the rich and poor are alike
made welcome, and there is no distinction in regard
to color. People of color here forget their com-
plexion. Frederick Douglass said that in the presence
of Abraham Lincoln he forgot that he was black. A
similar compliment has been paid to the Centennial
Baptist Church. Dr. Fulton is an able writer, and has
published a great many works and pamphlets principally on religious subjects. Among the more notable
of his works are the following : "The Roman Catholic
Element in American History," already mentioned ;
"Life of Timothy Gilbert, the Founder of the
Tremont Temple" (Boston) ; "The True Woman,"
"The Way Out," "Show Your Colors," "Sam
Hobart, the Railroad Engineer," etc. A tract from
his pen on the Sabbath has had a circulation of over
one hundred thousand copies. In all the great reforms of the day he takes an active interest. His
voice is one of the strongest in the land in urging

temperance, and his pen has done noble work in connection with this reform. As a lecturer Dr. Fulton
enjoys an extended and deserved fame. He seldom
leaves his church duties for service in the lecture
field, and never, excepting at the call of patriotic
duty, or to do a needed work. Previous to beginning
his labors in Brooklyn he had a wide reputation in
New England as a brilliant, magnetic, and forcible
speaker on temperance and other reforms, and this
was increased by his subsequent experience in the
South. The subject he chose for presentation in the
lectures of this Southern trip was the duties of citizenship, which he ably set forth in a discourse entitled
"The American of the Future ; Shall he be a
Partisan or a Patriot ?" It was the endeavor of Dr.
Fulton in this lecture to recall attention to the patriotism which distinguished the people in the days of
Washington, glance at the perils which grow out of
partisanship, and inquire what can be done to help the
growth of an American who shall compass the interests
of the entire nation in his love and work ; not to
advance one section at the expense of another, but to
enable the people to fulfil God's great purpose in
building a nation that is to bless mankind. Other
lectures of his, which have excited the most favorable
comment from the press, are entitled, " Witnessing
for Truth : the Overthrow of the Papacy," " The
Perils and Possibilities of American Womanhood,"
" Bismarck and the Conflict in Europe," " The
Force that Wins," " Whom shall we Trust ?" etc.
These lectures show Dr. Fulton to be a vigorous
thinker, an excellent word-painter, and possessed of a
fine sense of humor. His illustrations are mainly
taken from life, and enchain the attention even of
those opposed to his deductions. He speaks rapidly,
" but his sentences are powerful and caustic, and are
generally aimed at a given point, which they inevit-
ably reach." Always an industrious student, his
ability in scholarship is enlarged and thorough, while

his gifts as an orator and writer are of that original
and splendid kind which cannot fail to command
attention.

AS A PASTOR.

In all his pastorates he has labored with great
success, constantly widening the scope of his influence and the bounds of his fame.   Peculiar,
marked, and effective in all his characteristics,
whether of the mental or physical nature, he occupies a position at once of prominence and power.   For
religion and reform he is ever a zealous champion,
doing battle on every hand without fear or favor.
With a conscience keenly sensitive to the demands of
duty, he has the talents, courage, and energy which
make his effort successful in whatever direction he
feels called upon to devote them.   Dr. Fulton believes
the Gospel of Jesus Christ with all it implies, and in
this lies the secret of his radicalism.   Principle rather
than policy rules him, and he finds in a "thus saith
the Lord" the highest motive and the most im-
perious command.   His heroic conduct in St. Louis, at
one of the most critical periods in American history,
was based on this principle.   A regard for it placed
him among the opponents of Spiritualism, when the
story of the Fox girls and "spirit rappings" were
turning the heads of so many Christians.   In Albany,
though he preached Christ and gathered a strong
church, he became a power in the city as the enemy
of slavery and the foe of a conservatism which he felt
was paralyzing the energies of some of our best men.
He arrived in Boston when the war was at its height.
Theodore Parker, as the avowed advocate of anti-
slavery and as the foe of the Christian system, had
made himself a mighty power.   So successfully had
he stirred the anti-slavery sentiment in the bosoms of
men, that many ministers were found who openly
declared that they would rather trust themselves with
Parker's faith in the hands of God than with the lives

of some Doctors of Divinity. Fulton saw his duty clearly, and never swerved. Fidelity to Christian truth made him the foe of Parker, though regard for the rights of humanity made him eloquent in defence of the principles of human liberty which Parker advocated. Unlike many clergymen about him, he used discrimination, and, true to his character, accepted the wheat while he rejected the chaff. He was called "orthodox to the backbone." As Bishop Haven said : "He understands the enemies of orthodoxy and knows how to handle them. He preaches Christ crucified—to the anti-sacrificialists a stumbling-block, and to the sceptically wise foolishness ; but to them that are saved of both these classes and of all others, Christ the power of God and wisdom of God. His success is due to a threefold cause. First, faith ; he believes the Gospel with all his heart, mind, and strength. He discounts no letter of the word of God. It is all yea and amen in Christ Jesus. He is thoroughly convinced of the total depravity of the human soul, its need of the provisions of the atonement, of the work of the Spirit, of the blessings of salvation here and hereafter. This makes him a bold preacher of righteousness. No inward conflict troubles him ; of the divinity of Christ and the Gospel he is fully persuaded. Second, his heart is in his faith. He enjoys the experience he proclaims. He is not only a Gospel believer and preacher, but he knows how to make others interested. Some men are warm-hearted, but fail to warm other hearts. Not so with Dr. Fulton. No one can hear him without being interested. He draws his hearers unto him. They may scoff, may criticise, may condemn, but they listen. The third and not least reason of his success is the adaptation of his message to the hour. He knows, as but few ministers, how to preach the Bible in telegrams. He holds the mirror of passing events, not up to nature but up to nature's God, who is Christ the Lord. He makes every current breath blow the

sails of the Gospel ship. This makes him a thoroughly
live preacher. There is no dead wood about his
forest. Everything is fresh and green and growing.
Young people go to hear the deeds of the hour put
into Christian hope. He is sure to point the daily act
with a Scripture text and a Christian explanation.
Temperance, European war, Papacy's fall, everything
a-going is made to illustrate the faith of Christ. This
makes him a centre of debate. Men never discuss
thoroughly dead issues or dead men. They must have
the breath of life in them, no matter what else they
lack, or they are buried from talk and thought. His
freshness breathes contention. He speaks his mind
and his antagonists speak theirs. He is, of course, a
strong Baptist. He could not be any other if he was
one at all. He is opposed to open communion and
of whatever he deems of anti-immersion tendency.
Yet his heart knows no sect, and no more genial or
cordial spirit exists in the world." He is a man of
remarkable courage in his convictions. Whittier
described him in the words:

> " All grim and soil, and brown with tan,
>   I saw a strong one in his wrath,
> Smiting the godless sins of man,
>   Along his path.

> " Fraud from his secret chambers fled,
>   Before the sunlight bursting in,
> Sloth drew her pillow o'er her head,
>   To drown the din."

His impulsive energy brooks no delay when he is
in hot pursuit of Satan or any other evil spirit. The
impetuous temperament of the man makes him eloquent in public speech, and his Cromwellian courage
leads him to the front and into the thickest of the fight
in the great battle of what he conceives to be right and
justice, against wrong and oppression. He seeks no
excuse for ease and shelter in camp ; when the war is
waging, he wears the white plume of Navarre and
not the white feather of the retreating combatant.

He is one of those who attempts to "chase a thousand," believing that "one with God is a majority." The Southern type of manhood has much in it which a man of Dr. Fulton's temperament would admire. In St. Louis he formed an extended acquaintance with the Southern ministry and a wide friendship, which has been maintained notwithstanding the war, which threatened the severance of so many strong ties.

The churches of the South have resisted bravely and effectively the encroachments of Romanism. The Southern ministry, more than their Northern brethren, have written and preached against the wiles and withstood the influence of Rome. It was in part the peril to which the negro was exposed from Romish propagandism that made Dr. Fulton welcome to Southern pulpits. They regarded him as a coadjutor in a most important work.

Incidentally just here we find an admirable illustration of how

KINDNESS BRINGS ITS REWARD.

The war had hardly closed when from Georgia there came to Boston a Southern statesman of acknowledged ability, for the purpose of interesting the capitalists of New England in the fertile lands of the Empire State of the South. A meeting was gotten up for him in Tremont Temple, and Governor Andrew had consented to preside. Some of the famed philanthropists of that goodly town were on the platform to welcome the returning prodigal from the Union, and kill the fatted calf and make merry because of a reconstructed country, of which the coming of this man from Georgia to Boston was proof. The speech was not a success. They came to hear a Southerner confess, and not to listen to a defence of the people of the South. They were not ready for the feast provided for them. As a result, the Abolitionists and philanthropists fled the meeting in droves. The platform was nearly deserted, and Governor Andrew himself grew impatient. The meeting was a failure. No land was sold, and no money was made. The pastor was going to his room the next morning, when Solomon Parsons, Esq., the esteemed superintendent of the Temple, came out and said, "I wish you would come into the office. Here is the Southerner who spoke last night. He is stranded. He has not money to pay his hotel bill, and is in utter despair over his failure."

Dr. Fulton went in, was introduced, and heard the story. He was to lecture that night before the Bay State Course, and for it was to receive $100. He said, "I will tell you what I will do. If the chairman of the Lecture Committee will consent, I will give up my place to you, and you shall not only have the money, but an introduction to the lecture-going community, which may do you good." The man looked perfectly dumbfounded, and asked the Doctor to go over it again, saying, "I can't think I hear correctly."

Colonel Parsons, with a smile, said, "Yes, you hear it all right. It is just like my pastor to make such a proposition."

"Do you mean to say that you will give me $100 and a chance to lecture before a Boston audience?"

"Yes, that is the offer."

"Well, sir, that one fact redeems New England, and proves true what we have heard of Northern chivalry."

It was a cold November morning, and the east wind was doing its best; the Southerner was thinly clad, which Dr. Fulton saw, and said, "Put on your coat, and let us go and see the chairman of the committee."

"I must be frank with you," replied the Southerner, "and say I have no overcoat."

"Then come with me."

Dr. Fulton took this entire stranger to his tailor, and had him try on an elegant overcoat. The coat cost $75. The Southerner asked for a cheaper one, but went back, at Dr. Fulton's suggestion, to the better one, put it on, and wore it off as a token of regard from a Northern Abolitionist to a brave Southerner. Years had gone.   Dr. Fulton was pastor in Brooklyn. This gentleman was a lawyer in New York.   Gilbert Haven, D.D., asked Dr. Fulton to go South to help work up a better sentiment toward loyal Northern men.   There was a send-off meeting held in Brooklyn. This Southerner presided, and told the story given above, and gave Dr. Fulton letters to Governor Brown of Georgia, and many more.

Transfer the scene to Atlanta, where Bishop Haven had been driven out of the great hotel for riding with a cultured colored man.   Here Dr. Fulton came. The ministers had held a meeting and voted not to receive " the restless agitator," as they called him. On Dr. Fulton's arrival he was made acquainted with the fact.   With a good-natured smile, he inquired, " Who is the head man who runs matters in the churches ?"

" Dr. So-and-so and ex-Governor Brown," was the reply.

" All right ; I will call on them."

To the minister he went first.   The pastor of the First Baptist Church was in his study, and said, " We have heard of your coming, and have had a meeting and resolved not to receive you."

" What is the matter ?"

" You have the reputation of having been a rabid Abolitionist."

" That is the truth," said Dr. Fulton.   " If that makes a man bad in your estimation, I am as bad as they make them, and I came to you because I knew you represented the most ultra pro-slavery wing of the Southern ministry ; knowing that you wrote a book to prove the divinity of slavery, which since the war you have destroyed.   But I have heard with delight that since the surrender at Appomattox you have been foremost in trying to educate the negro, and I thought

that perhaps a rank Abolitionist, one that prayed for
the freedom of the slave and for the victory of the
Union arms, might come to the South and get down at
the foot of the cross of Christ and there strike hands
with an acknowledged representative of the ultra South
in striving as best we might to help Christ's poor."

THE SOUTHERN MINISTER

arose, stretched out his hand, and said, "You can,
Brother Fulton. I invite you to preach in my pulpit,
and will aid you all in my power."

"All right; introduce me to Governor Brown."

"He is the last man you want to see. He opposes
your coming."

"So did you; but it is all right. I have a letter to
him."

The two went together to the Governor's office.
The Governor has a face like Henry Clay. He is a
born gentleman, and a Southerner to the backbone.
Upon being introduced, Dr. Fulton said, "I have a
letter for you from a former Georgia Congressman,"
giving the name.

Governor Brown took it eagerly, and began reading
it. His eyes glowed with feeling. In a few mo-
ments he looked up and asked, "Are you the man
that gave that welcome to —— in Boston?"

"I have not read the letter, but I suppose I know
to what you refer."

"You are the one who gave him the overcoat. He
wrote me of it at the time." He laid down the letter, rose, crossed over to the visitor, and said, "Dr.
Fulton, you are welcome to Atlanta. My house is
your home, my carriage is at your service. I will
see my pastor, and you shall preach for us on Sabbath
morning."

"No," said the Southern minister, "he is to preach
for us in the morning, and he can preach for you at
night."

It was this Southern minister, occupying this prominent Southern pulpit, who wrote this description of the preacher, after he had ministered in the various pulpits of the city of Atlanta,* Ga., and had been introduced by Governor Brown to one of Atlanta's most cultured audiences :

" A tall, stout, finely-formed man, somewhat bald, with black whiskers and mustache, sat in the pulpit, and all eyes were turned toward him, for his fame had preceded him, and, in fact, had marked him as a distinguished pulpit orator in all parts of the land. Dr. Fulton's oratory is somewhat peculiar. He is a man whose heart rules his speech as it warms with his theme, flashing out and throwing its sudden light upon the brain and sending its currents of feeling into each gesture. When he looks upon his notes you recognize the New England orator in the careful turn of the period and in the excellent rhetoric. When he turns away from them to enlarge on some topic or sudden thought, there is at times a dash and carelessness in manner and matter that would captivate a Western man. And then again he is like a Frenchman—all passion, rushing in a whirlwind of words all on fire—his manner impetuous, literal, abrupt, telling more sometimes in a gesture than could be told in a thousand words. Recognizing art, but obeying genius, swayed by one burning thought, he impresses you as a man who is earnest in his faith, and whose faith makes him happy from the depth and power of his own sincerity. . . . He has won a wide reputation as a clear and compact writer of incisive English, and as a forcible and fluent speaker, who has something new to say and the courage to say it without ' fear or

* Dr. Fulton spoke out from a full heart, there as elsewhere in the South. His words met with a warm response, and at the close Governor Brown commended the lecturer and the lecture in the most emphatic terms, saying, " Georgia could afford to pay the preacher a good salary to go through the State and talk to all regarding the marvellous openings for thrift and prosperity, providing love could take the place of hate."

favor.' Not satisfied with his attainments, which are
of a high order, he studies hard, and continually adds to
his store of thought. His hatred of tyranny, intemperance, injustice, and selfishness kindles his combat-
iveness and inspires him with the aggressive energy of a
soldier in the storm of war. His firmness seems to cul-
minate in obstinacy, especially when conscience comes
to the rescue. He seems to be endowed with the spirit
of the old martyrs, and would not shrink from suffering and death if they stood in the path of duty. He is
a living representative of the heroic men who stepped
from the scaffold and the wheel of torture and the
flames of the stake to the sweet heaven, whose golden
gates swing on welcome hinges to receive them. We
give only a hint of his masterly sermon in his leading
thoughts. It was an hour long, but was listened to
with avidity by the vast congregation from beginning
to end. His text was Luke 19 : 22 : ' If thou hadst
known, even thou in this thy day, the things which
belong unto thy peace, but now they are hid from
thine eyes.' His subject might be said in one word
to be Possibilities, and he introduced it by saying,
' There were possibilities all about us—possibilities of
good and possibilities of evil, of misery and happiness,
of hope and despair.' The following thoughts in
substance were presented : *The greatness of the
possibility only enhances the greatness of the loss.*
Jerusalem was the holy favored city. According to
the Jewish Rabbi, the world is the eye, the white of
the eye the ocean surrounding the world, the dark
portion of the eye the land thus surrounded, the pupil
of the eye Jerusalem, and the image in the pupil the
Temple. With all its advantages, we cannot tell what
Jerusalem would have been had it improved its day,
as we cannot tell what the world would have been had
man not fallen, only that Eden would have blossomed
on Eden and beauty in ever-increasing stages filled the
earth.

   " No mortal can tell what possibilities were seen by

Christ as He stood on the brow of Olivet—possibilities that were trembling, falling, and fading away into everlasting night—her day gone forever—when He beheld this favored city and wept over it. He had been rejected. Imagine the scene of that great day of the feast, when, having climbed the eminence, the white-haired sire in front and behind him the younger, the priest held up a little vial of water, and instantly from every heart went up a prayer that in their marches in the year to come God would provide water in the desert, and that as they passed through the Valley of Baca they might go from well to well and from strength to strength. At this solemn juncture the voice of Christ is heard, clear, soft, melodious, and inspiring, sounding out over the multitude, echoing and re-echoing as it rolls through the Temple, saying, ' If any man thirst, let him come to me and drink.' They had heard. That was the moment of opportunity they rejected. That was the beginning of an infinite and an eternal loss, and now their day was gone ; it was night evermore. The anguish of a heart that mourns over lost possibilities is of the intensest character.

" Think of David. What cares he for victory ? His boy is dead. His palace is a prison. The shout of triumph tells of the overthrow and death of Absalom, ' My lost boy Absalom,' and thus does God feel for sinners lost. It is not alone what they may suffer that engages God's thought, but what they have enjoyed ; how they might have been built up in love, in culture, in manhood, in soul development. Then the preacher pictured a redeemed man growing as Paul grew, climbing the steep of praise, his soul being fashioned after the similitude of Christ, and being made wholly conformable to His mind and will.

" 2. *There are possibilities placed within reach of living men, as great as ever were seen by our fathers.*

" Then the preacher told why he was in the South, and spoke of the duty pressing upon us in regard to

the negro.   There was a moment of extreme nervous-
ness.   A Northern abolitionist in a Southern pulpit—
in the pulpit occupied by one of the most ultra of the
pro-slavery men of the South before the war—was in
a critical place.   The preacher had measured his task,
and knew the Lord God, whose providences had made
liberty possible, would carry him through.

" He said, so goes the report, ' Since I have come
South I have seen with mine own eyes the vast resources of this beautiful country, and felt in my heart
the true spirit of the people.   The work for the
colored people must be undertaken by the white people of the South.   Northern money cannot do it.
Northern men and women cannot do it.   There must
be a *we* in it.   It is a work for all of us to engage in.
Dr. Fuller, of Baltimore, after traversing South
Carolina after the war, came back to his people and
declared that he felt an irrepressible longing to go
there and preach to the people, black and white, and
devote his life to this one work.

" ' Romanists of all the world, from the Pope in
Rome to priests in the South, are engaged in the business.   In the streets black nuns are to be met, and
black priests are to be educated and sent forth by
Roman Catholics ; the most beautiful temples are
built by them and given to these nuns and priests to
entice their race by the glitter of its worship, into its
communion.   They will succeed if we do not pre-
occupy the land with the truth.'

" 3. *Simple faith in God is the spring of Christian
power, the source of the greatest possibilities of doing
good.*

" A banker whose financial plans have been swept
suddenly into ruin, and who on Saturday night stood
in his elegant mansion amid his beloved family on the
verge of bankruptcy, comes as usual to his Bible-
class on Sabbath morning, his face as calm and happy
as it ever was, his trust in God perfect, his interest in
his duty and class just as absorbing ; a merchant in

New York who, amid financial convulsions that shake
the whole country, is seen retiring frequently to a
little room for the refreshing of the heart and the re-
lieving of the burdened brain by a verse in God's
Word, and a swift assent in spirit to His presence in
prayer ; another merchant prince inducing an acquaintance and brother merchant to attend for five
minutes a prayer-meeting to the saving of his soul ; an
assistant cashier in a bank detecting the cashier in a
fraudulent transaction, and acting in a spirit of prayer
and obedience to the commands of Christ in this
emergency. These incidents of Christian life and
Christian power flowing out in streams of benefit, in
currents ever broadening and deepening, were related
with a simple earnestness and a touching pathos that
will not be easily forgotten. And each illustration
was sent home to each swelling heart with the question, Have you a faith like that ? Is your hand in
God's hand like that ? Is your love for Jesus like
that ?

" Throughout the entire discourse, the one awful
responsibility of the text was held up to view and
managed by the preacher with a master hand—the
possibility of the sinner's day ceasing and an eternal
night of despair closing around him even in this
world. While the possibilities of his turning to God
and opening his heart to Christ were urged in every
aspect and with winning sweetness, this fearful possibility of the text was held up as a dark background ;
not argued, but suggested ; not presented in a torrent
of words as a distinct menace, but depicted with a
touch here and there as a shadowy form, yet distinct
and ominous.

"It was a beautiful scene illuminated with the sunshine of God's love, set in a dim bordering of clouds
gleaming with the red tongues of death, muttering
with poisoned breath, and flashing up, now and then,
in threats of a night of clouds and tempest and everlasting doom."

The secular press thus spoke of the lecture on "The American of the Future" at James Hall :

"One of the most superb of lecturers met Atlanta in one of her best auditories, best both as to intelligence and numbers, at James Hall.

"Governor Brown introduced the distinguished gentleman to those present in a happy speech. He said we had heard Dr. Fulton as a minister of the Lord in the Lord's house on yesterday ; now he comes to us as a patriot. He comes to us as a messenger of peace ; as such we welcome him ; and while he would say, lest he be misunderstood, that we could not tolerate legislation looking to social equality between races who were made to be distinct, yet, with this proviso, he assured him that the great majority of the people of the South were willing to accept, abide by, and defend the Constitution of the country as it was now ; that we were all convinced that the South could not be prosperous without prosperity at the North, and that the North and West could not be prosperous without prosperity at the South. He then presented Dr. Fulton, who was greeted with applause.

"How shall we describe the unmistakable, or weave to the imagination the bow which nature herself paints with her inimitable fingers upon the heavens ?

"Such would be the attempt to reproduce the lecture of this wonderful speaker, flashing with eloquence, spiced with most exquisite humor, and clothed with words that shone with beauty and rose as flame. It was not sectional. The heart of a man that loved both North and South beat in it, while some things were said in all honesty, to which in all honesty some of his hearers demurred, yet nothing in word or spirit could be really objectionable to a fair-minded man. The idea of a broad, brotherly spirit, an unsectional love of country, a patriotism that was all-comprehending, all-embracing in its intellect and heart ; and a higher, universal education of the masses ; a recognition of manhood in work in all its departments—

this idea, intensified by every form of language and argument, and literally clothed and glistening in the gems of eloquence, was the lecture."

On his return, at the request of friends in New York and Boston, he delivered a lecture entitled, " The Outlook, or Some of the Lessons Learned in my Trip South." In it he used this language :

" It is said that in the days of the adventurous pioneer a trader pushed his way toward the slopes of the Pacific, and at last reached the chasm formed by the torrent of the Columbia rushing between Mount Hood and Mount Helen, where it breaks through the ridge of the Cascade Mountains. The magnificence of the scenery filled him with surprise. He spoke, and the result astonished him. He heard his slightest tones repeated and re-echoed with a larger utterance in reverberations that lost themselves at last amid the surrounding and distant hills.

" With something akin to this feeling of apprehension do I come to refer to what mine eyes beheld and my heart felt as I journeyed in that realm so lately traversed by armies, where business, modes of thought, and the forms of industries have all undergone a radical change.

" It is known that I went South to ascertain if there would be a welcome given to the conception of an American broad enough, generous and noble enough to take the interests of the whole country to his heart. It is with pleasure that I report the people in the South as ready to be generous, broad and noble in their views and operations as are the people of the North. Sentiments cheered and welcomed in Boston were cheered and welcomed in New Orleans.

" THE KEY TO THE POSITION

is our treatment of the negro. This was my faith before I started, and this is my solemn conviction on my return. For his deliverance from bondage this war was waged. God delivered him, and now commits to the care of His children the keeping of his destiny. Let us not deny it. The duty has its bright and dark side ; the North has seen the bright, and the South is compelled to see the dark. It is the privilege of the North and South to see both sides, and so engage in the work placed before us that love shall lighten labor and that God's blessing shall link the cross to the crown."

It was in 1855 he wrote and published in his " Roman Catholic Element in American History," ten years before liberty became a national birthright, and while to say it was to cast away favor and friendship, these words : " The influence of our free institutions is working out important results. Labor deserves protection. It has built up this Republic and made it strong. . . . The interests of the laborer are all opposed to despotism, as may be seen whether we look at Italy or South Carolina. In this fact there is hope. Though truth falleth in the streets, and error Haman-like rides its gay palfrey, yet the Christian does not despair, for he beholds the hand of his God shaping and controlling all things, and in the stirring events of the hour he greets a movement which is working out the disenthralment of the race. The patriot does not despair, because from a thousand sources the fiat has gone forth that the march of aggression shall be stayed, and that if the battle continues long enough the sun in his shining course shall light a race of freemen without falling upon a bondman's home. For broad and grand and mighty is our Republic, it has not yet attained its zenith, nor will it until the seedlings of despotism, translated from a foreign soil and nurtured in our own, shall be uprooted, and then it will flame the splendor of its orb over an area of freedom broad as an ocean-girt continent."

THE MAN AT WORK.

Rev. H. A. Delano in a recent letter describes the

man as he found him in his study in 1882, just previous to the evening sermon.   He says : "It was a
sight to gladden the eyes and stir the heart to the
utmost to see the swarm of people swarming to the
Temple on Sabbath evening.   We were invited to the
study—a beautiful room—and sat with the genial doctor talking of the work, while without was the cease-
less tramp of the multitudes who were pressing into
the great place to hear a radical and well-defined gospel from a man who is a force and a study to everybody who knows and feels him.   Young men came to
see him and ask after his work.   They came to tell
him of somebody anxious for salvation, to ask him if
he wanted any help for the evening, to breathe a word
of encouragement, and to receive a blessing.   Like a
father among his children sat this brave-hearted man,
and in the name of the Master dispensed the Master's
blessing.   The same power that made Tremont Temple under God what it was while Dr. Fulton was in
Boston seems present and operative here.   The doctor
is intensely himself, superlatively individual.   You
can only classify him with himself.   He keeps his
heart as a garden, watered and green, and tender and
beautiful.   He has no fence around it.   He has no
signs up cautioning men against trespass and tramping.   All is open welcome, generous, and great.   So
it falls out often that somebody takes advantage.
But when somebody goes ruthlessly tramping through
and upon and over all the flowers of the generous soul,
somebody gets suddenly shaken up and put out.   As
a member of the church said, 'the doctor is impulsive and peculiar, and won't stand any foolishness.'
Another said of him : 'He must work, and he does
his best work in his own harness.' "

Rev. James B. Simmons, D.D., thus described
him when he came to Brooklyn : "Many suppose
they know my friend Fulton who do not know him.
They think his successes spring from his eccentrici-
ties.   They are mistaken.   He has an inner and hid-

den life—a life hid with Christ in God, a life habit
of walking with God, of which those who misunder-
stand and censure him seem to know nothing. He
means always to be for God, even though it arrays him
against his brethren. He holds the truth to be
superior to men. If he conceives that God requires a
given thing of himself and his brethren, his view is
that not doubts and debates, but straightforward obedience is the first thing and the only thing next in
order. And he is apt to rebuke sharply those who
pause to discuss the propriety of obeying God's commands."

Dr. Fulton has been bitterly assailed in Brooklyn
because of his fidelity to the truth. In the midst of
this opposition, Rev. David Moore, D.D., then pastor
of the Washington Avenue Baptist Church of Brooklyn, entered a plea to give him "fair play," saying:
" He has not had it in Brooklyn. I have been in this
city almost twelve years, and have known no man so
bitterly misrepresented, against whom there has been
directed such unreasonable opposition and such per-
sistent and malignant hatred. What has he done to
deserve this treatment? Granted that he is impulsive, often injudicious, and harsh. This is the worst
of him. On the other hand, he has intellectual
power, is well-informed, is an eloquent platform
speaker, a powerful and faithful preacher, and a tireless worker. He has also a large, tender, loving
heart, and is as loyal to Christ and the truth as ever a
man was, and wants to do his best for Jesus and mankind. Those of us who know him best love and prize
him most."

To this, Rev. Edward Bright, D.D., editor of the
Examiner, added these words:

" Every man has a side to his nature in which
faults predominate, and it is only by taking him as a
whole, setting his virtues over against his admitted
failings, that any man retains the respect and self-con-
fidence of his fellow-men. Such a balancing of human

character is more than charitable. It is a JUST and the only JUST method of estimating the worth of people. And their character is to be judged by their aims more than by their ways of pursuing them. . . . We sincerely believe that the current of few men's aims more uniformly sets in the direction of that which is genuine, and true, and good, and noble. He has a warm, philanthropic, and God-fearing heart. He believes in and loves the truth of God, and sees no reason why all others should not believe in and love it. He has a vast conviction, too, that God has commissioned him to avow and propagate what he believes. His way of doing it may be open to criticism, but it is his own way, the way that is in harmony with his moral and intellectual nature, a nature that can undergo no radical change. He is especially a man to be taken as he is, having never sought to be fashioned into somebody else, and could not be if he would.''

"Such a man,'' said George W. Bungay in his description of Dr. Fulton in his " Cameo Cuttings ;" " such a man cannot easily be put down. He is like the fabled giant, who, when beaten to the ground, sprang to his feet with greater strength than he had before he received the blow. A small field of labor is not at all satisfactory to him. He desires to speak through types as well as through his lips, and the press, and the pulpit are heights or mountain-top pulpits from which he is ambitious to preach to the multitude. The doctor is human, and has faults. He was born to lead, and he knows it, hence he will ; he drives, and he will not be horse. He wants to have his own way, and he stubbornly adheres to the verdict he brings in his own favor, and the other eleven obstinate men cannot move him.

" Rev. Dr. Fulton is a combative theologian, and will take even a Pope's bull by the horns. When Monsignor Capel came to this country, the fighting parson pitched his hat into the ring and squared for battle.''

THE INFLUENCE OF TRUTH WAS SEEN IN HIS
OPPOSITION TO MONSIGNOR CAPEL.

For weeks the rumor ran from lip to lip, and the
press gave it wing, that the Catesby of "Lothair"—
the great converter of wealthy Protestants—had
arrived in America. It was said that a daughter of a
distinguished citizen had been led into the toils of
Rome. The press hailed Monsignor Capel as a
"member of the Pope's household"—the representative of the Vatican—and declared that he was to be
the feature of fashionable life in our fashionable world
during the coming winter. At the request of friends,
the lecture on "Monsignor Capel and the Methods of
Rome" was delivered. Capel was shown, not to be
the Marquis of Bute or Lord Somebody Else, but the
servant of the cardinal ; that he had fallen from favor
in England, and, as the New York *Tribune* said, was
the subject of more or less unpleasant talk, and "that
a silly section of our fashionable society gave their
guest the greatest consideration here about the time
he seemed to be in the least esteem at home." The
eyes of the people were opened. Capel, who began
by preaching the Popery which had enslaved Europe,
changed his tactics. The man who had posed as the
Catesby of "Lothair" was proved to be of humble
origin and without prestige at home. Though he
threatened lawsuits and denied that he had had trouble
in England, as was charged by Father Chiniqui, he
came to Brooklyn and lectured without the slightest
reference to his boasted threat, showing that, in his
estimation, "discretion was the better part of valor."
His power to do mischief is broken as much as was
that of the loud-mouthed Tetzel when Luther exposed
him. Tell the truth. It is the truth that kills and
makes alive.

For his fearless attacks on Romanism Dr. Fulton
has borne reproach, and still bears it. He moves on,
for he believes that the only way to overthrow

Romanism is to tell the truth about it and apply the truth to it. He said, in a letter defending his position: "We are in a great fight at this great world-centre. Rome has in New York more brains, more culture, more money, and more hearty devotees than dwell in the Eternal City. Romanism is almost master here in politics, in literature, and in religion. The methods practised in Europe are being introduced into our own land. We need not fear them if we will but expose them. Silence gives consent to error and permits it to live. Preaching the truth makes truth omnipotent, and in its province error hides, and its power to do mischief dies. Error lives because we let it. Few warn Romanists of their danger, because the average minister feels that he must preach the Gospel and build up his church in praying for the conversion of heathen in India, Italy, and in Ireland, and in neglecting those in his immediate vicinity. Not so thinks Dr. Fulton, and so he is anxious to rouse the churches to the possibilities within their reach, and believes that millions of Romanists are in this land to be led from darkness to light, and be made share-holders with us in the inherited blessings of the past, and in accomplishing the work for God in the present which shall make the future luminous with a new glory and radiant with the bright beams of hope.

For this let all Christians pray.

R. S. MacArthur.

INTRODUCTION.

CAN WE HOPE FOR THE CONVERSION OF ROMANISTS?

PERHAPS another question deserves consideration before the first be answered—viz., Do Romanists need conversion? There are those who are prepared to treat Romanists as they would treat any other Christian sect. They reckon them as a part of the Christian world. Are they right, or are they wrong? Answer this, and then the first question is in order.

Evangelical Christendom feels and believes that a work should be done for Romanists in Europe. Missions have been planted in Rome, and are being sustained by the various churches of Christ. Some of these missions are under the very shadow of the Vatican. In Rome, where it was impossible, previous to the advent of the army of Victor Emmanuel, to hold a religious assembly, God's Word is being proclaimed, the evils of Popery are being set forth, and hundreds and thousands are coming from darkness into the light. It is thus proven that the claim so often made here, that Romanists have a place as a Christian denomination in the evangelical world, is absurd. Romanists are in peril because of the errors that blind and destroy them, or else sending missionaries to Rome is an insult. If they are in peril in Rome, they are in peril in America. For, bad as Romanism is in Italy, in Ireland, in Germany, and in France, it is in purpose and in power more to be dreaded in America.

Consider some facts. 1. Romanism is the foe of

liberty, because its votaries subscribe not only to an absolute despotism, but submit to the dictation of a ruler in utter antagonism to free institutions. It is American to believe in religious liberty. Pius IX., August 15th, 1854, declared in his Encyclical Letter that "Liberty of conscience was a most pestilential error." It is American to believe in a *free press* and in *free speech;* this is called by the Pope "*the liberty of perdition.*" It is American to believe in the free circulation and open reading of the Bible. The Roman Catholic Church claims "to be the only living authority which has the right to interpret the Bible; its interpretation should be the only one allowed, should be protected by law; all others should be condemned and disallowed."

It is American to foster our public-school system. Romanism seeks its overthrow. A free people claim that the Constitution is the supreme law of the land. The Pope reserves the right to absolve his subjects from allegiance to it. The genius of our institutions is opposed to a state religion. Priest Hecker says, "There is ere-long to be a state religion in this country, and that state religion is to be Roman Catholic."

He who runs may read. "The ascendency of Romanistic principles implies the downfall of the Constitution." It is becoming more and more apparent that Lafayette prophesied truly when he said, "If the liberties of the American people are ever destroyed, they will fall by the hands of the Roman clergy."

2. The growth of Romanistic power should cause us to ask the question, Can we hope for the conversion of Romanists? In 1785 there were but 25,000 Romanists in America. They are now reckoned by millions, though it is estimated that, because of the influence of our institutions and the power exerted by the telling of the truth as it is in Jesus, over 17,000,000 Roman Catholics have taken their departure from the Roman Church and have joined other com-

munions or are in the slough of infidelity ; yet it remains true that to-day they rival in numbers any of
our largest evangelical denominations, and because of
their wealth and power, which are unified and wielded
against liberty, temperance, education, and Christianity, they deserve to be opposed and if possible to be
redeemed.

3. The policy of Rome should create alarm. She
is a law to herself in America. Rome wields political
power for the increase of the influence and wealth of
the Church. The effect of this is seen in New York.
The Roman Catholic Church has acquired in New
York City real estate and other property to the
amount of over $60,000,000 ! In eleven years it has
received from the public treasury of the same city
$5,827,471.19, an average annual donation of $529,-
750.10.

The Roman Catholic Church, because of its political
power, sets at defiance the laws which provide that
ecclesiastical property be held by boards of trustees of
the laity. At present $250,000,000 of property is
now held in this country by sixty Romish bishops under
the absolute control of the Pope.

"On Blackwell's Island $30,000 was voted by the
city to erect a church for the inmates of the island, to
be used by clergymen of all sects. A Roman Catholic
priest took possession of the church, erected his altar,
and refused to allow ministers of evangelical denominations to preach in it. The matter was referred to
the authorities. They dared not interfere, for fear of
losing the votes of Romanists.

"The St. Vincent de Paul Church, on Twenty-third
Street, refused to pay its assessments for paving the
street. Protestant churches were compelled to pay
their assessments on the same street, but the authorities, for fear of losing votes, paid the assessment out of
the general fund. In 1857 the City Council of New
York gave to the Church of Rome a tract of land,
valued at $4,000,000, on which the Fifth Avenue

Cathedral is built. Let Rome get more power, and there would be more gifts, more usurpations, and more abominations." ("The Future Conflict," p. 13.)

WHAT MAY BE.

If nothing can be done to head against this growth, it is believed that in thirty years Romanists will number one third of the population, in forty years two fifths, and in fifty-two years they will outnumber all non-Catholics. What has caused this increase? Emigration; annexation of Louisiana, Florida, and Mexican territory, with their Catholic population, and the fertility of the foreign population and the influence of the sentiment so destructive to child-bearing, which is delivering over to Romanists large areas of country as is found in the Western Reserve, simply because American families refuse to raise children, and foreigners shame us in this regard; finally, through the management of the penal institutions and the reformatories, being given over so largely to the control of the Church of Rome as was done by the Geghan bill in Ohio, engineered by the priesthood under the direction of the Archbishop of Cincinnati. Similar bills are on the statute-books of other States, which take out of the control of the State the direction of our reformatories and give over thousands and tens of thousands of children to the absolute control of the priesthood. They have captured nearly all the town and city officers in New York and New England towns and cities, and their blows fall thick and heavy upon our Republic.

Can we hope for the conversion of Roman Catholics? We answer, Yes, for these, among other reasons.

1. *Because of the Christ we preach.* The Christ of prophecy is the world's hero in imagination. The Jesus that came from Galilee to Jordan is the world's hero in history. No other character has stood the

tests of trial and remained the perfection of goodness
and the model of perfection.   From birth to death He
alone was faultless; from death to the Millennium
He alone increases in power.   Jesus is the world's
Saviour.   Romanists need not go to a priest, who
tires of his senseless service, nor to the Mass, which is
the poorest sort of idolatry, nor to a church, full of
corruption from centre to circumference, but to Jesus
Christ; not by the aid of Mary, but through the Holy
Spirit.   "He shall testify of Me," said Christ, "and
reveal Me to them."

An uplifted Christ is a conquering Saviour.   If
ever a being's path was blocked, Christ's was.   The
Jews were in power.   Ye who think nothing can be
done for Romanists, look at the world at that time.
There was no printing-press, no books or tracts for the
millions, no way of reaching the lost through the unnumbered sources of influence now under the control
of the Christian Church.   Christ's followers depended
upon Christ's Gospel and life, and with these Judaism
was overthrown and Paganism was vanquished.

They preached Christ.   They carried the doctrines
of the Gospel to the lost, and they triumphed.   It was
not different in the days of Zwingli and Luther.
Preachers of Christ stood up in Roman Catholic
churches and charged Romanists with "idolatry."
Excitements were produced, but the truth had free
course, and was glorified.   To-day we are afraid to
speak of Christ to the worshippers of Mary.   The in-
timation, "I am a Roman Catholic" closes the mouth.

2. Because of the adaptability of the Gospel to refute the errors of Romanism.   It saves all that is
good in Romanism, and demolishes all that injures.
Peter claimed to be infallible; said, after Christ had
foretold His trial and death, "This shall not be done
unto Thee," and so foolishly exalted himself above
Christ.   Jesus would have none of it, but replied,
"Get thee behind me, Satan, for thou savorest not the
things that be of God, but those that be of men."

Paul foretold the doom of the ripened fruit of this seedling in 2 Thess. 2 : 4–10, which, after having exalted himself above all that is called God or worshipped, " The Lord shall consume with the spirit of His mouth, and shall destroy with the brightness of His coming." It is possible to reach Romanists through kindness, through common-sense, and by taking the Christianity of Romanism under the protection of Christianity, while the curiosity of Romanists is aroused to study the Scriptures to see if the things said be true. The Bible is the plague of Romanism. To arouse this curiosity will tax all the ingenuity of man, but it can be done. Let it be said that we do not differ essentially from Roman Catholics who believe in the Christ of Scripture, but only from those who turn from God to Mariolatry and idol-worship.

For Romanists we have love and persuasion. For Romanism, which is a political parasite, a monster fastened on the back of primitive Christianity, eating out its very life, a system that works with all deceivableness of unrighteousness in them that perish, we have bitter and implacable opposition.

It is ours to show that Christ is the only Mediator between God and man ; while Romanism has saints by the score, the Virgin Mary, the intercession of priests, and what not. Tell Romanists of this, and they will heed it. It is ours to call attention to the peril growing out of the forbidding the clergy to marry, while the Scripture declares that the minister of the church shall be the husband of one wife. It is ours to show that Romanism is a conspiracy against Christianity and the Bible in all lands. The Pope and the clergy are, and always have been, on the side of tyrants and against the liberties of the people.

While Romanism is unconquerable and almost unapproachable, yet it will go down when struck with the Word of God upon its vital point. The moment the truth of Revelation shines in upon Romanists, their errors disappear as mists before a rising sun.

We must pray and work for the conversion of Romanists. Christ, in Luke 22 : 31 and 32, in speaking of Peter, said, " Simon, Simon, behold Satan hath desired to have you that he may sift you as wheat, but I have prayed for thee, that thy faith fail not ; and when thou art converted, strengthen thy brethren." Let us go to Romanists in the same spirit. Encouragements abound.

All recognize the fact that Romanists in Italy, in France, in Germany, in Austria, and even in Spain, may be converted. To them we send missionaries, for them we print Bibles, tracts, and newspapers. But in America we surrender them to themselves, as if our theory of religious liberty somehow compelled us to leave errorists to the undisturbed control of error and all that it implies.

Who prays for the conversion of Romanists ? Who ever thinks of handing them a tract, or of asking them if they have a Bible ? Who cares as to what they believe, or what their belief is doing for them ? After the sermon, " Can we hope for the Conversion of Romanists ?" a friend rose in the second meeting and said, " These sermons have opened my eyes to the imperilled condition of Roman Catholics." On last Friday I chanced to visit a friend who lives near the Catholic cemetery ; the road was crowded with people, old and young, some carrying children in their arms, and others leading them. I inquired what was the cause of so great an excitement. My friend replied, " This is All Saints' Day ; it began yesterday. It will last until the Sabbath. Come up and look at the place of burial." I went and saw it, black with people, the gravestones nearly hidden.

" WHY ARE THEY THERE ?"

" To pray for the souls of the departed, now suffering purgatorial fire." This is so every year. It was not worse in the days of Tetzel than it is now in

enlightened America. The Romanism of the dark
ages is here. Indulgences are sold on the street cor-
ners in Brooklyn as they are at Rome.

A man, formerly a member of an evangelical
church, married a Roman Catholic wife, and in due
time surrendered to Rome. He came and heard the
sermon, "God's Word against Romanism," and with
streaming eyes went out at the close of the service,
saying, "I never knew this before; I will come
again."

A Roman Catholic, having heard the same sermon,
said : "I am convinced there is no more religion in
Romanism than in these paving-stones. I am a member of the Roman Catholic Church, in good standing ;
I go to mass in the morning, and spend the rest of the
day in pool-rooms and rum-shops, and am usually
drunk every Sunday night, without injuring my standing in the church. That cannot be the religion of the
Lord Jesus Christ."

The sermon, "Is Romanism good enough for
Romanists ?" was given to a Roman Catholic in New
York. He lived in the upper part of the island. On
Sabbath morning he read it, and called in two or three
friends and read portions of it to them. They asked
for copies that they might read it to their friends, and
that night this man came to the Temple in Brooklyn
that he might get copies of the sermon for distribution. All this proves that Roman Catholics are accessible to the truth, and that, unless Christians bestir
themselves in their behalf, the blood of immortal souls
will be found in the skirts of their garments. If
Christians do tell the truth in the fear of God and love
of souls, without doubt, uncounted thousands may be
brought to Christ.

CHRIST MADE OF THE PEOPLE.

He went to them in love and in helpfulness. Let
us do the same. Romanists as a rule are poor. They

find little help in the Church or from the Church. Be kind, be courteous, be true ; Christ was beautiful in the home. He made Himself of no reputation that He might help the lost and the undone. Magnify Christ. Let us have more worship. Never do I enter a Roman Catholic Church but I feel they have something we have not. Infidelity belittles Christianity and attempts to dwarf to the stature of man the Son of God. Lift Christ up. Praise and glorify Him. Speak of His divine endowments and of His marvellous power. It is said He had a noble and well-proportioned stature, with a face of kindness and yet firmness, so that beholders both loved and feared him.

THIS CHRIST LIVED AND WROUGHT AMONG MEN.

Men saw Him. Faith sees Him now. Those who believe Him see Him in His beauty. Those who see Him not now shall never see Him in the glory of His graciousness, but in His majesty when the heavens and the earth flee away. This is our opportunity to introduce Christ to Romanists, to infidels, to all, for He is the brightness of the Father's glory and the express image of His person, the King of kings, and the Lord of lords.

ENCOURAGING FACTS.

In 1500, Rome had 80,000,000 adherents in Europe. Protestantism was without a representation either on a throne or among the people. Since that time Romanism has gained in that territory 69,000,000, and Protestantism 73,000,000. Protestantism has had a phenomenal growth, until to-day it plays a far mightier part than Romanism in dominating the world. It is certainly making great and rapid advances in all the leading Roman Catholic countries of Europe, as Spain, Austria, France, Portugal, and Italy, in Mexico, and in the countries of South America. Catholic Spain and Portugal, the leading countries of Europe at the beginning of the Reformation, are now barely third-rate powers; while England and Germany, then weak, are now the leading powers of Europe and among the foremost in the world.

Coming to America, we find that in Canada in 1820 the Roman Catholics were to the Protestants as three to one, but now there are one and a half more Protestants than Romanists. Dr. Dorchester, the great Methodist statistician, declares that of the 8,000,-000 immigrants who came to our shores between 1850 and 1880, 4,800,000 were Roman Catholics—a number nearly 50,000 more than the total increase of our Roman Catholic population. These figures show that the advance of Protestantism is a great historical fact. In 1500 there were 80,000,000 people under Roman Catholic governments, and none under Protestant. In 1700 there were 90,000,000 Romanists and 32,000,-000 Protestants. In 1830 Romanists ruled 134,000,000, and the Protestants 193,000,000. In 1876 the numbers were respectively 180,000,000 Romanists and 406,000,000 Protestants, while to-day nearly or quite 500,000,000 of the human race are governed by Protestant rulers, while Catholic governments control scarcely more than two fifths as many.

Romanism fosters ignorance, immorality, and crime. The religion of Christ promotes education, virtue, and good-will to man. In Rome, under the very shadow of the Vatican, the people are going into blank atheism; they reject Romanism and are not yet instructed to exercise faith in the Gospel. On the fifth anniversary of the death of Victor Emmanuel, January 9th, 1884, King Humbert and wife visited the tomb of the great deliverer of Rome in the Pantheon. The papers of the day reported that a mass was said by a priest before the high altar; the Queen knelt reverently, but the King remained standing during the entire service. As the representative of the government of Italy, he scorned to bow the knee in a Roman Catholic church; and he is only one of the prominent leaders in Italy who are giving up all their old faiths, but receiving nothing in place of them. It is not the fashion to become Protestant, but it is the fashion for men to proclaim themselves "unbelievers." Many parents would deem it a great humiliation if their son should become a Protestant, but a confession of the most outspoken atheism is regarded by them wholly in order. Here is the point. Recently the audacious statement was made that communism comes from Protestantism. The *Presbyterian* asks, "Where are there any Protestant communists? From what church come the assassins of our coal-regions? On whom do they call for spiritual succor? Without a single exception, on their priests. Our hope is in the proclamation of the Gospel to Romanists. Once led to Christ, they will help in securing good laws for the protection of the community against the vices of licentiousness, gambling, intemperance, stealing, robbery, and murder; they will support good schools for the education of youth; the open Bible will lead to reverent inquiry, and faith in Christ as the only source of hope and pardon will take the place of a dead ritualism; the conscience of mankind will be emancipated, and all men will come to the knowledge of the truth."

SAFELY INVEST IN ROMANISM?

---

2 Cor. 6: 17.

" Wherefore come out from among them, and be ye separate, saith the Lord, and touch not the unclean thing, and I will receive you."

WERE I a Roman Catholic I should pursue the policy that has been adopted by the Church of Rome. But I am not, and instead I believe in a church whose foundation and plan were laid and perfected by Christ Jesus the Lord. Romanism is described in the word of God as antichrist. It is to this age what paganism was to the apostolic age. The paganism is here as it was there. The idols, the ceremonies, the genuflexions, the rejection of Christ the one and only mediator, everything that characterized pagan Rome in the first century characterizes the Rome of the nineteenth century and the Romanism of the nineteenth century, no matter where it is taught or practised.

Towards this system we sustain relations either of antagonism or friendship; which is it, and which should it be? To the law and the testimony we are driven by the command of God; to expediency, to political sagacity, to what pays, we are driven by the teachings and behests of men.

What saith the word of God? Much everywhere; more on this subject than on any other; and yet such is the gravitating power of interest that men are silent when they should be outspoken; they are mixed up in enterprises sinful in fact, though they may be harmless in appearance, when God commands us " to come out from among them and be separate." Is it not my duty and that of every Christian to adopt these words of John, saying, " That which we have seen and heard deliver we unto you, that ye also may have fellowship with us; and truly our fellowship is with the Father and with his son Jesus Christ. This then is the message which we have heard of Him, and deliver unto you, that God is light and in Him is no darkness at all "? Wherever God is known and worshipped in spirit and in truth, there is progress in science, in art, in literature, and in the development of man physically, mentally, and spiritually; but wherever God is rejected, men grope in darkness as if there had been no light. Hence said the apostles, and the words should have weight, *" If we say that we have fellowship with Him and walk in darkness, we lie and do not the truth. But if we walk in the light, as He is in the light, we have fellowship one with another, and the blood of Jesus Christ cleanseth us from all sin."*

It is because those who give their money to build Romish Institutions, lend their influence to support this system which has shrouded so much of the world in moral darkness, and so disobey God and walk in darkness, even while they profess to have fellowship with Christ, that we ask the question: *" Can American citizens safely invest in Romanism?"*

In considering the question we shall notice: 1. Some of the reasons why people give to build Roman Catholic Churches and Cathedrals. 2. What they do by this support; and, 8. Why it should not be given.

I. Why Citizens invest in Romanism.

American citizens give their money to aid in building Roman Catholic houses of worship, because they claim that the priesthood exercises a restraining and healthful influence over their people. Said a member of an Evangelical church, I gave to build a Catholic church, not because I think Romanism right, but to make it pleasant for my hired help. They want their church privileges, and though, poor things, they may be lost through error, I think the church helps them to be contented in our neighborhood.

Romanism not good enough for Romanists.

Others declare that the Romish church is after all better suited to the capacities and wants of the people worshipping at the shrine of Mary than was the Church Christ founded; forgetting not only that it is Romanism which degrades the people wherever its baneful influence is felt, but that it was Romanism which made the ages dark, centuries ago, and that of the religion of Christ alone can it be said, " It is good enough for Romanists." The Plan of Salvation is infinite in perfection. Christ came to the lowest and most benighted, and His Grace lifts the Irishman, the Chinaman, the American, and African alike out of the horrible pit and miry clay, and places their feet on the rock, and puts a new song in their mouth.

Many contribute to this church who have little or no sympathy with their views, but to avoid the charge of bigotry. Others do so because of the influence they hope to obtain in this way; politicians have thus brought untold injury upon the interests of liberty and humanity. Romanists are not confined to servants, as was formerly the case. They fill many of the important offices of the commonwealth and the land; their votes are at a premium, for in many places they hold the balance of power, and politicians seem to think that the shortest road to promotion and power is through the favor of the Romish priesthood and the Romish people. *It is the duty of American citizens to make that road very long and tedious to any aspiring politician. A man that must betray liberty, Christianity, and humanity to serve his country, had better be retired from service, and give place to one better and truer than himself.*

Fashion has also much to do with it. Romanism conforms to the world and administers to the behests of the carnal heart. Majorities are pleased by it, fashion thrives in its presence, and the religion proclaimed permits the votary to serve God and Mammon, to please self, conform to the claims of appetite and minister to pleasure, and yet obtain salvation because of the holy sacrifice of mass and the seven sacraments, which are all so many pretended channels, through which the graces that flow from the wounds of the Redeemer are conveyed to the souls of Catholics of every class, in every condition and at every period of life, *solely because of the power exercised by the priests.*

This statement was illustrated only the other day in Boston. A woman dying with delirium tremens was visited by the priest. He prayed over the crazed, unconscious woman as she was dying. Her breath ceased and the poor votaries of the church went out to collect money for the priest, saying, "he has saved her."

Thousands held in ignorance of truth, of Christ, of the plan of salvation, yield ready assent to a faith that allows them to live for pleasure and obtain entrance into heaven through the instrumentality of a priesthood and the infallibility of the church.

For instance, to two churches at the North End of Boston, twenty thousand communicants are said to belong. Many drink, get drunk, fight, swear, perhaps violate other commands of God and laws of the land, and yet they remain members of the church, and if they receive holy unction before they die, are said to go direct to heaven.

Let us not be deceived. Thousands are thus deceived and deluded. Get men to hear Christ, and this system would go down before truth as did the temporal power of the pope before a few cannon shots fired at the instance of Victor Emmanuel.

False ideas concerning the state and the design of the state exert their pernicious influence upon the minds of the masses of Romanists.

Father Hecker declares that "ere long there is to be a state religion in this country, and that state religion is to be Roman Catholic." Bishop O'Connor, of Pittsburg, says: "Religious liberty is merely endured until the opposite can be carried into effect, without peril to the Catholic world." The Archbishop of St. Louis declares: "If Catholics ever, which they surely will, gain an immense numerical majority, religious freedom in this country will be at an end," The pope speaks of "*the delirium of toleration*," and asserts the right "*to punish criminals in the order of ideas.*"

The state is more than a police force. It is more than a house which is inhabited. It is more than an employer. France was compelled to employ her working men in self-protection. "Paint the dome of the Tuileries," said the great Napoleon, when a revolt was threatened, as the next wonder to save the children of France from revolution. But Americans believe in the state as an idea which has a mission to fulfil, and a work to accomplish.

The state is that organization in which man tries to realize the highest interests of humanity. In it all are entitled to life, liberty, and the pursuit of happiness. Here men can grow in body, mind, and soul, without let or hinderance. The Romanist and the Protestant are protected in their theories and plans so long as they do not conflict with the rights of neighbors and communities.

Romanists do not believe in this liberty. Hence, wherever the church rules supreme, as in South American republics, civil and especially religious liberty is unknown. The Roman church treats her votaries as minors. A free church in a free state welcomes free and independent men as the hope of the state and the glory of the truth.

It is because Romanists cherish this view, that riots such as disgraced New York occur. The citizen is nothing. The church is everything; and for her sake those who should be proud to be citizens, trample upon the rights of the majority because they are taught to betray the state for the sake of the church.

II. *Consider in this connection what is done by this support given to build Romish structures.*

Those who countenance the delusion by attending their fairs, supporting their schools, or contributing to the building of their pretentious cathedrals and institutions, say to every deluded Romanist, "You are right. You are as safe in your church as we are in ours. There is no radical difference. You honestly believe what we claim to be a falsehood, and it is as well for you as though you as honestly believed a truth." By so saying, in act if not by word, such are guilty of bringing irreparable injury upon the rights and immunities of every citizen of the republic. Lower this standard in one place and you lower it in all. Citizens of New York once felt that the country could save the city. The city has destroyed or contaminated the country, and spread blight and misery everywhere. Put yourself in the place of an ignorant devotee to Rome. You enter a fair. You have not much money, nor much of comfort: the church has the largest share of your earnings. You build houses of worship, but do not control them; their titles and deeds are all vested in the bishop. He is master, you servant; you cannot have a Bible. Your children are compelled to give up the public schools; or if they attend them, as in New York some do, there is little taught beside the catechism and breviary, so that your children grow up in ignorance. You see them neglected on the Sabbath; they riot and revel in pleasure, while other children keep God's day holy, and you wonder that the priest never rebukes them, and is content to see you in poverty, in degradation, in indebtedness, while ministers of Christ seek to reform and help you; and in a muddle you go to the fair, and there see educated Protestants, politicians and wives of politicians, editors and their wives, people of fashion who attend upon what is called the ministry of the word, and you say, "After all these people must believe me safe or they would warn me." "They must have respect for my religion or else they would not countenance it." "My surmisings are groundless. My faith in the church has the sanction of men who can read the Bible, and who have enjoyed advantages denied me and my children; therefore it ought to be without reserve. I am wrong, the priest is right." Thus do men and women lend their sanction to error, and acquiesce in a delusion which is leading astray millions, and peopling the realms of sorrow with a vast multitude whom it is their duty to warn, and whom they must warn if they would not have the blood of immortal souls on the skirts of their garments. If there is a Romanist whose ear is open to these words, let me ask you not to be deceived by these manifestations of regard. They are given not because Protestants believe in Romanism, but from the conviction that it is wise to live in peace with it. You are in peril because you are without the truth; the Gospel is your hope; seek it, study it, follow it.

III. *Let us call attention to some of the reasons which should dissuade American citizens from investing in these structures which help Rome to propagate her errors.*

1. Because of the character of the church. She is arraying herself against liberty, against education, against temperance, against the Bible, and against the institutions which are the outgrowth of the teachings of the Word of God. This, we are aware, is a serious charge, but do not the facts justify the declaration? We do not deny that men are often better than their system. Individual Romanists may be Christian, though Romanism is unchristian. There are many private members of the church of Rome for whom we feel genuine sympathy. Especially among the lowly and simple-hearted there are those to whom God has revealed himself in Jesus Christ, though their minds are clouded by superstition.

Never do I enter these carpetless and miserable homes, see the faith of the poor creatures, and recognize the fact that they feel they are pleasing God, even while they are, at the beck of the priests, keeping their children in ignorance, and emptying their homes of comfort, that these great cathedrals may arise in magnificent proportions,— structures which are like cancers preying upon the life of the republic, impoverishing the government, and eating into the very heart and life of the people without feeling an almost irresistible desire to beseech men of greater light who come in contact with them, to undeceive them by honest speech, and lead them into the more excellent way. Talk kindly to them of the contrast between a Protestant and Roman Catholic community. Look at the difference in the appearance of the faces, of the dress, and of the behavior. Ask them to see what our institutions and our religion have done even for their own people, compelling their priests to preach Christ, and to live lives of decency and propriety, and give up the scandalous practices which degrade Europe, and which characterize some of the benighted portions of America.

It is with the system we war, because as citizens we find ourselves at once in conflict with it. While it was comparatively modest; while it pleaded for a place among our modes of worship as a need of the foreigners who thronged our shores; while it demanded only what was granted by our liberties to every denomination, it passed unnoticed. We had forgotten what it was. It walked among us in disguise. Large numbers of our most enlightened people seemed oblivious to its spirit and to its aims. With many it was regarded as a harmless institution; with others as an ordinary variety of the Christian religion. At last it feels the clutch of power. It throws off disguises, and becomes arrogant and aggressive. It claims exclusive privileges. It meddles with our schools, influences the press, padlocks lips that once dare speak for truth and righteousness. It organizes proselytism. It interferes with private liberty. It spreads publications which contradict the Gospel, and falsify history. It accumulates wealth in the hands of ecclesiastics. It insinuates its influence into municipal affairs, and obtains special grants of the public money for its exclusive uses.

Think of it. We have been ashamed, as American citizens, at the corruption revealed in New York. We have known that every department of the municipal government was reeking with wickedness, and yet there was no feeling of hope general enough among the citizens to enable them to rise up against it. Law was dead, and justice was but a name. Robbery and crime sat in the places of trust and judgment. The worst day of old Rome's wickedness when the empire was put up, at auction, seemed to have returned. Millions of money flowed into the coffers of the church of Rome. Magnificent churches, cathedrals, hospitals, and other structures rose on every hand, while taxes increased, and robbery and crime stalked defiantly abroad. Why was it? There is but one answer. Romanism had infected the city, filled the offices, and ruled the hour. The result was there, what it was in Rome in the year 1516, before modern Protestantism was born, when Machiavelli wrote: "The nearer the people are to Rome, the less devotion they have. By the scandalous example of the court of Rome, Italy has lost every principle of piety, and every sentiment of religion." Is it not so in New

York? Will it not be so everywhere? Pulpits of Protestant churches have thundered against corruption, while Rome laughs and pardons the thieves, if she is permitted to share in the spoils. And why? Because as New York sinks in infamy, in corruption, in degradation, Roman Catholic institutions rise on every hand, *as monuments of a people's shame, and as gravestones of liberty.*

I am not unmindful that Romanists claim that they possess the true faith. We admit that the church of Rome has the whole truth in possession and on record, and this is the weightiest count against her. Paul, in Rom. 1 : 18, declares " *the wrath of God is revealed from heaven against all ungodliness and unrighteousness of men who hold the truth in unrighteousness.*" Rome hides the truth from mankind, and institutes rites, traditions, and figments of her own for that pure word of God, after which men everywhere hunger. She claims that a man is infallible, and pretends to be the sole trustee of the divine anointing, so that all office and ordination in the church of God must be derived in succession from his hands. And now this system of delegated power must be imposed on the body of believers. The priest must, by some visible operation, be raised above the people into a supernatural reverence and dignity. This is accomplished through the doctrine of mass which claims that by priestly invocation, the wafer of bread and the wine are changed at every celebration into the actual body and blood of Christ, and that he is thus offered anew in sacrifice every day for the sins of men, and that the priest can give forgiveness through this instrumentality to whomsoever he will. Nothing could more obscure and destroy the whole truth of a completed redemption through his blood, who on the cross exclaimed, " *It is finished!*" Add to this the doctrine of confession to a priest, of purgatory by which the tender sorrows of mourners are played upon to secure for a price the deliverance of the dead, out of misery; add the theory of indulgence, by which forgiveness of sins may be obtained and the doctrine of the intercession of saints and of the Virgin Mary, and you have a system of religion which has actually nullified the Gospel, dethroned the Son of God, destroyed the power of his great sacrifice, and placed the hearts of men under bondage to human mediators, who are powerless to guide and save; and this system is sanctioned and sustained by every one who, by word or deed, gives it countenance and support.

Financially it is a mistake to invest in Romanism.

As a mere matter of speculation, we cannot afford to foster it. Around every Roman Catholic church, drinking, poverty, and crime go on, if rebuked, still unchecked. Nine-tenths of the rumshops in all of our cities, are under the control of Roman Catholics. The property in such localities is depreciated in price, and Evangelical churches find it very hard to maintain a foothold, because the vast portion of the population around, or near, are given up to rum or Romanism. Splendid squares have been invaded in Boston and New York, by nuns and sisters of charity, and at once the value of real estate is deteriorated. It is said that a Washington Street Evangelical church would be a failure at the South End of Boston, because of the fact that so large a section of the city has been abandoned to Romanists. In some cases houses in the neighborhood have fallen one half of their value, when a Protestant church is sold to Romanists. This may seem strange, and may strike the reader with surprise, but it remains a fact. Now as these large squares and plats of ground could be purchased, none of these magnificent structures could be built by the money which Romanists earn or give, it seems to be foolhardiness itself, which causes capitalists and citizens to destroy the value of real estate, the thrift and prosperity of the city, simply to secure the favor of those who keep votes on sale, and power for the highest bidder. Romanism, the product of the natural heart, is like weeds in the garden. It absorbs the strength of the soil, and kills the harvest which might else be grown. As a great cathedral is proof positive of the degeneracy, the ignorance, and the blindness of the people rearing it, every up-going structure of the kind is a sure precursor of the lack of thrift, of enterprise, and of advancement. Why is it that mission schools are failures at the North End of Boston? Not for the lack of children, but because children are under the control of Romanists who profane the Sabbath day, and prefer pleasure to piety, and selfish indulgence to the worship of God.

Our Duty to Christ and Humanity.

But there is another and weightier reason still. Christ came to save men, and it is our duty to help on the work, not to retard it. In the New Testament we are supplied with a model after which we are to pattern. Christ declares, "One is your Master, even Christ, and all ye are brethren." The qualification of membership is faith in Christ, which results in a new life, that is proof of a new birth.

Love was the characteristic of the primitive church. In it all occupied a common level. The object of the church was to bring the world back to Christ, and give to King Jesus his rightful place as Lord of Lords. This we know, and this we are to preach, saying, "Whosoever believeth and is baptized shall be saved, and whosoever believeth not, shall be damned."

Whoever sanctions error betrays truth. Whoever fosters a system antagonistic to the Gospel, is recreant to the Gospel, sides against God, and betrays the highest interests of the immortal soul. We must take sides for Christ and humanity, against sectarian bigotry and Romish heresy. Wherefore says the Apostle, "Come out from among them and be ye separate." Do it now by speech as well as by deed. Do not sanction any betrayal of liberty, or country, or Christ.

"Touch not the unclean thing."

That is God's command; obey it, and then shall the promise, "and I will receive you," be yours in time and in eternity.

CHRIST'S RECOGNITION OF PETER.

Matt. 16: 18.

"And I also say unto thee, That thou art Peter; and upon this rock I will build my church; and the gates of hell shall not prevail against it."

A TEACHER in a mission school asked the question, "On what does the church rest?" "On Peter," said a child of tender years. The teacher said, "Very well. On whom did Peter rest?" "On *Christ*," was the answer. That is right, said the shepherd of that young soul; let us all get on Christ, and we shall be safe as was Peter. The child spoke in accordance with the instructions she had received at home. The child was taught in accordance with instructions received from Rome. The Pope, in the decree published July 18th, 1870, declaring the infallibility of the head of the Romish church, declares "that Christ placed Peter before the other apostles," and quotes the words of Christ, recorded in Matt. xvi: 16–19, as authority for the claim. There can be no doubt that Romanism rejoices to find its reason for existence in this Scripture.

Do the words of Christ warrant the claim? Rome answers in the affirmative. Hence, we are not surprised to find in the notes of the Doway Bible this language: "As Peter by divine revelation here made a solemn profession of his faith in the divinity of Christ; so in recompense of this faith and profession, our Lord here declares to him the dignity to which he is pleased to raise him, viz.: That he, to whom he had already given the name of Peter, signifying a rock (John 1: 42), should be a rock indeed, of invincible strength, for the support of the building of the church; in which building he should be next to Christ himself, the chief foundation stone, in quality of chief pastor, ruler, and governor; and should bear, accordingly, all fulness of ecclesiastical power, signified by the keys of the kingdom of heaven." This language does not surprise us. We freely and gladly admit that Peter was recognized as a steward of the mysteries of God. In my opinion, a great mistake is made when attempts are made to ignore the place accorded Peter by Christ on this occasion. It was a wonderful moment. In the speech of this rude fisherman, a thought had stepped forth, which in Christ's estimation was the seedling of hope for a lost world. Peter had voiced it. Christ at once associated him with himself, and said for this confession, "*Thou art the Christ, the Son of the living God*," made thus openly, thus unequivocally, — I will make you the honored instrument of making known my gospel to Jews and Gentiles, and will make you a distinguished ally in building my church.

The humanity in Christianity obtained everywhere a recognition from Christ: "Ye are the salt of the earth," "Ye are the light of the world." These and kindred passages show how Christ regarded the agencies of man in carrying forward the work of Christ amidst the devastations wrought by sin. Under the new as under the old dispensation, God draws by the cords of a man.

To associate Peter with him in work is one thing. To distinguish him above the apostles is quite another. To declare that his name was Peter, or rock, or to promise to build the church on this apostle rather than on Christ, are two widely different utterances. Christ applauded Peter because of this confession of his divinity. The confession was made at an opportune time, and marked the inception of the organization of the church, which is to-day the pillar and ground of the truth. It was a moment of wondrous and portentous import. "The God Man was uncovered to the eye of the world."

Confession of Christ the Rock.

The confession of Jesus Christ was then and there declared to be the rock on which the church was to be built. The confession was grandly made. There was no equivocation or doubt in it. "Thou art Christ, the Son of the living God." Welcome words. They are for the first time heard. They prove that Christ's mission is to be a success. The light of God shining through Christ has left its imprint on the heart of the disciple, and he utters this sublime truth as a result. "Flesh and blood did not reveal it." It was not a human product, but a divine enactment. My Father who is in heaven is the originating cause. Said Christ, "No man cometh unto me except the Father who hath sent me draw him." The work has begun. Peter steps to the side of Jesus Christ, recognizes his Messiahship, confesses the truth. This is not the result, Christ says, of my appearance, nor of my social communion. God is at work. Peter saw God in Christ, reconciling the world unto himself. In this confession the church finds its corner-stone. This is the fundamental doctrine of salvation : " Whosoever confesseth me before men, him will I confess before my Father and his holy angels." Again, Christ declares, "I am the way, the truth, and the life." "No man cometh unto the Father except by me." Christ elsewhere declares himself to be the well-spring of life, and whosoever drinketh of the water that I shall give him, shall never thirst again. He is also the bread of life. Whosoever eateth of this bread shall live forever. Peter, on the day of Pentecost, held up the crucified to the gaze of the people from every land and every tongue, and proclaimed that God had made that same Jesus whom ye have crucified both Lord and Christ

Paul, in his letter to the Romans, makes confession of Christ essential unto salvation, saying, Rom. x: 8-10, "The Word is nigh thee, even in thy mouth, and in thy heart; that is the word of faith which we preach, that if thou shalt confess with thy mouth the Lord Jesus, and shalt believe in thy heart that God hath raised him from the dead, thou shalt be saved. For with the heart man believeth unto righteousness, and with the mouth confession is made unto salvation." Clearly, then, Christ referred to the confession made by Peter of himself as the Son of God, rather than to Peter the man, when he said, "upon this rock will I build my church."

Christ the Rock.

From Genesis to Revelation, Christ is everywhere represented as the rock or stone of Israel, as in Gen. xlix: 24. Isaiah, xxviii: 16, uses this language: "Behold I lay in Zion for a foundation, a stone, a tried stone, a precious corner stone, a sure foundation;" he that believeth this testimony and rests all his hopes of salvation on Christ shall never be put to flight or confusion as one in haste to escape impending danger, for he shall be safe, and quietly wait the salvation of the Lord.

In harmony with the teachings of the Old Testament and the declaration of Christ, are the inspired words of Peter recorded in his First Epistle and second chapter, where we find these words: "Wherefore laying aside all malice, and all guile, and hypocrisies and crimes, and all evil speaking, as new-born babes desire the sincere milk of the Word that ye may grow thereby; if so be, ye have tasted that the Lord is gracious" Peter believed in the gospel. The words of Christ give life. Men grow thereby. The Bible was to him what it is to us, the power of God unto salvation to every one who believeth, because it revealed Christ Jesus the Saviour of the world. "To whom coming as unto a living stone, disallowed indeed of men, but chosen of God and precious; ye also, as living stones, are built up a spiritual house, an holy priesthood, to offer up spiritual sacrifices acceptable to God by Jesus Christ." Then quoting the words of Isaiah, he adds: "Unto you, therefore, which believe, he is precious; but unto them which be disobedient, the stone which the builders disallowed, the same is made the head of the corner. And a stone of stumbling and a rock of offence, even to them which stumble at the Word, being disobedient whereunto also they were appointed."

It being proved by the words of Peter that he rested his hopes of salvation upon a confession of Christ, let us proceed to notice the reasons therefor. Peter knew for what Christ came. That Christ was the foundation of his hopes he was everywhere ready to declare. "For other foundation can no man lay than that which is laid, which is Jesus Christ."

He knew that Christ did not in these words confer on Peter a prerogative which God himself does not exercise. For neither God the Father, nor God the Son, nor God the Spirit, can remit sins except on the condition of confession of faith in Jesus Christ, which includes a reliance upon the atonement, made by his death, and the hopes builded on his resurrection, which are unfolded in the Gospel.

If Christ had given Peter power to remit sins capriciously, then he would have conferred authority upon man which does not belong to God, and which it were impossible for Christ to conceive of, or design or do. That Peter never dreamed of exercising the power claimed by his pretended successors, is shown by his words on the day of Pentecost, and by his subsequent efforts. To the Jews and Gentiles he preached with unwonted boldness Jesus after his resurrection, and never more did he claim infallibility for himself, nor was infallibility claimed for him.

Peter differed from his pretended successors in that he led about a wife with him in his journeys. She shared his trials and joys, and was blessed in having her mother healed by Christ. He differed from his pretended successor in refusing worship even in Cæserea, where Christ said, "Thou art Peter," when Cornelius, a servant and notable Jew, fell down at his feet and worshipped him, Acts x: 25, Peter took him up, saying, "Stand up; I myself also am a man." But when the keeper of the House of the Angel Guardian was in Rome, he boasts of having repeatedly kissed the Pope's foot, and declares, "I would gladly have kissed the very dust it rested on. Here, seated on his throne, — the throne of St. Peter, — sat St. Peter's successor: the bishop of Rome, to whom all patriarchs and bishops of the world owe obedience, the head of the church militant, the vicar of Jesus Christ; yet I, an obscure, unknown stranger, from a distant land, far over the great waters, was permitted to approach him, to kneel before him, and even to kiss his feet. St. John, the beloved disciple, leaned upon the bosom of Jesus himself; the traitor Judas kissed his cheek; the Magdalene his feet. I could not do either, but I did what I could, — I kissed the feet of his vicegerent on earth."

Nor did he kiss the foot of the Pope alone in the sanctuary; but when as a man he sat at his breakfast-table, this man-worshipper, to whom the State of Massachusetts commits the keeping of very many of our youth, bowed three times, and absolutely worshipped the man. The contrast between the Peter to whom Christ spoke and the pretended successor of Peter could not be more marked, while the power of superstition over the mind or heart seeks in vain for a better illustration.

In the council in Jerusalem, the record of which we find in Acts xv: 16–29, it was evidently not Peter, but James, who presided and shaped the decision, while the epistles of Peter unequivocally proclaim Christ as the living stone on which all hopes of growth and usefulness were built.

Peter not superior to the Apostles.

The difficulty in our path is reached. Rome refuses to be governed by Scripture. Here Luther stood and said, "Confute

me by plain passages of Scripture, else here I stand, God help
me." If Romanists would bring their claim to Scripture, and
would abide its decision, we could argue with them, agreeing that
the conclusion reached should bind us.   It is not Scripture, but
tradition, on which Romanism rests its authority for existence.
That Christ honored Peter we declare; that he honored the other
apostles in like manner is abundantly apparent.   Indeed it might
be proven that he honored others more than he honored Peter.   John leaned on his bosom, and was called the disciple
whom Jesus loved.   To Peter alone did Christ say, "Get thee
behind me, Satan, thou art an offence unto me, for thou savorest
not of the things that be of God, but those that be of men."
Matt. xvi: 23.   This language is recorded in the same chapter
where Christ said, "Thou art Peter."   Again, the idea of placing
one disciple above another is opposed to all of Christ's teachings.
In Matt. xx: 20–26, the mother of Zebedee's children seeks posts of
honor for her two sons; yet Christ refused the request, and said,
"Whosoever will be great among you, let him be your minister;
whosoever will be chief among you, let him be your servant."

Other apostles are as truly the foundation of the church, as is
shown by Eph. ii: 20, where Paul declares Christians "are built
upon the foundation of the apostles and prophets, Jesus Christ
himself being the chief corner stone; in whom all the building
fitly framed together, groweth unto an holy temple in the Lord."
"And the wall of the city had twelve foundations, and in them
the names of the twelve apostles of the Lamb."   Rev. xxi: 14.

Peter, instead of being ruler, was rebuked by Paul, as is recorded
in Gal. ii: 11, where he said, "When Peter was come to Antioch,
I withstood him to the face, because he was to be blamed."

The Keys.

But, says the devoted Catholic, did not Christ give Peter the
keys?   We reply, he did, but no more than he gave them to the
other disciples.   To Peter he said, "And I will give unto thee
the keys of the kingdom of heaven; and whatsoever thou shalt
bind on earth shall be bound in heaven; and whatsoever thou
shalt loose on earth shall be loosed in heaven."   In these words,
Christ gave to Peter official recognition of his stewardship, and
authorized him to proclaim officially the remission of sins on the
terms set forth in the Gospel.

In the eighteenth chapter of Matthew the truth is illustrated.
The disciples are taught that they occupy a representative position.   Their actions on earth are to be ratified in heaven because
their deeds are the blossoming forth of God's thought.   The
disciples came to Christ and asked, Who is greatest in the kingdom of heaven?   Perhaps Peter may have been envied because
of the attention bestowed upon him by the Saviour.   "And
Jesus called a little child unto him and set him in the midst of
them.   And said, verily I say unto you, except ye be converted
and become as little children, ye shall not enter into the kingdom
of heaven."   Then comes the question as to what was to be done

with a brother who trespassed against them? Christ replied, go and tell him his fault between thee and him alone; if he shall hear thee, thou has gained thy brother; if he does not hear thee, then take one or two more, and if he will not hear them, tell it unto the church; and then follows language identical with that used with Peter. "Verily I say unto you, whatsoever ye shall bind on earth shall be bound in heaven: and whatsoever ye shall loose on earth shall be loosed in heaven."

The minister, in his official capacity, as is the church in their official capacity, are engaged in solemn business. What they do on earth is ratified in heaven. The truth deserves consider- ation. Men have no right to trifle in the work of God. They are not to add to or substract from the Gospel. "For I testify unto every man that heareth the words of the prophecy of this book. If any man shall add unto these things, God shall add unto him the plagues that are written in this book; and if any man shall take away from the words of the book of this prophecy, God shall take away his part out of the book of life and out of the holy city, and from the things which are written in this book." These words close the volume of Scripture, and are recorded in the last portion of the last chapter of Revelations. Notwith- standing this, Rome rejects the Scriptures unless they can be accompanied with the notes and comments of men. There is to-day a standing offer from a merchant, to furnish for the mill- ions of Romanists in Italy and America, any copy of the New Testament, no matter by whom translated, which the Pope will sanction as a true version of the New Testament, to be given to all who will accept of it, providing it be circulated without note or comment.

It is not done, and why? "The Bible," said Chillingworth, more than two centuries ago, "the Bible only is the religion of Protestants." The confessions of all Evangelical churches echo this sentiment, and declare "the holy Scriptures containeth all things necessary to salvation." But Roman Catholics express themselves differently from Christians in this matter. They re- ceive the Bible indeed, but they want something more than the Bible for their guide. Thus the creed of Pope Pius IV. declares, after repeating the Nicene Creed, "*I most steadfastly admit and embrace apostolic and ecclesiastical traditions and all other observan- ces and constitutions of the same church.*" This opens the door to tradition and to innumerable errors. "I do also admit the holy Scriptures, according to that sense which our holy mother the _urch has held and does hold, to which it belongs to judge of the true sense and interpretation of the Scriptures; neither will I ever take and interpret them otherwise than according to the unanimous consent of the fathers." The Council of Trent placed the unwritten traditions of the church on a par with the re- corded word of God, and thus added a vast amount to Scripture, while such were the contradictions resulting therefrom, that, in self-defence, Rome has been obliged to restrict the circulation of the Scriptures to a fearful extent. In Italy, where Rome was supreme, the Bible was banished. John Wickliffe, the herald of the Reformation, and the earliest translator of the Bible, made his translation from the Vulgate; but the Council of Constance, in 1415, more than thirty years after his death, anathematized him as a notorious and scandalous heretic, and ordered his bones to be disinterred and cast out from ecclesiastical burial. William Tyndale, another English reformer, and a translater of the Bible from the Hebrew and Greek originals into clear and simple English, was condemned as a heretic, and finally, after his last prayer, "Lord, open the king of England's eyes." was strangled and burned at the stake in Belgium, Oct. 6, 1540.

Bible burning and Bible hating characterizes priests in America as in Europe. The opposition felt towards the Bible being read without note or comment, in the public schools, is one of the saddest features of the times. Catholics owe it to themselves and their children to remonstrate against priestly opposition to the word of God. According to Pius IX., the church of Rome rests upon Peter because of the word of God. If the word of God is true at all, it is all true. If we admit its binding power in one instance, we must admit it in all. This truth is pervading the minds of thousands of the more intelligent Catholics in our land. They resist whatever separates them from the word of God, and in so doing they are right. Let God be true, for as Peter said, "*We must obey God rather than men.*"

Peter Dear to the Heart of the Church.

Because of the attempts to exalt Peter by Romanists, and to prove that he was not in any way superior to the other apostles, by Protestants, it is to be feared that we are losing from our thought and heart the grand place Peter held in the esteem of Christ. He was a bold and fearless man. His impulses at times carried him away, but he was a man of power and influence. Christ loved him and leaned on him. His confession of Jesus before all was like him. His sermon and bearing on the day of Pentecost, entitle him to the admiration and love of the Christian world. The risen Christ whom he had denied had been in their midst. He had asked Simon, — not Peter, but Simon, — saying, "Simon, Son of Jonas, lovest thou me?" Peter's heart was broken. And he said, "Lord, thou knowest all things; thou knowest that I love thee." Jesus said unto him, "Feed my sheep and lambs." The crisis had come. The Lord had ascended to his throne on high. Fifty days had passed since the Lamb was slain and captivity was broken. Forty days he had been with them after his resurrection; the rest he had passed within the vail.

The second Lord's day after the ascension found the entire company met with one heart to renew their oft-repeated prayer. We know not where was the room, nor who was praying. The disciples all prayed when one prayed for the descent of the Spirit.

"Suddenly there came a sound from heaven as of a rushing, mighty wind." Shaken by this supernatural sign, we may see each head how low. They raise their eyes. Peter sees James crowned with fire. James sees Peter all aglow. The Holy Ghost has come. Jesus is the Christ. "And they were all filled with the Holy Ghost, and began to speak with other tongues, as the spirit gave them utterance." The noise and the rumor flew forth. God had come. The people from far and near flocked together. Nothing draws people like the power of the Holy Ghost. Let Christ come in the spirit, and the people come also. The crowd surged about them. The people ask what meaneth it. Then Peter opens his lips, not in Rome, for it is questionable if he ever was in Rome; but in Jerusalem, he stood forth as God's ambassador, as Peter, as Christ's associated laborer, and preached Jesus and the resurrection with such power that multitudes were pricked in the heart, and cried out to Peter and to *the rest of the apostles*, "Men and brethren, what shall we do?" Then Peter said unto them, "Repent and be baptized, every one of you, in the name of Jesus Christ, for the remission of sins, and ye shall receive the Holy Ghost." Thus was he honored as a preacher of righteousness. He knew his work, and boldly he entered upon it, and adhered to it until his death. Let us imitate his example. Keep the two facts before you. Peter's confession, "Thou art the Christ, the Son of the living God," was the begining of the church, completed on the day of Pentecost, when Christ was preached, and men believed and were baptized.

The confession of Christ is the rock on which faith builds the superstructure of hope. Preaching Christ is the means by which this world is to be subdued and brought back to the rule of the Most High. Peter's confession and Peter's preaching are suggestive facts. The one pointed out Christ the rock and foundation of faith. The other pointed out the tongue as the instrument which was to be the most potent instrument of the grandest war ever waged. Man's speech to his fellow man; a message in human words to human faculties; from the understanding to the understanding; from the heart to the heart. Blessed symbol! Let us make of it and honor it. Prayer had brought the spirit's presence, and with God came a people prepared to receive the Gospel, and a man prepared to preach it.

Have we confessed Christ as did Peter? If not, let us learn that this is our first business; Make Jesus ruler. Abandon all for him. Think how Christ came to Peter and blessed him because of his confession. Such a blessing is in readiness for all!

Have we prayed for the Spirit's presence? Think what would be the result; the tongue of fire would once more be seen, and Christ's Gospel would be the power of God to the subjugation of man.

Do we preach Christ, not only here, but from man to man? If not, take Christ's gospel and go with it to men as did Peter, and soon the cry will be heard, *Men, what shall we do?* and we can with Peter reply: "Repent and be baptized, every one of you, in the name of Jesus Christ for the remission of sins, and ye shall receive the gift of the Holy Ghost."

THE MISTAKES OF PETER, TYPES OF THE MISTAKES OF ROMANISM.

LUKE xxii : 31, 32.

"And the Lord said, Simon, Simon, behold, Satan hath desired *to have* you, that he may sift you as wheat. But I have prayed for thee, that thy faith fail not: and when thou art converted, strengthen thy brethren."

THE loving and omniscient Christ addresses more than Peter in these words. It is the wonder and the glory of the Bible, that it meets the wants of humanity. Christ spoke for the ages, as well as spoke to the ages. There is a prescience in the words which followed the rebuke administered to Peter, which is seen in the light of subsequent events, and understood when we consider that the mistakes made by Peter prior to the resurrection of Christ were types of the mistakes of the church in subsequent ages, out of which grew Romanism. Christ was not deceived. His eye beheld the danger, and his example furnishes us a grand illustration of the best way to meet it and overcome it. How tender was his utterance. How full of love his admonition. How encouraging his exhortation. To obtain the full meaning and significance of his words, we must hold the conception in our thoughts, that the omnipresent and omniscient God was speaking. It is a tendency of our nature to judge God by human standards. Christ cannot be understood, judged in this manner. We cannot understand Christ's dealing with Peter, if we lose sight of the Divinity which looked through the eyes of our common humanity, and ranged through all the subterfuges and hiding places of the human heart with an exactness, a comprehensiveness, and an omniscience which made it impossible that he should lose from his speech a single thought, or add to it a single shade that should imperil the future of truth. The more we study the drifts and purposes of humanity, — seeing that it is a tendency with Christians, as it is a habit with the unregenerated, to make God like unto themselves, — the more we are impressed that Christ, who knew what was in man, knew this, and needed not to have any one tell him what was to be, because the future, with all of its mysteries and possibilities, was actually present to him; the more we observe the care exercised in the composition of the Gospels, a care which placed in them everything now needed to refute error and support truth, the more we are impressed with the absolute need of a Divine Founder for a Divine Faith. Christ saw in the mistakes of Peter premonitions of Romanistic error, and so he rebuked the tendency, and used language which must have been hard for him to bear, while he was ignorant of its significance; but which, studied in the light of Romanistic pretension, clearly enunciates a truth deserving serious consideration.

Notice in this connection that Peter's first mistake appears in the Papal claim of infallibility, the root-error of the system.

The Saviour had been showing "unto his disciples, how that he must go unto Jerusalem, and suffer many things of the elders, and chief priests and scribes, and be killed, and be raised again the third day." " *Then Peter took him, and began to rebuke him, saying, 'Be it far from thee, Lord; this shall not be done unto thee.'*" This spirit of presumption, "which opposeth and exalteth itself above all that is called God, or that is worshipped;" or, in other words, this spirit which induced Peter to exalt himself above Christ, and to declare what should be done to him, is so like that dread vision of which Paul prophesied in 2 Thess. ii : 4-10, and which Christ saw darkening the sky of the future, that we can understand why he should turn to him and say, "Get thee behind me, Satan; thou art an offence unto me; for thou savorest not the things that be of God, but those that be of men." If Christ was overjoyed when he recognized the working of the Father in the heart of Peter, causing him to confess "that Christ was the Son of God," Christ was filled with sorrow when he saw Satan holding possession of the soul of Simon, and even then plotting the ruin of the race.

Notice the charge.

"Thou savorest not the things that be of God, but those that be of men." Strange words! Ponder their meaning. They shine forth not only as revelations of the character of a man, but of the character of the church that claims the man as founder. Was ever prophecy more clear-eyed. That Romanism builds on Peter, we do not deny. As we study the early life of the man, we are surprised that there is so much in his character, in his words and disposition, calculated to supply the irreligious system with material for a foundation. May it not be so with all of us? How perilous to let go of Christ! How full of danger is the act of presumption which permits us to attempt to take God's work out of his hands! Christ said, "I must suffer many things of the elders and chief priests, and scribes, and be killed, and be raised again the third day." Peter said, "Lord, this shall not be unto thee." That pretentious spirit infests Romanism. Christ commands us to "search the Scriptures." Romanism expresses its disbelief in the Scriptures, and applauds its votary for declaring "that the doctrines of Scripture, if believed in, would send the believer to hell."

The pretentiousness of Peter, which caused him to declare what Christ should do and what should not be done to him, was matched by the effort afterwards made to set aside the work of Christ, and substitute therefor the work of a man. The claim that priests have the power to forgive sins, is but the outcropping of the same disposition which said unto our Lord, "This shall not be done unto thee."

Do Priests claim the power to forgive sin ?

A Roman Catholic priest, in an article published in a secular paper, denies that priests claim the power, and quotes as proof the reply to the question: "In what manner can sins be forgiven by the sacrament of penance?" "By the priest's absolution, joined with confession, contrition and satisfaction." Confining our attention to this statement, it is not difficult to perceive, that two of these conditions are derived from the priest; namely, absolution and confession. We might ask, of what value would this sacrament be to a Catholic if there was no priest, no confession, and no absolution? Will Romanists assert that a sinner can go to Christ direct and have his sins forgiven, and that the confessional is a luxury to be enjoyed, rather than a necessity? Christ said, "Where two or three are gathered together in my name, there am I in the midst of them." Rome denies the statement, and claiming that God can be communicated with only in a consecrated place, builds a church, or erects an altar, before she tries to win votaries, or to perform an act of worship. The disciples were sent into all the world and were commanded to preach the gospel to every creature, saying, "Whosoever believeth and is baptized shall be saved." They found Paganism enthroned in pomp and show, ministered unto by rites and ceremonies and glorying in the achievements of architecture. Pictures decorated their temples; and idols built by human hands, consecrated them. Rome adopted Paganisms, gorgeous rites, mitres, tiaras, wax tapers, crosiers, processions, lustrations, images, gold and silver vases, holy water and temples. The result was, Paganism was Romanized. Let us not deny it. Paganism, the religion of the natural heart, finds in Romanism its embodiment, and is a power which lives and exerts its influence. Christianity declares that God is not confined to any place, that communion with him is possible at any time and anywhere. For there is one God and one Mediator between God and man, the man Christ Jesus. Rome claims that salvation is impossible outside the church, and "that Christ gave power to forgive sins to the apostles and their successors, — the bishops and priests of the church."*

2. The second mistake of Peter consisted in his ignoring the necessity of Christ dying to the world, which is involved in the idea of conversion. Paul said, "God forbid that I should glory save in the cross of our Lord Jesus Christ, by whom the world is crucified unto me, and I unto the world." Peter did not understand the purport of his speech, and did not comprehend, as he afterwards did, that if Christ had not died for all, then were all dead. Rome does not comprehend it, even now. She does not believe in a dying to the world that we may live to Christ. But on the contrary, by precept and practice, inculcates the belief that man can be saved without a change of heart. Religion with them is not a life inwrought in the soul that bears fruit, but a life apart

---

* Boston Catechism, approved by Bishop Fitzpatrick, p. 17.

from it, inhabiting an organism called a church Men are saved,
not because they confess Christ with the mouth, and believe in
their hearts that God raised Christ from the dead, but because a
man has baptized them, and a man has confirmed, and a man has
fed them with the bread and wine in the eucharist. Christ said,
"Verily, verily, I say unto you, except a man be born again, he
cannot see the kingdom of God." *"That which is born of the flesh
is flesh, and that which is born of the spirit is spirit."* "And as
Moses lifted up the serpent in the wilderness, even so must the
Son of Man be lifted up; that whosoever believeth in him should
not perish, but have eternal life." These words declare the need
of a change of heart, wrought by the Spirit of God, in order that
man may know Jesus, the author and finisher of our faith.

Do we comprehend the peril of Romanists? Millions of them
in this and other lands are trusting to man, to an organism
rather than to Christ. They are taught that they are safe, even
though they continue in sin. We hear them swear; we see them
growing up apparently without faith, and without hope; they
claim that they are sincere, and are, therefore, safe. Look at
the man in yonder rapids. He believes he can escape. You
know his peril. He will not heed your cry, fancying that sincerity is salvation. He is in the current. It is mightier than
the man. What does sincerity avail him? Yonder is a blind
man approaching a precipice. The way is smooth. He claims
that he is safe. But he is blind, and you strive to arrest his
march. Romanists are blinded by superstition. Go to them in
love. Be in earnest. A leading merchant accepted Romanism.
When asked, "On what do you rest your hope of salvation?"
he replied, "On the fact of my baptism into the Roman Catholic church, my confirmation and communion." — "Then," I said,
"it is on what man has done for you, rather than on any sense
of pardon received from Christ?" He replied, "Yes." I tried
to show him his peril, and quoted to him Peter's words : "Neither is there any other; for there is none other name under
heaven given among men, whereby we must be saved, except
the name of Jesus Christ of Nazareth, whom the Jews crucified,
and whom God raised from the dead." In vain. It seemed impossible to get him to let go of man. "Suppose you are lost
because of your rejection of Christ?" — "Then," said he, "I
will hold the priest responsible to all eternity, — for I pay him so
much a year for prayers and indulgences."

You remark, how wonderful the blindness of the man! His
blindness was no greater than is that of others. Millions are influenced by the same delusion. This man died in a few weeks by
sun-stroke, and went home to God. leaning on man and rejecting
Jesus Christ because Rome held his conscience and faith. It is
declared to be the doctrine of the Catholic Church, "that man is
spiritually born by Baptism, strengthened by Confirmation, nour-
ished by the Holy Eucharist, and restored to spiritual health by the
sacrament of Penance." Now, it is known to every scholar that
there is no such word as "penance" to be found in the Bible.

The Catholic, or Doway version, misleads its readers; for the word *metanoeite* is from the verb *metanoeo*, meaning, to change one's mind, to feel penitence, or repent. To this definition, Rome adds and includes penance, not only penance and amendment of life, "but also punishing sins by fasting, and such like penitential exercises." Thus again does Romanism savor of the things of man. That Jesus Christ came to earth and died that we might have life, Rome admits. Romanists should search the Scriptures and see if they are not in danger because they reject Christ and accept man instead as a mediator.

3. *Peter's third mistake was in seeking the pre-eminence.*

The language of the text intimates that Peter had been making the attempt to prove himself to be the greatest. The recognition Christ gave to Peter may have emboldened him; and so, when the strife began as to who was to be greatest, Peter assumed a position which did not belong to him. Christ singled him out and said, " Simon, Simon, behold Satan hath desired to have you, that he may sift you as wheat." Was there a prophetic outlook in these words? Do they mean more than they seemed? Was Christ directing his attention to the disposition that was to distinguish them who were to rank themselves as his followers? Was it to be their distinctive feature to seek to be chief, to claim supremacy absolute over men in temporal and spiritual affairs? Christ was prescient. He saw the things of to-day as much and as clearly as he saw the things of that day. And so, when he spoke to Peter, did he not speak to his followers, saying, " Satan desires to have you."

I will not ask, Has not Satan obtained control of the church of Rome? Let us rather see if we cannot find a ground for hope and of expectation, because the church of Rome resembles Peter in his mistake. He courted power, pre-eminence, and position. So does the Papal See. No one can review the conduct of Romanists, and see how Satan hath used the machinery of the church of Rome to stifle liberty, to oppose education, to cover humanity with a pall of night, and lock up their hopes in the castle walls of superstition, without seeing reasons why Satan should desire to have such a power, and to keep such a power under his control. But as there was a noble nature lying side by side with the ambitious nature in the character of Simon, so are there not seedlings of hope lying side by side with seedlings of doubt and despair in the present condition of Romanism?

4. *The fourth mistake of Peter was made when he denied Christ.* How little did he know himself. He had just said, " Lord, I am ready to go with thee, both into prison and to death." Christ said, "I tell thee, Peter, the cock shall not crow this day before thou shalt thrice deny that thou knowest me." The words were literally fulfilled. Peter turned his back on Jesus to gain the favor of a wicked world. The same thing was done by the church before she took the name of Rome, when she gave up fellowship with God and leaning upon the truth, for the sake of the power and patronage of men. At first, the supremacy of

the church of Rome was limited. But the rank which this imperial city held in the world offered to the ambition of its early pastors a prospect of wider sway. "All the inhabitants of the earth are hers," said Julian; and Claudius declares her to be the fountain of laws. When heathen Rome fell, she bequeathed her power to the representative of this church, and the trident of a Nero became the tiara of the pope. At first, the Roman bishop was one among brethren, and by all was regarded as an equal. Exhortations grew into commands, and fraternal epistles were converted into bulls; or, in the words of D'Aubigne, "Men suffered the precious perfume of faith to escape, while they bowed themselves before the empty vase that held it." Thus was Christ deserted, and the living faith in Jesus was compelled to retire to the lonely sanctuary of a few solitary souls, as Christ, after looking at Peter, found refuge in himself, and rested his hope upon the truth sown broadcast in the world. In the beginning of the gospel dispensation, whoever had received the Spirit of Jesus Christ was esteemed a member of the church. The order was inverted by the church of Rome, and no one unless a member of this church was counted to have received the Spirit of Jesus Christ. Salvation by grace was lost sight of, and salvation by works was substituted. The pope exalted himself as God. He dispensed pardons and indulgences to the living and the dead. The evil was at its height, and then Luther the Reformer arose. During this night of years we are not to conclude that all followed one path and that the faith of Jesus had died out. Far from it. The church of Rome was not universal then, no more than it is universal now. Brave and devoted men preached Christ and contended for the faith once delivered to the saints, and won mighty victories in the name of God, as is proven by the millions of martyrs who died witnessing for the faith, and by the records and results which come down to us as an inheritance from the past.

Our ground of hope for Romanism

Finds its support in the words of Christ addressed to Peter. "But I have prayed for thee, that thy faith fail not; and when thou art converted, strengthen thy brethren." Study the language, "*I have prayed that thy faith fail not.*" Peter had faith in Christ, which was evidenced by his confession. Romanists have a kind of faith. They confess Christ in the sign of the cross, in their prayers and in their speech. For this they are loved by God and should be loved by us. They are nearer us than are thousands who revile Christ. Let us feel this and imitate Christ's example and pray for them. The assurance would do them good.

Do we pray for Romanists?

Rather, do we not feel disposed to fight them, and say hard things of them, and quote against them the persecutions of the past and the hatreds of the present. Suppose the spirit of Christ possessed us and induced us to pray for them in faith;

can we not believe that thousands of them would come to the light, as did Luther, and millions more beside?

Let us pray for them in hope.

They have some faith. Let us pray that it fail not; but that they hold on to that as the sinking man holds on to the line thrown to him, while the life boat is on its way to save him. Love thaws the ice which the hammer cannot break. There are many reasons why we should have faith and hope in this land. The gospel is exerting its influence upon the masses. The ministers of the Romish church preach now as they did not once preach. The sermons of some of their priests are full of gospel truth, and must exert a salutary influence on the lives of their people. They see, with us, the need of temperance, and in many of the priests this cause finds its noblest advocates. Pray that they hold on.

Let us pray for their conversion,

And let us preach and talk as we pray. Their church teaches, as we have seen, that there is no need of this. But the lives of its membership reveal the necessity. As our Lord and Saviour said to Nicodemus, so say we, not to Romanists alone, but to all, " Ye must be born again." The heart is at enmity with God. It must be changed. The heart of stone must be melted, or broken, and for it must be substituted the heart of flesh that shall delight to do the will of God. Do you ask how can this be done? We reply, faith exercised in Jesus Christ; such as came to Peter when he saw Christ after his resurrection; a faith preceded by confession of the lips, and completed by believing in the heart, that God raised Christ from the dead.

Can anything be more plain? Romanists trust to what men or organisms can do. By so doing they dishonor Jesus Christ. Their duty is similar to our own. They must reject all mediation except that which comes through Christ Jesus. By this we approach God, and have fellowship with him. How clearly John places this truth before us in the first chapter of his gospel: " There was a man sent from God, whose name was John. The same came for a witness, to bear witness of the Light, that all men through him might believe. He was not that Light, but was sent to bear witness of that Light. That was the true light which lighteth every man that cometh into the world. He was in the world, and the world was made by him, and the world knew him not. He came unto his own, and his own received him not. But as many as received him, to them gave he power to become the sons of God, even to them that believe on his name, which were born, not of blood, nor of the will of the flesh, nor of the will of man, but of God." Let us bless God for this gospel, which is as a lamp to all our feet.

We have spoken of our ground of hope for the conversion of Romanists, and have intimated that Christ gives us a reason for it in the words addressed to Peter. Let us for a moment look out upon the world and study its condition in the light of prophecy. We are told that the mystery of iniquity doth already work; only he who now hindereth will hinder until he be taken out of the way. "And then shall that wicked one be revealed, whom the Lord shall consume with the spirit of his mouth, and shall destroy with the brightness of his coming." Has not God uncovered his hand the past year? Let us hope, then, in the preaching of the gospel. Romanists only need to throw away error, and seek God with their whole heart, through the merits of Christ's redeeming grace, and they shall be saved. Already, many of the errors of Rome are seen by such men as Hyacinthe, Dollinger, of Europe, and thousands in America. Let the work go on. Pray mightily for the conversion of the leaders, as well as of the followers, and then shall the testimony of Christ sound forth from the lips of the redeemed in all lands, as it was sounded forth in France and Europe, when the altars of superstition were deserted, and Bible readers and Bible preachers spoke to listening thousands, who were called by this gospel to the obtaining of the glory of our Lord Jesus Christ.

Then shall the true character of Romanism shine forth, and men shall see that its coming was after the working of Satan, with all power and signs, and lying wonders, and with all deceivableness of unrighteousness in them that perish, because they received not the love of the truth that they might be saved.

A word to converted Romanists.

Preach in love to the blinded. Thou hast been converted as was Peter, that thou mightest strengthen thy brethren. Go to them in the love of Christ, and with the constraining power of the gospel, and you shall see of the travail of your soul and be satisfied. In vast numbers they shall come to the knowledge of the truth. This is my faith, and for its consummation let us all devoutly pray.

> Jesus my all to heaven is gone,
> He whom I fix my hopes upon;
> His track I see and I'll pursue
> The narrow way till him I view.
>
> The way the holy prophets went —
> The way that leads to banishment;
> The King's highway of holiness, —
> I'll go, for all his paths are peace.
>
> This is the way I long have sought,
> And mourned because I found it not;
> My grief, my burden long has been
> Because I could not cease from sin.
>
> The more I strove against its power,
> I sinned and stumbled but the more;
> 'Till late I heard my Saviour say,
> "Come hither, soul, I am the way."

THE GREAT SPEECH AT THE VATICAN.

ATTRIBUTED TO BISHOP STROSSMAYER.

THIS speech has been widely circulated in Europe and America, as translated by Rev. Leonard W. Bacon. We can imagine better than we can describe the effect produced upon the Roman people. Nothing like it has been witnessed since the king of Babylon beheld on the palace wall the words : *Mene, mene, tekel upharsin,* weighed in the balances and found wanting. It was said that the bishop of Bosnia, in Croatia, had been studiously applying himself to the examination of the Holy Scriptures on the question whether the holy pontiff who presides in the council is really the successor of St. Peter, the vicar of Jesus Christ, and the infallible teacher of the church. The effect of this inquiry whether raised in the Council or outside was startling. This is the language as circulated in Rome.

I open these sacred pages. . . . But what! shall I dare to tell it? I find in them nothing to justify, however remotely, the ultramontane view. Nay, more! to my utter astonishment, I find nothing said about a pope, successor of St. Peter and vicar of Jesus Christ, any more than about a successor of Mohammed.

Yes, Archbishop Manning, you will say that I blaspheme; and you, Bishop Pie, that I am out of my senses. No, no, my lord bishops! I am not blaspheming; I am not beside myself! But having just risen from the reading of the New Testament from beginning to end, I declare to you before God, lifting my hand towards yonder great crucifix, that I find in its pages no trace of the papacy as it now exists.

Do not refuse to listen to me, venerable brethren! Do not, by your murmurs and interruptions, justify those who declare with Father Hyacinthe, that this council is not free, but that our votes are imposed upon us in advance. If this were so, this august assembly, towards which the eyes of the whole world are turned, would fall into the most shameful contempt. If we would be great, we must be free.

I thank His Grace, Bishop Dupanloup, for that nod of approval! It gives me courage to go on.

Reading, then, the Scriptures, with such attention as the Lord has made me capable of, I have not found in them a single chapter, a single verse, in which Jesus Christ commits to St. Peter lordship over the apostles, his fellow-laborers.

If Simon, son of Jonas, had been appointed to be what we understand His Holiness, Pius IX, to be in our time, it is astonishing that Christ did not say to the apostles: "When I am ascended up to my Father, ye all shall obey Simon Peter as ye have obeyed me. I appoint him vicar upon earth."

Not only is Christ silent on this point, but He has so little thought of giving the church a chief, that when He is promising thrones to His apostles, to judge the twelve tribes of Israel (Mathew 19: 28), he promises twelve of them — one apiece — without saying that one is to be higher than the rest, and is to belong to Peter. Surely if He had wished this to be so, He would have said so. What must we infer from His silence? Logic tells us: Christ did not intend to make Peter chief of the apostolic college.

When Christ sent forth the apostles to the conquest of the world, He gave to all alike the power of binding and loosing; to all, the promise of the Holy Ghost. Let me repeat it: if He had meant to make Peter His vicar, He would have appointed him commander-in-chief of His spiritual army.

Christ, says the Scripture, forbade Peter and his colleagues to have rule and lordship, and power over believers, like the princes of the Gentiles. (Luke 22: 25.) If Peter had been made pope, Jesus would not have spoken thus, for according to our traditions, the papacy holds in its hands two swords, the symbol of spiritual and temporal power.

One fact has profoundly impressed me. When I observed it, I said to myself: If Peter had been pope, would his colleagues have suffered themselves to send him with St. John to Samaria to preach the gospel of the Son of God? (Acts 8: 14.)

What would you think, venerable brethren, if, at this moment, we were to permit ourselves to depute His Holiness, Pius IX, and his Eminence, Monsignor Plantier, to betake themselves to the Patriarch of Constantinople, and adjure him to put an end to the Eastern schism?

But here is another fact, of greater importance still. An ecumenical council was assembled at Jerusalem to decide on questions on which believers were divided. Who would have convoked this council, if St. Peter had been pope? St. Peter. Who would have presided over it? St. Peter, or his legates. Who would have formulated and promulgated the canons of it? St. Peter. Well, now, nothing of the kind took place. The apostle was present at the council, like all his colleagues. But it was not he who framed its conclusions, but St. James; and when the decrees of it were promulgated, this was done in the name of "the apostles, the elders and the brethren." (Acts 15.) Is this the way we manage things in our church?

The deeper I go, venerable brethren, in my examination, the more I am convinced that in the Holy Scriptures there is no appearance of the primacy of the son of Jonas.

While we teach that the church is built on St. Peter, St. Paul, whose authority cannot be questioned, tells us, in his Epistle to the Ephesians (2: 20), that it is "built upon the foundation of the apostles and prophets, Jesus Christ himself being the chief corner-stone." The same apostle is so far from believing in the supremacy of Peter, that he openly rebukes those who say: "I am of Paul and I of Apollos" (1 Corinth. 1: 12) in the same terms as those who would say: "I am of Peter." If, then, the latter apostle was vicar of Jesus Christ, St. Paul would have taken good care not to censure so violently those who held to his colleagues.

The same apostle Paul, enumerating the offices of the church, mentions apostles, prophets, evangelists, teachers, pastors. Is it credible, venerable brethren, that St. Paul, the great teacher of the Gentiles, would have left out the greatest of all the offices — the papacy — if the papacy had been founded by divine Institution? It seems to me that this omission would have been no more possible than a history of this council that should make no mention whatever of His Holiness, Pius IX. (*Voices in the Assembly — Silence, heretic! silence!*)

Keep calm, venerable brethren! I have not got through yet. By hindering me from going on, you will show the world that you are in the wrong, and that you have gagged the humblest member of this body.

I proceed: The apostle Paul in not one of his letters addressed to the various churches, makes any mention of the primacy of Peter. If this primacy had existed, if in short the church had had a supreme head, infallible in teaching, would the great teacher of the Gentiles have omitted all mention of it? Nay! He would have written a long epistle on this important, this vital subject. When, therefore, he is rearing the edifice of Christian doctrine, is it possible that he leaves out the foundation and the key-stone? Now, unless the apostolic church is to be reckoned heretical, which we neither wish nor dare to say, we are constrained to acknowledge that the church has never been more fair, more pure, nor more holy, than in the days when it had no pope. (*Voices — It is false! it is false!*)

Monsignor de Laval cannot contradict this; for if any of you, venerable brethren, should dare to think that the church which at this day has a pope for its head, is stronger in faith, or purer in morals, than the apostolic church, he must say it openly in the face of the world; for this room is the centre from which our words fly from pole to pole.

I proceed: Not in the writings of St. Paul, nor in those of St. John or St. James, have I found any trace or germ of the papal power. St. Luke, the historian of missionary labors of the apostles, is silent on this vital point. The silence of these holy men, whose writings are part of the canon of the inspired Scriptures, is as inexplicable, if Peter had been pope, as that of Thiers would have been if he had omitted the title of emperor in the history of Napoleon Bonaparte.

I see before me a member of this body who says, pointing at me with his finger: "He is a schismatic bishop who has got amongst us under false pretences."

No, no, my venerable brethren, I did not come into this august assembly like a thief by the window. I came by the door just as regularly as yourselves. It is my right as a bishop, as it is my duty as a Christian, to speak and declare what I know to be true.

But the thing which astounds me beyond all expression is the silence of Peter himself. If he had been what we say — the vicar of Christ upon earth — he must have known it. If he knéw it, how does it happen that he never once — not one solitary time — acted as pope? He might have done it on the day of Pentecost, when he pronounced his first discourse; but he did not. He might have done it at the council of Jerusalem; but he did not. He might.have done it at Antioch; but he did not. He might have done it in his two epistles to the churches; but he did not. Imagine such a pope as this, O my venerable brethren!

If, then, we would maintain that Peter was pope, it necessarily follows that we must maintain that he was not aware of it at the time. I put it to any man with a head to think, and a mind to reflect, whether these two suppositions are credible.

To sum up, then: During the life-time of the apostles, the church never thought of the possibility of a pope. To maintain the contrary, it would be necessary to put the Holy Scriptures into the fire, or out of the mind.

But I hear from all sides the question, "Was not St. Peter at Rome? Was he not crucified here head downward? The chair from which he taught, the altar at which he said mass — are they not in this Eternal City?"

Venerable brethren, the sojourn of St. Peter at Rome has no other proof than tradition. But even if he was bishop of Rome, what argument can be drawn from his episcopate here to prove his supremacy? A scholar of the highest rank, Scaliger, has not hesitated to say that the episcopate and sojourn of St. Peter at Rome must be classed among ridiculous legends. (*Repeated cries* — "*Silence him! silence him! Down with him from the platform!*")

Venerable brethren, I am ready to be silent; but is it not more becoming to such a body as this to prove all things, as the apostle enjoins, and believe that which is good?

In the midst of such a storm of disapprobation, the bishop reached the close of his main Scriptural argument. The interruptions he encountered, and the retorts he made upon the overwhelming majority that roared against him, are not the least interesting and instructive things about the speech. But nothing could check the torrent of voluble Latin, in the fluent use of which no man in all the council could compare with Strossmayer. The historical argument which followed was not less notable than the beginning. — *Christian World, July,* 1871.

THE APOSTLE PETER
THE OPPONENT OF ROMANISM.

ACTS 4:10.

"Be it known unto you all, and to all the people of Israel, that by the name of Jesus Christ of Nazareth, whom ye crucified, whom God raised from the dead, even by Him doth this man stand here before you whole."

WE have seen that the mistakes of Peter were types of the mistakes of Romanism. We have charged upon Satan this mystery of iniquity, the cunning and craft which caused the deluded to claim that Christ declared his purpose to found a church on Peter rather than on the confession of Himself, who is everywhere referred to as the stone which the builders rejected, but which has become the head of the corner. The mistakes of Peter prior to the day of Pentecost, were grievous and grave. On them, Rome builds her pretentious superstructures. Let us now study the life and the teachings of the apostle Peter after he came into the fulness of the light, and began the work of *strengthening his brethren.* The day of Pentecost had passed The city of Jerusalem was under the spell of its influence. A mighty revival had shaken it to its centre. Thousands of converts, from every land and of every tongue, were singing the praises of the risen Christ. The lie which had been spread far and wide, that his disciples stole away his body, was refuted. The power of God on yesterday, felt everywhere, seen everywhere, and known everywhere in the city, proved that the high-priests were parties to a fraud, and that the disciples were the God-appointed leaders of the people.

The morning came. Peter and John, the orator of yesterday, and the acknowledged favorite disciple of Christ, go together "into the temple at the hour of prayer, being the ninth hour of the day." A man, lame from his infancy, was lying by the gate Beautiful. He was well known. Daily, for years, he had occupied that position, and had asked alms. He saw Peter and John, and, true to himself, he cried to them for help. Notice, this is the first miracle after the day of Pentecost.

If Peter was conscious of any special trust reposed in him by his divine Master, if he had a right to think that " he was placed before the other apostles, and that God had established in him a perpetual principle of this twofold unity, and a visible foundation on whose strength the eternal temple might be built, and in whose firm faith the church might rise upward until her summit

reach the heavens," as was claimed by Leo the Great, and as is
quoted by Pius IX. in his dogma of Infallibility, now is the time
for Peter to reveal it. It need not be argued that Peter's modesty
made him ignore his claim. One of the distinctive characteristics
of Christianity is the endowment which causes the mouthpiece
of God to assert himself. The apostles were bold to claim for
themselves the respect which belonged to their offices and positions. Peter did it on this occasion. Paul and others did it on
other occasions. But neither Peter nor Paul ever thought of
taking the place or accepting the honor which belonged to Christ.
Let us examine the language. "And Peter, fastening his eyes
upon him, with John, said ' *Look on us*'" — *not look on me, the
rock on which Christ is to build his church.* The conception never
entered his mind. But "look on us." The man looked, and
Peter said, "Silver and gold have I none; but such as I have
give I thee; in the name of Jesus Christ of Nazareth, rise up
and walk. And he took him by the right hand and lifted him up;
and immediately his feet and ankle bones received strength. And
he leaping up stood, and walked, and entered with them into
the temple, walking, and leaping, and praising God." It was a
wild time, the power of God, which shone forth in Jesus Christ,
lived on the earth. God was in their midst, and they knew it
when they saw the lame man, which sat for alms at the gate
Beautiful, leaping and praising God. "And as the lame man
which was healed held Peter and John, all the people ran together unto them in the porch that is called Solomon's, greatly
wondering." Whence came this power? *Is it of God or of
man?*

Peter refuses to be regarded as the Cause,

And asks: "Ye men of Israel, why marvel ye at this? or why
look ye so earnestly on us, as though by our own power or holiness we had made this man to walk? The God of Abraham, and
of Isaac, and of Jacob, the God of our fathers hath glorified his
Son Jesus; whom ye delivered up, and denied him in the presence
of Pilate, when he was determined to let him go. But ye denied the Holy One and the Just, and desired a murderer to be
granted unto you; and killed the Prince of Life. whom God hath
raised from the dead, whereof we are witnesses. And his name,
through faith in his name, hath made this man strong, whom ye
see and know; yea, the faith which is by him, hath given him
this perfect soundness in the presence of you all."

Peter authorizes faith in Christ rather than in an organization.
Rome claims that the church and the church alone is the depository
of the truth of God. Adam Moehler, in his work on Symbolism,
says: "The church is the Christian religion; so that Christ
himself is only in so far an authority as the church is an authority. The faith existing in the church, from the beginning
throughout all ages, is the infallible standard to determine the
true sense of Scripture." Says Archbishop Manning,* "It is impossible to reject the indissoluble union of the spirit of truth

* Sermon on Ecclesiastical Subjects, p. 24.

with the universal church and His perpetual guidance of the same, without rejecting a main and vital part of the office of the Holy Spirit, and therefore, of the economy of the Holy Trinity in relation to the redemption through Jesus Christ." Of this claim which Rome persists in making in the name of Peter, the apostle knew nothing and said nothing.

Peter preached Christ rather than the church, or a man, and quoted the words of Moses predicting the coming of Christ, and said: "It shall come to pass that every soul which will not hear him, shall be destroyed among the people." As they spake unto the people, the priests, and the captain of the temple, and the Sadducees came upon them, being grieved that they taught the people and preached through Jesus the resurrection from the dead; they laid hands on them and put them in hold until the next day. A vast multitude of dignitaries came together in Jerusalem. Among them was the high-priests, and the rulers, and elders, and scribes, and they bring the prisoners before them, and they asked, "By what power or by what name have ye done this?"

Peter gives the glory to Christ. Then Peter, filled with the Holy Spirit, speaking not as a mere man, but for God, said unto them, "Be it known unto you all and to all the people of Israel, that by the name of Jesus Christ of Nazareth whom ye crucified, whom God raised from the dead, even by him doth this man stand here before you whole. This is the stone which was set at nought by you builders, which is become the head of the corner." Thus did Peter preach Christ. And as if he were looking down the ages and saw the monstrous errors which were to confront this truth and darken the world with their shadows, as if he saw how men would claim the right to pardon sin in their own name and because of their derived right, he added, "*Neither is their salvation in any other; for there is none other name under heaven given among men, whereby we must be saved.*" Thus did Peter in the boldest, fullest, and most unequivocal manner refute the pretension that the true church was built on him, and thus did he declare Christ to be the sure foundation. Here Romanists part company with Peter and the true church. They claim that "as Christ is prior to Peter, so is Peter prior to the congregation of the faithful under the new law." Says Dr. O. A. Brownson, "The church is not, as many suppose, a mere aggregation, or association of individuals; she is an organism, living and operating from her own central life, derived from the indwelling of the Holy Ghost; and it is the failure of non-Catholics to recognize and appreciate this fact that renders it so difficult for us to make them understand the importance of the unity of the church, and that salvation is not attainable out of the communion of the Church." The reason for this failure arises from the neglect of Peter to proclaim this so-called truth. He does not even mention the church, or the life of the church, or the necessity of the church; but instead, declares that Christ is the life of the soul, and "even by him doth this man stand before you whole."

Peter the Opponent of Romanism.

Does any one doubt that the Apostle Peter was selected by the Holy Spirit to do valiant service in opposing the errors which afterwards entered into the growth, and gave solidity and power to Romanism? Then follow down this stream of gospel history from this point onward until Peter's work was done. See him as he confronts Ananias and Sapphira "who have kept back part of the price." Deception, which is the stock in trade with Rome; deception, which begins in mutilating scripture, and then in rejecting it altogether; which substitutes error for truth, and is forever hiding the priceless message of Christ to dying men, — is rebuked by Peter, and both Ananias and Sapphira fall dead in his presence, smitten by the wrath of God.

Look into St. Peter's Church at Rome, where the Pope is worshipped rather than God. He is seated on his throne. Cardinals pass, bow and kiss his toe. Priests kneel before him at the commencement and close of each service. Incense is offered before the throne and him that sits on it. A Romanist thus describes a scene he witnessed in Rome: "Last of all entered the Pope himself, seated in the gestatorial chair, and borne on the shoulders of members of his household. This was Pope Pius IX. Glorious Pius IX., the exile of Gaeta, the head of the Christian church on earth. His holiness wore a mitre of cloth of silver." It was Palm Sunday, and the Pope distributed leaves of the Palm-tree. Said the devotee, "I had the pleasure and the honor to be one of these last, and received my palm, advancing like the others to the throne, first kissing the Pope's foot and then the palm as his holiness presented it."

"I have used the expression, 'the Pope's foot,'" continues the writer, "and I have done so intentionally. Some writers like better to soften it down, and they talk about kissing an embroidered cross, and are vastly anxious that all Protestants should be informed that there is a cross on the pope's shoe which is kissed, — just as if they (Protestants) cared a penny for an embroidered cross! For my part, I yield to none in my respect for the cross, be it embroidered or not embroidered, — be it on a shoe or on a diadem. But it was not that I kissed. It was his foot." Thus does the pope exalt himself above all that is called God or worshipped.

Popery in the past was bad enough. The popery of to-day is worse. Never were papal pretensions more bold, more pretentious, more blasphemous, than now. No arrogance that the world has ever witnessed can compare with that of the Romanism of to-day. Though the pope has been called "the Vicar of Christ," "our Lord God, the Pope," though Prospero Fagnani, the oracle of the court of Rome, in his commentaries on the Decretals, declares that the pope may make laws and institutions for all men; that he *may dispense with the observance of the divine laws, and the gospel precepts,* that "*he is king of kings and ruler of rulers,*" "*the judge of all men,*" that "*he can create a law where before there was none;*" though Bellarmine wrote: "If the pope should err by enjoining vices, or prohibiting virtues, the church, unless she would sin against conscience, would be bound to believe vices to be good, and virtues evil." Though Innocent III. declared himself, in his coronation sermon, to be "*the Christ of the Lord*," yet it was reserved for Pius IX., in the year of our Lord 1871, to declare himself infallible, despite the opposition of Hyacinth and others, who protested against a man assuming divine attributes, and yet on the mountain peak of the nineteenth century, this man stood up and boldly, with pomp and parade, declared himself Infallible Pontiff. No wonder that the sheeted lightning rent St. Peter, and that the puny man was hurled from his exalted position, and is to-day the subject of King Victor Emanuel, the weakest man in Europe, and on a par in rank with the Patriarch of Constantinople.

Rise and Progress of Romanism.

The assumptions of popery, like her mummeries, had no existence during the first three centuries. During the lives of the apostles, and in times immediately subsequent, the church was comparatively pure. Believers worshipped God, and God alone, and relied on salvation entirely as the merit of Christ's death. The religion of the humble Nazarene had none of those unmeaning rites, imposing ceremonials, and debasing customs of Romanism. In A. D. 306, Constantine succeeded to the throne of his father. Having seen, as he claimed, the appearance of a cross in the heavens, exceeding bright, bearing the inscription, "By this Conquer," he at once changed front, became the champion of the church, defeated Maxentius, and in 313, by formal edict, confirmed and extended the privileges of the Christians. Then Romanism blossomed. The substitution of Paganism began. A profession of the gospel being no longer accompanied with danger, the churches being richly endowed, the clergy loaded with honors, it was but natural that upon the pure spiritual worship of him who came to abolish all forms, should be engrafted the superstitions of the ignorant heathen. Of a conversion of heart there was not even a pretence. When Peter and John were seen the people took knowledge of them, that they had been with Jesus and learned of him. Look at Romanism and you see it has been with Paganism and learned of it. The people then saw in Romanism the spirit of Anti-Christ. They opposed their pretensions. Irenæus declared that the bishop of Rome was but a presbyter, for Jesus was the only bishop of souls. Maurus affirmed that all ministers were bishops, and all bishops were of equal rank. The early councils resisted papal supremacy. The council of Carthage, A. D. 418, resisted three popes; that of Chalcedon, A.D. 450, Pope Leo, and St. Ibar, the Irish divine, wrote, "*We never acknowledge the supremacy of a foreigner.*" Says Theodoret: "*Christ alone is head of all.*" Notwithstanding, in A.D. 606, the emperor Phocas conferred upon Boniface III. the title of universal bishop. Thus Romanism, after a desperate struggle of three centuries, established itself, though Gregory, Pope, author and canonized saint, in his contest with the bishop of Constantinople, two years

before, denounced the title of universal bishop as "vain," "dia-
bolical," "anti-Christian," "blasphemous," "execrable," "infer
nal," and said: "Whoever adopts or affects the title of universa.
bishop has the pride of anti-Christ, and is in some manner his fore-
runner in his haughty quality of elevating himself above the rest
of his order." Salvation by grace was lost sight of, and salvation by works became the doctrine of the church. Baptism
became a saving ordinance. It was the initiation into the church,
and who ever took shelter there was safe.

These are the steps taken to reach the position described by
Paul in his letter to the Thessalonians. The pope exalted himself as God. He dispensed pardons and indulgences to the living and the dead. The doctrines of saints, of works, of priestly
power and influence, became the articles of faith on which the
masses rested their hope. Sins were pardoned, and favors dispensed by the pontiff, who took to himself the title of supreme.
Pilgrimages were instituted in 1300 by Boniface VIII., by whom
it was declared that all who should at that time, or thenceforth,
make the pilgrimage to Rome, which should take place every
hundred years, should receive a plenary indulgence. From all
Catholic countries the aged and the young toiled on to Rome, —
two hundred thousand in a single month visited the eternal city.
All these foreigners brought with them rich offerings which re-
plenished the treasury. The avarice of the pontiffs increased
these pilgrimages from fifty to thirty, and from twenty-five
years to the establishment of both the jubilee and the indulgence
in the market houses of all the nations of Christendom. It was
no longer necessary to abandon one's home to obtain an indulgence. What others sought beyond the Alps, might now, with
money, be obtained everywhere.

Turn now to Acts 8: 18-23, and read. Peter had laid his hands
on converted men, and they had received the Holy Ghost. Simon
the sorcerer saw it, and offered Peter money, saying, "Give me
this power that on whomsoever I lay hands, he may receive the
Holy Ghost." But Peter said to him, "Thy money perish with
thee, because thou hast thought that the *gift of God may be
purchased with money*."

Let Peter speak these words to-day in any Roman Catholic
church, in Rome, in Boston, or in New York, and he would not
be tolerated.

To set up a single caste as mediator between God and man,
and to barter in exchange for works, and penances, and gold,
the salvation freely given by God, — such was popery.

To open wide to all, through Jesus Christ, and without any
earthly mediator and without that power that called itself the
church, free access to the gift of God, eternal life, — such was
Peter's mission and constant endeavor.

The church of Rome, though opposed in the 16th century,
though humbled and mortified in the 17th, though its power was
broken in the 18th, and though the head of the church was driven
a homeless wanderer from his pontifical chair in the 19th, and is
now the subject of a king, is the same to-day as formerly. In
doctrine, in practice, and example it is unchanged.

Their Claim is this:

"The pope holds, as successor of Peter, immediately from Christ, in whom is the original priesthood, and all teaching and governing authority. He is not evolved from the internal operations of the church, nor created or commissioned by the episcopacy, but is the central unity whence the whole hierarchy takes its rise." United to the successor of St. Peter, every Catholic claims with St. Ambrose, "Where Peter is, there is the church." This is their boast. From such language we would be led to suppose that the succession had been natural and uninterrupted; that one pope gave his cloak to his successor, as the prophet let fall his mantle upon his follower prior to taking his passage in his chariot of fire. History, however, informs us of endless controversies; of two or three popes, at one time battling with swords, not of truth, but steel, for the supremacy. D'Aubigne has well said of the 11th century, "The throne which affected to exalt itself above the majesty of kings was sunk in the filth of vice. Theodora and Marozia installed and deposed at their pleasure the pretended teachers of the church of Christ and placed on the throne of St. Peter their lovers, their sons and their grandsons." These too well-authenticated charges may have given rise to the tradition which places upon the papal throne a girl named Joan, who had taken refuge at Rome with her lover, and whose sex was betrayed by the pains of childbirth coming upon her in the midst of a solemn procession

In the commencement of the 11th century, Rome was one vast scene of debauchery, wherein the most powerful families in Italy contended for the pre-eminence. The counts of Tuscany in 1033 placed a boy, brought up in debauchery, upon the pontifical throne under the name of Benedict IX. This child of twelve years of age continued, when pope, in the practice of the same scandalous vices that had characterized his youth. Another party elected in his stead Sylvester III., and Benedict, with a conscience loaded with adulteries, and hands stained with homicide, at last sold the papacy to a Roman ecclesiastic. The emperors of Germany, moved to indignation by these enormities, purged Rome with a sword. In 1047, a German bishop, Leo IX., possessed himself of the pontifical throne.

Henry III. deposed the three rival popes, and pointing with his finger, on which glittered the ring of the Roman patricians, designated the bishop to whom the keys of St. Peter's should be confided. Such is the comment of history upon the succession claimed by the church and its defender.

It is amusing to see assumption bolstered up by assumption in which arrogance confutes itself. Now we are told that the pope "is not evolved from the internal operations of the church," and in three lines we are informed that "Christ may use bishops, priests or the faithful in designating the bishop." Whoever is acquainted with the history of cardinal elections, knows that scenes have transpired in Rome while filling the papal See, which history blushes to record. Bribes are freely used to obtain votes, and oftentimes foreign armies have declared on

whom the pontifical robes shall fall. No wonder the leaders of
Romanists understand the art of buying votes. The leaders of
this class became proficients of the business in Rome.

Much is said about the unity of the Roman Catholic church.
If we study history, we shall find less of unity there than elsewhere. Evangelical Christians of every name are united in
Christ in the support of truth. Our Tract and Bible societies
show it. Romanists are united in the support of error. Let
any man preach Christ and discard tradition, or declare in
favor of the Bible as did Peter, when he besought Christians to
desire the sincere milk of the word that they might grow thereby
(1 Peter 2: 2), and at once he is disturbed; but let him say as did
a Catholic at Hunter's Point, when the Lord's prayer was being
read, " *Damn that, take the Bible and go to hell with it,*" or let
them express their unbelief in the Scriptures and claim, "*that
its doctrines, if believed, would send them to hell,*" and the priest
will uphold and applaud them, and declare, as did Father
Cummins, that the attempt of civil authorities to force the reading
of the Scriptures was a piece of Mahommedanism. Rome, in
every age, has feared the Bible and denounced its indiscriminate
use as the corrupter of Christian integrity.

Christ taught us that it is a heart unity which is required, not
a unity in name, or form, or semblance. Belief is the foundation. That is a heart matter. It comes from an acknowledgment
of Christ as head, from following in the path marked out, and
from heeding the instructions received, that we may do the will
of Christ, as did our leader that of his Father.

This unity of the Father and Son was a type of the unity which
does subsist between Christ and the believer. We are not to
inquire whether we are in unity with men,— whether we agree
with them or follow their leadership or direction. But are we in
unison with Christ? As Christ is the same to all, a unity existing between him and the follower will unite the followers together
by an inseparable bond of undying love, which will form an unbroken and undisputed link, not to the pontifical chair of the
Seven Hills, but to the throne of God.

" O, turn ye, O, turn ye, for why will ye die,
When God in great mercy is coming so nigh ?
Now Jesus invites you, the Spirit says come,
And angels are waiting to welcome you home.

How vain the delusion, that while you delay,
Your hearts may grow better, your chains melt away;
Come guilty, come wretched, come just as you are,
All helpless and dying to Jesus repair.

The contrite in heart he will freely receive,
O, why will you not the glad message believe ?
If sin be your burden, why will you not come ?
'*T is you he makes welcome ; he bids you come home.*

Come, give us your hand, and the Saviour your heart,
In him once united, we never shall part;
O, how can we leave you, why will you not come ?
We 'll journey together, and soon be at home."

PETER VERSUS TRADITION;

OR,

HAVE ROMANISTS AN AUTHORIZED VERSION OF THE SCRIPTURES?

---

2 PETER 1: 16.

"For we have not followed cunningly devised fables when we made known unto you the power and coming of our Lord Jesus Christ, but were eye-witnesses of his majesty."

PETER believed in the Scriptures and opposed tradition, and spoke of it as of a "*cunningly devised fable.*" Rome believes in tradition and opposes the Scriptures and calls the Bible a "*mischievous book.*" To prevent and remedy the mischief and guard against error, "*it was judged necessary for Romanism to forbid the reading of the Scriptures in the vulgar languages without the advice and permission of the spiritual guides whom God has appointed to govern his church.*" So reads the admonition prefixed to every copy of the Doway Bible. Christ said, Matt. 22: 29, "Ye do err, not knowing the Scriptures." He makes ignorance of the Scriptures the source of heresies. Rome makes knowledge of the Scriptures the source of heresies. In the catechism it is asked, "Have any great evils ensued from an unrestricted reading of the Bible in vulgar languages by the unlearned and unstable?" A. "Yes; numberless heresies and impieties; as also many rebellions and civil wars." No better proof is required to show that Rome is anti-Christ.

Have Romanists an authorized version of the Scriptures?

Ask the question and they will reply they have, and claim that the Doway Bible is the true and authorized version of the Scriptures. In support of this they will quote the approbation of priests and bishops. Is it true? It becomes us to reach a safe and just conclusion. In the catechism it is claimed that the revealed word of God is their rule of faith. "But of what does the revealed word consist?" The answer is, "Of two parts; the written word called the Holy Scriptures, and the unwritten word called divine tradition.   Are these two parts of equal authority? Yes; because they have been equally revealed of God." The Council of Trent declares "that the discipline of the church is contained in the written word and in the unwritten traditions which the apostles received from the mouth of Christ himself, or from the apostles themselves, being the dictate of the Holy Ghost to them, and delivered as it were from hand to hand, come down to us."

The Bible contains then the written word, the church contains the unwritten word, and as the unwritten word is claimed to be a part of the Scriptures which cannot be found, and which has never been seen, *there can be no authorized version of the Scriptures.* As further proof of this fact, consider these facts.   The Doway Bible is declared to be an admirable translation from the Vulgate, which is the edition of the Bible translated by Jerome from the Hebrew and Greek into the Latin.   The Doway Bible is the transla-tion of a translation, and is not from the original languages in which they were written, as is our Bible.   Final proof, the Irish Catholic prelates declared upon oath in their examination before the British Parliament that there was NO AUTHORIZED VERSION OF THE HOLY BIBLE IN ENGLISH; because it never had been sanctioned by the Pope, as indeed it could not be for reasons given.

Romanists Oppose Resting on Scripture.

They claim that the Bible is hard to be understood; that the ignorant fall into errors for want of knowledge, and the learned through pride and self-sufficiency.   Peter calls tradition a fable, and preaches the Gospel.   The professed follower of Peter claims that the word of God contained in the Holy Scriptures properly consists " *not in the mere words of the sacred text, but in the mean-ing of it, as the Holy Fathers teach;* that many persons who are the most assiduous in reading the Bible, yet do not attain to the truths of religion taught by Jesus Christ, and are really igno-rant of the word of God.   That others who have learned the essential truths of Revelation, as to what they have to believe, and what they have to practise, from their pastor's instructions and their catechisms, have really attained to the knowledge of God's word, even though they should never read any portion of the Bible."   This is what Romanists dare print in Bible-loving America.   The burning of Bibles at Champlain, N. Y., illustrates the meaning of the language.

The Root-Error of Romanism

is before us.   Because of it professed Christians are ignorant of Christ, and thousands and millions of Catholics are as destitute of the Scriptures as are the Pagans of China and Japan.   The priest goes with his cross and breviary, and leaves the Bible be-hind him.   Catholic countries are empty of the Bible.   Because of it the people are dwarfed in intellect.

The Fruits of Tradition and Scripture

deserve notice just at this point. We stand now on the border of the wilderness of Romanistic error. On the one side is ignorance, gloom, superstition, and crime; on the other is intelligence, the blessed light of the Bible, enlightenment, and faith in the Lord Jesus Christ. Compare Ireland with Scotland, Spain with England, Italy with Prussia, Rome with Edinburgh, Belfast with Cork; how wide the difference! Come across the Atlantic, and continue the comparison in our own Western Continent. Compare Mexico to New England, Brazil to these United States, the city of Mexico to that of Boston or New York or Cincinnati; how great the contrast! Come yet nearer home. Compare the worshippers in churches where the Bible is ignored, with congregations who gather to listen to the gospel, and behold the contrast intellectually, socially, and morally. This cannot be seen in America as in Europe, for the influence of the gospel compels Romanists to preach the gospel in part, if not as a whole, in the United States. In Ireland, in Europe priests seldom, if ever, open a Bible and preach the gospel. Dr. Murray, in his letter to Archbishop Hughes, asks, "Why is it that Papal countries and communities thus suffer, and so sadly suffer, when contrasted with other communities where there is an unshackled conscience and an open Bible? The traveller in Europe need not be told when he crosses the lines that separate Papal from Protestant States; the obvious marks of higher civilization declare the transition with almost as much plainness as would a broad river or a chain of mountains. Popery with infallible certainty degrades man. Do you ask how?

"In this wise: it takes from him the Bible, the revealed will of God, with all its clear light, with all its high motives to excite the soul to high and holy action, and without which neither civilization nor religion can be long maintained. It withholds from the people all right moral instruction; it suppresses the preaching of the Gospel and substitutes for it the dumb show of the Mass. The Apostles turned the world upside down by preaching the Gospel, but in Papal countries there is generally no preaching. I never heard a sermon in a Catholic church in Ireland. I venture the assertion that there are multitudes of Catholic churches in Catholic countries where a sermon would be as great a rarity as would be the saying of mass in a Scottish kirk."

Romanism is a System of well-constructed Logic.

Give them one proposition, concede to them one single premise, and the whole of their faith follows most legitimately and logically. Convince me out of the lids of the Bible, which I recognize as absolute and infallible authority upon the point, that Jesus Christ, when on earth, founded the church on Peter; that the Holy Ghost, on the day of Pentecost, descended upon the Apostles and made them the witnesses of his mysteries, the partakers of his thoughts and depositaries of his intentions, so "that there arose within the living consciousness of the truth, which has descended lineally in the mystical body to this hour; the divine tradition" (as Archbishop Manning calls it) "of the light of Pentecost in which all the revelation of God hangs suspended in its symmetry and perfection," and I bow before it as I do before my Maker, and I believe everything that it teaches, no matter what it is. It is because I believe that God embodied his mind and will in Scripture, and not in a church; because the prophecy came not by the will of man, but God descended by the Holy Spirit, on whom he would and when he would, and they spake as they were moved by the Holy Ghost, and then stopped, having no more right to add to their speech a single word or subtract from it a single word than have we, because they spoke out God's mind; and the word spoken which was written under the command of God for our instruction, contains all that it is important for us to know, that I claim, with Chillingworth, that the Bible, not the church, not the traditions of the church, but the Bible, God's word, miraculously written, miraculously preserved, and miraculously illumined and endowed with power, is the embodiment of my faith, the light of my feet, the solace, the joy, the support of my being. In the Bible I find my supernatural unity — not in a church. In the Bible I see preserved what God has revealed and perpetually offers the world as truth, which in the beginning He shed abroad for a brief moment as a message to mankind. The Bible — not the church, but the Bible — is the fountain and channel of light to the world; the exposition of law and the interpreter of the truth of God. Does a man ask for guidance, we give him God's word. Does a man go to a Romanist for a light, he sends him to the church. Herein lies the difference. With Peter we declare "we have not followed cunningly devised fables," we have not permitted what somebody else says to usurp the place which belongs to what God says, but we take what we know to be God's word, what Romanists admit is God's word; and we preach that and rest on that "when we make known the power and the coming of our Lord Jesus Christ."

The Christian Church is with Peter and Paul.

It is evident that Peter rejected the oral law of the Jews, just as we reject the traditions of Rome. It is noticeable that Peter never uses the word tradition. Paul *does*, but Peter *does not*. As though God would guard Romanists from being led astray by any such delusion, he caused him to pronounce the oral law a cunningly devised fable, in order that the hint might save Romanists from this monstrous error.

Paul uses the word translated tradition, which means oral instruction, as follows, in 2 Thess. 3 : 6 : "Now we command you, brethren, in the name of our Lord Jesus Christ, that ye withdraw yourselves from every brother that walketh disorderly, and not after the oral instructions that ye have received from us." In this there can be no reference to the unwritten law of Christ, because he speaks expressly of the instructions received from himself. Besides, as though God would shield the church, He has Paul in the most positive manner refer, in 2 Tim. 3: 15, 16, to the holy Scriptures instead of tradition, "which are able to make them wise unto salvation, through faith which is in Jesus Christ." He does not stop there, but adds: "All Scripture is given by inspiration of God, and is profitable for doctrine, for reproof, for correction, for instruction in righteousness, that the man of God may be perfect, thoroughly furnished unto all good works." If tradition, or the part not communicated in the gospels, were essential to make a man's education perfect, or to thoroughly furnish him, Paul would have said so. But he did not say it. He requested us rather to rest wholly on Scripture, through faith, which is in Christ Jesus.

To this utterance of Paul, Rome adds this note: "Every part of divine Scripture is certainly profitable for all these ends. *But if we would have the whole rule of Christian faith and practice, we must not be content with those Scriptures which Timothy knew from his infancy, with the Old Testament alone; nor yet with the New Testament, without taking along with it the traditions of the apostles and the interpretation of the church, to which the apostles delivered both the book and the true meaning of it.*"

Where is this Unwritten Word?

It must be somewhere. Did God hide it from the masses and give it to the priests or apostles? No; for he commands all to search the Scriptures, and declares that they, without priest or bishop, are able to make men wise unto salvation. How do we know that the unwritten word is God's word? May it not be the word of man? The common law, if not in the statutes, is found in the opinions and decisions of the courts, and is written. Are the men who have called the written word a mischievous book, who have burned it and chained it and trampled upon it, the men to guard and preserve the unwritten word? It is claimed that this unwritten word may be found in the writings of the fathers; but were they inspired men? The history of tradition refutes the pretensions of its advocates. The early church clung to the Scriptures. The use of tradition works the decline of piety and of knowledge of God in every age of the church.

The abuse of tradition is seen in the fact, that when men seek to ignore the written law, they reject revelation and its truths, and become a law to themselves. To ascribe infallibility to tradition, casts the Bible into the shade. Two infallible standards of truth cannot exist; since, if they differ, one must be wrong, and if they do not differ, then they are the same thing. Hence, when Romanists claim that there is an unwritten Bible which the church holds, and which the priests have access to, but which was never seen, and which conflicts with God's written word, they become anti-Bible, and therefore anti-Christ. Notwithstanding this, it cannot be denied that Romanists believe in tradition in preference to Scripture. They teach the doctrine that truth becomes truth because it is believed, and that it is first believed and then true; whereas, independently of its being believed, it has an unchanging and everlasting existence. In other words, Romanists declare that the fact of a certain doctrine having at all times been believed and taught by the church, is conclusive evidence of its truth, because the church cannot err. The difficulty growing out of this false and untenable position is apparent to every student of history. Gregory the Pope, and so the mouthpeice of the church, declared against an infallible pontiff. Leo XIII declares in favor of an infallible pontiff. The church must have been wrong in the sixth century, or it is wrong in the nineteenth century. Galileo was persecuted because of his claim that the earth revolved round the sun. The infallible church declared him wrong. Science declares him right, and the church is compelled to follow in the wake of science. Thus the church is proven to be fallible, and tradition a false and unsafe guide. That the Scriptures do not contain an account of all the things which Christ did, is declared by John 21 : 25, in his gospel. To enumerate them all, and what grew out of them, the Evangelist said, "I suppose, that even the world itself could not contain the books that should be written" In John 20 : 31, we find the same admission made, and the purpose stated in positive terms, why the gospels were written, viz., "That ye might believe that Jesus is the Christ the Son of God, and that believing ye might have life through his name." To declare that the Bible is not sufficient to reveal the truth as it is in Jesus, so that men may go to God through Christ, is to impeach not only the veracity, but the goodness of Almighty God.

Rome builds on tradition instead of Scripture, and quotes scripture whenever it is possible by it to bolster up tradition. Christians build on scripture rather than on tradition, and if tradition harmonizes with the scriptures, so much the better for tradition. We place in the hands of the converted man the gospel, and he at once is endowed of God to be a workman that needeth not be ashamed. The plan, the purpose, the guidance essential to his work, are found in the gospel. Hence we care not for an apostolic succession, but glory in being united to Christ by a living faith.

Rome confronts us here with her traditions, makes of none effect the teaching of scripture, and opens the floodgates of error. Through the door of tradition come priestly intercession, transubstantiation, and all the distinguishing errors of Roman sm. Archbishop Manning, after saying that it had been declared by the Church, in Council assembled, that the Virgin Mary was immaculate, adds : "It does not say that it is true, it offers no logical or historical proofs of its truth, it declares that it is revealed : that *it was contained in the revelation on the day of Pentecost.* And we receive it, not upon argument or criticism, I ut upon the testimony of the church, the sole witness of the mind of God." The same reason is adduced for believing in the dogma of Papal Infallibility, and for whatever other error it may suit the whim or caprice of the Pope, or the Jesuits who rule him, to propagate. This is that falling away that must come, this is the revelation of the man of sin. Tradition becomes the sheet anchor of Romish hope. Thus the door is thrown wide open to errors of every conceivable kind, and the blinded and deluded followers grope their way in the darkness of error down the steeps of ruin. The power of Rome thus organized is fearful. Satan inhabits the entire scheme, and its coming "is with all deceivableness of unrighteousness in them that perish, because they received not the love of the truth *that they might be saved.*"

The Law and the Gospel contained in the Scriptures.

Is it not reasonable to suppose that in accordance with the express declaration of Paul, an infinitely wise God has given to man all that is essential to make him wise unto salvation through the guidance of the Holy Spirit?

Reasoning from analogy, we should be compelled to look for our sufficient guide in the inspired word. Everything which has come from God's creative hand is admirably adapted to the end sought to be reached. The machinery of the universe, vast and intricate as we know it to be, is controlled by known laws, and with all its complications careers forward without a jar from age to age. Seasons come and go in regular order. Man is so constituted that it is impossible to suggest an improvement. Can it be possible that God would be thus careful to provide for the wants of the body, and leave man in ignorance in regard to the wants of his soul? All governments see to it that the law of the land be understood by all the subjects. Every proposal for the benefit of the masses is published and placed before them. No government can secure the confidence of the people that pursues a different course. Hence every intelligent man feels, that if God is his ruler, he has a right to read God's law and become acquainted with His will as it is revealed in the Scriptures. For this reason the tramp of Victor Emanuel's soldiers was no sooner heard in Rome than her priest-ridden populace demanded the word of God. They bought it with eagerness. For this reason, and because Romanism would not trust the people with the Scriptures, there is no place on the earth where the Pope and Romanism is as unpopular and as bitterly hated as in Rome.

The people see that they have made the commandments of God vain through their traditions. They have practised and are practising the grossest of impositions; for in vain do they worship Christ: teaching for doctrines the commandments of men. Peter, schooled and educated by his Lord, declared we have not followed cunningly devised fables, when we made known unto you the power and coming of our Lord Jesus Christ. *Rome has,* and as a result she departed from the true path, and became, under Gregory the Great, a consolidated despotism. The Lord Jesus Christ was banished from their worship, and Mary was substituted. Images and pictures, under the pretence that they were needed to represent the spiritual truths of religion to the eye, were set up in the most holy places. The word of God was exchanged for the traditions of men and the decisions of councils. The church claimed infallibility, and so adopted or rejected whatever was felt to be for her interest.

Thus is the word of God set aside for the opinions of men. Tradition is a subterfuge — a sham and pretence. Rome, because of it, rejects God's word, builds up her colossal power in obedience to the dicta of the devil, without regard to the Gospel. Christ is set aside, as is the Bible, and for the same reason, and the priest boasts the power to forgive sins. The catechism of the Council of Trent says : " The power with which the priests of the new law are invested is not simply to declare that sins are forgiven, *but as the minister of God really to absolve from sin*, and this not because of the authority of Scripture, but of tradition. In the minister of God who sits in the tribunal of penance as his legitimate judge, the votary of Rome venerates the power and person of our Lord Jesus Christ. This is his language : "I confess to Almighty God, to the blessed Mary, to blessed John Baptist, to the holy Apostles Peter and Paul, and to all the saints, and to you, father, that I have sinned exceedingly in thought, word, and deed, through my fault." Thus does Romanism, through tradition, teach for doctrine the commandments of man.

Paul in his Epistle to the Galatians deals heavy blows against the tendency to error, and declares, "If any man preach any other gospel than that ye have received, let him be accursed ;" and Christ said, Go ye into all the world, and preach the gospel to every creature, and whosoever believeth — not in the church, nor in the man who bears the glad tidings, but the gospel — and is baptized, shall be saved. For this reason with Peter it is our boast that "we have not followed cunningly devised fables when we made known unto you the power and coming of the Lord Jesus Christ. But we have a more sure word of prophecy whereunto ye do well that ye take heed, as unto a light that shineth in a dark place until the day dawn, and the day star arise in your hearts." Beautiful language ! Glorious privilege ! Let us commend this gospel unto all by our lives, by our testimony, by our prayerful solicitude, that those who have rejected the light of the Sun of Righteousness for the taper-light of tradition, may on reflection be induced to return unto the Lord their God who speaks, saying, "Incline your ear and come unto me; hear and your soul shall live, and I will make an everlasting covenant with you, even the sure mercies of David." God in tenderness and love says to all, "Seek ye the Lord while he may be found; call ye upon Him while he is near; let the wicked forsake his way, and the unrighteous man his thoughts; and let him return unto the Lord, and he will have mercy upon him, and to our God, for he will abundantly pardon." "Come unto me," said Christ, "all ye that labor, and are heavy laden, and I will give you rest." Sinner, let go of man, give up tradition, accept the offer of salvation through Christ, as revealed in the Scripture, and thy soul shall live.

PETER AND THE PRIESTHOOD;

OR

FALSE TEACHERS, THEIR INFLUENCE AND THEIR DOOM.

2 PETER 2:1.

"But there were false prophets also among the people, even as there shall be false teachers among you. who privily shall bring in damnable heresies, even denying the Lord that bought them, and bring upon themselves swift destruction."

THE tramp of the cohorts of error has been heard all along the line of the centuries. The battle began before Eden; it will go on after time shall be no more. The phases of the fight changes and its scenes are ever shifting; but the cause remains. which is rebellion against God and hatred of the truth. False teachers are the allies of Satan. No matter where they stand, whether in Christian pulpits, so called, or on platforms where infidelity is the boast and glory: no matter whether robed in the vestments and canonicals of the priest, or in the costly garments of fashionable life; false teachers who deny the Lord that bought them, deserve to be warned against and withstood. The apostle Peter, whose mistakes prior to the day of Pentecost were patterned after by Romanists, seems to have been chosen by the Holy Spirit, by pen and speech, to outline the danger and warn against the evils which threatened the church and which have cursed the world.

As the traditions of Judaism were in the path of the gospel, so false teachers were in the way of Christ. Peter made bold to speak out against them both as a true man of God. Notice the language: "But there were false prophets among the people." They claimed a Thus saith the Lord, for their message. They deceived the people. Their prophecies failed. The people became infidel. Though God said, "Let him that hath a dream tell a dream, and he that hath my word let him speak my word faithfully; what is the chaff to the wheat, saith the Lord?" yet men everywhere neglected to weigh truth in the scales of Scripture. They did not compare prophecy with prophecy. They did not lay judgment to the line; they sought a gospel pleasing to self, rather than honorable to God, and were led astray. When Christ came, the Jews were not ready to welcome him. Tradition and the teachings of men had blinded their eyes, so that as a nation they could not see the sky of hope reddened by the light of fulfilled prophecy, and vocal with the songs of the angels singing, "Glory to God in the highest, peace on earth, good will to men."

They regarded Christ as an usurper, or an imposter, and tried to chase away the spectre that haunted them, and predicted the close of the old dispensation and the dawn of the new. The evils which confronted Peter, confront us, and will confront our children. Error does not die. The poet sings, —

> "Truth crushed to earth will rise again;
> The eternal years of God are hers;
> But error, wounded, writhes in chains,
> And dies amid its worshippers."

This is good as prophecy, but bad as history. I wish error had died. Error lives. It opposed the disciples as it opposed the Jews. Peter said, "There shall be false teachers among you." False teachers came. They were not bold enough to attempt to dethrone the God of truth, nor to prove that Jesus Christ had not been in their midst (Satan waited centuries before he had Strauss, of Germany, attempt that); but they quoted the word of the Lord to feather the barbed arrow of error; they tried to prove that Christ was not what he claimed to be; that his disciples were ignorant men, and had attempted to deceive the people; that the miracle of the resurrection was a mere pretence; that the disciples stole away the Lord's body, and pretended that he rose from the dead and ascended on high; and then they referred to Christ's words and praised them; they spoke of his life as a man, and glorified it by their speech, while they spurned his teachings and rejected his example, and so they brought in damnable heresies. Ponder the meaning of the word. Heresy is a fundamental error in religion. It does not purport to be in opposition to religion. It is simply an opinion in regard to truth which a man expresses and stands for, though the teachings of God's word rebuke the man and reject his theory. A damnable heresy is one which denies Jesus Christ, or which, followed to its legitimate conclusion, substitutes error for truth, and the human for the divine. But, says some one, does God deny a man the right to his opinions? Is private judgment a sin? If I am honest in a belief, am I not safe? Many a man who forgets God and seeks the favor of an irreligious world, knowing that Baal has worshippers as devout and sincere as any who bow before the altar of Jehovah, and that the cold and lukewarm, the wanderers, those who know that thrift follows fawning, will not disturb him because of any neglect of the fundamental truths of Christianity, is prone to seek the favor of the world by the expression of opinions respecting some fundamental doctrine of religion in such language as will win the favor and secure the regard of the ungodly, even though by so doing he grieves the heart of the faithful, crucifies the Lord of glory, and puts him to an open shame in the house of his friends. The seed sown brings forth fruit. "For when they speak great, swelling words of vanity, they allure through the lusts of the flesh, through much wantonness, those that were clean escaped from them who live in error. While they promise them liberty, they themselves

PETER AND THE PRIESTHOOD.   55

are the servants of corruption; for of whom a man is overcome
of the same is he brought in bondage."

In these words the apostle holds up the peril arising from false
teachers and false teaching. Thousands have been wrecked upon
this rock. Servitude is the consequence of sin. The man who
tampers with error, who claims the right to investigate, to hear
both sides, to weigh truth in the scales of human judgment, who
rejects the teachings of revelation, and accepts in their stead
human opinions respecting religion, loosens from the moorings
of truth, and drifts into the current of error, and goes down the
steeps of death. There are heresies, to which attention is invited
by the words of the apostle, which deserve to be uprooted   First,
that one which substitutes a man for Christ; second, that which
grows out of the first, auricular confession; and third, the heresy respecting the word of God. Let us notice them in their
order.

1. *The Heresy respecting the Priesthood.*

The Lord Jesus instituted two orders, — apostles, ministers,
elders, or presbyters (terms used interchangeably in the New
Testament), and deacons. An attempt has been made to prove
that Christ instituted three orders, — apostles or bishops, presbyters or priests, and deacons; though the most eminent students of ecclesiastical history have declared with Dr. Holland,
King's professor of divinity at Oxford, England, that to affirm the
office of bishop to be different from that of presbyter is false and
contrary to Scripture; yet the heresy has gained a footing, and
holds its place in the world; and the opinion that man is made
a priest, with powers similar to those possessed by Christ, lives
and exerts its influence upon mankind.

A priest is a person set apart for the performance of sacrifices
and other offices and ceremonies of religion. He had a place in
the old dispensation, but he has none in the new. There were
four kinds of priesthood. 1st. That of kings, princes, heads of
families, and the first-born. This may be called a natural priesthood, because nature and reason teach us that the honor of
offering sacrifices to God should belong to the most mature in
understanding and the greatest in dignity. 2d. The priesthood
according to the order of Melchisedek, who was at once king,
priest, and prophet; that is, authoritative teacher in every sense
of the term. 3d. The priesthood of Aaron and his family,
which subsisted as long as the religion of the Jews. 4th. The
priesthood of Jesus Christ, and of the new law which is infinitely superior to all others in its duration, its dignity, its prerogatives, its objects, and its power. The priesthood of Aaron
was to end; that of Jesus Christ is everlasting. That of Aaron
was limited to his own family, was exercised only in the temple,
and among only one people; its object was bloody sacrifices and
purifications, which were only external, and could not remit sins;
but the priesthood of Jesus Christ includes the entire Christian
church spread over the ages of its existence, and among all

nations of the world. "Seeing, then, that we have a great high
priest that is passed into the heavens, Jesus, the Son of God, let
us hold fast our profession; for we have not an high-priest which
cannot be touched with the feelings of our infirmities; but was
in all points tempted like as we are, yet without sin. Let us,
therefore, come boldly unto the throne of grace, that we may
obtain mercy and find grace to help in time of need." Heb. 4:
14–16. "Being made perfect, He became the author of eternal
salvation unto all them that obey him." Heb. 5:9. "Who, his
own self, bare our sins in his own body on the tree, that we,
being dead to sin, should live unto righteousness: by whose
stripes ye were healed: For ye were as sheep going astray, but
are now returned unto the Shepherd and Bishop of your souls."
1 Peter 2:24–25.

Thus, is it established by Scripture that we have access to God
by Jesus Christ, the one mediator between God and man. Whosoever will come, may come and taste the waters of salvation.
Romanists reject the teachings of Christ; substitute a man in
the place of Christ; draw attention away from the Creator to the
creature, and so openly deny the Lord that bought them.

God lives in Truth, not in Organizations.

Rome declares "that as Christ was not to remain in his own
person upon earth, he therefore chose twelve disciples whom he
called apostles, and he communicated to them all those sacred
powers necessary for bringing others to salvation, which he himself had received from his Father; with powers, moreover, to
communicate the same power to others who might succeed them,
and carry on the same by a perpetual succession, to the end of
time." In this, as in every heresy, there is, if not a mixture of truth
with error, an opinion concerning truth which conceals and
sows broadcast an error. Christ did call about him apostles,
and he did communicate to them power, and he did commission
them to speak. Miraculous power was given them, that by its
use they might enforce their speech. Christ did not commission
them to transmit this power to others. The power to work
miracles died with the apostles. The power possessed by them
was in the Holy Spirit, and animated not their persons but their
speech. That power animates their speech at this hour, and will
while time shall last. Hence, the gospel is the power of God in
this world; and Paul had reason to declare, I am not asha ned of
the gospel of Christ, "For it is the power of God unto ss vation
to every one that believeth." Père Hyacinth, and millions besides, are disposed to feel that this power to which Paul referred,
inhabits a man, or an organization, rather than the gospel. That
God draws by the cords of a man, is our glory and our hope. It
is God that draws, not man. That the Word was incarnated in
Jesus Christ and walked in flesh among men, we are bold and
glad to preach. But that the Word is so incarnated in the
priesthood, as that a man can safely usurp the prerogatives of
Christ and take his place in the scheme of salvation, is a heresy

that is damnable, because it denies the Lord who bought us, and has consigned to eternal misery all who have turned from the Creator to the creature, and who have forgotten that it is the gospel in man, and spoken by man, which makes him and his message a power. *"For therein is the righteousness of God revealed, from faith to faith."* God lives in his Bible. The truth of the gospel is freighted with life; and if received into the soul, it carries life there, and a man who is a new creature in Christ, will exclaim with Paul, "I live, yet not I, but Christ liveth in me; and this life I now live in the flesh, I live by the faith of the Son of God."

The idea of the priesthood connects itself in all its forms, pure and corrupted, with a consciousness of sin. Men who accept the office of a priest, feel that they have broken the law of a power above them which they dare not approach without the intervention of some one holier than themselves. Hence, among the most ignorant and benighted, altars have been built, sacrifices instituted, priests installed to offer up prayers in their behalf. A priest, in the estimation of the suppliant, is a kind of mediator between God and man. He claims to represent God. He lives apart from man. He surrounds himself with mystery, utters a strange language, and professes to belong to a superior class and to possess supernatural power. From this it is apparent that the idea of a priesthood can only be tolerated amidst great ignorance, or great superstition. The church of Rome ascribes to every priest a mysterious dignity which entitles him to the reverence of the people.

A minister is a brother in the Lord. He is chosen by the church to serve them, and is also appointed over them. He proclaims Christ the mediator between God and man, and endeavors by the aid of the Holy Spirit to lead men to embrace the offers of the gospel. This truth was revolutionary in its character and levelling in its tendencies. It broke down the middle wall of partition between Jew and Gentile, overthrew the altars of heathenish superstition, and banished from the minds of true believers every claim set up by man to the office work of the priesthood. The apostles proclaimed everywhere, that as the priesthood had been changed and as Christ was made priest, not after the law of a carnal commandment, but after the power of an endless life, he is able to save to the uttermost them that come unto God by him, seeing he ever liveth to make intercession for them. For centuries this doctrine held sway. When superstition, the fog that rises from the lowlands of ignorance and vice, usurped the throne of reason, the old leaven of caste once more displaced the new leaven of fraternity; the sanctity of the clergy became a dogma of the church, the Bible was banished, and Mary, the so-called queen of heaven, took the place of Christ, the Saviour of the world.

Christianity does not dwarf manhood or restrain development. It is an added force. It promotes the growth of the whole man It blesses the body with the products of temperance, raises the

1*

mind to the contemplation of the words and works of God, and
thrills the soul with a new life which brings it into harmony with
its own highest interests, and enriches it with an heirship with
Christ to an inheritance of the "all things" of God.

Contrast the relative position of a minister and a priest. A minister is a servant of Christ. A priest is the servant of the
church. The one preaches Christ. That is his distinctive work.
The other ignores the gospel, prays in a foreign tongue, and
gladly banishes the Bible from the public schools and from the
homes of those who worship at the altar. The minister serves
the church through Christ. The priest serves the church through
Mary.

"Who, asked Gavazzi, is the master in a Catholic family?
The confessor! Sons and daughters obey their confessors before their father and mother, and often displease their parents
in order to please their confessor; husbands are only secondarily obeyed by their wives, first in command over them is always
the Father confessor. Believe my words; they speak the experience of more than twenty-five years among Popish clergy.
The great work of Jesuits is always with women in the confessional. Here they dispose of society. So that not in Italy only,
but even in America, many Catholic husbands, practising big-
otries to your astonishment, will tell you that they do so in order
to preserve the peace of the family, such being the will of the
Father confessor, expressed by means of their wives, who become furies if their holy masters are not obeyed. The last warfare of the priests is at the dying bed. From that death-bed all
friends, all relatives are purposely excluded; the priest alone
remains. What weapons he has in his hands; fear of hell, remorse of conscience, the flame of purgatory, all are used to
induce the dying penitent to make the church partially or totally
his heir." *Shame upon the imposition.*

The minister is one of the people. He mingles with them, is
known to them and rules in love. A priest lives apart from the
people, is selected by an order above him, and by education, by
habit, as by oath and inclination, he holds the people aloof. Pro-
fessing great sanctity, and claiming intercessory power. his rule
is almost supreme. This fact in a government where the ballot
exerts a controlling influence is never forgotten; and so, though
he is hidden from sight, he touches cords of influence in secret
which move men and parties in the most open manner to block
the wheels of progress, crucify truth, and stab liberty.

A minister must keep with, if he does not keep in advance of,
the people. A priest may keep behind them and can oppose
them and tyrannize over them, without peril to himself or danger to his order.

That a minister is the natural opponent of the priest is proven
by the effect wrought in Italy. Her priest-ridden millions began
to emerge into the light as soon as true messengers of salvation
passed through her gates. Truth knocked off fetters from the
mind and limb, and permitted the captive to go free. Gavazzi

and others, learned that it was possible for a clergyman to have a burning heart toward his duties as a minister; and yet, when called to be a man, a citizen and a soldier, knew how to bind the Bible to his heart and lift the sword and the musket in defence of the truth, believing that there is nothing incompatible between Christianity and patriotism, between the freedom of the soul and of the body; — that to be right with God, man must be right towards man, and they thundered forth these doctrines of the cause of freedom and republicanism until the gates of Naples and Rome have been opened before the advancing hosts of Bible-readers and teachers of the word of life.

We see God in Jesus Christ, and can hold him up, not only as the being who went to the heart of men and took possession of the very centre of their being, and reinfused that with new life and with extraordinary power, but as God manifest in the flesh, to whom we look for life and hope; who tore away the vail of the future, opened heaven to our view, and laid bare hell to our gaze. The interest felt in his life is wonderful. No other life interests as does this life. The facts reported by the evangelists are windows through which we behold wide and fertile plains of being, veined with life and flowered with beauty.

2. Auricular Confession; or, the Heresy respecting the Power of the Priesthood,

is most alarming in its character. The priesthood claims the power of forgiving sins. Out of this claim has grown auricular confession. Confession is defined in the Catechism of the Council of Trent to be "a sacramental accusation of one's self made to obtain pardon by virtue of the key." Said Rev. Joseph Blanco White, a converted priest of Seville, Spain, "One of the greatest evils of confession is, that it has changed the genuine repentance preached in the gospel — the conversion and change of life which is the only true external sign of the remission of sins through Christ — into a ceremony which silences remorse at the slight expense of a doubtful, temporary sorrow for past offences. As the day of confession approaches, the Romanist grows restless and gloomy; he mistakes the shame of a disgusting disclosure for sincere repentance of his sinful actions. He at length goes through the disagreeable task, and feels relieved. The old score is now cancelled, and he may run into spiritual debt with a lighter heart. This I know from my own experience as confessor and penitent." Converted priests, in speaking of the confessional, are unanimous, here as in Italy, in declaring it immoral in its nature and in its effects. The earliest trace of confession is found in the case of apostates from the church, who, seeking re-admission, were compelled, as the scandal they had given was public, to make a public confession (not an auricular confession) of their apostacy before being received again. "Auricular confession" is a confession breathed into the private ear of the priest. Christ commands us to go direct to God through prayer. "When thou prayest enter into thy closet, and when thou hast shut the door, pray to thy Father, which is in secret, and thy Father, which seeth in secret, shall reward thee openly."

Men may confess to each other the sins that they have committed against each other, and to God the sins committed against the Most High. To Christ alone was the power given to forgive sins.

"Immorality," said Gavazzi, "in the Roman church, commenced with her confessors. The confessional is, to the young, unmarried priest, a suggester of impurities; there he contracts the stain; outward from the confessional it travels until it is scattered on every hearth, and met in every cross-way." Auricular confession is said to be a religious institution; but practically it becomes, in astute hands, a political instrument. Master of the secrets, of the conscience, and soul of his penitent, the priest is a more effective tool of despotism than armed legions. In this free land the power of the priesthood is felt to be among the greatest of our perils. They not only claim the power to control votes, but they claim that it is their duty to use that power to subvert our free institutions, and plant in their stead the despotism of the Old World; that beneath the arch of its power superstition may supplant the Bible, and become the lever, while ignorance here, as there, becomes the fulcrum of Romanism. "Where confessors are, there real and permanent liberty cannot be. To condemn the system, to make it abhorred and despised, it is enough to name its first patron, Pope Innocent III, the brigand of all European kingdoms, who excommunicated John of England, that he might lay his hands upon his sovereignty; that Cannibal who taught men to thirst for one another's blood; that founder of the Inquisition, — he was the imposer of auricular confession."

Its Character

is best seen in the work accomplished through its aid. Under Gregory XVI, sisters were forced to accuse brothers, wives husbands, mothers sons, to obtain absolution. Confession to man is always bad. If it exist in a country not popish, it introduces popery; if it exist in a popish country, it introduces slavery and misery. In theory and practice, Christ was against auricular confession. He never spoke of the apostles as confessors, or of Christians as penitents. Everywhere we find the Saviour forgiving sinners and healing the sick. Christ always declared, "Your faith has made you whole," not your confession. So spake Gavazzi; and none knew the tendencies of Romanism better than did the bold prelate who has since preached the gospel with such effectiveness in Rome.

The immorality of the confessional is proven not by apostates from Romanism, but from its most honored sons. The late Rev. Francis P. Kenrick, D. D., bishop of Baltimore, one of the ablest and most learned Roman Catholics in America, previous to his death in 1863, published a Latin work which has been introduced as a text-book into the Roman Catholic seminaries of this country.   In this he devotes seven pages "to the crime of solicitation," in which he gives the papal legislation respecting seduction by the confessional, — legislation which was, of course, demanded by the existence of the very crimes therein prohibited, because such laws are not made for the righteous, but for the lawless and disobedient   He specifies as many as nineteen ways of seducing women in connection with the practice of confession. Such as "solicitation during the act of confession," "before the act of confession," and "immediately after it"; solicitation to which confession furnishes an occasion, under the pretext of confession in the confessional, and outside of the confessional." The laws in some of these cases are thus given: "Anything written on paper adapted to excite love, or a love-letter delivered in the tribunal, is equivalent to solicitation in the confessional." We will only quote one more: "If a priest suggests to a female refusing to comply with his desires on account of exposing her reputation to peril, that she should send for him under a pretext of desiring to confess to him, he is to be regarded as soliciting under pretext of confession."   To this and many other things which we care not to write, Archbishop Kenrick prefaces these words: " We scarcely dare to speak concerning the atrocious crime in which the office of hearing confession is perverted to the ruin of souls by impious men under the influence of their lusts.   Would that we could regard it as solely a conception of the mind, and as some theme invented by the enemies of the faith for the purpose of slander."   But it is not fit that we should be ignorant of the devices of the enemy, for the archbishop declares that " *no one is to be condemned to those most severe punishments on the accusation of one witness.*"

The priest who attempts to seduce a woman by means of the confessional, may therefore laugh at human penalties; no one knows the fact but himself and his victim; and, if she communicates it to others she only publishes her own shame, and becomes a slanderer of her spiritual guide and intercessor with God. He cannot be convicted of sin on her testimony, but she may be punished without mercy for bringing up an evil report of the priesthood, the government, and the church. The priest knows all the secrets of every female heart in the parish; not a girl or a woman, within his jurisdiction, but must blush and tremble before him; she must confess to him every unchaste thought or desire or action under pain of eternal damnation. Auricular confession is a human invention, unscriptural and anti-scriptural, an engine of immense power placed in unworthy hands, and employed to throttle liberty, to destroy chastity, and is fraught with the most dreadful danger, temporal and spiritual, to priest and to people, to the church and to mankind, for this world and the world to come. Is it any wonder that thousands in the Romish church object to their wives and daughters en-

tering the confessional, and that some refuse to have their wives
meet the priest except in their presence?

3. *The Heresy respecting the Word.*

The heresy respecting the priesthood of Jesus being exchanged
for the priesthood of man, is matched by that other heresy that
the words and opinions of men may safely be substituted for the
teachings of the gospel.

Theodore Parker and his imitators claim the right of a minister
of religion to improve upon the teachings of the Bible as well as
upon the example of Jesus Christ. In his "discourse on the
function of a teacher of religion," he declares it to be a duty to
destroy faith in a miraculous communication of doctrines on
matters pertaining to religion, and to show that there is no phi-
losophic or historical foundation for this vast fiction; it is such
stuff as dreams are made of. There is, he says, "no supernatural, miraculous or infallible revelation; it is not in the Bible, but
the universe is the only Scripture of God, material nature is the
Old Testament, human nature the New, and in both fresh leaves
get written over every day." So much for the theology which
he is to overthrow. A word as to the doctrines to which he
must be opposed.

There are five doctrines common to the theology of Christendom, viz.: the false idea of God, as imperfect in power, wisdom,
justice, benevolence, and holiness; the false idea of man, as
fallen, depraved, and by nature lost; the false idea of relation
between God and man, — a relation of perpetual antagonism, man
naturally hating God, and God hating fallen and depraved man;
the false idea of inspiration, that it comes by a miracle on God's
part, not by normal action on man's; and the false idea of salvation, that it is from the wrath of God." All these a minister is
to oppose, said Theodore Parker, all these and much more.

These extracts will suffice to show the relation that naturally
exists between Romanism that rejects part of the Bible, and
Theism that rejects the whole. The one claims that the wisdom
of God is enshrined in the church; the other, that it is enshrined
in human nature. Theodore Parker died worshipping himself,
and believing that he was to be the author of a new religion,
and Brahminism in Calcutta, as in Boston, adopts him as the
founder of Theism. There is but a step between a faith which
claims that theology is a human science, as does Theism. and a
faith which claims that the product of man possesses infallibility.
If a church made up of men uninspired can reach decisions which
are incontrovertible, then theology is but a human science, and
there is no real disagreement between men who hope to be saved
by their own good works or those who hope to be saved by the
good works of somebody else employed by them to work for
them. It follows, naturally, not only that heresies help each
other and that lovers of heresy applaud all new-comers, but that
the union of these forces stand opposed to the church of Christ,

and must be resisted and opposed by the lovers of truth, else they prove derelict to duty and openly betray Christ.

The Influence of false Teaching.

Who can calculate or describe this influence? It finds monuments in jails and prisons; it speaks in the hoarse and harsh dissonance of the cannon; it flashes in the light of the glittering sabre; it glasses itself in fashion; it permeates with life and hope the schools of vice, and the dens of shame; it nerves the arm of the rebellious to resist God, and applauds the courage of the sceptic that reviles Jehovah; it cheers to the echo every irreligious sentiment falling from the lips of the atheistic believer; it encourages the press to give to every error a trumpet tone, and to padlock the lips of truth, or hush its voice. In Italy its harvest is ignorance, degradation, poverty, immorality, weakness, decrepitude, monkish legend and superstition; while in America it ministers to crime, to lust, to the profanation of the Sabbath, to intemperance, degradation and death of body and of soul. "For many have followed their pernicious ways, by reason of whom the way of truth is evil spoken of." Through covetousness, because it pays to-day to be bad, they have made merchandise of their followers. Millions are bound by the chains of error, and shrouded in the night of superstition, who are lost unless the light of the gospel can irradiate their night, and bring deliverance to their captive souls. Said a converted Roman Catholic, "Could I address myself to every papist upon whom the sun shines, I would say to them all, the doctrine of confession is a priestly device to gain an absolute authority over your consciences. If bishops and priests will not, in this day of light, cut in pieces the net woven in the dark ages to confine and trammel you, it is in your power to rise and tear it in pieces." Let Christians pray that the eyes of Romanists may be opened to the deceptions practised upon them, and turn from error to truth, from tradition to Scripture, and from the priesthood of man to the royal priesthood of Christ Jesus, our Lord.

Their Doom.

God says leaders and followers bring upon themselves swift destruction, their judgment lingereth not, their damnation slumbereth not; they are known, they are described. It is your fault if you reject God's word for error. It is your duty to believe that your creator and preserver is your rightful ruler. If you are wise you will accept his law and heed its voice. It is worse than folly, it is madness to go contrary to this.

A wicked man who trampled upon God's law and defied his power, ploughed his field and planted his potatoes, hoed them and dug them on the Sabbath. When he dug them he found them good, and so called a Christian farmer and said to him: You believe in God? Yes. You believe it is wise to obey

him and perilous to disobey him? Yes. Well, you see those
potatoes, are they not good? Yes. How do you account for it?
I ploughed this ground on Sabbath, planted my potatoes on Sabbath, and hoed and dug them on the Sabbath, and yet they are the
best crop I ever raised. How do I account for that, said the
farmer?—in this way: *God does not settle all his accounts in
October.* Men look at Romanism, at the power of the world, at
the weakness of the church and the apparent helplessness of
truth, and inquire how do you account for it? Is there not a
reason to think that the *vox populi*, or the voice of the majority
arrayed against the truth may not be, after all, the voice that
shall stand? We reply, No. The judgment of an ungodly
world may for a long time linger. But it is made up, and the
time hastens to deliver it. Romanism is described in the New
Testament, and its doom is predicted. Prophecies long ago
made are blossoming into fulfilment. Truth is gaining ground
every hour. Thrones and dynasties are crumbling before the
aggressive strides of the champions of the cross of Christ. The
judgment of God is influencing the opinions of men. Romanism
dead at the heart will die at the extremities. Be not deceived.
God is not mocked and the time cometh to reveal it.

It is perilous to believe wrong.

The damnation of errorists slumbereth not. The voice is
sounding through all the world, "Come out of her my people, that
ye be not partakers of her sins and that ye receive not of her
plagues. For her sins have reached unto heaven and God hath
remembered her iniquities." "And he said unto me, It is done,
I am Alpha and Omega, the beginning and the end. I will give
unto him that is athirst of this fountain of the water of life freely.
He that overcometh shall inherit all things, and I will be his
God and he shall be my son. But the fearful and the unbelieving
and the abominable and murderers and whoremongers and sor-
cerers and idolaters and all liars shall have their part in the lake
which burneth with fire and brimstone. Behold, all ye that
kindle a fire that compass yourselves about with sparks; walk
in the light of your fire and in the sparks which ye have kindled, this shall ye have at my hand, *ye shall lie down* in sorrow."
To these solemn admonitions of God's Word it is impossible
to add anything. Whoever rejects Christ is lost. "And this is
the will of him that sent me, that every one which seeth the Son,
and believeth on him, may have everlasting life, and I will raise
him up at the last day."

THE MEASURING ROD.

Rev. xi. 1: "AND THERE WAS GIVEN ME A REED LIKE UNTO A ROD; AND THE ANGEL STOOD, SAYING, RISE, AND MEASURE THE TEMPLE OF GOD, AND THE ALTAR, AND THEM THAT WORSHIP THEREIN."

To uncover the meaning of this passage, and to study the lessons which attach to it, forms the business of the hour. The gospel, or this *good news* of Revelation, has been strangely overlooked. Thousands, knowing that it contains mysteries difficult to be understood, ignore the great truths it unfolds, the promises it breathes and the grand hopes it places before the children of God. There are clouds of wrath banked up along the future, but approach them and you find among them rifts and windows which open to the eye such visions of delight as can nowhere else be found. In the tenth chapter, God places before the church the implements of warfare by which we are to be blessed in gaining conquests over sin and self, over the world, the flesh and the devil. They are the *voice*, the *book*, the *experience* and the *prophecy*. In regard to the importance of the voice, the distinguishing characteristic of the herald of salvation, there is no question. The voice was the implement of power of the banner-chieftains of the cross from the days of Peter down to the present. The Bible is the garner in which seed is stored, which, sown upon the heart acres of mankind, produces the only harvests essential to the world's life, thrift and happiness. The experience of the child of God is a manifest power; when related it serves as a lamp to the feet of the stranger, as a source of encouragement to the child of God, and permits the church to supply the world with proof that they have been with Jesus and learned of him. About the use of prophecies, there is at present much doubt.

Why is it? The Apocalypse is simply the uncovering of the chart to the eye of man, in accordance with which the church is to sail the open sea of the future. It is the order-book in which Christians find the intimations and commands of the Most High. For this reason it is written on the title-page of the book of Revelation, "Blessed is he that readeth and they that hear the words of this prophecy and keep those things which are written therein; for the time is at hand." What shall be said of those Christians who never read or ponder these sublime truths? What would have been thought of the different corps commanders about Strasburg, if, on the morning when the attack was to be made all along the lines, they had slept upon their posts, having failed to read the orders sent them, because of their indifference to the commander-in-chief? Imagine him waiting for the sound of the conflict, and waiting in vain, because his orders had been ignored. Would not he, and the nation and the world, have united in the declaration, *"Cursed be that commander who fails to read and heed the orders of his chief."* The prophecy of the Apocalypse has to do with this work of the church. Jesus is commander-in-chief. These instructions are given by his order to the church militant. They sound clear and distinct the truth, "He that hath an ear to hear let him hear what the spirit saith unto the churches."

If the tenth chapter points out the instrumentalities to be employed in the conversion of the world, the eleventh chapter places before us the work to be accomplished and the distinctive characteristics of the workmen to be employed in its execution. The thoughts, though clothed in apparent mystery, are easily understood by the help of the key supplied by Scripture.

THE TEMPLE — WHAT IS IT?

1. In the first verse, the angel of the covenant places in John's hand a reed, and commands him to measure with it the temple of God and the altar, and they that worship therein. This language must be understood metaphorically. The word "temple" refers to that in the new dispensation which the temple would represent in the old. The temple was the abode of God on earth: and under the new dispensation, that peculiar residence was transferred to the church, and God is represented as dwelling in it. "Know ye not that ye are the temple of God, and that the spirit of God dwelleth in you." *Thus it appears that particular and congregated churches are called temples.* These are to be measured by "the reed," or rod, which is described to be the Word of God. The Scriptures furnish the true measure of the church of worship and of the ordinances. This measuring is to be done more and more. Men may call God's commands non-essentials, but in the light of Scripture they do so at their peril. As we approach the millennial days, the people of God will be compelled to have their church organizations, their rule of faith and practice, measured by the "reed" of Scripture truth and example, and those who do not conform to it must be set aside.

THE ALTAR IS TO BE MEASURED.

2. He is commanded to measure the altar, which declares that the church is to be judged with reference to its notions of sacrifice to be made for sin, and the method of reconciliation with God. This command teaches us that the theory which claims it is no matter what a man believes if he is sincere, is exploded.

A man must accept the offer of salvation according to God's plan, and believe in Christ's propitiation and atonement for sin, or he is lost. The Scripture rule is clear and pronounced. Whatever people ignore the sacrifice made by the death of Christ on Calvary, strike out the sun from the system, and leave nought but gloom and night behind.

THE WORSHIPPERS ARE TO BE MEASURED.

3. The temple and the altar are not only to be measured, but the worshippers are as well. What do they believe in regard to church order and church building? What has been their practice? Do they obey the behests of Scripture in regard to the ordinances? *It is our business to know.* The command is definite. Measure the worshippers, and "be not unequally yoked together with unbelievers; for what fellowship hath righteousness with unrighteousness?"

"But the court which is without the temple leave out, and measure it not, for it is given unto the Gentiles, and the holy city shall they tread under their feet forty and two months."

This enables us to explain why it is that those portions of Christendom which revolted from Christ and refused to conform to the measurement of Scripture are shrouded in the night of error. The Gentiles are the paganized churches who introduced into their service forms which do not belong to the altar, and objects of worship, such as the Virgin Mary, angels and saints, in imitation of the demon worship of the heathen. In this manner they utterly opposed the measurement of the altar, and the plain and positive commands of the gospel regarding Christ, who is the express image of the Father, the only begotten Son of God, the Alpha and Omega, the Prince of the kings of the earth, who loved us and washed us from our sins in his own blood.

By "the holy city" is meant the kingdoms of Europe, or so-called Christendom, which the papal and paganized power is to tread under foot for 1260 years, the exact time, during which the "two witnesses" are to be clothed in sackcloth, and are to prophesy.

THE MEANING OF THE OLIVE TREES.

4. "The two witnesses are the two olive trees, and the two candlesticks standing before the God of the earth."

A practical truth is here proclaimed which the church is in great danger of ignoring. In Zachariah 4:2 and 3 verses, we perceive that in the old dispensation the candlesticks were seen first, and after that the olive trees. John sees the olive trees first and the candlesticks last. Now, as the two witnesses of the old dispensation were Israel and the ministers at the altar, in the new dispensation they are the ministers and the church. If this truth teaches anything, it declares that the ministry hold by far the most conspicuous place in the world's redemption. They are the olive trees which pour from their abundance, the inspiration, the purpose, the resolve, which shall make the church instinct with life and power. Let those who feel that the work of the ministry is over, and that the church is to give way to other organizations, ponder this truth. It is unmistakable in its declaration. Previous to Christ's coming, the Israel of God was the distinguishing feature of the life of the world. Since that time the olive trees have towered above the church, and have not been hidden behind. It was Paul and Peter and other apostles who preached the gospel and administered its ordinances, that form the distinguishing feature of the new dispensation. It is the "Acts of the Apostles," not the acts of the church or of the churches, that engage our attention. Rome makes much of the church. The gospel makes more of the preacher. We think of Novation, of Donatus, of Constantine, who became the head of the Paulicians; of Arnold of Brescia, of Luther of Germany, Calvin of Switzerland and John Knox of Scotland, as of the olive trees who stand on the mountain peaks of history, looking down the line of the centuries and blessing us with their influence. It is the ministry of to-day that is either the hope or the curse of the world. They are to bring down blessings or barrenness, health or sickness. If they are valiant for the truth, the church will be brave. If they are cowardly, disasters are sure to come.

5. Note the protection given to the witnesses. "And if any man will hurt them, fire proceedeth out of their mouth and devoureth their enemies; and if any man will hurt them, he must in this manner be killed." This language implies that Christians have been overcome because they were silent. They consented to error, or error would have been slain.

Is this true? Then what shame and condemnation belongs to the churches of Christ. Had they been braver they would have been stronger. Had Luther preached the whole truth, Europe had been free. If we are weak to-day, it is because we smother the truth. Do we feel this? It is the fault of the ministry and the church if God's law concerning the Sabbath is made of no effect. Those infidels who profane the Sabbath by opening the theatres for paid lectures and concerts on Sabbath evenings have no power if we will but speak and act as becomes the upholders and defenders of the truth. Let us not be deceived. It is the fable of the camel and his driver over again. The driver was in his tent, the camel thrust in his nose; he struck him, and bade him retire. "Pray let me breathe the cool air, the sun is fierce outside," said the camel. Then came the head, the shoulders, and at last the body; the driver was driven out, and the camel held possession, because at the outset he was not successfully repulsed. This opening of theatres for the purposes designated, is but the entering of the camel's nose. The enemies of our faith mean the destruction of the Sabbath, which has been our inheritance and the fountain source of our strength, and hope that the opening of the theatre for lectures and concerts will abrogate the Sabbath. Citizens and patriots, if they care for the safety of our country, should unite with God's children in preserving the Sabbath inviolate, — that matchless benefaction which has made our land glorious. The battle against intemperance is to be waged by the church of Christ. Let the ministers and the church take a stand in favor of temperance and against the manufacture and sale of intoxicating drink, and this idol of Dagon would fall down before them. Measure the worshippers, ministers of Christ, by the rule of the Scripture, and though pews will be emptied of rum-sellers and rum-drinkers, the church of God will be clothed with fresh strength, and will shine bright as the sun, fair as the moon, and terrible as an army with banners. It is because Christian men connected with the secular and religious press are dumb, that those who are infidel to the family and to the Sabbath, the only institutions of God which survive the wreck and ruin of Eden, invade the sanctities of the day and prostitute it to the purposes of pelf and self. The instrumentalities for saving the world are committed to the two witnesses. If they treat them with disrespect, cast them aside; then error will triumph at the expense of the truth.

If there is nothing done for Christ, it is the fault of those to whom God has entrusted the interests of his cause. This is distinctly stated in the sixth verse, which delares, " These, the witnesses, have power to shut heaven, that it rain not in the days of their prophecy." The ministry are largely responsible for the present condition of Europe. Had they, in the past, proclaimed the whole truth fearlessly, and warred against the deceptions and errors of Rome; had they explained the ordinance of baptism in accordance with the teachings of Scripture, and rested there, the famine of hearing the word of God had not raged so fearfully. As it is, a judgment on a nation or a city, not to be rained upon, so it is a spiritual judgment upon a people when there is a withholding of the truth of revelation. Oncken and others are doing for Europe the necessary work. The Bible is being scattered and read. The spirit of life from God is entering into the people. The morning light is breaking in upon them. Already the power of the witnesses is felt to be the most potent of earth. Nothing is so empty or feeble as a lie. Nothing is so weighty and potent as the truth. The time of conflict is predicted. " The beast that ascendeth from the bottomless pit is to make war with the witnesses and silence their voice. This is to be followed by a period of merriment and rejoicing on the part of the enemies of the church. Despair not. It is but for a day."

THE PROMISE OF DELIVERANCE.

7. "And after three days and one half, the spirit of life from God entered into them and they stood upon their feet; and

great fear fell upon them which saw them." This declaration brings us face to face with the central fact in the history of a sin-cursed earth, viz, the resurrection from the grave of our Lord Jesus Christ.

In regard to the particular time designated by the three years and a half, there have been many conjectures. The truth seems to me to be this : God shows us, in this language, that though sin may seem to gain a victory over the church, it is but momentary at the best. On the third day the spirit of life from our God shall enter into the apparently dead, and they shall stand on their feet and be clothed with power. Their enemies shall look upon them with fear. The children of God shall rejoice because of them. Would you behold an illustration of this truth? Go back to Jerusalem. Jesus is in the grave. The Roman soldiers are keeping watch. The morning of the third day arrives. How Jerusalem was startled, as they found that the earthquake shock had done more than shake the city to its foundations; it had rolled away the stone from the door of the sepulchre, when the spirit of life from God entered into the helpless body, and it arose, and Jesus took his morning walk in the garden. What a change was wrought! Timid disciples became brave. Denying Peter was transformed into the boldest of preachers. Doubting Thomas cried " My Lord and my God !" and the standard-bearers of Christ Jesus were clothed with sal-vation as with a garment. Behold the result on the day of Pentecost, and wherever they went. Everywhere their preach-ing was attended with power. This same experience has been repeated over and over again. The mists of error have been rolled back, and the sun of truth has shone forth. It was so in the days of the Arian controversy, when all at once, God's spirit of life gave the church resistless power. It was so in the days of Luther. It was so with the leaders of France, when the Hugue-nots became a power and an inspiration. Take this one fact as an illustration. The Latern Council assembled on the 5th of May, 1514, and they rejoiced over the death of the witnesses. " *Heresy*," said their orator, "is *extinguished, the church is tri-umphant, exclusive and supreme.*"

From the 5th of May, 1514, to the 31st of October, 1517, when Luther first appeared, is exactly three years and a half. "Then the spirit of life from God entered into the witnesses. And they heard a great voice from heaven, saying unto them, come up hither. And they ascended to heaven in a cloud, and their ene-mies beheld them. And the same hour was there a great earth-quake, and the tenth part of the city fell, and in the earthquake were slain of men seven thousand, and the remnant were affrighted and gave glory to the God of heaven." There are those who find the explanation of this passage in the condition of the church which succeeded the advent of Luther. At once, strangely and mysteriously, as in a cloud, Protestantism passed from obscurity into notice. Kings became enamored with the Bible, and whole provinces threw off the Roman yoke. William,

Prince of Orange, of the Netherlands; Henry of Navarre, of France; and Elizabeth, Queen of England, lifted up the banner of Protestantism from the valley of humiliation to heaven, or the heights of kingly power, and their enemies beheld them. Their influence resembled the throes of an earthquake. Consternation pervaded Europe. The strong portions of papal power gave way, and the people sang glory to God. This. though it may not be the explanation of the truth taught, illustrates it, and shows that the hope of the church is in the keeping of God. When men degrade it with doctrinal corruptions and an unholy life, so that its ruin seems inevitable, God comes with the spirit of life, and Christianity lives again, strong, fruitful and beneficent. After every period of decay it revives to fresh power. After every attack it springs up with renewed energy. The very blows aimed against it seem but to quicken and animate it. Troubled on every side, it is not distressed; perplexed, it is not in despair; persecuted, it is not forsaken; cast down, it is not destroyed.''

Its one assurance of life is, that it displays the banner because of the truth, and bears about in the body the dying of the Lord Jesus. It proclaims that the temple, the altar and the worshipper are to be measured by the Scripture standard, and fearlessly holds up the truth, backed up by the eternal and unalterable purposes of Almighty God. As the Saviour impressed upon the minds of the disciples that the end of the world was at hand, and as the people of every age have been made to feel that they stood upon the threshold of important events, so this proclamation of the gospel of Revelation belongs to Christians of every age. Think of those places where it seemed as though truth was dead and buried. A new feeling takes possession of the heart. The olive tree is seen. Some minister, in the fear of God and the love of souls, spake, and at once there is what is called a revival. The spirit of life from God enters into them, and they stand upon their feet. If this be the true interpretation, then what minister can confront his responsibilities and fail to cry, '' Who is sufficient for these things ?'' It is the duty of the ministry to preach, and of the church to illustrate those teachings by a well-ordered life and a godly conversation. When they do their duty, life is enjoyed. They have power to shut heaven, that it rain not in the days of their prophecy. In other words, the responsibility of saving the world rests on the church; where they go, Christ goes. When they pause, the work of God is hindered.

This portion of God's word devolves great responsibilities upon the ministry and the church. If declensions abound, it is your fault; if revivals, they are your glory. It shows also that God is the protector of his truth and it reveals to us the power of the truth.

In this light, survey the field. Who prays for the ministry as though they were the olive trees through whose instrumentality the influence of the church was to be seen and felt? Evangelistic success is what it is, largely because of the concentration of prayer upon such labor. Pray for the ministry. They are to

preach Christ to dying men. Bind about them your love. Think
of the value of a faithful ministry, and you will pray for those
ou love; and pray for God to set apart the best material of the
Fhurch to the use of his sanctuary. Think of a dying world.
The blood of souls is ou the skirts of the garments of a dead
ministry and church. They do not warn sinners of danger.
They do not proclaim the truth. Let us bless God that there is
so much faithfulness, and be encouraged to work as never
before. God is on the giving hand. Let sinners be affrighted
at their past conduct. Repent of sins committed and of a
Saviour scorned, and come with us, and give glory to the God
of heaven for the matchless love that planned for us redemption,
and seeks to save all who will believe on Christ's effectual work,
and trust to the offering of his shed blood.

> To-day the Saviour calls,
>   Ye wanderers come;
> Oh, ye benighted souls
>   Why longer roam?
>
> To-day the Saviour calls,
>   For refuge fly;
> The storm of justice falls,
>   And death is nigh.
>
> The Spirit calls to-day,
>   Yield to his power;
> Oh, grieve him not away,
>   'Tis mercy's hour.

---

1. Sinners, will you scorn the message
     Sent in mercy from above?
   Every sentence, oh, how tender!
     Every line is full of love:
       Listen to it:
     Every line is full of love.

2. Hear the heralds of the gospel,
     News from Zion's King proclaim:
   "Pardon to each rebel sinner;
     Free forgiveness in his name:"
       How important!
     "Free forgiveness in his name."

3. Tempted souls, they bring you succor,
     Fearful hearts, they quell your fears;
   And with news of consolation,
     Chase away the falling tears;
       Tender heralds!
     Chase away the falling tears.

ROMISH SUPERSTITIONS — THEIR IN-FLUENCE IN AMERICA.

2 PETER 2:21.

"For it had been better for them not to have known the way of righteousness, than after they have known it to turn from the holy commandment delivered unto them."

ROMISH superstitions live in America as in Europe. Their influence in the present as in the past, is bad, and only bad. They covered the nation's cradle with their gloomy shadows; they kindled martyr fires in the wilderness of the New World, as amid the monuments of ancient civilizations; and now that the nation has attained gigantic proportions, they seek to cramp its mind, fetter its limbs, and blot out the stars of hope shining in its sky. Are we helping or hindering in this work? The words of the apostle indicate the originating cause of Romish degeneracy, and of the malign determination to oppose the good and true in all lands. It was not because they had not the truth, for this they possessed, while they rejected its teachings, and turning to tradition, placed the words and will of man above the words and will of God.

"Superstition means an excess or extravagance in religion: the doings of things not required of God, and the belief of what is absurd." We have shown that there were two parties at the outset. One believed in God's word; they accepted the teachings of the Bible as their rule of faith and practice. The others claimed the right of altering God's word and becoming a law to themselves in consequence of the power given to them on the day of Pentecost. Those two parties confront each other at the close of eighteen centuries as they did at the commencement of the Christian era. Baptists contend for the law: Romanists for the church. Baptists find God living in truth and animating the words of inspiration by his Spirit. Romanists believe that God tabernacles in an organization called a church. The result is before us. The Bible meets superstition and contends against it. America is the sanctuary of truth and the asylum of liberty. Our fathers left untouched "what here they found — freedom to worship God." Romanists came to escape persecution, famine, and slavery. They have brought with them their superstitions. In noticing their characteristics, consider, —

1. *The Idolatry of Rome.*

It is seen not in crosses, in robes, in crooks and crosiers alone, but in images as well, though the worship of them are violations of the command, "Thou shalt not make unto thee any graven image, or any likeness of anything that is in heaven above or that is in the earth beneath, or that is in the waters under the earth." How does Rome avoid the issue? As she avoids every other, by claiming, first, a divine right to disobey God, and then by professedly quoting God's word as authority, saying, in a note in the Douay Bible, "All such idols or images as are worshipped with divine honor must be given up. But otherwise, images, pictures, or representations, even in the house of God and in the very sanctuary, so far from being forbidden, are *expressly authorized by the word of God.*" To prove which, references are made to the brazen serpent in Exodus, to the cherubim in Chronicles. See Exodus 25 : 15; 88 : 7. Numbers 21 : 89. 1 Chron. 88 : 18, 19. 2 Chron. 3 : 10. Few, of course, will be expected to look at these references. Your surprise will be great to see how utterly and unblushingly truth is falsified by this declaration and by these quotations. In Ex. 25 : 15, reference is had to the construction of the tabernacle, and the verse reads, "The staves shall be in the rings of the ark; they shall not be taken out of it." Now, how staves *can* have anything to do with idols or graven images it is difficult to conceive. Yet Rome finds here a warrant for worshipping the manger, or crib, which is preserved in the Basilica di Santa Maria Maggiore, in Rome, consisting of five boards of the manger in which the infant Jesus was deposited at his birth, inclosed in an urn of silver and crystal, with a fine gilt figure of the child at the top. Ex. 88 : 7 refers to the ephod, the sacerdotal habit, or dress, and could have nothing to do with images, but is quoted as authority for their dress. Numb. 21 : 8, 9, refers to the brazen serpent lifted up to heal Israel from the bite of the fiery serpents. In Chronicles, the reference is to the cherubim that guarded the mercy-seat. It is plain why priests are afraid to trust the people with the word of God. No one can read even the Douay version without seeing that the priests are untrustworthy. What God commands them not to do, the priests teach should be done. They fill their churches with idols and images, and teach their people to turn from the living and true God to beings made by human hands which can neither see nor understand.

For an illustration go to any Roman Catholic Church. All the old superstitions of Greece and Rome have taken refuge among them. Idolatry is the foundation of the faith of the worshippers. Here, as in Naples and Rome, it is true that the masses have no idea of worship without some statue or picture to bow down to. A God that is not visible to the eye is altogether unknown to them. In the editions of the Bible published for use of Romanists in Italy, the second commandment, as it is given in 'he twentieth chapter of Exodus and the fifth of Deuteronomy, is wanting. This one fact being brought to the attention of the people during the revolution of 1848, and now that Victor Emanuel has entered Rome, has done more and is doing more to open their eyes to the deceptions practised upon them by the church than anything else. They perceive by a reference to the Bible that the Jewish and Pagan elements are so mixed up with both the doctrines and practices of the Roman Church, that there hardly remains a shade of primitive Christianity; and hence, they come to feel that the Bible, and the Bible alone, is sufficient to destroy the whole edifice of popery. In Rome the Bible itself is heresy, as the priests assert, it is from it that all heresy proceeds. Therefore a man who studies it is suspected of doing so in order to find a pretext to separate himself from the Romish church. So general is the idea that the Sacred Scriptures and the papal church are not in agreement.

Said a Bible distributor in Rome, in distributing the Word of God among the Italians, "We dwell on its value to those not acquainted with it, and explain the mode of reading it so as to understand it. The chief rule is that the Bible never contradicts itself; obscure passages should be explained by others more clear. 'The Bible explains the Bible,' is the canon of Augustine. It is not true that the Fathers are necessary to interpret it." The church of Rome orders the study of the fathers in preference to that of Scripture; and this she does because in the diversity of their opinions, the reader becomes bewildered, and is obliged to have recourse to her for explanation. How significant the fact that as soon as Italians obtained the Bible they emerged from the darkness of superstition into the sunlight of truth. They renounced their idol worship, and through faith in Christ passed to the embrace of the Father's love.

In America, such is the influence of the priests over the minds of the deluded votaries of Romanism, that idols are openly kept on sale, and the people bow down to stocks of wood and stone in Boston with as devout worship as characterizes the blinded devotees of pagan lands, while the Bible is seldom found in a Romanist home. It is said that they do not worship the image, but the God represented and behind it. This may be true of some, but that it is not true of the multitudes is apparent from the sacrifices they make to obtain an image and a candle for their homes. It is known that many a poor Irish family in Boston took the money given them by the city to purchase food for their families, and bought instead a candle consecrated by the priest, and to be burned before their idol on Christmas. When remonstrated with, they reply, "The city has no right to interfere with our religion. If we go hungry to save our souls, it is nobody's business." Thus, while Rome neglects her poor and builds great establishments which are but nurseries of Romanism, American citizens, by a tax, support and feed the fires of Romish superstition.

Mariolatry.

2. The worship of the Virgin Mary is a Romish superstition. It is difficult in this land to form a conception of the extent to which this worship of Mary is carried in Roman Catholic countries. To the Romanist, here as there, Mary is God, and worship is simply the adoration of the Virgin. Viewing Romanism in the light of the Bible, this is its crowning sin; viewing it as a system combined to seduce and enslave, this is its masterpiece.

Though Christ when dying on the cross refused to call Mary his mother, but in addressing her said, " Woman, behold thy son," and in addressing John, said, " Behold thy " — not my — but " *thy mother*," yet Rome declares that *Mary is the mother of God and is immaculate like Jehovah.* Popery thus blots out the God-man as mediator, and in his stead presents us with Mary, who is to the devotee " the one living and true God; for though the Father and Son are known, they are accessible cnly through Mary, and they stand so far behind and beyond her, that to the Romanist they are vague, shadowy, and unknown. Mary is the first name to be lisped in childhood, the last to be uttered by the quivering lips before they are closed in death. Around the neck of the infant is suspended a small image of the Virgin; when the babe seeks the breast it must kiss the image, and thus literally does it draw in the adoration of Mary with its mother's milk " " Were the New Testament to be written at this hour, Rome would blot out the name of Christ and substitute that of Mary. Take a proof: The church close by the Vatican has upon its marble pediment, graven in large letters, ' Let us come to the throne of the Virgin Mary, that we may find grace to help us in our time of need.' The Roman sees, Heb. 4: 16, quoted, but cannot verify it if he would, seeing the Bible is forbidden to him." Pius IX, at the foot of the column of the Immaculate Conception, erected to perpetuate the fact that he was permitted to decree the dogma, has Moses, David, Isaiah, and Jeremiah casting crowns before the Virgin, saying: " Thou art worthy; for thou wast slain and hast redeemed us to God by thy blood." When it was announced that the French occupation of Rome should cease, the pope published a decree calling on all Rome to go with him to the feet of Mary, if happily by cries and tears they might prevail with her to avert from the throne of God's vicar the dangers that threaten it, and in that act the pope led the way. Though Christ guarded against Mariolatry, and never answered a prayer that she offered lest he should seem to give countenance to the supposition that she holds a position toward him different from that of others, yet Rome rejects the teachings of Scripture, and glories in her shame, by substituting prayers to Mary and the saints as though Christ had vacated the mediatorial throne. That they know better is apparent from the fact, that they have the Scriptures. ' Peter says: " It had been better for them not to have known the way of righteousness, than after they have known it to turn from the holy commandment delivered unto them." Jesus being the way, the truth and the light, it follows that whosoever attempts to attain heaven through the aid of Mary, rejects Christ and brings damnation upon his soul. Think of the millions thus deluded in our land, and you will perceive a reason why we should bestir ourselves to give to them the knowledge of the truth, and warn them to escape the perils which surround them. The peril that confronts us is best seen when we look abroad. Though it is true that ignorance, degradation and crime increase in inverse ratio as we approach the city of Rome, and that beneath the shadow of St. Peter's beggary and misery rule supreme; yet if we would find a virgin field where Romanism has luxuriated and spread its dogmas free from all contact with heresies, — a field filled with revolution and ever threatened with anarchy as a proof that Romanism is the bitterest and most implacable foe of liberty and of republican institutions, — we must turn to Mexico, that land invaded by Fernando Cortez in 1519, where, beneath a flag bearing the inscription, "Let us follow the cross, for under this sign we shall conquer," deeds of blood were performed under the eyes of priests fresh from Rome, which even now curdle the blood and fill the soul with horror.

Robertson records the fact, that fifty nobles who bore food to the Spaniards with friendly intentions, were seized, their hands cut off, and they with their bleeding stumps were sent back to their fellows. At last, crazed by fear and shocked by the inhuman cruelty practised towards them, the Indians sent a delegation, saying, "If you are divinities of a cruel and savage nature, we present you five slaves that you may drink their blood and eat their flesh. If you are men, here is meat, bread and fruit to nourish you. If you are mild deities, accept our offering of incense and variegated plumes." Mexico is a magnificent country, abounding in mineral and agricultural wealth, extending from the Gulf of Mexico to the Pacific, over territories stretching about fifteen hundred miles from east to west, and six hundred from north to south, embracing territory not inferior in fertility and opulence to any in the torrid zone. Mexico is Catholic. Its condition when contrasted with the United States, presents in bold relief, not only the contrast between the effects of Romanism and Christianity, but its condition exposes to our gaze the results of papal rule when undisturbed by dissent. Mexico was free from the seeds of the Eleatic philosophy which the school of Xenophanes, Parmenides, and Zeno had drawn from physical speculations. It was free from the scientific deductions which Aristotle had planted in the Old World. The church of Rome did not have to dash aside in Mexico such theories as the opening of the Egyptian ports had spread over Europe. There was no contact with extraneous elements, no Pantheism to the east of them, no Greek philosophy, no Mohammedanism to overrun some of the fairest territory of the church; no sects to distract the faithful, no Trinitarian controversy to set the mind in action.

The religious force which had concentrated itself in the Old World swept over the virgin soil of the New, without opposition. The fanatical monk penetrated with the crucifix into the midst of the most savage tribes, while sword, fire, and massacre were the instruments used in the propagation of the faith. What is the result? Mexico is in total night. Schools have been the exception. The masses are in ignorance of science, of history, and of the Bible. Do we contrast its condition with India, where the Gospel met every opposition, we find India becoming civilized and enlightened. Schools and colleges abound. Papers are printed, Bibles are circulated, and prosperity begins to bless her degraded millions. In Mexico, said Hon. Thomas Corwin, our late minister to that sister Republic, "The great want of the people is, that public opinion which is so omnipotent in the United States; and this again arises from the want of education. Hence, in the last fifty years Mexico has passed through thirty-six different forms of government, and has had seventy-three presidents. The cause of causes that itself originates and gives force to all other causes, and which has destroyed public opinion is Romanism." The church is the power which blocks the wheels of progress, muzzles the press, obstructs the circulation of the Bible, prevents all systematic provision for general education, and left the mass of the people in as profound ignorance of the progress of knowledge as they were forty years ago. The church has been the instigator of all the cruelty and oppression, all the intrigue and disorder, all the internal weakness and dis-organization, which have made the name of Mexico a by-word over the world. Would you gain an estimate of the influence of the church, consider the wealth arrayed against the Republic and in favor of absolutism. In 1860 it cost Mexico $8,000,000 to sustain her clergy, while the estimated value of her church property was $300,000,000, about one third of the valuation of the whole country, the income of which is about $20,000,000.

The Dawn of a Brighter Day.

Though the church party has arrayed itself against the government, though revolt follows revolt, let us rejoice in the appearance of a fresh reason for revolution; the Bible has appeared in Mexico, borne by converted priests and laymen. In Monterey and vicinity, Rev. T. M. Westrup, who came to New York to be ordained as a Baptist minister, with a company of devoted co-laborers has planted churches in the cities and towns, while in Mexico itself ex-priest Aguas has in the cathedral preached and argued against Romanism in a manner worthy of a Luther. The priest who challenged him to a discussion did not appear, because the Archbishop declared "he had no right to do so except by special permission of the Pope." Aguas showed that the real reason was because he dare not confront Rome's greatest enemy, the Bible.

In Spain, in Mexico, and elsewhere among the old Latin races, there seems to be a movement which promises mighty results for the truth. What Westrup has done in Mexico, Rev. W. J. Knapp attempted in Spain, Van Meter in Rome, and so the work goes grandly on, and out of the mouths of her disinthralled subjects Rome is proven to be idolatrous; "I have read," said Aguas, "in your hearing the great precept that forbids idolatry, 'Thou shalt not make.'" Is it not clear that the figures we have hitherto worshipped are likeness of things in heaven or on earth? Who placed these idols in the temple? Who tempted us from infancy to adore them? Who made us bow down to them? Rome, heretical home. When, therefore, God says, "Thou shalt not bow down before them nor adore them," there can be no intellect, however powerful and perverted, that can successfully defend the practice. The field is literally white for the harvest in all South America. The people, to a very great extent, have thrown off the yoke of Rome, discarded their false system of religion, and are waiting and looking for something better. Let us see that they have it in the Gospel which Christ commissioned us to give them. The influence of Romanism is not confined to Italy or Mexico. It is this which lies back of the barbarism of New York, the desecration of the Sabbath in Chicago, Cincinnati, St. Louis, and its attempted abolition in New Orleans. Romanism is the foe of education, of the Bible, of a general system of education. That it will destroy us we have no fear. It has been said, "The lion that eats the ox does not become an ox, but the ox becomes the lion." Education and the Gospel go together. Wherever Christ is preached there is enlightenment, progress, and growth. The educational value of the Bible cannot be estimated. It is the ploughshare that ridges the fields of thought on which literature and science grow their richest harvests.

Mariolatry encourages Sinners.

There is another effect of this worship of Mary which should not be ignored or lost from sight. Sinners find encouragement because of it. Christ's worship is built on the teachings of the Scriptures. To obtain forgiveness of sins through Christ, there must be a change of heart, a new birth, a new life. Old things must pass away, and all things become new. Romanists believe that they can be saved more easily through Mary. Christ requires repentance. Mary, devotion. Faith in Christ demands submission to the will of God, reformation of life, and devotion of heart, as required by the Gospel; while devotion to Mary consists in prayers to her, or some external practices in her honor. St. Bernard had this dream: "There were two ladders reaching from earth to heaven; at the top of one was Christ, at the other Mary; a great number of people on both tried to reach heaven, but from Christ's ladder all fell back; not one from that of Mary." Therefore, according to this father, salvation is a certain and constant fact when people apply to Mary; to apply to Christ, salvation is almost impossible." Father Liguori taught *that damnation is impossible when there is devotion to the Virgin Mary*. Hence, the worship of Mary encourages sinners and multiplies sins. All that is said of the worship of Mary is applicable to that of the saints, which is derived from Paganism.

Saint Worship.

The Pagans had their gods, as Papists have their saints; Paganism had expiations for the dead, so has Rome; Paganism had its purgatory with material fire, Rome has the same; Paganism had vestal virgins, Rome has her nuns; Paganism had its *pena-*

tes, Rome has saints for every street of the town and corner of the country. What can saints do? *Mediate* is the answer. Cardinal Bellarmino says, they see our necessities *through God*. The Gospel invites us to go directly to God through Jesus Christ. Well did a converted Romish priest declare, " Papists, not satisfied with Christ, have the Virgin Mary as co-mediator; nor yet content, they create some millions of sub mediators to increase the strength of their supplications to God. To prove the effect of medical springs, the water must be drunk directly from the fountain; if it pass from bottle to bottle, it loses all its power. So in the case of Romanists. You pray to Mary, to saints and angels, to carry your demands to Christ, while he opens the way to himself direct, saying, "Come unto me all ye that are weary and heavy laden, and I will give you rest." Romish superstition blinds the eyes of the deluded votary, and destroys both soul and body."

St. Patrick a Protestant.

The Irish bishop is called a Roman saint, and is claimed to have been the champion of popery. Processions are held in his honor, and faith is exercised in his power to help in America quite as much as in Ireland.

Patrick was not even a Romanist. He was not a messenger of the pope, but of Christ. He went to Ireland of his own accord, and established a church independent of Rome. Churches on the model of the great apostle were established in France and Germany, and were persecuted on the continent as in Ireland In A. D. 602, the Irish Columbanus was ordered to leave France by a council to which he wrote, pleading for liberty of conscience; and five centuries after the time of Saint Patrick, Saint Bernard reproached the Irish for being Pagans, unconnected with Rome, because every little town had its independent bishop; and it was not until 1148 that Rome obtained a secure foothold in Ireland, when the clergy suicided their independence, and sacrificed themselves upon the altar of Rome. Irishmen worship the Virgin Mary. Not so with Patrick. A glorious hymn remains as composed by him the day previous to his controversy with the Irish prince, but not a word in it to Mary; all his beautiful aspirations, all his warm affections, all his victorious hopes, are to and from Christ alone. If Irishmen would follow Patrick as he followed Christ, they would leave the altar of Mary and turn to the cross of Christ, and lift their island from beneath the heel of priestly superstition into the sunlight of God's favor.

Transubstantiation.

3. The doctrine of Transubstantiation is a Romish superstition prevalent in America. The sacrifice of the mass is an inheritance from the heathen. The word of God is expressly contrary to it. In all of Paul's epistles we are told that Christ effected our redemption on Calvary, — died once to atone for human sins, and that man's guilt was thereby cancelled; that he justified by his

death all the generations of the earth, that his blood alone saves the world. According to the Council of Trent, the mass is the continuation of the sacrifice on Calvary. Continuation! there was no need of any. "We are sanctified through the offering of the body of Jesus Christ *once for all.*" And every priest standeth daily ministering and offering oftentimes the same sacrifices which can never take away sins; but this man, after he had offered one sacrifice for sins forever, sat down on the right hand of God; from henceforth expecting till his enemies be made his footstool. *For by one offering he hath perfected forever them that are sanctified.* Whereof the Holy Ghost also is a witness; for after that he had said before, this is the covenant that I will make with them after those days saith the Lord. I will put my laws into their hearts, and in their minds will I write them, and *their sins and iniquities will I remember no more.*" Heb. 10: 10–17.

Notwithstanding these positive utterances of Holy Writ, we find in the Roman Catholic's catechism, approved and in use in Boston, these words : —

Q. What is the Holy Eucharist?

A. The Holy Eucharist is a sacrament which contains really and indeed the body and blood, the soul and divinity of our Lord Jesus Christ, under the forms and appearances of bread and wine.

Q. Does anything remain of the bread and wine after consecration?

A. No; the substance of the bread is changed into that of the body of Jesus Christ, and the substance of the wine is changed into that of his blood.

Q. What is this change called?

A It is called transubstantiation.

Q. How is this change effected?

A. It is effected through the almighty power of the words of Jesus Christ spoken by the priest in mass. (p. 45.)

This is the boastful claim. It is pretended, and Romanists are superstitious enough to believe, that *a priest can make a God, an Omnipotent, Infinite, Omniscient, Almighty, Eternal, Invisible and Omnipresent God, whenever he so chooses and wills.*

Without characterizing the claim, let us examine it. Are the words, "This is my body, this is my blood," to be understood in a literal sense? On another occasion Christ said, "I am the bread that came down from heaven;" and no one ever supposed that *he* was actually bread, and subsequently changed or transubstantiated.

Said a Romanist recently, whose attention was called to the absurdity of this claim, "A little examination was sufficient to shake my belief in that doctrine which I had hitherto professed. Would Jesus Christ have told us things that were impossible to be? Now, it is impossible, absolutely impossible, that what is bread should, at one and the same time, be his body, and that what is wine should contemporaneously be his blood. This cannot be either simultaneously or successively. The church of Rome saw the first to be an absurdity, and, therefore, held to the second. But how can the body of Christ become bread, and his blood wine, if such change be not in accordance with the laws of nature? Could Christ deceive us? Now, it is not true that bread and wine, according to nature, has ceased to exist in the sacrament, *for we see they do exist;* that which we see and touch and taste, are natural bread and wine. Can there be faith against nature? And yet that is against nature which neither is nor can be; whatever is must be according to nature's laws. There may be substances of a higher nature, and subject to superior laws, than those with which we are acquainted; but they can never exist in contradiction to them, since Nature herself, in that case, would be destroyed. Therefore, what is bread and wine cannot — *not be* bread and wine; God, omnipotent as he is, cannot order it otherwise. But the sacrament, after consecration, is always natural bread and wine; therefore, it is not the substance of the body and blood of Christ."

Transubstantiation is not only Illogical, it is Unnecessary.

Paul truly said, the kingdom of God is not meat and drink, but righteousness and peace in the Holy Ghost (Rom. 14: 17). Christ said, It is the spirit that quickeneth, *the flesh profiteth* nothing; the words that I speak unto you, they are spirit and they are life (John 6: 63). Corporeal substances may be a type, a figure of the spiritual, but nothing more. The words of Christ are full of truth and wisdom. The interpretation of the Romanist is a grovelling conception, full of error, falsehood, and absurdity. Christ could not better symbolize the effect of his passion and death than by the bread and wine. And we cannot more grossly abuse it than by attributing to a sinful priest the virtue and power of the Saviour; with the additional enormity, that what Christ has been able to do once, a wretched priest can repeat as often as he chooses. No wonder that many priests in this land refuse and declare that the mass is nothing but a lie, a solemn imposture, an actual sacrilegious assault upon Christ.

The dogma which constitutes the mass, with its double element of transubstantiation and propitiatory sacrifice, is the most fatal of Romish doctrines, the most detestable of all heresies, and the most abominable of all practices. Around this as their sun revolves all the rest of the papal system. If there is no propitiatory sacrifice but through the Eucharist, if the priest controls it, and has it in his power to make Christ, or to refuse to do so, every worshipper is bound to the priesthood by his every hope of salvation.

Contemplate the use made of this alleged sacrifice. Money, said Gavazzi, is the end of all popish practices. Money procures masses for the repose of souls in purgatory. In proportion to the alms, the mass, it is said, has more efficacy, because God regards the money given, and in proportion grants more suffrages to the souls in torments. Because of this pretended claim to power, millions of money have been won for Rome, and millions more are forthcoming. Here rests the power of control which enables priests to build these magnificent institutions and churches, despite the poverty of their people and the blasphemous character of their boastful pretension. "The ancient pagans worshipped their god under material forms; the Assyrians the sun; the Egyptians, reptiles and vegetables; the Greeks, heroes; the Romans, emperors; and the modern pagans, under the form of a stone, or a tree. These were called and are called pagans, because they worship God under material forms. But the Roman Catholics, according to the Boston Catechism, worship God under this material form of bread and wine; therefore, are we not justified in pronouncing Romanism as no better than paganism?

It is because of this superstition that Rome holds in her hand the destiny of the soul. The dying wait for extreme unction and rest their faith on a bread-God which a man makes, rather than on the atonement of the Lord Jesus Christ, slain on Calvary that every believer may have life. Because of this, the sermon has been largely excluded from the sanctuary, and instead of the bread of life furnished in the gospel, there is a forest of candles burning at the altar; people are counting their beads and praying before pictures; mummeries take the place of worship, and chants to the virgin the praises to Almighty God.

This superstition is here, and its influence is felt. That it should be tolerated is a surprise to the reflecting. Enter a Catholic church on Christmas. There is the archbishop in his robes, with his cross, his crook, and his crozier; there are priests in numbers moving about making their crosses, obeisances, and genuflections. When the bishop rises, crook and crosier move before him, and priests follow after; the book is shifted from side to side, and is read and chanted in a language which none understand. There is the elevating of the host and the bowing down of the people; the waving of incense, prostrations, lustrations, and all the usual accompaniments of such a service, no better than a pantomine, and not much different from a play at a theatre. If mass thus performed, with all the splendor and pomp of ritual, is thus unmeaning, how insipid must it be when performed in country chapels by ignorant priests "who hunt up the sheep to shear off the wool." For, be it remembered, the people cannot obtain the forgiveness of their sins only in the church and at the hands of their priest. Hence, in lands most full of superstition, their churches throng with worshippers, and in lands illumined by the Gospel, the learned become infidel, and the women go to mass.

On the contrary, behold the faith of the gospel with those who believe in Christ rather than in the surroundings of Christ; with those who recognize the fact, that Jesus, not the manger, — not Mary, — not the gifts, but Jesus, the child Jesus, the man Jesus, the crucified, — Jesus the risen and ascended Lord is our hope; the bread and wine symbolizes the body and blood of Christ. Approaching the Lord's supper, we enjoy sacramental union with Christ in this last supper, and commemorate his death till he come; thus we escape all the false consequences of stating "you have the real presence of Christ in this wafer;" thus we save ourselves from the charge of being cannibal, or Christ eaters; thus we do God's will and obey Christ's commands, and can pray, Oh, Christ! be all in all, that all may profit by thy blood! Christ, teach all by thy inspired Word, to worship Thee accordingly; open all eyes by means of Thy truth to escape the delusions of human doctrines towards Thee! Thus do we receive all from Christ; give all to Christ; labor all for Christ, and Christ becomes all in all, and is for all. Christ in life, Christ in the hour of anguish, Christ in the time of tribulation, Christ in death, Christ our joy and glory forever!

The Superstition regarding Christmas.

Christmas, called the great festival of the Christian world, was a Pagan feast to the Sun and Saturn, which was Romanized, adopted, and transformed into a part of the church, as was the statue of Jupiter in the Pantheon, called afterwards the statue of the Apostle Peter, and made to serve a purpose in popish ceremonies. Previous to the year A. D. 500, the *Christi messa*, or mass of Christ, from which Christmas is derived, began with the festival of St. Thomas, December 21st, and extended to the feast of Purification, February 2d, and included many lesser festivals.

The Pagan festival was mainly a day of riotous indulgence, universal license, low masquerades, and all sorts of vulgar sports. The throne, for the time being, was generally surrendered to misrule and wassail. No wonder that the old Puritan Prynne, referring to these disorders, said, "that they should cause all pious Christians eternally to abominate them."

"The Eastern church appears to have originally celebrated Christ's baptism, while the Roman division commemorated the nativity; but towards the close of the fourth century the two branches of the church agreed to unite on the latter, and to celebrate it uniformly on the 25th of December.

"The rites of Christians in the early days were simple and impressive. Bells were rung and masses said at midnight, carols sung and the churches dressed with evergreens. Friendly visits were made and presents given, and thus the foundations laid for the world-wide observance of the season which has come down through all the ages with only trifling modifications.

"In more modern times, England and Germany have taken the lead in the celebration of Christmas, though very recently, America, uniting the practicable features of the customs of both countries, has made the keeping of Christmas national and almost universal."

There is no evidence that Christ was born on Dec. 25th. Newcome claims that the event occurred in October, Paulus in March, Weisler in February, Lichtenstien in June, Griswell in April,

Lardner and Robinson in autumn; while Newton, because of the prophecy of John the Baptist, "He must increase and I must decrease," declared the church placed John's birth at June 24th, and Christ's at Dec. 25th, when the days began to increase. There is but one reason for making it a holiday. As observed in our churches and among our people, it is calculated to promote a friendly state of feeling. But as a day to commemorate the nativity of our Christ, there is neither warrant for the festival nor reasons for its observance. Christ never intended that it should become one of the institutions of the church.

The Sabbath,

Which is the commemoration of his resurrection from the dead, He has required us to hold sacred as the manifestation of our love to him, and for the confirmation of our faith in his atoning blood. He has taught us to look to the cross rather than to the manger when we would see our Christ. In this we glory, and in this we are in harmony with the primitive church who never thought of keeping the day of his birth holy to the Lord.

The superstition that made Christmas a festival day was an after-thought of Romanists, and by adopting it we are in danger of dishonoring Christ's commands, which forbid our adding to "the things written in his word." The list of Romish supersti tions which hold a place among us might be indefinitely extended. They pervade the realm of art, they permeate literature, and are seen exerting their influence upon our daily life. The halo over the head of Joseph and Mary in pictures welcomed to our fire-sides and libraries, the respect paid to the crucifix, its introduc-tion to many of our churches, its use in the realm of fashion, the robes worn by the clergy, the respect paid to Lent, and to days made sacred by the canon of Rome, but utterly repudiated in the Scripture; the countenancing the introduction of images into the sanctuary, — mark the departure from the primitive sim-plicity of the Gospel, and indicate the tendency to turn from the Gospel way, and to seek the favor of the world at the expense of God's glory and humanity's weal.

Ignorance and Romanism

Go hand in hand. The opposition to education, to reading the Bible, is but half of the plan. Rome is not content with mere opposition, as are too many of the professed followers of Christ. Rome acts. Already priests are traversing the South, and are seeking to gain an influence over the uneducated freedmen. Their peril is iminent.

Cardinal Barnabo, Prefect of the Propaganda at Rome, in his letter of instructions to the Baltimore Plenary Council, said, "It is the wish of the sacred congregation that the bishops of the United States, in fulfilment of the charge which has been entrusted to them, of feeding the Lord's flock, should consult

together respecting some uniform method of providing salvation for the blacks."

The Romish church in England has inaugurated a mission to
our land, — the first foreign mission ever sent out from that
branch of the Papacy; and a few days ago, a number of missionaries were set apart by Archbishop Manning, at St. Joseph's
College, near London. A letter published in the "Irish World,"
says: "The same ship which carries this letter will bear to your
shores the vanguard of a body of Roman Catholic priests, who
have received from the propaganda of Rome the special and exclusive mission of converting to the Roman Catholic faith the
negro population of the United States, who will be followed before long by forty other priests, who are now preparing themselves for the same work, and who have already been given by
the Archbishop of Baltimore a house and grounds for the head-
quarters of the mission. The forty will before long be followed
by four hundred," etc. These missionaries take with them neither wives nor children, and scarcely two coats. It won't cost
much to keep them. Their wants will be of the fewest and sim-
plest, and, without exaggeration, they will have nothing to do or
to think of but the work in which they are to engage.

The Archbishop in his address said: "The missionary college
of St. Joseph has been founded, not for the education of priests
for ordinary work, but for the special work of conducting a mission in America. In the heart of a great Christian nation, there
are to-day five millions of people who are indeed within the
warmth of civilization, but at the same time are left out in the
cold by neglect. These priests go as the vanguard of others
who will soon follow, inflamed with the love of souls not lovable for their intelligence and virtue, but souls black with ignorance and vice, lovable only because your Master died for them.
You give yourselves forever," said the Archbishop to the priests,
"to be the fathers and servants of the negroes, and to labor ex-
clusively for them until your death, in the spirit of Peter Clavor,
who announced himself as forever the slave of the slave." The
Archbishop then rose from his throne, prostrated himself before
each missionary, embraced his feet, and then arising, kissed each
upon both cheeks, receiving a similar kiss in return.

To the superficial glance there is nothing more nor less in this,
than a noble desire to bless the black race with the light of Papal
Christianity. Look deeper. Hitherto, Rome has rested her hope
on the uneducated Irishman. She perceives a new ally in the
uneducated Negro. We must bestir ourselves. The Negro is
not easily deceived. A love for the Bible possesses his soul.
Whatever wars against it is suspected. In Louisiana, the Sisters
of Charity tried to banish the Bible; the Negroes heard of it and
banished them. The field is ours. A thirst for knowledge per-
vades their minds. Accustomed to the preaching of the gospel
in the past, they love it and find in the message of salvation
their meat and drink.

The fact is full of significance. If education and the influence of the gospel of Christ preserve men from the contaminating touch of that power, which holds in its hands the ballot of an ignorant Irishman, then we perceive the basis of hope for the nation. Let the principle rule supreme. Let education for all classes and races become the purpose of the nation, and an influence will be exerted which shall exercise a controlling influence upon the destinies of the country. The waves of barbarism and ignorance will no longer threaten to submerge the altars of political hope, but intelligence and virtue will remain the bulwark of free institutions.

Rome builds on nature, and ignorance is the sheet-anchor of her hope. Free schools and a free press are the power which destroys her system, and undermines the foundations upon which she rests her hope.

The colored population of the North have been affected by the denunciations of the Evangelical churches, which have fallen from the lips of liberty-loving and Christ-hating infidels.

Let Rome step forward, and by appeals to the pride of the carnal heart, open to the African a road to ascendancy over his former master, and we perceive the power to be arrayed against the higher interests of this unfortunate race. For behind this attempt, slumbers a war upon free schools, upon a free press, and a free pulpit, and the purpose to build up a power which dooms its hapless victims to a slavery whose fetters bind the conscience, and whose bars shut out the light of the Gospel.

The effort to educate the colored ministry should be encouraged. An educated ministry is their future hope. Like minister, like people, is peculiarly true among them. Now, their leaders are within our reach. They can be taught the doctrines of the Gospel, and established in the faith. They can be aided to preach as were our fathers, and so they will becomes guides for the people, who will in time demand a higher grade of ministerial ability than is required at present. To further this object, let Christians bend their energies. The work cannot be postponed. Wait a few years and this people will be beyond our reach, as they were in the West Indies where they refused all aid of the whites, and preferred an uneducated to an educated ministry.

Let it be ours to uncover error and proclaim the truth; then shall the superstitions of Rome be exposed, and the people who seek here an asylum from the dwarfing influences of Romanism and Paganism in the Old World, find that the religion of Christ that empties the soul of the disposition which attempts to fetter truth, while it unbars hope, strikes off fetters and unlocks prison doors, introduces the emancipated to the truth which gives freedom, and to the light born of love which begets life and peace and joy.

THE INTOLERANCE OF ROMANISM.

To say that Rome is intolerant is to utter a truth as self-evident as an axiom. Popery cannot change. The past binds it. While it remains Popery, it must war upon Protestantism. For the Romish church, the alternative is simple — Popery or the Gospel.

In a popish tract, entitled "Religious Toleration, a Question of First Principles," we find this admission: "It cannot be denied that Catholic governments have persecuted. In old Catholic times, heresy was an offence of which the law took cognizance; the teachers of heresy were sometimes committed to the flames; and what is more, the ecclesiastical authorities sanctioned the proceeding, and Catholic priests formally defended the principle of non-toleration."

This is a frank admission. It saves us the necessity of proving what every one knows to be true. This spirit is unchanged. In the recent canons, *De Ecclesia Christi*, which have been passed in the Œcumenical Council of 1870, we find canons 6 and 12 read as follows: "Whoever says that the authority with which the Catholic church proscribes and condemns all religious sects separated from its communion is not proscribed by divine right; or that about religious truths only opinions, not certainties, can exist, and that therefore all religious sects are to be tolerated, let him be anathematized." "Whoever says that Christ, our Saviour and sovereign, has conferred upon the church the power to direct only by advice and persuasion those who turn aside, not to compel them by orders, by coercion and by external verdicts and statutory punishments, let him be anathematized." This is certainly frank and to the point. It is our fault if it is not understood.

It is worthy of notice, however, that the priest, having admitted a truth, links it to a falsehood. He says, "The champions of Protestantism never attempt to show that Catholics were tolerated by Protestants while they had the power to persecute; whether at the period of the Reformation or in later times." The reverse of this is true, to an extent almost to create an impression that the priest wilfully prevaricates. Wherever the principles of the Gospel have taken root, popery has been tolerated and defended. In Rhode Island, from the earliest period, Romanism was tolerated, and as soon as the principle ruling there permeated the nation, the same was true everywhere within the bounds of our ocean-washed republic. A sojourner in this land made this declaration concerning the extent of our toleration: "When a papist speaks against Protestantism, the

Romanist exclaims: 'Oh, he is right. Free discussion, toleration of opinion, is the law.' When a Protestant speaks against popery, the cry everywhere in America is, 'This is a crusade against Roman Catholics; this is to excite citizen against citizen.'" In other words, Rome may persecute, revile, and denounce; we must bear it.

Rome charges God with Intolerance.

In justification of the intolerance of Rome, this language is used. "They who believe in revelation and acknowledge the divine authority of the Jewish laws, cannot deny that religious intolerance was sanctioned, or rather enjoined by God himself. Offences against religion, revolts against the spiritual power, were punishable with death. The law of Moses knew nothing of liberty of conscience. It no more tolerated religious dissent or spiritual independence than it did disobedience to parents or rebellion against the civil rulers."

There is in this utterance much of the cunning of the priest, little of the honesty of a Christian. Intolerance is the feeling which refuses to allow an opinion to exist adverse to itself without persecuting it and those who adhere to it. In this sense there was no intolerance under the administration of God in the ancient theocracy. There is not a single instance on record where men were persecuted for opinion's sake. Abram was called of God to be the father of a great people. But Abram was tolerant and the very pattern of kindness. He listened to God, he obeyed him in many things rigidly and well, but he did not persecute those of an opposite faith. The only wars he waged were for the defence of vested rights, represented either by himself or by those called to obey God. Jacob and his posterity were far too tolerant of error. The sons forgot God and longed after the society of those who rejected his rule. They were not intolerant of their descendants in Egypt when Moses went out to them, and plead with them to return to God. Much might be said in proof that they were rather neglectful of God, than disposed to extend the faith of Abraham by the sword.

They were commanded to be rigid in discipline and to punish with death the violators of God's command; but this came not from their intolerance, but from the disobedience of men to the divine injunctions. Men are under obligations to obey God, remembering, under His rule, disobedience is death. Indeed, the evils resulting from the tolerance of the Jews are numerous. They were not as separate from the godless nations as they should have been. Slavery, polygamy, and idol worship are all proofs of the attempts made by the people to harmonize in faith and practice with the nations about them. Hence, it is a well-understood fact, that many of the errors tolerated under the old dispensation were in consequence of the infirmities of the flesh, the weakness of the faith, and the lack of moral character. God governed and guided them as best he could until the time came for the appearance of the Shiloh, when the law was preserved;

but the errors resulting from tradition, and association with an unbelieving world, were warred against. "Think not," says Christ, "that I am come to destroy the law or the prophets; I am not come to destroy but to fulfil." Christ came to bring the world back to God, so that the commandments given on Sinai should be lifted out from beneath the mountain of tradition and superstition, and should find a welcome in the heart and a rule in the life. This, every intelligent student of the Word of God knows, whether he be a Papist or a Protestant.

It is false to assert that the rule of God was overthrown at the coming of Christ. The ruler became visible and explained his government. The Romanist, in his tract, declares to the contrary, saying, "That dispensation, indeed, has passed away forever, — the law of love has superseded that of fear; but with the Bible Christian, the believer in revelation, I would insist most strongly on this one fact : a principle sanctioned and enjoined by God himself, cannot be a wrong principle. It may not be always applicable, or always expedient, much less always obligatory in its fullest extent; but wrong in itself it cannot be, or the God of truth and holiness would never have given it the force of law. It is a great point gained to make people see and admit this; in fact, once concede the principle of what is called religious intolerance to be abstractly not wrong but right, and this question is narrowed to this very simple point, — whether in particular instances it was justly, mercifully, or expediently applied or enforced. It can no longer excite that moral disgust which men now feel at the bare mention of the thing; nor, I may add, will it be any longer available as a theme of anti-popery declaration."

We take issue with the Romanist on this point, and say that the principle underlying God's government is always applicable, and always expedient. If intolerance was ever right, it is right now. If it was ever expedient, it is expedient now. There is no Jesuitism in Revelation. That commodity finds its home in Romanism.

To say that God is intolerant, is to deny not only history, but to ignore the results of observation. Intolerance refuses to permit opinions to thrive or live, which are opposed to those dear to us. Can this be charged on Jehovah, who commands the sun to shine on the evil and the good? We have not the time to detail the history of God's dealings with Israel. Could we do it, we should find that His rule was disciplinary, but not intolerant.

Notice the shrewdness of the wily foe. God, he claims, is intolerant. Therefore intolerance is not wrong in principle, and Rome is justified. Second, God varies in his government. He is now tolerant, and now intolerant, as the case may be. Here, again, Rome is justified. We deny it. The Bible has one voice for all classes and conditions; for God is the same yesterday, to-day and forever. But supposing it to be true of God, the Infinite Ruler, it does not become the finite subject of God's government to claim the right to usurp the power and rule of the

Most High. A third position is now taken. The writer claims that the principle is universally recognized. "*Universal tolera-tion is simply an impossibility; it never has been practised and never can be.* Let a government be ever so indulgent, there must be a point at which the law interferes to prevent certain opinions being published and acted upon. Every government recognizes some first principle, — at any rate, it is possessed with the in-stinct of self-preservation, and without coercion, — in other words, without intolerance, no government could exist a day or an hour." This apparently fair statement ignores the funda-mental principle of our government, in which the principle of toleration finds its fullest and most unequivocal recognition. Let us quote again the covenant which every inhabitant was required to sign in Rhode Island : "We, whose names are here underwritten, being desirous to inhabit in the town of Provi-dence, do promise to submit ourselves in entire or passive obe-dience, to all such orders or agreements as shall be made for public good of the body, in an orderly way, by the major consent of the present inhabitants, masters of families, incorporated together into a township, and such others whom they shall admit unto the same *only in civil things.*"

This covenant is the corner-stone of our free government. It is against this principle Romanists rebel. Irishmen, Italians, Spaniards, and what not, come here. They find a government; they seek to become members of the body politic. They take an oath in accordance with that covenant. They find that the majority have decided upon a system of education. The Roman-ist not only wars against it by speech and pen, but he rebels against it. He will not submit to its requirements. He is so intolerant that he becomes rebellious, and keeps his children out of the schools, and compels them to grow up as ignorant and bigoted as himself, though the majority are against him.

The government rules in civil matters only. Religious opin-ions are not proceeded against. Laws enter into the framework of the government; they are published and known. People can live under them or live elsewhere. The Romanist claims that he has a right to live under them and war against them. He calls punishing for theft intolerance. That is not intolerance. Steal-ing is not religion. The right to steal is not a religious opinion. The laws on the statute book are for the protection of society, — of every individual. Punishing for theft is protecting the peo-ple. The right to compel the children of the people to obtain an education is based on the fundamental law of protection. It is in keeping with the advice of George Washington, who, in his farewell address, said, "Promote, then, as a matter of primary importance, institutions for the general diffusion of knowledge. In proportion as the structure of the government gives force to public opinion, it is essential that public opinion should be en-lightened."

For this reason States punish offences against morality, but not against religion. We allow Mormonism and Romanism to enjoy the utmost liberty of opinion, but deny their right to violate the laws of the land by offending against the laws of God which supply the authority in the legislation of the State. The principle is enunciated in the words of President Grant's famed message, in which, speaking of Mormonism, he says: In "Utah there still remains a remnant of barbarism, — repugnant to civilization, to decency, and to the laws of the United States. Neither polygamy nor any other violation of existing statutes will be permitted within the territory of the United States. It is not with the religion of the self-styled saints that we are now dealing, but with their practices. They will be protected in the worship of God according to the dictates of their conscience; but they will not be permitted to violate the laws under the cloak of religion."

Tolerance true, and false.

It is to be feared that the idea of tolerance, which means primarily "the capacity of enduring," is to be used to prevent our resisting error by the proclamation of the truth. We are in danger more of neglecting the liberty, and of refusing to use it wisely, than of anything else. Intolerance confronts us. Error is busy sowing its seed and mustering its forces. The friends of error are active. The friends of truth are commanded to be quiet; to permit the Bible to be banished from the schools, to permit the Sabbath to be desecrated, the teachings of Scripture to be ignored, lest they become intolerant. Rome, boasting her intolerance, must be tolerated. Protestantism boasting its tolerance, must be persecuted, beaten, and abused, and be silent. Error and superstition demand toleration now and always. Tolerance does not imply the absence of opinions or a disregard for opinions, but a faith in God and in truth so great that it dare trust to truth in the battle with error, rather than to force, as applied and wielded by the supporters of the right. Said Chief-Justice Story, in his Commentary on the Constitution: "It yet remains a problem to be solved in human affairs, whether any free government can be permanent where the public worship of God and the support of religion constitutes no part of the policy or duty of the State in any assignable shape. The future experience of Christendom, and chiefly of the American States, must settle this problem as yet new in the history of the world, abundant as it has been in experiments in the theory of government. But the duty of supporting religion. and especially the Christian religion, is very different from the :ight to force the consciences of other men, or to punish them for worshipping God in the manner which they believe their accountability to him requires."

These utterances harmonize with the requirements of the Gospel. Support religion; use liberty not as an occasion to the flesh, but in love serve one another. As a nation we are forgetting this command and are imperilled thereby. We seem to be forgetting that this land was created by the Most High; that his rule extended over it before man occupied it; that it has been peopled with a wise reference to its being held for the purpose of building here a nationality that should obey God rather than man; that we have reached the solution of the problem, the most perplexing, the most difficult to be understood by the carnal heart, viz.: Can religious liberty harmonize with the enforcement of regulations essential to the well-being of society? Divide church from state, and can you have religion protected by the state, or is intolerance essential to good government? This question must be answered by us. We are to show to all the world that religion is not dependent upon the state, but derives its inspiration and its victories from God.

This is our duty and opportunity. The field is before us. In the name of our God we are to set up our banners. Some one has said Rome puts her faith in majorities. Let us meet Rome in the fear of God and in the love of man. In the spirit of the Swiss magistrates who said to the Roman clergy, "Answer these men's arguments; preach better; make it impossible for our Swiss to become Baptists." We say, answer the arguments of Rome, preach the gospel more faithfully than they or any other class of errorists preach it, believe in its success, and so make it impossible for this nation to be given up to evil influences.

It is not our duty to stand still and see the ship of state scuttled, but rather to see that vigilant commanders be placed on her deck and a faithful crew man the yards. This work rests upon the individual; stand up for the truth, for the ordinances of the Gospel, for the kingship of Jesus Christ.

The difference between Protestantism and Romanism lies not so much in opinions concerning the obligations under which men are placed to government, as to what is the government to which they owe allegiance. The Christian coming here recognizes the obligations to be ruled by the laws of the land. The Romanist ignores this obligation and claims that the Pope is his ruler, and the government of the church the only one to which he owes allegiance. Hence, the Papist is as intolerant towards the government as towards anything tolerated by the government. This makes of every Romanist a common enemy. Said John Milton, "Men at first united into civil societies, that they might live safely and enjoy their liberty, without being wronged or oppressed; and that they might live religiously and according to the doctrine of Christianity. They united themselves into churches, civil societies, have laws and churches, have a discipline peculiar to themselves, and far differing from each other. And this has been the occasion of so many wars in Christendom, to wit: because *the civil magistrates and the church confound their jurisdiction.*"

Here is our peril to-day. Romanists, as religionists, are tolerated. Romanists, as the enemies of legislation and of the genius and spirit of our institutions, should be opposed. Because England under Cromwell regarded Papists as a common enemy to good government, they were not welcomed to the privileges of the body politic. "Therefore, we do not admit of the papist sect, so as to tolerate papists at all; for we do not look upon that as a religion, but rather as a hierarchial tyranny under a cloak of religion, clothed with the spoils of the civil power, which it has usurped to itself contrary to our serious doctrines. No Protestant of what sect soever, following Scripture only, ought by the common consent of Protestants to be maltreated for religion. But as for popery and idolatry, why they also may not hence plead to be tolerated, I have much less to say. Their religion, the more considered, the less can be acknowledged a religion; but a Roman principality rather endeavoring to keep up her old universal dominion under a new name, and mere shadow of Catholic religion, being indeed more rightly named a Catholic heresy against the Scriptures, supported mainly by a civil, and except in Rome, by a foreign power; justly, therefore, to be suspected, not tolerated by the magistrates of another country." Can we doubt as to whether John Milton knew Romanism? Can we suppose Romanism to have changed?

Rome is intolerant, because intolerance is its life, and tolerance is its bane. Hitherto the punitory discipline has been tacitly received and acted upon, as the tenet of infallibility has. But the canons quoted and recently passed by the council of Rome, the Index and the Inquisition, became matters of faith. Henceforth Romanists must believe, under pain of damnation, that it is right to punish with torture and death those who dissent from papal teachings. This for America as well as for Italy. Let your sister or son be torn from the home, confined in a convent which is only a prison; let the thumb-screw, the rack, the implements of torture be applied until death results; arrest the murderers; break through their gates; enter their chambers of death, and put a stop to this work of horror; and at once the cry is raised — this is the religion of Rome. You must suffer it to kill and to destroy because the Catholic principle of faith is this: "Heresy is not an error of judgment merely, but the breach of a divine first principle,"—an "outrage upon absolute truth; therefore, in punishing its propagators and abettors, he does not punish men for errors of opinion, but for an offence against faith."

We declare to Romanists that they are welcome to live in the enjoyment of all civil rights; but they must restrain their conduct, and not tamper with the right of opinion, call it by what name they choose.

Let us now, by a narration of facts, expose the intolerance of Rome. Heresy is the death of Romanism. Now that the Inquisition is to become a part of the faith of Romanists living about us, let us see under what name and in what spirit persecution is to be waged; for it will be admitted that it is the boast of the Romanist, that the church has never relinquished her authority over all persons in all places. Repression goes hand in hand with conversion. The Inquisition is an organized institution whose chief is the pope. It is called the *Holy Office*. As late as 1825 new prisons were built for the holy office in lieu of those humanely destroyed by the French. These gloomy piles excite the wonder of the traveller who comes suddenly upon them after visiting St. Peter's and the Vatican close by; for this blood-stained prison is under the pontifical roof. When the present pontiff fled to Gaeta in 1849, the populace burst open the prison. No instruments were found, for they were all destoyed by the army of the republic. In one cell was a furnace, a woman's dress, and long tresses of hair pulled out by the roots. The cell was of peculiar construction and suggestive of horrible things, being large enough to contain a human body. The general impression of the people was, that it had been used to consume the remains of victims. Near the luxurious apartments of the Primo Custode, a Dominican friar, was found a deep trap, — a shaft opening into unknown depths. This was the *Vade in Pace*. Beautiful names are given in Rome to hellish deeds. As soon as the accused had confessed his offence, he was sent to the commissary, the trap lying directly in the way. The words "*Go in peace*" were a signal to loose the catch, which at the least pr ssure opened a yawning tomb. The earth found at the bottom of the pit was chemically analyzed, and proved to be a compost of common earth, decayed bones, etc., fetid to the smell and horrible to the sight. In 1860 it was thought necessary to examine this prison, as the foundations had become insecure from the constant overflow of the Tiber. The architect was not allowed to go alone, lest he should make plans; so two priests escorted him, one of whom describes the terrible scenes which they beheld.

The writer in these words lays bare the picture. "Leaving the custodian's apartment, we entered a vaulted corridor, very gloomy, dirty, and damp. It was a *cul de sac*, leading nowhere. The prior unlocked a small door leading to the prison of the newly arrested. The cells were small, six feet by four, grimed with age and dirt, horrible as the dens of wild beasts in the Coliseum. There was no window except a little grating, high up in the wall, about the size of an octavo volume; no outlet but the little low door; through this grating food and water were passed to the captive. The cells were living sepulchres. In one of them a large number of skeletons, minus skulls, was discovered buried in lime. This is the bath of quicklime. In it the sufferers are immersed up to the neck, and it is slowly increased until, with the suffocation of the smoke and the anguish of suppressed breathings, they die in unspeakable agonies. After a little time, the heads would roll off into the hollows left by the shrinking of the lime. These were found collected in a hamper. The first tier of cells seemed to complete the prison; but our chaperon pulled an iron ring in the stone floor, and revealed a small cavernous pit, with an iron ladder to it. It looked like descending a coal shaft. Descending the ladder, they found themselves in a low corridor which baffles description. Damp dropped from the slimy walls; vile reptiles and horrible vermin held carousal. Rats, emboldened by impunity, scampered about and stopped to stare at the intruders. The cold in that hot day penetrated the skin. As before, no cells and no opening in the walls, as above, could be seen. The plashing of the river was audible. There was a still deeper depth. The friar pulled one of a line of rings inserted in the wall, and a small door opened. By introducing the legs first, says the writer, we managed to get in. Imagine a cell level with the bed of the river. A small grating looking upon it, but far above reach, admitted light enough to reveal a foul den of torture. Could any human soul exist in such a place! The odor was horrible. Into these prisons the condemned were sent. At the least enlargement of the capacious river the cell was filled with water and the prisoner drowned. The despairing cry for help and mercy died away unheard; or, worse than this, rats entered from the river and devoured the victim. No inquiry was made for them after imprisonment. Rome makes hell felt in this life, though she does little to introduce the joys of heaven."

This charge against Rome is not made in a corner. Nor is it made of the fact, that this prison is under the roof of the Pontiff. For all we know, witnesses for Jesus may be uttering their despairing cry at this moment. Now, the trouble is here. Rome admits and justifies her intolerance. In Rome, Protestants may be silent and stay; but if they speak out for liberty, they must escape or perish. Not so in America. We can speak, and speaking is a duty. *As the heart is, the man is; the heart of Rome is laid bare. Study it.* This Romanism is in our midst. It plots against our liberties and determines to undermine the foundations of the government. Let us not forget that eternal vigilance is the price of liberty. Let us open the cell and look upon a victim.

On a bright June morning in 1848, the tramp of Garibaldi's followers was heard in Rome. The bright radiance of liberty penetrated for a moment the depths of despotism; Rome was free. While yet the heap of pontifical carriages was burning in the Piazza di St. Petre, an armed crowd presented themselves at the gates of the Inquisition. They were soon battered down, and a hush of awe fell on the assemblage as it entered those remoter portals. Pass at once to the cells in the lower regions. They are dripping with damp and overrun with rats. Look. Two prisoners are discovered alive, half demented with silence, darkness, and famine. They were unable to speak or comprehend that they were free. With tears in their eyes and low murmurs of pity, the crowd conducted them up-stairs on their shoulders, for they were unable to walk. The first discovered was a nun about thirty-five years old, and still bearing traces of beauty and loveliness. Her monastic habit was so worn and ragged, that it scarcely covered her. She had had no change of linen for five years, and in winter and summer the same food and bedding. The former consisted of a half a loaf of bread, sour and black, per day, weighing a pound; and at noon a small pannakin of stewed haricot beans. The bedding was laid on an erection of brick, and consisted merely of a heap of straw, perfectly rotten and mildewed, with a blanket in like condition. The other prisoner was a bishop, and still wore his faded purple cloak. He was nearly seventy, and it was a pitable sight to see his wretched and uncared-for age, and the settled expression of hopeless despair on his countenance. His left side was paralyzed. The multitude that only a few hours before shouted, down with the priests, knelt and kissed the old man's hand with passionate fervor. They hoisted the two victims in chairs and carried them through the city, with the hair and other relics of torture. These facts are known about Rome : let us be sure that we do our part to keep them before the people.

But it is not alone of Rome I would speak. John the Revelator "saw the kings of the earth as well as the beast" gathering their forces to make war with the Lamb. In other words, error is intolerant, and hence between all forms of error there is this band of unity.

Do we seek the cause? we find it in its lack of faith. Rome has a creed, but no faith. It dare not trust. Power enforces doctrine. The freedom of the will is ignored; the freedom of thought is warred against. Error is empty of trust because it is without a just claim.

Truth is built on a claim. Have I faith in God? I have it either because of merit in myself or because I may be permitted to plead the merits of another in receiving blessings from God. Jesus Christ is our claim; we trust in him and to him. He, the God-man, undertakes for us. We leave our interests in his hands, because we have in him an advocate with the Father, and a helper in the world. Errorists have not faith. They must have power to take its place. They seek it and secure it as best they may.

This intolerance of error is not only seen in the way it seeks power, but in the spirit it advocates and exhibits. In the rural districts of New England it is perilous for any Romanist to become a believer in Christ, and desert Rome for the church of Christ. The intolerance of Rome is intolerable even here. What must it be in countries where she has power? Contrast the writings of the apostles and of Christian men with the writings of the champions of error. In the one class you detect evidences of the peace of God which passeth knowledge; in the other, of persecution which ignores knowledge, right, and justice.

There is, then, to be a battle. Error is aggressive. Infidelity unites with Romanism not only in resisting truth, but in advancing error.

This foe must be met. How? By force contending with force? No; but by Christ's children showing the more excellent way, and, in the spirit of the Master, leading the thoughts of the deluded and ignorant into the sunshine of love and truth, and by insisting upon the maintenance of religious freedom in this land.

VICTOR HUGO TO THE PRIESTS : " *We know you ! We know the clerical party. It is an old party. This it is which has found for the Truth those two marvellous supporters, Ignorance and Error. . . . There is a Book—a Book which is from one end to the other an emanation from above ; a Book which is for the whole world what the Koran is for Islamism, what the Vedas are for India ; a Book which contains all human wisdom, illuminated by all divine wisdom ; a Book which the veneration of the people call* THE BOOK— *The Bible ! Well, your censure has reached even that. Unheard of thing ! Popes have proscribed the Bible ! How astonishing to wise spirits, how overpowering to simple hearts, to see the finger of Rome placed upon the Book of God.*"

ROMANISM A PLAGUE, IF NOT A PERIL.

ROMANISM is the masterpiece of Satan. It embodies and unites the forces of evil against truth It is the plague of Christianity in the sense that it is troublesome and vexatious, and if it is not a peril to Christianity it is because God is the author of truth; and Christianity, deriving its life from the God-man, shall live, because it is impossible to kill out or imperil this life of God in the world.

Romanism is a plague, in that the Roman Catholic Church claims " to be a body of Christians," while they do not " obey from the heart that form of doctrine" which they profess to have received from Christ, and are, in form and in spirit, representatives of ancient Paganism. Paul described their influence when he said, " For the name of God is blasphemed among the Gentiles through you."*

Romanism is a plague, because those who reject the teachings of Christ, and care but very little about any form of worship, in a half-approving way speak of Romanism as " an ancient form of Christianity," forgetting that, though the bark in its first launching might have borne some resemblance to the Christian church, Christ abandoned her when she abandoned Christ; and the bark, so beautiful at the outset, has been bored by the worm and clogged by the barnacle of every sea over which it has sailed, and is now water-logged and worthless. One refers to Romanism as being the mother of Protestanism, ignoring the fact that the logic which reaches this conclusion would compel him to recognize the devil as the author of Christianity; since sin came by the devil and death by sin, and Christ came to save the lost; and, as he would not have come had none been lost, Satan is the author of Christianity. How absurd! No wonder that, after such an admission, the same writer should predict " that the Catholic church will work with the Protestant churches, like sisters, for a common cause and one end."

Romanism is a plague, because of her power to appear in sheep's clothing, though, as a wolf, she seeks to devour the flock of God, and attempts " to seduce even the very elect."

By claiming that Rome is a plague, we describe her characteristics. A plague is a source of perplexity, of pother, of disease. So Rome is a plague now as it has been in the past; but to the cause of Christ, to Christianity, whether you speak of the present or of the future, Rome is a plague, if not a peril. We rejoice to believe that there never will be a time when the power

* Romans 2: 24.

"that opposeth and exalteth himself above all that is called God
or that is worshipped, so that he as God sitteth in the temple of
God, showing himself that he is God," will not be under the control of the Almighty, and will be made to subserve the purposes
of truth.

The fear, not without a show of reason, is widely felt, that
Romanism is a peril as well as a plague. We are told of what
the Romish church has achieved in the past; of her colossal
power; of what she is doing; of what, judging from the lights
of history, she will do. With the Inquisition and its horrors
the world is more or less familiar. It is apparent that Rome is
unchanged, and that she is full of the same persecuting hate to-
day which characterized her when the bones of Waldensian martyrs whitened the mountains and valleys of Italy. We are
aware that Rome is a living power. Proofs of this power lie all
about us. It is everywhere apparent. We see it in the unblush-
ing attempts made to control public opinion; we see it in the
conduct of venal, truckling partisans; we see it in the magnificent structures built or being built, planned or being planned, not
only on our Atlantic coast, but in every considerable town and
city on this continent. Footprints of her power are seen in
New York, "where the common rights of the community at
large are invaded by the public processions of Roman Catholic
societies in the streets of the city, on the Sabbath day, disturb-
ing with noise and clamor the worship of Christian citizens, and
impeding them in their progress to and from their respective
churches. The same power is seen in the grants of money made
by the municipal or by the State government for the support of
Roman Catholic schools and other institutions, which grants are
in direct opposition to the fundamental principle of our system
of government, which recognizes no form of religion to be aided
by the State.

The mystery of iniquity doth already work; we know and see
it; and yet with Paul we exclaim, "Only he who now hindereth
will hinder until he be taken out of the way, and then shall that
Wicked be revealed whom the Lord shall consume with the
spirit of his mouth, and destroy with the brightness of his coming; even Him whose coming is after the working of Satan, with
all power and signs and lying wonders, and with all deceivableness of unrighteousness in them that perish; because they received not the love of the truth, that they might be saved. And
for this cause God shall send them strong delusion that they
should believe a lie: that they all might be damned who believed
not the truth, but had pleasure in unrighteousness."

John the Revelator had a vision, as did Paul the apostle. Carried away into the wilderness, he saw a woman sitting upon a
scarlet-colored beast, full of names of blasphemy, having seven
heads and ten horns. "And the woman was arrayed in purple
and scarlet-color, and decked with gold and precious stones and
pearls, having a golden cup in her hand, full of abominations and
filthiness of her fornication, and upon her forehead was a name

written, 'Mystery, Babylon the Great, The mother of harlots and the abominations of the earth.' I saw the woman drunk with the blood of the martyrs of Jesus." The mystery of the woman and the beast that carried her, was explained to the Revelator. "The seven heads are seven mountains, on which the woman sitteth," and are supposed to represent the seven powers that give support to the church of Rome. "The beast" is the power on which she rides, and "the ten horns" are ten kings, which shall "receive power as kings one hour with the beast. These have one mind, and shall give their power and strength unto the beast. These shall make war with the Lamb. and the lamb shall overcome them; for he is Lord of lords and King of kings, and they that are with him are called and chosen and faithful."

In the Christian soul there is a fortress held of God, and impregnable to Rome. The Lord's Christ was master and conqueror even in the dark ages. Prophecy proclaims Jesus to be the conqueror of all opposing forces in the future. There are times when it becomes us as Christians to survey the world from the watch-towers of the Bible and of the church, and to note the leadings of Providence, and gather up proofs that, no matter how high the barriers of opposition may be reared in the path of the stream of spiritual Christianity, that river, finding its fountain-source in God, shall rise higher than them all, and sweep them all away. God has done great things for his people, and now, as in the past, our hope is in God; and so with the prophet we exclaim, "Only fear the Lord, and serve him in truth with all your heart." The words of John are in harmony with this ancient faith. Jesus Christ is to overcome all opposition, not only because he is King of kings and Lord of lords, but because they that are with him are called and chosen and faithful. They were called of God and chosen of God, and are faithful because of the power of God that keeps them. Hence victory is sure.

The two Tendencies.

It is said that "there are two overpowering tendencies at work everywhere in the religious world, and that all effort to find a logical foothold between these two tendencies has been ineffectual; that the one leads to the Catholic church, and that the other leads off into rationalism and atheism."

The first part of this utterance is true. There are two overpowering tendencies at work everywhere, and there is no logical foothold between them. But it is not true that one of these tendencies leads to the Catholic church, and the other to infidelity and atheism. The Catholic church, infidelity, and atheism are on one side, and the Evangelical churches with *the gospel are on the other*. Wherever Romanism thrives, atheism and infidelity flourish. Let Romanism gain supremacy in a land, and the religion of the New Testament disappears; the Sabbath is overthrown; the Bible is burned or banished, and the truth as it is in Jesus is unknown. For proof of this assertion, go to Rome,

or to Paris, or even to the Romanized portions of any city, or
any part of our country, where Rome is dominant.

" The greatest outbreak of atheism in moden times," says one,
" was in France shortly before the French Revolution. Now,
the Protestants had been extirpated by Louis XIV, the Hugue-
nots were driven out of France, and it was left purely Catholic.
In two generations nearly the whole intellect of the country had
gone over into atheism. Dr. Priestly says, almost the only men
of eminence not atheists were Voltaire and Rousseau. Rousseau
was brought up in Geneva; Voltaire was a great student of
English Protestant writers, like Locke, Newton, etc. As soon
as free thought broke out of the Catholic church, it went directly
into atheism. There was no stopping-place. Blanco White tes-
tifies the same about Spain. Protestantism was rooted out of
Spain by the Inquisition. The same thing was true in Italy.
Protestantism is the safety-valve for free thought. The Roman
Church fastens it down, and the result is an explosion."

To say that Christianity has no independent existence outside
of the Catholic church, is to deny history and to ignore reason.
Romanism is against Christianity. It has no more right to call
itself Christianity than has a wolf to call himself a lamb because
he has attempted to devour a lamb.

Romanism Paganism Revived.

It is a mistake, born of a spirit of toleration, that speaks of
Romanism as even a part of Christianity, or as a branch of the
Christian church. Romanism is paganism revived. When the
founders of Rome forsook the path marked out by the New Testament and entered upon their work, they wrested the sceptre
from pagan Rome, and under Gregory the Great, in the name of
a church, built up a consolidated despotism, which first enslaved
and then beggared Europe.

It has been said " that, if you take the truths which Protestantism retains of Christianity and carry them to their logical
consequence, they would lead to a return to the Catholic
church." This is either true or false. If true, we sin if we
contend against Rome. If false, we sin if we countenance
Rome. Protestantism is the result of a protest against Rome,
against " indulgences," " penance," " purgatory," " the power of
'he priest to forgive sins," against " substituting Mary for
Christ," " tyranny " and " earthly dominion " for Christianity and
a kingdom not of this world. A glance at the teachings of
Christ and history proves this claim, no matter by whom made,
to be false as false can be. Christ commissions men to preach
his Gospel in all the world, saying " whosoever believeth and is
baptized shall be saved." Rome commissions men to burn the
Gospel in all the world, and declares that whoever believes, not
in Christ, but in the infallibility of the Romish church,—a church
that substitutes Mary for Christ, —shall be saved. The assumption that Romanism is Christianity is monstrous in its absurdity, and absurd because of its monstrosity. The Bible is against

Rome, and so Rome is against the Bible. History is against Rome, and so Rome belies history. As Gavazzi said, "Light and darkness, hell and heaven, God and Satan, Pope and Bibles, cannot go together, and therefore the Popes have always absolutely prohibited the reading of the Bible.

Having shown that Romanism has been and is the enemy of Christianity, let us notice a few of the many proofs going to show that Romanism and paganism are the same. Those who are familiar with the letters of Dr. Middleton, will remember that in 1724 he went to Rome, to visit the genuine remains and venerable relics of pagan Rome. Educated at Cambridge University for the ministry of the Church of England, chosen at the age of twenty-three a fellow of Trinity College, and a few years later, on account of his vast and varied learning, appointed principal librarian of the University, he went to Rome fitted by general studies to search more particularly into some branches of its antiquities, and to lose as little time as possible in taking notice "of the mummeries and ridiculous ceremonies of the present religion of the place." His surprise was great when he found that "all the ceremonies appeared plainly to have been copied from the rituals of primitive paganism, as if handed down by an uninterrupted succession from the priests of old to the priests of new Rome."

The testimony of Dr. Middleton was given in the former part of the eighteenth century. Let us now turn to Rev. Henry Alford, D. D., late Dean of Canterbury, Eng., who writes in the latter half of the nineteenth century, and declares under the head, "Rome Essentially Pagan," that "Rome is essentially a pagan city. Her churches, numerous as the days of the year, rise everywhere around you. Bells are continually going; the commemoration of saints and martyrs is endless. Yet, with very rare exceptions indeed, the *worship of the people* in those churches has nothing in common with Christianity. It is not even the one God of the Jews and Christians, who, as a matter of fact, is adored in them; it is not he whom Christians believe to be God, blessed for ever, incarnate in the flesh of man. God has passed out from the practical worship of this people; the Son of God has, as matter of fact, ceased to be an object of their adoration. The Eternal Father is found in their pictures as an old man, — the Divine Saviour as a little child; but both are subservient, and nearly all their worship is subservient, to one purpose, — to the glorification of a great goddess, and, after her, not of the Father, Son, nor Spirit, but of a host of men and women, made into objects of adoration by themselves, and, whatever may be alleged to the contrary, clothed, as she is pre-eminently clothed, with the incommunicable attributes of the Godhead." *

Gavazzi, than whom none knows Rome better, insisted that "the popish church is but a pagan church, which has transubstantiated the gospel into the flesh and blood of ancient pagan-

* Romanism in Rome. By Rev. John Alford, D. D., Dean of Canterbury Am. Tract Society, pp. 6, 7.

ism. It is evident that Rome has adopted three branches of
paganism; viz., gods, priests, and things."

First, of gods. St. Augustine, in his book entitled "Town of
god," shows that there were not less than 22,000 pagan gods.
In Rome there are, according to the martyrology, more than
100,000 gods, — *i. e.* saints, — real substitutes for the pagan gods,
having the same names and attributes or functions. The ancients
worshipped the *Dii Tutelares*, gods who protected the nations.
Belus was the Deus Tutelaris of the Babylonians, Isis and Osiris
of Egypt. Among Romanists, St. Louis is the patron saint of
France, St. Stephen of Hungary, St. Patrick of Ireland. The
ancients worshipped the *Dii Præsides*, who presided over towns.
So do Romanists. Juno was over Carthage; Minerva over
Athens. Every town had its own. The pagans had their *Dii
Patroni;* so have Romanists. In Baltimore, in the Church of St.
Alphonsi Liguori, there are two altars, on one of which is Mary
with the babe; on the other the Virgin, with the breast open, so
that the immaculate heart is shown. This is more than pagan.
Pagans had rural divinities; so have Romanists. In Italy you
find very little of Christ. All are Marys or saints. In ancient
Rome there was a temple to Romulus, where he was suckled by
the wolf. On his anniversary it was the custom of Roman
nurses to go in a procession, bearing children, to put them over
the altar, in order to pray to Romulus to be their patron during
their infancy. When Rome became professedly Christian, the
nurses were in despair. The church substituted Saint Theodorus, in the identical temple, by merely changing the name of
Romulus to Theodorus, and the nurses were happy. Jupiter of
the pagans is now St. Peter of Rome; and the Pantheon, a
heathen temple, with all its gods, was converted into a church,
and the names of the apostles were given to the heathen divinities. Thus, though with different names, there are the same
gods, the same miracles, the same attributes, the same devotions,
the same paganism.

Second. There is a similarity in priests. The pagans had
Pontifices, majores, and minores, and at the head of those the
Pontifex Maximus; in the Romish priesthood are the major and
minor clergy, and at the head the identical Pontifex Maximus.
The following are some of the points of identity between the
Roman and Pagan priesthood: —

The Romish Cardinal, clad in the same scarlet dress and invested with the same function, viz., to approve the acts of the
Pontiff, has taken the place of the pagan flamen.

The ancient Emperor, uniting to his imperial dignity the High-
priesthood, styled himself Divus, Pontifex Maximus, and Cæsar.
The Pope claims to be High-priest and King-god over earth, and
Prince in the Roman States. Hence again, we declare that Papal
Rome is no less nor more than the church of Pagan Rome.

Third. As to things. Wax candles are common to both
systems.

The pagans had holy fountains, holy wells, holy father Neptune, holy father Tiber, holy ocean, and holy Naiads; they have their Ganges now.

In Rome there are two sacred fountains of St. Peter, — one in the Mamertine Prison, where he is supposed to have been confined, and one in the Santa Maria, in Via Lota.

There are three holy wells of St. Paul, where it is said his head touched the earth after his execution, and whither multitudes resort; also the sacred waters of St. Patrick in Ireland.

At the entrance of the pagan temple was a vessel containing holy water; so in the Roman Church. Both are used in the same way, and alike are made of salt mixed with water.

The amulets and talismans employed in the superstitions of Egypt, Greece, China, and Hindostan, are fully matched in the Roman system by her rosaries, scapularies, relics, and medals.

Truly did Dean Alford say, "With nine tenths of living Romanists, the whole of the faith once delivered to the saints is set aside, and is as if it had never been; and this goddess-worship (for such it is in reality) has taken its place. Everything is done by, everything is sought from, the Madonna. As to our blessed Lord, he is but a helpless infant in her arms. The burden of their prayers to her is to show herself to be a mother, and command him to do this and that."

If we are correct in our conclusion that Romanism is paganism revived in form and in spirit, then it is a duty we owe to Christ and to fair dealing to resist the claims which it puts forth of being considered Christianity, or in any way akin to it. It is to be tolerated because our government tolerates all religions, even the heathenism of the Chinese; but it should not be supported or encouraged by the State, any more than Mormonism or Mohammedanism.

Wisely did the synod of New York remonstrate against the practice of those parents who place their children in the schools of the Roman Catholic Church, and especially in view of the fact that it is publicly alleged by one of the distinguished teachers of that church that seven out of every ten Protestant children under their tuition becomes Catholic." I have elsewhere* called attention to the influence exerted by the Roman Catholic servants in our homes, where, alas! too frequently the nurse teaches the child the use of the beads, and familiarizes him with the crucifix as an emblem of worship. With many, a Roman Catholic servant is a barrier to discussion, or even to conversation, concerning Roman errors. The result is, our children grow up either in fear of Rome, or ignorant of her devices, and it becomes fashionable to smother opinions on this subject. Let Americans be unmuzzled. Talk freely in the house and at the table, and so honor God and protect liberty.

The Purpose of Romanism.

Having considered its character, a word will suffice to define

* Woman as God made her; The true Woman. By Rev. J. D. Fulton. Published by Lee & Shepard.

its purpose. Its purpose manifestly is, to establish a religion
opposed to the teachings of the Gospel and to the spirit of
Christianity. It resembles those forms of faith born of the
earth, and derived from the uninspired teachings of the carnal
heart, distinguished for their lust after temporal dominion. In
its spirit and agencies it is in direct opposition to civil and religious liberty, and in every country where it has had or now has
control, it tramples upon the rights of man, and just in proportion as it flourishes, true civil liberty disappears. Garibaldi described it as a "cancer," "an imposture," as a "formidable
enemy, because it exists among the ignorant classes, and is
everywhere the foe of education, of enlightenment, and of progress. It rules by falsehood, because it is sacrilegiously covered
with the cloak of religion. Its smile is the smile of Satan; its
embrace is the embrace of death!" That it may be possible for
the light of Christ to find its way to the heart of a Romanist, we
will not question. With Gavazzi, I hope that many thousands
may be saved; "yet their salvation is made more difficult even
by their own system, because it is made to depend upon super-
erogatory works, which are far too numerous." It is because
Christ is not the foundation of the superstructure that we believe in its final overthrow. Prophecy describes it as the *agency
of sin*, as "*the harlot riding the beast*," to which kings shall give
their power as they make war with the Lamb, and declares that
they shall be overcome by the Lamb.

Proof from History that Rome is not Master.

In 1550, Rome was saying in her heart, "My dominion shall
encircle the globe. Asia, that world of the hoary past, — America, that world of the brilliant future, — shall meet at my footstool, Europe, and worship me as God. My throne shall overtop
the Rocky Mountains and the Himalayas. The Missouri and
Ganges shall float my revenues. The waves of every ocean shall
waft the gold and homage of the gorgeous East and the mighty
West to this Eternal City. Beyond where Alexander trod,
beyond where floated Cæsar's ensigns, shall stand the pillars of
my dominion, — a dominion to which all heathens and heretics
shall submit or perish, — a dominion over all kingdoms of the
world and the glory of them." Such was the hope of Rome, but
such a hope was never to be realized. How inspiring at this
point the teachings of history! How wonderfully the victories
won over Romanism prove God's omnipotent power of control
over this iniquity!

In 1554, Philip, the heir of Charles V, was made King of Naples,
of Sicily, and also of England, by his marriage with Queen Mary,
known in England as Bloody Mary. In 1556, he ascended the
Spanish throne. Then it looked as though Europe and Great
Britain were alike lost to Protestantism. Everything that
human ingenuity could devise was done to bind England to
Rome, but in vain. Philip was not crowned king. Mary did
not live; when she died, Elizabeth, her sister, was in prison.

Proudly does the Englishman point to the robes she wore from her cell in the tower to the throne of England. In vain did Philip try to win her favor. Failing here, he determined to wrest the sceptre from her grasp, and regain the throne which he had lost by the death of his former wife. But the love of truth was deep in the English heart. The Reformation was in full blast on the continent, and large dominions had been severed from the dominion of the Pope. Spain was now at the zenith of her power. By discoveries and by conquest she had gained control of Peru, Mexico, New Spain, the West Indies, and the richest portions of North America, while rich provinces in Asia and Spain bowed at the foot of the Spanish throne. The Roman church, by the Holy Office of the Inquisition, burned alive, in Spain alone, from 1433 to 1808, 31,912 persons; Torquemada burned in fifteen years 8,800; Deza, in seven years, 1,664 persons; and Cardinal Ximenes, in ten years, 2,530 persons.

In France, the war was raging between the priests and the people. In the Netherlands, Philip was exerting his utmost strength to destroy the power of William, Prince of Orange, the leader of the Protestant forces.

Foiled in these attempts, though 36,000 martyrs for liberty of conscience had evidenced how much dearer than life was their love for God's word, Philip II determined, as a last resort, to destroy England, in the hope of prostrating forever the reformed faith.

The monarch of an almost boundless empire, supported by enormous wealth, and by the best disciplined army in the world, encouraged by the Pope and the priests, impelled by superstition and the most unrelenting bigotry, he declared himself supreme; and, determined to attack Protestantism in its stronghold, he fitted out the armament against England known as the "Spanish Invincible Armada," which for pride, wealth, magnificence, and the munitions of war it contained, and the provisions and resources of all kinds it carried, and the number and character of the men who accompanied it, was never excelled by any armament that ever floated upon the sea.

But God was against him. His invincible fleet was scattered as by the breath of the Almighty; England triumphed; Protestantism, liberty, and religion were established on a surer foundation than ever before.

The strong arm of Spain was broken; Henry IV was fighting Philip successfully in France; and the war of the Netherlands — after lasting sixty-eight years — cost Spain $800,000,000, despoiled her of her treasures, bereaved her of her best men, and caused her to sink to that despicable position which she has since occupied among the nations of the earth; while Protestantism was gaining in Europe and in Great Britain. Thus was the New World delivered from the hand of the oppressor.

In 1610, Henry IV, the Abraham Lincoln of France, was assassinated. The interests of Protestantism began to suffer at the hands of his descendants. But what was loss to Europe was gain to America. The power lost by Spain in the New World passed for a time into the hands of France, only to be wrested from her by England, whose sons were to control America.

The work left unaccomplished by Philip II was resumed by Louis XIV, who, uniting under his sceptre the empires of Francis I of France and Charles V of Spain, extended his empire over the Netherlands, Sardinia, Sicily, Naples, Milan, and other possessions in Italy; over the Philippines and Manilla Islands in Asia; and over the greater part of Southern and Central America, California and Florida. It looked now as though Rome was to be master. The throne of Louis XIV was the embodiment of the power of Rome. The Protestant nations were fully apprised of this fact, and had already formed an alliance against him. England was to Protestantism what France was to Popery; and consequently the subjugation of England was the darling project of Louis.

The spirit of the man is evidenced in his revocation of the Edict of Nantes, made by Henry IV, which gave Protestantism equal rights with Romanism. By a single stroke of his pen fifty thousand families were banished from their homes.

For a time, to the natural eye, it looked as though a gloomy shadow was to rest upon the prospects of America; for, at this time, Louis the XIV, the right hand of Rome, claimed as his nearly the whole of the New World. The French flag was seen on the shores of the St. Lawrence and the Great Lakes, along the rich prairies of the West to the Mississippi; and the whole of the wide and beautiful valley, from the Falls of St. Anthony to the Gulf of Mexico, was, by reason of French dominion, the land of the priest and the crucifix. The question to be decided was, Shall North America be Protestant, or Catholic? All know that freedom found a hope in Protestantism, and a grave wherever Catholicism ruled supreme. France declared, "America shall be Catholic." So said the Pope; thus spake Montcalm; for this the Jesuit labored everywhere, in the thronged city and in the solitudes of forests, amid the haunts of civilization and by the cabin and tent-fires of the red man. Soldiers who invoked the Virgin and adored the wafer, gave battle to the power of Britain on the waters of Champlain and far away on the banks of the Ohio. French forts belted the homes of Englishmen, while they extended along the table-lands of Mexico, overlooked the mines of Peru, reached the broad plains of the Amazon and La Plata. Northward, southward, from pole to pole, from ocean to ocean, these missionaries extended the dominion of the Pope, until in the New World none disowned his sceptre save a few red brethren in the woods, and a few white brethren along the shore. It is not necessary to describe the work wrought by Clive in India, where, at the battle of Plaissey, French dominion was overthrown and English dominion was established. It is enough to declare that in one hour of battle the deed was done. Thus did Jehovah smite the scarlet hand stretched out to grasp the Eastern hemisphere. The power of Rome in the East was broken, — the cita-

del of her strength was in the dust. Rome could not burn heretics in India, for England held the reins of government; and
where the tread of the English lion is felt, there is freedom to
worship God.

Come back fifteen thousand miles, and enter the Prussian
territory. It was in the month of August, 1756, that the Seven
Years' War commenced. The English were fighting the French
in India and the French in America. The world was like a ship
madly tossed upon the billows and beaten by tempests. The
Protestants of Europe rallied about the standard of Frederic the
Great. They went to battle with psalm-tunes on their lips, and
with a love for the Bible in their hearts. At last they fought the
battle of Leuthen, animated by their love of truth and by a spirit
of revolt against the aggressions of Rome. *Victory was won.*
From that eventful period in history dates the political ascendancy of the Protestant element. The ark of the national covenant was for the first time intrusted to the hands of unshackled
freemen. Protestantism, victorious in India and in Europe, now
began a new work. Popery was no longer master. "It had felt
the power of truth, when preached by a line of cannon encircling
half the globe."

The war of the sword being over in Europe, the war of words
began. The pulpit's voice was heard. The Bible began to be
circulated, and the press uttered its inspiring voice. Voltaire,
writing history as a partisan, made the annals of his race a con-
tinuous sarcasm against the hierarchy of the Roman Catholic
church, and did effective battle. It gives us confidence in
humanity's progress, in the wisdom and almightiness of Providence, when we see all, both friend and foe, brought into a common field, and made, by an unseen hand, laborers and co-laborers
together for a common object. What Voltaire was in the domain
of literature and with the pen on the Continent, that James
Wolfe was with the sword in America, who, in 1759, received the
command of the expedition against Quebec. The glory of the
ascent up precipitous cliffs, by means of hanging boughs and
projecting crags, until they stood upon the Heights of Abraham,
upon the very summit of the supposed impregnable fortress, is
familiar to all. How he led on his troops; how by perseverance
and military stratagem he overcame the difficulties of the enterprise; how he disregarded the wound in his wrist, and still,
sword in hand, pressed forward against overwhelming odds
from victory to victory; how, pierced by a second ball, he fell
into the arms of an officer, and said, "Don't let my brave com-
panions see me fall," — all this has been committed to immortal
record. "Night, silence, the rushing tide, veteran discipline,
the rare inspiration of genius, had been his allies; his battle-
field, high over the ocean river, was the grandest theatre on
earth for illustrious deeds; his victory, one of the most momen-
tous in the history of mankind, gave to the English tongue, and
the institutions of the Germanic race, the unexplored and seem-
ingly infinite West and North. He crowded into a few hours

actions that would have given lustre to length of life; and, filling his day with greatness, completed it before his noon." Amid
the gathering gloom and incoming night of the tomb, amid the
roar of cannon, the clash of arms, and the moans of the dying,
a shout borne on every breeze reaches his ear. Louder and
still louder grows the swell, and it runs along the victorious
lines. " *They fly!* they fly!" sounds clear above the roar and
din of battle on the Heights of Abraham. The expiring Wolfe
half starts from the repose of death's stupor to ask, "Who
flies?" " *The French fly.*" "Then I die contented," says the
soldier, and expires. Little did the dying hero understand the
significance of that shout. It meant that North America was
lost forever to the Pope; it meant that the scarlet lady of the
Tiber should never have control of the destiny of the Western
hemisphere; it meant that America should become Freedom's
citadel and the heritage of Truth. How surely all history displays the glorious providence of God! How sublime and beneficent is the grand drift of human affairs as controlled by that
Providence! How dark and deplorable is the world's history as
the designs and characters of men are displayed! — how bright
as the plans and agency of God are revealed!

Proofs drawn from recent Events.

The history of God's providential acts in favor of the truth do
not stop with the victory on the Heights of Abraham. We behold
proofs of His power in later struggles with this bitter and implacable foe. To-day, we are to a large extent what these conflicts have made us. Our love of freedom, our hatred of oppression, our opposition to prelacy, is not an ephemeral feeling; it
is the tree which has been grown during centuries of struggle.
Care has been bestowed upon it. Its roots have been moistened
by the best blood of the race, and its trunk defended by the
brawny arms and courageous hearts of as gallant and devoted a
band as the world ever saw. Had we time to review the history
of religious freedom in the United States, we should see how
God's providence alone brought together antagonistic creeds,
and made deadly foes bear arms together in defence, perhaps, of
the only principle on which they could then have united. Romanists were compelled to adopt the Gospel platform to save
themselves from destruction.

Is Romanism on the increase?

Emigration has done much for Rome, more than it will ever
do again; and yet, with it all, the growth of the Roman Catholic church has not kept pace (considering the help it has received from abroad) with the Baptist or Methodist Churches,
which have grown from within. The principal current of conversion affecting the Roman Catholic church in this country is
a current out of it. Their own statistics show that out of two
Catholics coming here they lose one, out of ten children educated in our schools they lose five. Over twenty millions of Catholics

have emigrated to this country; there are but six millions now in the country. In Rome there is everywhere decay. "Year by year," says Dr. Alford, "the old ceremonies are less attended, and less cared for by those who attend them. Whether it be Carnival or Christmas or Easter, the remark of the Romans universally is, that it is nothing to what it used to be a few years since. But yesterday I witnessed the processions of the confraternities coming to adore the Easter sepulchre in St. Peter's. There was lamentation round me that, where we saw ten or twenty members, there used to be hundreds. And the aspect of that vast building during the most solemn services I can never forget. It was thronged by thousands, come to hear the Miserere, and see the ceremonies. But general reverence there was none, and I speak not now of the behavior of *strangers*. While one *Roman* was kneeling. twenty men were walking, and talking aloud, even during the Miserere itself. Inquire wherever you will, and you find, beneath a fair semblance of religion and purity, a reeking mass of falsehood, oppression, impurity, and selfishness, the details of which must be incredible except to those who, like myself, have had the means of substantiating them. It is not too much to say that the present moral and religious state of Rome is a foul blot on modern Christendom, and hardly to be paralled even among the darkest passages in the history of our race."

Not so among the Protestant churches. Never did evidences of inherent vitality more abundantly abound. Never were revivals more general, or conversions more frequent. "Besides the nimble, strong, and multiform working of the Protestant faith, there is the great fact that the Protestant nations are the ones that wield the principal civilizing influences of the world. They carry the torch for mankind; and it is Protestantism in them that supplies and lights the torch. Take the Protestant nations out of the world, and who could have any hope for it? and take Protestant Christianity out of them, and there would be no hope for them.

"As I stood on a beautiful summer morning, in front of the magnificent monument which the citizens of Glasgow have reared to the memory of John Knox, the 'man who never feared the face of clay,' and studied the face of the statue, so calm, so earnest, and beheld the Bible which his hand holds forth as the source of power that wrested Scotland from the dominion of the Pope and gave that land to Christ; as I gazed upon the tombs of the martyrs, and beheld proofs of God's power in the changes wrought there and elsewhere in Great Britain, my thoughts winged their way westward and homeward. For the first time I was made to understand why Roman Catholic cathedrals and structures are being built in America. Just such a people, in the past, reared the magnificent structures of Great Britain as are now carrying brick and mortar in our own land. Let them go on. ' *The Lamb shall overcome them.*' These splendid structures shall yet be filled with the sounds of the Gospel, and with

the praises of worship, as are those far-famed cathedrals once
the boast of the Roman, and now the pride of the English
church. Let those who feel that the country is imperilled by
Romanism go back a few years in their recollections. Behold
proofs of the power of Rome in elections, in legislatures, and in
government! The American movement which desired to place
'none but Americans on guard,' in compliance with the instructions of Washington, grew out of the peril that threatened the
ark of our liberties. Rome was pretentious and insolent. The
people believed that the alien born were slaves to a power antagonistic to liberty, and that the foreign vote, controlled by a foreign
potentate, not only proposed, but elected, presidents, — that this
directing force vested in the bishops of the Romish church in the
United States, dictated treaties, claimed cabinet appointments,
placed its hand upon the free thought of the nation, and strove to
muzzle the press, and kill out the vital independence of the people. Hence, the opposition to a despotism whose tyranny knew
no limits, and was restrained by no barriers. It was shown that
demagogues bargained for the Catholic vote, — a vote which procured seats in the cabinet and on the supreme bench, chaplaincies
in the public service, foreign missions and embassies, seats of
honor and emolument at home and abroad, places by the thousand in the revenue service, and the confiding to the hands of
a Roman Catholic the entire postal service.

At times the sky was overcast with clouds. It was proved then
that a majority of Romanists, though they find protection under
our flag, are, after all, alien in heart as in birth. The Pope is
master, though the President is professedly ruler. The struggle
was severe, but the followers of the Lamb were again equal to
the emergency; and though riots arose, though orphan asylums
were torn down and innocents were murdered, though our largest
city seemed given up to violence, yet the cause of truth again
triumphed, and the fell power of despotism was broken, and
Romanism, which has always been a plague, ceased to be a peril.
To-day, in the South as in the North, the Bible is freely circulated,
the press is unmuzzled, and 'the called, the chosen, and the
faithful' are at work as never before. From State to State in
the South revivals of religion have gone, blessing thousands and
bringing untold numbers from darkness to light. Truth goes
forward in straight lines. It mocks the slavish fear of the task-
master, and proudly claims Freedom as her child. After all, our
hope of humanity, of civil freedom and political freedom, rests on
the omnipotent working of the Holy Spirit. Rome may control human votes, venal legislators, but there is one thing Rome
cannot do: she cannot wrest the power of God's Spirit. She
cannot hinder revivals of religion, those pentecostal showers
with which so large a portion of our land is blessed. She cannot
retard the progress of truth as taught in the Sabbath school, the
Bible class, and the family circle, nor can she change the immutable purposes of Almighty God.

THE WAR ON THE BIBLE IN OUR PUBLIC SCHOOLS.

EPH. 6: 4.

"Bring them up in the nurture and admonition of the Lord."

ROME'S opposition to the Bible proves that her character is unchanged. The power that beggared Europe is arraying itself against the genius of our republican institutions and the spirit and teachings of the gospel of Jesus Christ. The battle has begun. Let it go on. Truth asks no quarters, and it gives none. If Romanists can overturn the altars of liberty in this New World, then it is proven that error is mightier than truth, and that those who are against it are more and mightier than those who are for it. This can never be true. God is the author of truth and is always for it. Liberty is the ally of truth, and liberty has devoted adherents. Education, that power that draws out thought and develops mind, is its constant helper; so is religion, and so are the people who have found in our sunny land a birthplace and a home.

The war on the Bible is a significant fact. Clubs lie thickest about the trees which bear the best fruit, and it is a law of warfare, that if you can destroy the centre of an assaulting column, you can easily scatter all that remains behind.

Rome knows that the Bible is the parent of all of our greatness; it is the fountain source of education, of morality, as well as of religion. Destroy the Bible, and you destroy the foundations on which the superstructures of hope are builded. I do not blame Rome for her hate. She must give way to the Bible or the Bible must give way to her. The fight is inspiring rather than dispiriting. When you want to rear a good tree, you take it out of the nursery, or hot-house, and place it on the open plain, so that winds may smite it and wrestle with it. The conflict helps the tree, compelling it to widen its base and deepen the hold of its roots, and increase the strength of its trunk and boughs.

See that oak on the mountain. The twig was wont to bend and yield; but years and conflicts added to its size, to its strength, and to its capacity to endure and withstand. Now behold it. Clouds blacken the heavens; the tempests burst forth from their prison chambers. They bestride the plain, they sweep up around the mountain, they grapple with the oak. Watch the conflict. The sturdy tree is undaunted. Roots hold firm, trunk stands true, boughs bend, creak, and groan; but with the exception of here a leaf and there a twig, that monarch of the forest comes forth master of the gale. The battle has helped it, and it will do better next time because of the sturdiness won in the fight of to-day.

The attack on the Bible means business. It points to the source of our strength. It is an indication of the power committed to the people and of the work they have to perform. It is God's way of saying to us, all you are and all you will be, comes from your devotion to truth. The Bible is attacked, — defend it. Let the world know by your action and your speech that you are glad of every opportunity to show your devotion to truth. Then let the conflicts increase. Victories for truth will be multiplied, and the American people will grow up to be a Bible-loving, a Bible-defending and a God-fearing nation, beautiful as Tirzah, comely as Jerusalem, and terrible as an army with banners.

The Schools are to be Managed not alone for Men, but for God.

The schools, like the atmosphere, are free to all. The influences of them surround all. Whatever taints them, injures us. Whatever ennobles, purifies, and exalts their character, blesses us. It will not do to stop with us. We are prone to do it, and naturally think that society is organized, nations are grown, civilizations are built up, to help the individual. Thus reckoning, we ignore God. Man is created to promote God's glory and advance the interests of truth in the world. Children belong to God. God commands us to bring them up for him, — that is, "*in the nurture and admonition of the Lord.*" Rome brings them up for the church first, and claims that she brings them up for God. Others bring them up for the state first, and so secondarily for God. Both classes make a mistake. The schools belong to God. We are to train the children to know him, to serve him, to love him, knowing that this accomplished good citizenship, loyalty to the church and to the institutions designed and built by God, will follow naturally, and as a matter of course: hence the command, "Bring them up in the nurture and admonition of the Lord." Romanists substitute the church for the Lord, — seek to bring up children in such a manner that they may be saved, not from their sins, not from death, not from ignorance, not from vice, but from Protestantism, and to the church. As education destroys the power of the priest, and dissipates the fogs and mists of superstition, Romanists war against it with all their power. The priests — *not the people, but the priests* — contend against education for mere existence. Education is the death of Romanism. Therefore, they oppose education.

Our argument is not, then, so much for them, as for those who believe that education of the mind and soul is essential to the growth which God designs for all. If priests of Rome argue that ignorance and degradation, such as is found in all Catholic countries, is preferable to the enlightenment, the intelligence, the culture, the prosperity of all Protestant countries, we must pass the priest, and, appealing to the people, not only point out a more excellent way, but by schools, by literature, by Christian enlightenment, we must urge all to follow us as we follow Christ. To do less is to ignore our manifest duty. It is impossible to divorce the Bible and education. Our literature is interwoven with religion. To attempt a separation is to destroy not only the child, but the mother. "Religion, or virtue, in a large sense, includes duty to God and our neighbor; but in a proper sense, virtue signifies duty towards men, and religious duty to God." Religion, not theology, not dogmas, not creeds, is to be taught in the schools, to the end that the pupils may become intelligent and virtuous citizens, competent to discern the path of duty in all the relations of life, and strong in the resolution to walk in it. Said the Abbe de Malby, in a letter addressed to John Adams concerning the government and laws of the United States, "It is difficult to avoid forming a conclusion respecting the relations of religion to our God, because they are enveloped by a multitude of mysteries; but the relations of religion to society are ascertained beyond the possibility of dispute. Who can entertain a doubt whether God hath intended to unite all mankind by the ties of morality and virtue, — ties whereon is founded the welfare of each citizen and of society?" Can Roman Catholics afford to dissent from the principle that God is ruler, that his word is authority in things moral and spiritual, and, therefore, that his revealed word be treated with the respect due to it.

It seems to me that in waging this fight against the school system, Catholics must take either one of two positions, —

1. That ignorance is better than enlightenment for Catholics. Or, 2. That the word of God is the death of Popery.

For it is admitted by Catholics that children educated in church-schools cannot compare with children educated in public schools.

The Pope uncovers his Hand.

In a letter written by Cardinal Antonelli, his Secretary, to the Bishop of Nicaragua, he says: "We have lately been informed here that an attempt has been made to change the order of things hitherto existing in that republic, by publishing a programme in which are announciated, 'Freedom of education and of worship.' *Both these principles are not only contrary to the laws of God and of the church, but are in contradiction with the concordat established between the Holy See and the Republic. Although we do not doubt that your most illustrious and reverend lordship will do all in your power against maxims so destructive to the church and to society, still we deem it by no means superfluous to stimulate your well-known zeal, to see that* THE CLERGY, AND ABOVE ALL, THE CURATES, DO THEIR DUTY.

By CARDINAL ANTONELLI."

This language needs no explanation. "Freedom of education and worship are contrary to the laws of God and of the church

. . . alike destructive to the church and to society." In-fallibility makes this declaration with respect to one American Republic; it holds equally with regard to all. It is Rome's fundamental principle. In the city of New York, $900,000 have been given in nine years to an institution which is the avowed enemy of the republic of liberty, of education, and of progress.

"The Priests must do their Duty."

This, in the light of the Hunter Point war, is a significant utterance. When the five villages now embraced in Long Island city were united, a department of education was organized under a Board of five Commissioners, — three Protestants, and two Roman Catholics. These Commissioners, by a unanimous vote, adopted the By-laws of the State of New York Board of Education, including article twelve, which requires that the schools shall be opened with the reading of the Bible. All assented to it. The children were delighted with it, and their parents saw them influenced by the teachings of truth, and rejoiced. The priest heard from the Pope through the Bishop and was commanded to do his duty. What is a priest's duty? To teach the truth, to preach the gospel? No, but to oppose the truth. He began his work, and the Board was at length induced to suspend all religious exercises at the opening of the schools for one month; at the end of which time the Board decided that the Lord's prayer, or the Ten Commandments, or both, at discretion of the principal, should be read each morning; thus, for the sake of peace, was principle trampled upon. In vain! The Lord's prayer might do, but what can Rome do with the Ten Commandments, when one of them condemns her idolatry and openly accuses the church of treason to God?

Hence, on Nov. 24, 1871, while the teacher was reading the Lord's Prayer, a girl arose from her seat and cried out, "I don't believe that." There is a lesson for us in the appearance of the girl. Rome can do little with the boys, but retains its hold of the girls. Ninety-nine of every hundred who attend the confessional are women. Put the ballot into women's hands and the priests will do their duty with a vengeance; but liberty and education may suffer more than is apprehended. The girl did not stop with mere dissent, but expressed her horror of the Scriptures, and said, "its doctrines, if believed in, would send them all to hell." The priest had evidently discharged his duty so far as that girl was concerned. On Monday following, Nov. 27, during the reading, thirty children commenced shouting, "Don't believe in that!" So the war went on. The parents sided with the teacher, and brought back the children who left the school in accordance with instructions from the parents. But parents and children were compelled by their priests to fight the school or suffer the perils of excommunication, which is claimed to be damnation.

This brings the question before us. It is education, with the Bible, which is the foundation of our moral and civil code, or it is ignorance and despotism and crime. On which side in this fight do you propose to stand? The Board of Education stood firm, and in open court it was decided that the Bible should be read, and that there should be no further disturbance. This is for the public. The hate of the priesthood lives, and the Pope cries out, "*Priests do your duty.*"

The priests evidently mean to obey. They are arrayed against our school system in the press, in the pulpit, and, more than all, in the confessional. One who has gone to the confessional for the last time said this: "At the close of my confession, the priest would ask, 'Is that all?' 'It is.' 'Not all,' said the priest. 'You keep your child in the devouring fire of the public schools, and will be damned unless you desist.' I replied, the child improved in morals and in mental power in the public school, and the reverse was true when he attended the parochial school." The priest in his anger grew violent. The woman left the confessional to return no more, but keeps her child in the public school, and finds in the word of God a light that leads her to Christ direct, without the mediation of a priest. In many of our cities, priests have carried their opposition so far that Romanists remonstrate and stand by the teacher in preference to the priest.

There could be nothing worse for the future of America than for the children of foreigners to be reared up in the ignorance of Romanists in Italy or in Ireland. Hence, Romanists owe it to themselves, to their children, present and future, to demand that the school system be preserved inviolate, and that their children enjoy the boon procured for them, by the devotion to liberty and to enlightenment for the entire population of America, which characterized the founders of our nationality.

Can Romanists in the light of history, of what the Bible has done, and of what it offers to do, — can they afford to break with the moral sentiment of this land, which makes Christ the bulwark of liberty, and the hope of oppressed and sin-stained humanity?

The decree has gone forth that Catholics who send their children to the public schools will not be allowed to partake of the Holy Sacrament. Will Catholics yield their children's hopes of the future to this despotic usurpation, or will they resist it in the name of God and in love of their children? Will Americans bend before this opposition, or defend enlightenment and Christian culture?

The common schools of America had been founded more than one hundred and twenty-five years before the Declaration of Independence, and we find that universally the reading of the Bible and religious instruction formed a part of the system of education therein. We find that the old Continental Congress which had charge of our affairs during the Revolution, provided that there should be imported from Great Britain, at the public expense, for distribution among the people of this land, 20,000 Bibles. We find that the first act of the first continental con-

gress was to provide for the appointment of a chaplain, and he
came in the next morning and read that magnificent thirty-first
Psalm of David, beginning, "In thee, O Lord, do I put my trust;
let me never be ashamed; deliver me in thy righteousness," and
then invoked the blessing of God in prayer upon the assembly
We find that every regiment of the American army of the Revolution was provided with a chaplain at the public expense. George
Washington, when he took the oath of office, reverently bowed
his head and kissed the Holy Book. Congress is opened by
prayer each day of session.

The Constitution of the United States, in providing for religious
liberty, expressly declares that no restraint should be exercised;
" that congress should make no law respecting an establishment
of religion or prohibiting the free exercise thereof," but recognizing the principle introduced to the notice of mankind by Roger
Williams, who repudiated toleration because the right to tolerate
implied the right to proscribe, who would not accept as a favor
from man what had been given to him as a right by God; who
held that when God made the eye he conferred the right to look,
and when he made the Bible he conferred the right to read it or
to have it read. So congress opened the way for the worship of
God and for the diffusion of the principles of the gospel without
prescribing any form of worship or any mode by which the gospel should be circulated.

Judge Story, in his Commentaries upon the Constitution, in
regard to the rights of conscience and the establishment of religion, says: "The promulgation of the great doctrines of
religion, the being and attributes and providence of one Almighty God, the responsibility to him for all our actions, founded
upon moral freedom and accountability; a future state of re-
wards and punishments; the cultivation of all the moral, social,
and benevolent virtues, — these never can be a matter of indifference in any well-ordered community. It is, indeed, difficult to
conceive how any civilized society can well exist without them.
And at all events, it is impossible for those who believe in the
truth of Christianity as a divine revelation, *to doubt that it is the
special duty of the government to foster and encourage it among all
the citizens and subjects.* This is a point wholly distinct from
that of the right of private judgment in matters of religion and
of the freedom of public worship according to the dictates of
one's own conscience.

This is the broad platform on which the people of this land,
with few exceptions, have found it in their hearts to occupy. They
have felt that religion, morality, and knowledge, being necessary
to good government and the happiness of mankind, therefore
schools and the means of education should forever be encouraged.
Up to this time, in the Northern or Free States, schools have been
encouraged. The South pursued a different course.

It will be remembered that shortly after the termination of the
war in 1781, the idea of establishing schools at the public cost in
South Carolina was abandoned on account of the expense, and

consequent unpopularity of the means. General Marion, when he was informed in advance of this probable result, with great earnestness declared his belief, that the chastisement of the Almighty would be visited upon the people if they neglected to provide for the instruction of the masses, and uttered this prophecy: "If the means of education are withheld from the people, if they are not bestowed by the government, ambitious demagogues will arise, and the people, through ignorance and love of change, will follow them; vast armies will be formed, bloody battles fought, and the country desolated with all the horrors of a civil war." The Southern States did fail to provide popular education, and the result followed. Everywhere the need of education is felt. Europe is providing it for her people. Italy is running a race with other nations in building up a system of free schools. In Rome much has been done, and much is being done; and in the United States, where our school system has been our boast and glory, we find the priesthood of the Roman church opposing education, and many of the descendants of the Puritans acquiescing in the conclusion that it is best to give up the Bible to save the school, even though Romanists declare their opposition more to the school than to the Bible.

The Command is, "Bring up the Children in the Nurture of the Lord."

"Nurture" is a beautiful word. It has arms that enfolds, and love that warms. It means nourish, or educate. To bring up children in the nurture of the Lord, is to educate them as they do in Prussia and elsewhere, by telling them of God, of the work of creation, of Providence as seen in history and in life.

Rev. Calvin E. Stowe, D. D., years ago visited Germany with a view to investigate the systems of elementary public instruction then prevailing, and personally inspected many schools of all grades. As there must be many Catholic and Protestant children together, it is well to notice the course pursued. He informs us that the methods of religious instruction employed are various, according to the creed of the neighborhood, the style of instruction of the teacher. Sometimes the teacher calls the class around him and relates in his own language the simple narratives of the Bible. Sometimes he employs the translation of the Scriptures in general use among the people. The higher classes receive instruction in the whole Bible history, finishing with a summary of Christian doctrine, in the form of a catechism, which is the one employed by the church to which the parents of the scholars belong. Religious instruction of some kind, like all the other instruction of the schools, is not optional, but compulsory. The teachers, however, abstain from sectarian peculiarities, or from casting odium upon any denomination of Christians.

The late Horace Mann says: "Nothing receives more attention in the Prussian schools than the Bible. It is taken up early and studied systematically."

In all the Protestant schools, Luther's catechism is used, and in all the Roman Catholic schools the Catholic catechism is used, and when the schools are mixed, they have combined literary with separate religious instruction; and here all the doctrines of the gospel are taught early and most assiduously.

Gambetta, of France, says in his speech of Nov 16, 1871: — "The only way for France to retrieve her place in Europe, is to improve and strengthen her internal position. The most pressing and urgent of all reforms, is a comprehensive measure of general education, which would finally abolish the class distinctions which unfortunately exist. I am for absolutely gratuitous, obligatory, and (I would use a word grating to many ears) lay instruction. History shows that in all times the rulers who had an interest in forming men for their own purposes, looked upon every man who could read as an enemy. I am not only for the separation of church and state, but for the entire separation of the schools from the churches. I consider this not only a question of political, but of social order." He utterly denied the force of the objection that partisans of lay instruction wanted to breed up atheists; and declared that in his proposition there was nothing hostile to religion. "Let religious education, whether Catholic, Jewish, or Protestant, be given in religious temples, according to the choice of parents; *but let not the Catholics, with their claims to exclusiveness, have anything to do with the propagation of necessary knowledge which it is the State's duty to see imparted to every citizen.*"

What education under priestly influence has effected for his country, Gambetta well knows. His cure is radical. Put it into the hands of the laity, and let it be absolutely gratuitous and obligatory!

"My wish," said Lord John Russell, "and hope is, that the rising youth of England may be taught to adopt, not the church of Rome nor the church of England, but the church of Christ. The teaching of Christ, whether dogmatic or not, is to be found in the Bible, and those who in their infancy read the Bible may, at their own choice, when they reach the age of fifteen or sixteen years, follow the teaching of the church of Rome or of any Protestant community they may prefer. In this manner, Christianity may in time be purged of the corruptions which, in the course of time and amid the conflicts of the sixteenth and seventeenth centuries, have stained its spirit of love and charity." Beautiful words coming from the lips of a statesman of ripe wisdom, full of the honors and fame of this world. In an atmosphere of freedom, — freedom of education, freedom of worship, — Rome cannot succeed. She must compress and mould the human mind while tender, after her own deformed pattern, against nature and against truth, or fail in the effort. Those who have the truth, who believe in the Divine Head of the church, and not in a pretended human head, can safely leave the mind to the influences of the truth divinely commissioned to regenerate the world.

There are many reasons why we should seek to bring our children to know God. Among which are the following: —

1. God is their Father and their best friend.

God so loved them that he gave his only begotten Son that they might be loved and saved.

Christ said, "Suffer little children to come unto me and forbid them not, for of such is the kingdom of heaven."

As an earthly father educates his children so that they may enjoy the home life, come in contact with the learned and cultured, and enjoy their society, so our Heavenly Father desires that our children should be so educated and trained that they may be fitted for the enjoyments of heaven, and the companionship, not only of their Redeemer but of the redeemed.

It is a Hindoo saying, that "Man is nothing until he becomes a triadman, wife and child." Then and there all the interest in life begins. Now, earth has no monopoly of the experiences of Heaven. It is a divine image, having its archetype on high, which God desires us to reproduce here in its purest and brightest form, in the hope of a Christian home.

"Little children," another has said, "are Christ's own nurselings." They love, and trust, and give, after the fashion that reigns in Heaven. Love is their sunlight; they ask for nothing but to bask in it. There is no glow for them when that sun is clouded, — no gloom when that sun is shining. They are sent to us that we might learn of the mysteries of love. Love is of God, for God is love. All love that is not self-love has God for its fountain and Christ for its pattern. Let this love of God through you find its way to the child and to the children. Educate them to know God, to love him, to worship him in spirit and in truth; and by so doing you take the tendrils of love growing spontaneously in the heart, lift them up from the decaying things of time, and find them a support in the cross of Christ, which, like the tree of life, shall reappear in all its beauty and glory in Heaven after its work is done and its mission is fulfilled on earth.

This is a work in which all can engage. Let Romanists teach their children to know Christ and to love him, and they will be sure to give them advantages in the arts and sciences which fit the mind better to comprehend the height and depth, and length and breadth of the marvellous works of God, and love of God as revealed in Jesus Christ His Son, and our Saviour.

Nurture means nourishment. Education is to the mind what food is to the body. It feeds, sustains, and endows it. Education is a duty binding on all, because God is the creator, upholder, and the rewarder of those who diligently seek him.

2. Knowledge of God builds up a man. Take the Bible as a book of ethics and nothing can take its place, and no man can afford to have its place usurped. Take it as a teacher of morals, and nothing can compare with it in worth or power. The world needs the Bible quite as much as the Bible needs the world. In my heart, if I wished to curse Rome (which I do not), I could wish her no worse thing than that she should succumb to this

demand of her priests. It is in opposition to the political, social, and religious interests of her people. Christ, the light, is an element of growth, of power. The Romanist and Protestant alike need it. Behold the weakly plant growing in the shadow. It is pale and feeble, without health and without beauty. Let it be brought into the sunshine, and the white gives way to green, the weakness to strength; and the plant which had only a sickly existence, gives promise of fruit and growth.

It is our duty to bring up children in the nurture or nourishment of this Infinite love that has found its way to the world and that seeks to bless the world. Christ is here. He is ready and waiting to bless. The word is nigh thee, — "In the battle which is raging, even in the young heart, every high thought, every holy purpose, every heavenward aspiration, is the work of His love; and every base thought, every impure passion, every worldly purpose, is the work of the enemy." Teach this, for whoever believes it is blessed, and whoever rejects the truth is cursed in time and impoverished in eternity. Education means drawing out, unwinding the faculties, developing the power. What can be compared with the influence exerted by those who open the eyes to the wonders of truth and fill the mind with thoughts of God? Then man becomes a fellow-helper with God. In every field of human activity in which the higher faculties find play, the power is of God. The intelligence, energy, and patience by which men win great successes, are ever formed and kept at white heat by the breath of God. In Him we live and move and have our being.

Why not say so? If His breath kindles the flame of life, the glow passes swiftly through every pulse and organ, and energizes them; if He withholds his inspiration, they fail and die.

The History of the Catholic School Question.

In 1822, the Bethel Baptist Church, of the city of New York, made application for a portion of the public funds to be devoted to the maintenance of certain schools under its supervision. The request was granted. After the lapse of three years it was reconsidered, on the ground that they were not strictly common schools. The decision of 1825 was regarded as settling the principles on which the school fund was thereafter to be distributed. On this ground the application of the Catholics in 1831 and '32 for an orphan asylum, was strenuously resisted by the trustees of the public schools. But, despite the opposition, and in the face of their own admission of the justice of the principles out of which it arose, the corporation of New York granted the Catholic petition, "out of pure sympathy," as they said, "for so interesting a charity." Here the war began. It was justice against injustice. In 1840, the Catholics, led by Archbishop Hughes, again took the field, and made the attempt to sweep our school system from the board. They demanded their portion of the school fund, and withdrew their children from the public schools. The intemperance of the Catholics revealed .

their hate to education, and opened to American eyes the perils threatening our institutions. The schools were denounced as "Anti-Christian," "heathen," and "godless." One declared that it was the duty of Catholics to get their children out of this "devouring fire." Another more recently has said, "We don't want our children to grow up like those around them and believe neither in God, man, or the devil," as though Catholics were in need of an education to make them believe in *the devil or in man!* The position was taken and is maintained, — 1. That this country, where government finds its corner-stone in the Word of God, is in duty bound to give the recognition that belongs to it as the Word of God; and so that there is no argument in favor of separate schools for Catholics which would not apply to the Chinese, the Mormon, or the Mahommedan. Romanism, the foe of enlightenment and of education, was beaten in New York, in Cincinnati, and wherever the battle has been fairly fought. The people declared with Hon. Rufus King, former president of the School Board in Cincinnati, that if it was desired to teach a child nothing but honesty, the precepts of the Bible should be selected beyond every book that ever was written. "Nay, more, if the object is not to teach morality, if I wanted a book which contained lessons of the purest English undefiled, I should take the Holy Bible as the best text-book that can possibly be found for that study in our public schools."

George R. Sage, son of a Baptist minister, and formerly a partner of Hon. Thomas Corwin, made a speech of immense power in support of the Bible, proving from a legal stand-point that the constitution of the State made it imperative to retain it. Others followed. It was shown that everything depends upon the Bible. It is the first image which takes possession of the mind, the first thought that lodges there which tells the story of a child's life. If that be of Christ and of the Word of God, its influence never dies.

Knowledge being power, it should be directed to useful purposes, to insure which the mind must be under the influence of religious principles, as fully as the body is under the influence of the mind. These influences being derived from the Bible, it should be a *school*-book, not to be opened and read in a gloomy way, but as the Word of God, presented to the minds of the children in its truly endearing sublimity; that they may see it as the spirit of wisdom directing to order, obedience, and true freedom.

It is very sad to see the extremes to which men fly in considering their relations to the Word of God. One class ignore its history, its philosophy, its morality, its love, its advice, as if it were hurled at them in condemnation or defiance. They call it hard names, and treat it as a foe rather than a friend.

The opposite extreme compel, or attempt to compel, attention to its claims as though it were a tedious task to be mastered, rather than the most delightful of reading and most entertaining of histories. The Old Testament is the most valuable ancient document in the world, and if we would incite the young to bring their fresh young appetites to bear upon it, they would have that lodged within them which would unlock for them the inner meaning of all the histories which they may be called upon to study, for it is, in a word, the key to the universal history of man.

"Take the Bible as a whole," said Prof. Huxley, "eliminate all that is not desirable for children to occupy themselves with, and there still remains a vast residuum of moral beauty and grandeur. And then consider this great historical fact, that for three centuries this book has been woven into the life of all that is best and noble in English history; that it is written in the noblest and purest English, and abounds in exquisite beauties of new literary form; and finally, that it forbids the veriest hind who ever left his village to be ignorant of the existence of other countries and other civilizations, and of a great past stretching back to the farthest limits of the oldest nations of the world. By the study of what other books could children be so humanized and made to feel that that each figure in the vast historical procession fills, like themselves, but a momentary space in the interval between two eternities."

The Bible as a Book to be Read and Studied.

It becomes us seriously to ask ourselves if the Bible should not be put back in the school to be read as a text-book. Good readers of Scripture are growing rare. The reason is, very little Scripture is read audibly. In the olden time I remember when the class in reading the story of Christ's death on Calvary were melted to tears, and the hearts of teachers and scholars alike were blessed by the morning lesson. We have given away to prejudice and priestcraft rights which it becomes us to regain and hold. Let our children be taught to be good Bible readers, and they will thank us for the boon so long as they live.

In opposition to this truth, John B. Purcell, Archbishop of Cincinnati, on Sept. 18, 1869, declared to the committee, "The entire government of public schools, in which Catholic youth are educated, cannot be given over to the civil power. We as Catholics cannot approve of that system of education for youth which is apart from instruction in the Catholic faith and the teaching of the church. If the school board can offer anything in conformity with these principles, as has been done in England, France, Canada, Prussia, and other countries, where the rights of conscience in matters of education have been fully recognized, I am prepared to give it respectful consideration." This is the position taken. The church is first, God and humanity second. A compromise was found to be impracticable. The Catholic priests declared, "We are far from agreeing with the gentlemen that there are thousands of Catholic children anxious to avail themselves of the advantages of the common schools. All we Catholics want is our share of the public money." Well did Mr. Sage say in reply to this, Catholics as Catholics have no share in the public funds, no more than Protestants as Protestants have it. Hon. Rufus King well said, "The right of conscience and equality, secured by our laws, do not contemplate that every sect or party is to dictate its own terms of participating with others in the common privileges, but merely that each may have and enjoy the same privileges and immunities which are granted to others." Here we stand sheltered by the constitution, and obedient to God. We have no morality which is not enjoined by our religion. We have no rule of conduct furnished by law touching the dealings of man toward his fellow-man, or by the State, which is not to be found more explicitly and more forcibly commanded by the Divine Author of that religion; and as the true strength of the government is its reliance upon the intelligence, patriotism, and morality of the people, the knowledge of the Bible should be encouraged, and its elementary truths made known to all. It is only in Christian nations that what we understand by the majesty of the law is recognized and felt in the administration of justice and the conduct of public officers, and nowhere upon earth is that majesty so exemplified as in these United States of America. Truly has it been said, " Exclude all religious instruction from the education of the child, and what sense of obligation will the man derive from the oath? Discard the Bible, prohibit all knowledge of religion, and what value could be attached to an appeal to a Being of whom the witness had no knowledge? How is it possible to administer without relying upon the religion of the Bible?" And let it be remembered, Romanists do not propose to use the Bible in their schools. " Within thirty miles of Cincinnati," continued Mr. Sage, " a wholesale murder was committed. A feeble old man and three children — one a babe upon its mother's arm — were the victims. The mother herself was felled to the floor and left for dead. One only of the household escaped unharmed, and she a child of seven years. She was the only witness of the fact of the murder. Without her evidence conviction was impossible. When the murderer was brought to trial, and the child placed on the stand as a witness, instantly came the objection that she was too young to testify. Now, the rule in such case requires the judge to ascertain whether the child has acquired such a sense of moral accountability to a Superior Being as to feel the binding obligation of an oath. That is the test of competency. The judge came down from the bench and took his seat beside the child. She had never been a witness. There was a startled expression when she was asked if she knew what would be the consequences if she should tell an untruth. Instantly she replied, ' God would be angry with me.' — 'My child, where did you learn that?' inquired the judge. — 'At school, and from my mother,' was the reply. There were tears in many eyes in the crowded court-room when the oath was administered, and not one who heard her but believed every word of her testimony. The murderer was convicted and executed because of the influence of religion in the schools." Richard Snell Edgeworth, induced by a noted French infidel, educated his son, from his third to his eighth year, according to the scheme proposed by those who would eject the Bible from the schools. He sums up the result in a single sentence: "He had all the virtues of a child bred in the hut of a savage, and all the knowledge of things which could well be acquired at an early age by a boy bred in civilized society." In advocating the keeping of the Bible in the schools, we do more than advocate the cause of religion, — that of the state and its citizens, the protection and security of life, liberty, and property. The Bible is the safeguard of all these. No free government now exists in the world unless Christianity is acknowledged, and is the religion of the country. Then, let us not be fettered or hindered. Romanists and Pagans are welcome to America, but they are not welcome to destroy America. They are welcome to enjoy the protection of the laws, not to destroy them, and so subvert our institutions. Let us make our schools worthy of the people, and believe that they will be sustained by the people despite the influence of their opposers.

There is Work in the Home.

3. We are commanded to bring the children up " in the admonition of the Lord."

The word admonition means counselling against a fault.

If we bring up the young in the nurture of the Lord we shall cherish all the good in them, and seek to plant good within them.

If we bring them up in the admonition of the Lord we shall point out their errors, their peril, their sins, and warn them against them.

The Bible is to our faults what the shears of the vine-dresser is to the branches that need pruning; what the words of a true friend are concerning our merits, etc. God, being our creator and benefactor, is interested in us as is no one else, and speaks to us as no else can.

Against this apostolic command three classes are arraying themselves. 1. The professed Christians, who think more of education than of Christianity, and who prefer a nation of atheists to a disruption of our school system.

2. Infidels who ignore the word of God and are hostile to it.

3. A class of Romanists whose bigotry has been excited, and whose fears have been disturbed by the apprehension that education and the plain and manifest teachings of the gospel are against the tenets of their church.

To such I would appeal: —

Think what your children leave if they turn away from the schools!

More and more, education and culture is felt to be a fortune. Ignorance and lack of skill reduces a man to a level with a brute, — makes him stationary as a post in society, even while the tramp of progress is all about him.

The True Ground.

I do not propose to defend the Bible. I believe it to be the inspired revelation of Almighty God to man, and argue, —

1. That the suppression of the Bible is the destruction of religious liberty, and that religious liberty is the only sure foundation of civil liberty.

2. That the exclusion of the Bible from the public schools is the first step towards the suppression of the Bible in our land.

3. That it is in exact accordance with the spirit and true meaning of this constitution that the Bible shall be read in the public schools, and shall be recognized as the bulwark of free institutions. Infidelity always fights under a mask. David Hume left some infidel manuscripts with directions that they should be printed and published after his death. "He loaded a blunderbuss," said Dr. Johnson, "directed it against Christianity, and sneaked into the grave, leaving another to fire it off." So it is here; the battle is more than against the Bible,—it is against religion, against progress, against education, against the genius of the republic and the spirit of liberty.

To this, certain ones object, saying to Romanists, "Gentlemen, if you object to such religious education as is now given, we are willing to waive that and remit all religious teaching to the fireside, the Sunday school, and the church; but common schools, at some rate, we must and will maintain."

When the two women came with the child, both claiming to be the mother, Solomon proposed to divide the child, knowing that maternal love would cause the mother to spare her offspring. The result was reached. The woman ready to have the child slain did not love it. Is it not to be feared that those who are willing to have our school system rent, broken, dissevered, are lacking either in devotion to the highest interests of the people, or are made to err in judgment because of a desire to secure the support of Romanists and at the same time preserve the schools intact. Make the public schools superior to private schools, and the children of America will overleap all sectarian barriers to reach them; and as this cannot be accomplished without the help of the Bible, patriotism demands that its influence be secured, for education is the cheapest police force which can be employed, and by this, under God, kings are to rule and princes decree, and without it no throne is stable and no national existence safe.

Let us, then, in the spirit of love for Christ and men, stand for the word of God in the public schools and in the home, and then shall we have the consciousness and comfort, if evils betide this Republic, that we are not to blame.

"Trust in the Lord, and do good, so thou shalt dwell in the land, and verily thou shalt be fed." The Son of God is working unseen and silently to defend his truth and advance his cause. Behind the curtains his hand is busy. From afar, converging lines are bringing up relief. Separate forces will unite at the point intended. That point will be, perhaps, man's utmost extremity; but at that point, hopeless destitution and the divine fulness will meet, and victory even will redound to God's declarative glory and to man's highest good.

ROME AS A PERFECTED ORGANIZATION.

To confront the despotism of Rome is to combat the *Prince of the Power of the air.* No matter who represents Romanism, who speaks or writes for it—he may be skilled or unskilled, learned or unlearned, wise or otherwise—the power behind him is the mightiest, the most extensive, the best organized of any form of error on the face of the earth. It is not child's play to tell the truth about Romanism. The Papacy, strong, colossal, reaching into every land and ruling over three hundred millions of people, is the monument of the father of lies. Error is its stock in trade. Human nature in its normal condition is its field of hope. Romanism employs men. It does not reform them. It marshals them into a perfected organization, which is a power because of these, among other facts :

1. All her ecclesiastical gatherings, from the meetings of the cardinals and œcumenical councils down to the meetings of her priests, including the great Society of Jesus and many of her lay organizations, are secret and oath-bound, and their doings are not known to the outside world.

2. Her military organizations, enabling the Cardinal Bishop of New York to wield the whole mass of her adherents in a solid body at his will.

3. The vast amount of wealth she is accumulating.

4. The title of her property, including churches, school property, convents, colleges, asylums, and so on, being held entirely in the individual name of the bishop of the diocese in which the property is located.

5. Her parochial school system, by which nearly all her children, from infancy to maturity, are thoroughly imbued with the doctrines and intolerant principles of the church.

6. Working under the infamous maxim that the end sanctifies the means.

Add to all this that the spirit and life of Romanism is intolerance and bigotry, which makes the organization thoroughly unscrupulous, and we perceive the danger to the Republic, saying nothing of Christianity, in permitting such a despotism, officered by foreigners, controlled and directed by a foreign despot, and wielded to uproot and destroy free institutions, defiantly to go on unchecked and unhindered, because in the name of religion she sets up her banners. We would not, we must not, disturb her in her sacred retreats of worship, but we must not permit her to scuttle the ship on which we sail. As a so-called religious organization, its principles are that the church, having been established by God Almighty, must necessarily be above all human institutions and laws ; that its devotees must obey the priests and other church authorities in all things ; that there is no salvation whatever outside of the church ; that the head of the church is infallible and cannot err in spiritual matters, which is stretched to include temporal matters.

Hence, when the Duke of Richmond, formerly Governor of Canada, declares " that the Government of the United States *ought not to stand and will not stand, but will be destroyed by subversion and not by conquest;*" and when we see priests at the dictation of their bishop swarming about a legislature as they did about the Legislature of Ohio in support of the Geghan Bill , when we see the majority of the voters of the city of New York controlled by the behests of a single man, and that man the right hand of the Cardinal Bishop, we gain an insight as to the peril which threatens this land, consecrated to freedom and designed by Providence to be the home of peoples.

HOW TO AVERT THE THREATENED DANGER TO OUR FREE INSTITUTIONS.

In the address of the Order of the American Union to the American People, we find this draft of a proposed amendment, which is submitted to the American people for their consideration :

" ARTICLE XVI.

"SECTION 1. No public money, property, franchise, or credit shall be appropriated, directly or indirectly, for the benefit of any religious or non-religious sect.

"SECTION 2. No special laws shall be enacted for the benefit of any one religious or non-religious sect.

"SECTION 3. All ecclesiastical property shall be held in trust by boards of trustees, numbering not less than five members to each board, to be appointed by and composed of members of the congregations owning or donating the property.

"SECTION 4. No property shall be exempt from taxation except public property.

"SECTION 5. All new voters after the adoption of this amendment shall be required to be able to read and write before exercising the elector's franchise."

In 1875 Ulysses S. Grant, twice President of the United States, and confessedly one of the foremost men of this age, said at Des Moines, Iowa : " Let us labor to add all needful guarantees for the most perfect security of free thought, free speech, and a free press, pure morals, unfettered religious sentiment, and of equal rights and privileges to all men, irrespective of nationality, color, or religion. Encourage free schools, and resolve that not one dollar of money appropriated for their support be used for any sectarian school. Resolve that neither the State nor nation, or both combined, shall support institutions of learning other than those sufficient to afford every child growing up in the land the opportunity of a good common-school education, unmixed with sectarian, pagan, or atheistic tenets. Leave the matter of religion to the family altar, the church, and the private school supported entirely by private contributions. Keep the Church and State forever separated." Among the many wise things said and brave deeds performed, this utterance and act claim a recognition as the bravest and the best.

It is not New York City alone that is in danger. The gateway of the western world was the stake played for by the representatives of this ancient despotism. It is not too much to say that there was a time when that magnificent metropolis was under the control of the Pope, as was not Rome, the city of his habitation. Money in uncounted sums poured into her coffers, valuable properties in land were placed under the control of bishop and priests, and for the benefactions, votes were sold and political power was conferred. As a result, there has been a despotism built up in the Empire State which at one time threatened its prosperity and darkened its future. The fight in New York epitomizes the conflict in the Republic.

THERE CAME AN UPRISING.

Thousands born in America, and others as patriotic, though born in foreign lands, partakers of the free speech engendered by our institutions, rose up against this monstrous usurpation, threw off its toils, and the rights of freemen were maintained and protected. The work achieved in New York is only matched by what has been wrought abroad.

The Papacy of the past is no more. Free thought, free speech, a free press, and a free pulpit has been its disease. Its death is sure to come.

The Papacy of the present imitates the Papacy of the past in allying itself to despotism, but its old power is gone. The lions asleep and caged in Central Park resemble the lions of the jungle in appearance, not in action. These we feed. Those devour. The Papacy of to-day depends on our favor. The Papacy of the past

> "Up from the ground uprose
> As from his lair the wild beast."

Legend has it that Charlemagne in his fight with the Saracens was outnumbered. The bravest and the best had fallen. The army of France was miles away in the valleys of the Pyrenees. What was to be done? There was his trumpet, and that was all. The men to wield the sword and battle-axe were few and far away. He took the trumpet and blew one more blast. It leaped from crag to crag, from mountain peak to mountain peak, and reverberated through the valleys and reached the ear of the army, and they came to his help. Our hope is in the Gospel trumpet. Let us give it voice and the inspiration will follow; lovers of the truth will rally, and the hosts of error will be dissipated, and Jesus shall reign as Lord of all.

IS ROMANISM GOOD ENOUGH FOR ROMANISTS?

ROMANISM has a place in the life of the world. Is it to be displaced, or is it to extend until in fact, as in name, it shall become universal in its sway and the representative of omnipotence in its might? The answer to this question is found in its intrinsic worth more than in its pretension, in what God's Word says about it, far more than in any claim it may make to infallibility. This we might admit in theory, but before it can have any direct influence we must reach a just and true conclusion as to whether Romanism is good enough for Romanists. The majority answer the question in the affirmative; they go further, and declare that it is good enough for the poor in Europe, and for the poor in America. For this reason they regard the Church of Rome as a part of the Christian world, and hold this organization, despite its history, as one of the Evangelical denominations. They rejoice in its growth and contribute to its prosperity by assenting to its pretensions, if not by contributing to its support.

The question deserves to be asked and to be answered in the spirit of love and not of fear. Seven millions of professed Romanists in this land, unnumbered millions in other lands, are not more interested in i s answer, or ought not to be, than are the millions of Protestants who enjoy the inheritance bequeathed to us by the sacrifices of our fathers and by the unmistakable providence of Almighty God. There is in Heidelberg, Germany, a meeting-house divided from cellar to roof by a thick wall. On one side meet Protestants, on the other assemble Romanists. There they worship, unmolested and undisturbed. Neither party think of yielding to the other or of trying to convert them from the error of their ways. Both cannot be right. One accepts of Christ and his teachings; the other substitutes Mary in Christ's stead. One clings to the Scriptures as the sheet-anchor of hope; the other rejects the Bible and rests the faith upon the authority of the Church or tradition. On one side there are bare walls, a pulpit and a choir, and people with Bibles in their hands, taking a " thus saith the Lord" for the rule of their faith and practice. On the other, there is an altar, a portrait of Mary, pictures or stations on the walls, images and confessional boxes, a priest at the altar, and people listening to a prayer they do not understand, bowing and crossing because they have thus been taught, without a reason for their faith, and without a thought as to whether it be true or false.

That Church with its Wall

illustrates the conduct of Protestants and Romanists in America. Protestants seldom think of preaching the Gospel to Romanists. They live beyond the wall—in our homes, in our stores, and foreigners are beginning to do so on our farms. In New England, in New York and in Ohio hundreds of farmers have sold out their homesteads, and have either gone West or removed to the cities and villages near by, and the places that knew worshipers of our Lord Jesus Christ in simplicity and truth, know Him no more.

Romanists have purchased the old homesteads, have divided up
the fields, and, instead of the farmer who kept the fire of a Christian's faith burning on the altar of the country or village church,
are Romanists and their chapel. Instead of the supporters of
liberty, of temperance, of the public schools, where the Bible was
read and the prayer was said, now there is a people who vote as
the priest bids them, who oppose temperance, the old school system, and the lecture so full of importance and thought, and live a
foreign life in our new republic. There they are beyond the wall.
No one preaches to them the Gospel. They are as much beyond
our thought, desire or hope as though they still dwelt in green Ireland or beside the beautiful Rhine, in Germany. The question,
Is Romanism good enough for Romanists? is literally seldom
asked.

If Romanism is good enough for Romanists, it is good enough
for everybody. If not good enough for Romanists, it is not good
enough for anybody. In this all will agree. If it be true that
Romanists reject or mutilate the Scriptures, that they accept error
for truth, substitute Mary for Christ, tradition for the Bible, and
the power of the Church for the salvation wrought out by the Son
of God, then it becomes us to say so, not to Protestants alone, but
to Romanists, and not to Romanists alone, who are in the dark and
are dead to Christ, but to Protestants, who are asleep concerning
the peril of their neighbors and friends, and ought to be waked
up and set to work, lest the blood of their fellows be found in the
skirts of their garments.

To-day the Wicked One is Hidden.

The eyes of the people are holden that they cannot see; their
ears are stopped that they cannot hear what the Scripture saith
concerning the Wicked to be revealed, " whom the Lord shall
consume with the spirit of his mouth, and shall destroy with the
brightness of his coming, even Him whose coming is after the
working of Satan, with all power and signs and lying wonders,
and with all deceivableness of unrighteousness in them that perish,
because they receive not *the love of the truth* that they might be
saved." There was a time when the world was stirred by the
peril threatening religion, liberty and morality because of the
machinations of Rome. A battle was fought and a victory was
won. The weapons of truth were laid aside. The artillery of the
prophetic portions of God's Word were silenced. The watchmen
who walked the walls of Zion and filled the air with the alarm
sounded out have been called down from their proud position;
and if Romanism were extinct and Romanists were all converted
to Christianity, there could not be greater indifference to this question, " Is Romanism good enough for Romanists ?" than there is
at the present time. There is no room for the discussion of this
important subject in the religious or in the secular press. But
Romanism is not dead nor are Romanists converted. Never was
Romanism more united, more determined, more powerful—politi-
cally, socially, or as an organization—than at the present time.

In 1785 Bishop Carroll estimated the Roman Catholic population at about 25,000. There was one Romish church in New York City, one in Philadelphia, and the rest were settled in Pennsylvania and Maryland. In 1790 there were 80,000; in 1810, 100,000; in 1836, 1,250,000; in 1870, 5,000,000, and at this present time not far from 7,000,000. According to this statement the Roman Catholics have increased two hundred and fifty fold. The question naturally arises, What are the causes that have produced this remarkable increase? First, immigration; second, annexation of Louisiana, Florida, and Mexican territory; third, the conversion of Protestant women through the convents and Romish educational machinery, resulting in their children being brought up in that faith; fourth, the children of mixed marriages, between Catholics and Protestants, generally being brought up Catholics, the priest requiring an ante-nuptial pledge to that effect before performing the ceremony; fifth, the constant inculcation by the priest in the privacy of the confessional (as well as publicly from the pulpit) of the necessity of multiplying children, ostensibly for the purpose of carrying out the Biblical injunction, but in reality for the purpose of increasing the political power of the church in the midst of a Protestant community. Sixth, the Woman's Rights craze, which tends to the barrenness of American women and to producing a hatred for children and a dislike to bearing them, which is resulting in the breaking up and utter extinction of thousands of our American homes and in supplying their places with Irish and German families whose parents still delight in olive plants about the table, and in the prattle of children's voices about the hearthstone.

The indifference of the Christian Church to the doings of Rome, is one of the saddest features of our times. Think of a professor of a theological seminary of the Presbyterian Church complimenting the Roman Catholic Church for taking children out of the public schools and giving them over to the tender mercies of a priesthood, sworn to fight all that militates against the propagation of errors that have beggared Italy, and gladly would imperil America. True it was voted down by an overwhelming vote, but the fact that it was offered shows how indifferent the people are to the perils that environ them. Rev. Dr. Binney, of London, recently said to his younger brethren in the ministry :

"Study Popery Anew.

The proper remedy against the threatened influx of Papal power is to read afresh the tenets of the Papacy, to understand its errors, to chronicle its crimes, to mark well that its character is as immutable, its purposes as unchanged, its ruling spirit as full of enmity toward God and to all that refuse to wear the mark of the beast, as its pretensions are arrogant, and that everywhere and always it has proved itself to be a thing which at once involves God and degrades man."

Romanists in this land need this quite as much as Protestants. They have no interest in being wrong, but every interest in being right. We have no interest in having them wrong, but every interest in having them become yoke-fellows with us in the Lord that with them we may conserve the interests of liberty, of education, and of mental and financial progress. They are our brothers. In the birth-throes of battle they were born into our American life. In clearing the wilderness, in building and perfecting the railway and telegraph systems, they have wrought side by side with Protestants. In press-rooms, in editorial sanctums, in stores and factories, in shop and on farm, their brain, their push, their generous bearing, their economy and industry entitle them to love and consideration. We cannot afford to have them cling to errors. Truth helps and blesses ; error dwarfs and hinders. Let us say so. God Almighty is the Father of us all. Jesus Christ the Saviour is for them as for us, the one Mediator between God and man, and the Holy Spirit the inspirer of the best life ; the comforter in sorrow and the guide in spiritual as in temporal affairs, is ready to wait on them as on us, and lead us all into the way of truth, of righteousness and of peace.

1. *Romanism is not good enough for Romanists, because it gives no place in its system for the unchangeable and unerring wisdom furnished by the Word of God.*

The love of truth is not with Romanists a passion. They are taught to love the Church even when not illustrating by its life the teachings of the gospel, and tradition even when it usurps the place belonging to the Scriptures. Every one should know that the Council of Trent, held on the 13th of December, 1545, and lasting until December, 1563, nearly eighteen years, is the highest authority, as to the present doctrines of Romanism. The council was held to uproot Lutheranism and establish Romanism. It had many sessions. In these they canvassed the situation and made many decisions which have to do with the welfare of millions. Then they decided that laymen ought to receive the faith which the Church dictated without disputing or reasoning, and that they had nothing to do but hear and submit. Their power to reason was set aside. Their access to God's Word was forbidden. They placed tradition upon an equality with the Scriptures, declared the books of the Apocrypha to be a part of the word of God, elevated the Latin translation of the Vulgate to an authority superior to that of the inspired Hebrew and Greek originals, and enacted severe penal laws against the liberty of the press. They placed a band of iron about the conscience, cramped faith, and tried to destroy all love for the truth as revealed by the Bible. In rule 4, they say : "Inasmuch as it is manifest from experience that if the Holy Bible, translated into the vulgar tongue, be indiscriminately allowed to every one, the temerity of men will cause more evil than good to arise from it ; it is, on this point, referred to the judgement of the bishops or *Inquisitors*, who may, by the advice of the priest or the confessor, permit the reading of the Bible translated into the vulgar tongues by Catholic authors to those persons whose faith and piety they apprehend will be augmented and not injured by it, and this permission they must have in writing. But if any one shall have the presumption to read or possess it without such written permission, he shall not receive absolution, until he has first delivered up such Bible to the ordinary. Booksellers, however, who shall sell, or otherwise dispose of Bibles in the vulgar tongue to any person, not having such permission, shall forfeit the value of the books, and be subjected to such penalties as the bishop shall judge proper. Can Romanism be good enough for Romanists that declares that the indiscriminate use of the Scriptures will be productive of *more evil than good?* This is not a doctrine belonging to the dark ages. Pius VII in 1816, Leo XII in 1824, Pius VIII in 1829, Gregory XVI in 1832 and 1844, published bulls against the circulation of the Scriptures. Whenever Rome has the power, the Church opposes the publication, distribution, reading and possession of the Holy Scriptures. Christ said: "Ye shall know the truth, and the truth shall make you free." Rome hates this freedom and fights it successfully only where she can banish or burn the Word of God. Now, when we remember that this is the land of the Bible ; that love for the Bible peopled it, and that adherence to the teachings of the Word of God has been the seedling, out of which has grown religious and political liberty, we find reasons for saying that a system which repudiates the Word of God is not good enough for any one living within reach of the enjoyment of the blessings resulting from the possession of the oracles of God.

2. *Romanism is not good enough for Romanists, because it is not what it claims to be, but is an apostacy from the only true, holy apostolical and Catholic Church of Christ.*

Romanism claims to be the ancient apostolic and universal church, the mother and mistress of all churches. The fact that Roman is prefixed, proves that it is a sect. The word catholic means universal. The word Roman means something local and particular. To speak of the Roman Catholic Church of America, is just as absurd as to speak of the Boston Church of New York. And yet Roman is the necessary affix to the boasted claim of Catholicity. In every bishop's, priest's and layman's oath Rome is used. Prophecy locates the system of error beside the Tiber. The mystical Babylon and modern Rome are the same. Rome is the center, the heart and the home of Romanism. It is Roman or nothing. Romanism names it as well as Roman Catholic, and Roman is essential to its designation ; this proves it a sect, and shows that it never was catholic or universal. The Greek Church is its rival. The Patriarch of Constantinople and the Bishop of Rome were each anathematized by the other. Both claimed universal supremacy ; and as it is impossible for two bodies to occupy a given space at a given time, the fact that both claimed it is proof positive that neither possessed it.

As proof that Romanism is not original Christianity, it is enough to declare that centuries passed before the system had a place in

the thought of mankind, and its pretended decretals were shown
to be spurious, because the names they used had no existence
when the gospels and epistles were written. The epistles of the
ninth century speak of archbishops, archdeacons, door-keepers,
and what not, when no such terms were known to the apostles.

Besides, all know that the church at "Jerusalem is the mother
of us all," and not the Church at Rome. The Church at Samaria,
at Antioch, and at Athens, are all older than the Church at Rome.
These had a place in the beginning of the Acts of the Apostles.
The Church of Rome is mentioned at the end.

Again, the Douay Catechism, in answer to the question, What
are the essential parts of the Church, answers, "A pope, bishops,
pastors, and laity." Now not one of the apostles ever dreamed of
a pope. The Lord Jesus planted the heel of his condemnation on
the pretension incarnated in the pope. In the Douay version
we read, "You know that the princes of the Gentiles overrule
them, and those that are greatest exercise power against them. It
shall not be so among you, but whosoever will be the greater among
you, let him be your minister." This rebukes the idea of a prince
among the apostles—a vicar of Christ, a law over the people of
God. Again, in Matt. 23, 8 : 'Be not you called Rabbi, for one
is your Master, and all ye are brethren, and call none father (i. e.
pope), for one is your father who is in heaven." What the disciples knew not, Christ foresaw and warned against the tendency
which cropped out when the question arose as to who should be
greatest. In Eph. 4 : 13, we read : "And he gave some apostles, some prophets, some evangelists, and some pastors or teachers." In this enumeration which contains the entire list of of-
ficials, there is no pope. In I. Peter 5, 1, we read, "The elders,
therefore, among you I exhort, who am a fellow elder and a witness of the sufferings of Christ."

In the 4th verse, the Douay version has this: "And when the
Prince of Pastors shall appear." In our version, "And when the
Chief Shepherd shall be manifested," referring, not to a pope, but
to Christ. The claim of a supreme head amongst the apostles is
not made in the New Testament. Up to A.D. 451, the patriarch
of Constantinople had the same power as the patriarch of Rome.
The papal head appears in 606; and in July 16, 1054, the Roman
head, or the Church of Rome, having been first anathematized by
the Greek half, obtained a name and a place. At this time the
Greek Church was larger than the Roman Church, and so the
Roman Catholic Church is proven to be an apostacy from the
primitive Church, which Christ established. Notwithstanding this,
Bellarmine, a Roman Catholic historian, centuries after Christ's
ascension, positively affirms that the right of succession in the
popes of Rome is founded in this, that Peter, by Christ's appointment, placed his seat at Rome, and there remained until his death.
History, on the other hand, shows that Peter never was at Rome;
that there is no succession in fact, that the entire claim is built
out of the necessities of the organization, not at all upon scripture
nor upon what did actually occur. As late as A.D. 588, St.

Gregory opposed the title of universal head, and said the bishop of Rome neither can nor ought to assume it. And adds: "Although Jesus Christ committed to St. Peter the care of all the churches, yet he was not called the universal apostle." It is not strange that good Catholics should have fought this pretension when you consider what was the conduct of some of the men claiming the title, and ruling as pope. In 498 Laurentius was elected pope. In this struggle, murders, robberies, and numberless evils were perpetrated at Rome. Such were the horrible scenes, that there was danger of destroying the whole city. In the schism between Popes Sylvanus and Vigelius, in the sixth century, the latter, though an atrociously wicked man, implicated in unnumbered crimes so that all virtuous men opposed him, was raised to the papal chair. Yet, says Baronius, he is not to be despised, though a bad man. For, said he, *Let every man recollect, that even to the shadow of Peter, immense virtue was given of God.*"

The same writer, in the year 1004, names three rival popes who committed the most hateful crimes, and bartered the Papacy, and sold it for gold. Filthy, indeed, was the face of the church when the most powerful and sordid harlots then ruled at Rome, at whose pleasure Sees were changed and bishoprics were given, and, which is horrible to hear and most abominable, their gallants were attended into the See of Peter, and made false popes; for who can say they could be lawful popes, who were intruded by such harlots without law? There was no mention of the election or consent of clergy, the canons were silent, the decrees of popes suppressed, the ancient traditions proscribed, best armed with secular power, challenged all thoughts to itself. For seventy years there was no pope in Rome, besides all the other interregnums. The pope resided at Avignon, in France, and left St. Peter's chair empty. For almost half a century there were two popes and two lines of popes existing at one time, one reigning in Italy and one in France. And at last there were three popes—Benedict XIII., the Spanish pope ; Gregory XII., the French pope; and John XXIII., the Italian pope. Then the Council of Constance met and deposed the three popes, and appointed a fourth pope. After this can any man have any confidence in any pope being the successor of St. Peter, who never was pope, who never was bishop in or out of Rome? But let us not needlessly exaggerate the shame of the Roman Pontiffs. The throne which affected to exalt itself above the majority of kings was sunk in the filth of vice. Rome was one vast scene of debauchery, wherein the most powerful families in Italy contended for pre-eminence. It is next to impossible to form a just and adequate conception of the state of things which tolerated such flagrant vices in the so-called leaders of public opinion. To-day Romanism is something about which the masses in the church have little or no care. The feeling is that Paul described them, "who changed the truth of God into a lie and worshiped and served the creature more than the Creator, who is blessed forever. For this cause God gave them up unto vile affections and the practice of the most scandalous vices." This is not pleasant reading. Is it strange that Archbishop Purcell, when his attention was called to these scandalous men, was compelled to admit *"that, without doubt, some of the popes were in hell!"*

Is so false a system worthy of Romanists? We would not intimate that all Roman Catholics rest their hope of salvation upon the succession of the popes of Rome. We think, with D'Aubigné, that Catholicism should be distinguished from popery. Popery is an erroneous and destructive system; but we are far from confounding Catholicism with popery. Catholicism confesses the great doctrines of Christianity, and acknowledges God the Father, Son, and Spirit—Creator, Saviour, and Sanctifier. In our own land many Roman Catholics read the Bible and believe in its teachings, even while nominally they retain a place in the Church of Rome. With us, they believe that Jesus Christ is God's purpose in the world's history and that the Gospel is the fulfillment of all hopes, the perfection of all philosophy, the interpreter of all revolutions, the key to all the seeming contradictions of the physical and moral world—it is life, it is immortality. "Since I have known the Saviour, everything is clear with him; there is nothing I cannot solve," said the historian, C. D. Bonnet. Jesus Christ is the true God of human history.

Instead of the Bible, Rome has 135 large folio volumes and the Apocrypha. These are composed of the following parts: Apostolical Fathers, 35 folios. 2. Eight volumes of Decretals. 3. Ten volumes of Bulls of the Popes. 4. Thirty-one volumes of Canons and Decrees of Councils. 5. Fifty-one volumes of the Acts of the Saints. All these must be understood and interpreted by councils, but are beyond the reach of the laity. To expound them is difficult, if not impossible. The true reason of infallibility is inspiration. Jesus Christ, Romanists admit, can give a perfect rule. He therefore inspired twelve apostles to form that rule and enjoined us to hear them. We both have a perfect rule, and that rule is the Bible. Where is the inspiration of the one hundred and thirty-five folios? and yet these are the embodiment of Romanism. Is it safe for men to throw away God's chart and accept the writings of fathers, bulls of popes, decrees of councils, &c.? Romanism that cuts adrift from the Word of God is not good enough for Romanists. Years ago the country rang with denunciation because a steamer filled with people, fastened to the shore of the Niagara River, was cut loose at night and was permitted to drift upon the rocks of perdition and plunge over the precipice into the boiling cauldron beneath. A few only were lost then. Millions are imperiled who are cutting loose from the teachings of Scripture, and pushing madly upon the thick bosses of Jehovah's buckler.

8. *Romanism substitutes Mary for Christ, and rejects the chief corner-stone on which the true Church is built.*

In the "Glory of Mary," by St. Alphonsus Maria de Liguori, the author of "Moral Theology," now the standard book in every

Romish library, he says: "It is the will of God that all graces should come to us at the hands of Mary." "God, to glorify the mother of the Redeemer, has so determined and disposed that of her great charity she should intercede in behalf of all those for whom His divine Son paid and offered the superabundant price of His precious blood, in which alone is our salvation, life and resurrection." St. Bonaventure says "that those who make a point announcing to others the glories of Mary are certain of Heaven," and this opinion is confirmed, not by Scripture, but by Richard of St. Lawrence, who declares that "to honor this queen of angels is to gain eternal life." "Since the flesh of Mary," says the Abbot Arnold, of Chartres, "was not different from that of Jesus, how can the royal dignity of the Son be denied to the mother? Hence, we must consider the glory of the Son not only as being common to, but as one with, that of His mother." "If Jesus is the king of the universe, Mary is also its queen, and as queen she possesses by right the whole kingdom of her Son." "Whoever asks and expects to obtain graces without the intercession of Mary, endeavors to fly without wings." "God has decreed," says St. Bernard, "that He will grant no graces otherwise than by the hands of Mary." Not a word of Scripture for proof or authority. "Nay, more," says St. Bonaventure, "whenever the most sacred Virgin goes to God to intercede for us, she, as queen, commands all the angels and saints to accompany her, and unite their prayers with hers." Mary is called "*the rainbow round the throne*," "for God, at the prayers of Mary, forgives the crimes of enemies;" and so this book goes on, relating what the fathers have said, and utterly repudiating the Scriptures, and refusing to recognize Jesus Christ, through whose cleansing blood alone salvation is possible: for there is none other name given under Heaven among men whereby we must be saved. Is a system of faith good enough for Romanists, or anybody, that thus betrays Jesus Christ? The question deserves to be pondered and answered.

"Nuns," says Liguori, "ought to have a special devotion towards St. Joseph, their guardian angel and their tutelary saint, and principally towards St. Michael, the universal patron of all the faithful, but above all toward the most holy Virgin Mary, who is called by the Church our life and our hope; for it is morally impossible for a soul to advance much in perfection without a particular and a certain tender devotion towards the most holy mother of God." "Let him who is in the habit of blaspheming be advised to make the sign of the cross ten or fifteen times a day upon the ground with his tongue and thrice every morning, and say to the blessed Virgin, ' *O Lordess, give me patience.*'" Nor does this faith in Mary distinguish the past from the present. A Roman Catholic woman brought to the writer a card headed

" *Important,*"

containing this language, "you will not miss the alms which will await you for a hundred fold reward at the great judgment. Offer it as a balance against past offences, to get grace to resist temptations, to bring a blessing and success on your affairs, and for the dear departed souls who may be relieved by this act of charity." In the center is a picture of the cross and crown surrounded by the words "*Saint Joseph pray for us.*" Beneath it are these words "The sisters of charity implore a little aid to enable them to pay for schools for children of the West and to relieve their suffering poor. They faithfully promise to those who give it themselves, or who assist them by procuring money from others for this purpose, a special intention in 300 masses offered for the souls in purgatory, as well as a daily remembrance in the prayers of the Sisters." On the other side are the letters "A. M. D. S.—All that we give in charity to the faithful departed is changed into grace for us, and after our death we shall find its merit doubled a hundred fold."—St. Ambrose.

"*Jesus, meek and humble of heart, make my heart like unto Thine.*" 300 days' indulgence each time.

"*Sweet heart of Mary be my salvation.*" 200 days' indulgence. Then comes a cross with 60 squares and beneath it these words: "Please collect five cents for each small square (piercing the same with a pin) till the sixty are full, you will have three dollars to send to the superioress of the convent—the sisters of charity." This card is being distributed now, because the faith reposed in Mary is an existing fact.

A brass medal bearing *an image of the Saviour* being taken down from the cross, was also brought by another Roman Catholic; on the opposite side are these words: "M *To all the faithful who shall recite an Ave Maria before this holy image an indulgence of* 1,080 *days is granted.*" Can it be possible that such pagan idolatry is good enough for those who are with us journeying towards the bar of God?

4. *Romanism is not good enough for Romanists because of the immorality taught by its ministers and tolerated by its members.*

The lusts of the flesh, the lust of the eyes, the pride of life are found in her communion. In all our public institutions meat is excluded on Friday, because the majority of the criminals are members in good standing of the Roman Catholic Church. The rule of faith of the Romanist repeals and annuls certain positive laws. Catechisms published by the authority of the Church expunge wholly the second commandment, so that it should not stand in the way of paying reverence to images.

The common cursing and damning which offends our ears in all the lanes and streets and highways, is authorized in the following words : "To curse insensible creatures, such as the wind, the rain, the years, the days, fire, sun, is no blasphemy, unless the one who curses, expressly connects them with the name of God, by saying, for instance, cursed be the fire of God—the bread of God."

Romanism gives a License to Vio'ate.

In some way or other every precept of the Decalogue, the Sabbath as a divine institution, is thus set aside. "The Pope claims the right and the power to decree that the sanctification of the Lord's day shall only continue a few hours, and that servile work may be done on that day." Hence, in Roman Catholic countries there is no Sabbath. It is mass in the morning, and work or pleasure the rest of the day. "Merchandising, and the selling of goods at auction on the Sabbath, is, on the account of its being a general custom, altogether lawful."

"Buying and selling goods on the Lord's day, and on festival days, are certainly forbidden by the Canonical law, but when the contrary custom prevails it is excusable." "He who performs any servile work on the Lord's day or on a festival day, let him do penance three days on bread and water. If any one break fasts prescribed by the Church, let him do penance on bread and water twenty days."

Three days on bread and water for disobeying the Lord, twenty days on the same for disobeying the Church.

In regard to the seventh commandment, says the casuist, let the Confessor ask the penitent if he has stolen anything, and from whom, whether it was from one person or from different persons, whether he was alone or with others. Because, if at each time he stole a considerable amount, at each time he sinned mortally. But, on the contrary, if at each time he stole a small amount, then he did not sin grievously, unless the articles stolen came to a considerable amount." A difference is made between small amounts taken from different persons and the same person, at different times and at one time. If a considerable time intervene between the thefts, for instance, two months, then the theft probably does not amount to a grievous sin." Absolution is granted for stealing money to pay for masses, though the priest is under obligation to say masses without reward. Is such a license to sin, given by the authorities of a Church claiming infallibility, and by priests of a Church who are said to represent Jesus Christ, good enough for citizens of this Republic, the foundations of whose prosperity is commercial integrity, saying nothing of its influence upon the hearts and souls of those who are to be judged, not by the Canons of the Church, but by the plain and positive teachings of the Word of God, which in positive commands thunders from Sinai, saying:

"Thou shalt have no other gods before me. Thou shalt not make unto thee any graven image, or any likeness of anything that is in heaven above, or that is in the earth beneath, or that is in the water under the earth. Thou shalt not bow down thyself to them, nor serve them; for I, the Lord thy God, am a jealous God, visiting the iniquity of the fathers upon the children unto the third and fourth generation of them that hate me, and shewing mercy unto thousands of them that love me and keep my commandments."

This is the command. See how it has been repudiated and disobeyed. In the fifth century, the practice of ornamenting the churches with pictures became general, and thus the door was opened for that torrent of idolatry which flooded the churches, and in three or four centuries carried away almost every vestige of spiritual Christian worship. Afterwards the Bible, being forbidden, Pope Gregory called these images and pictures "*Books for the ignorant.*" In 713 Pope Constantine issued an edict in which he pronounced those accursed who "deny that veneration to holy images which is appoint d by the Church." In 787 it was decreed in the General Council held at Nice, "that holy images of the cross should be consecrated, and put on the sacred vessels and vestments, and upon walls and boards in private houses, and in public ways, *and especially th it there should be erected images of the Lord God, our Saviour Jesus Christ, of our Blessed Lady, the Mother of God, of the venerable angels, and of all the saints.* And that whoso ver should pr sume to teach or think otherwise, or throw away any painted books or the figure of the cross, or any image or picture, or any genuine relics of the martyrs, they should, if bishops or clergymen, be deposed, or, if monks or laymen, be excommunicated." Thus was the system of Popish idolatry established by law, and confirmed by a general council in direct opposition to both the letter and the spirit of the Word of God. Idolatry is stamped on the forehead of the Papal Anti-Christ. There it is, at this hour, in America as in Europe.

Romanism claims in the *worship of the host* power to create God; this is the meaning of the doctrine of Transubstantiation. For more than six hundred years after the institution of the Lord's Supper the bread and wine were typical of the Lord's broken body and shed blood. In 787 the second Council of Nice declared that the sacrament, after consecration, is not the image and anti-type of Christ's body and blood, but is, properly, *his body and blood.* The Cardinal in New York, every bishop and priest in the land, teaches that Jesus Christ's body and soul is in a crumb of consecrated bread.

In 1215 this dogma became an article of faith; it was called the "*burning article;*" it was the test doctrine of the Inquisition. Millions were put to death because they would not declare that the very God they worshipped could be eaten and devoured by them. Heathens, Mahometans, Jews and Christians have with one voice declared that it is the extremity of madness and stupidity for any man "*to worship what he eats, or eat what he doth worship.*" If any man could have changed the bread and wine into the body of Christ, the Apostles might have done so; yet Paul said (1 Cor., 11:26) the supper was instituted to shew forth the death of Jesus Christ, and not to sacrifice him. The supper was instituted by Christ at a table, and not at an altar. Christ offered nothing to God, but distributed the bread and wine to His disciples. In it there was no elevation of the Host, nor the adoration of the sacrifice, nor anything that cometh near to the ceremony of the mass. It was a rule that while the Chief Priest was in the sanctuary no sacrifice could be offered. As Jesus Christ has entered into Heaven, and while He occupies the mediatorial throne therecan be no true and proper sacrifice offered.

The time has come again and again when this truth has rolled like the voice of a trumpet over the land, casting down the disobedient, and lifting up the faithful. Rome heard it when Luther's tread shook Germany, and when the image breakers wrought their terrible work in Antwerp and in the Netherlands. We have heard it in America, when the spirit of loyalty to God stirred the hearts of the people, and it shall grow louder and louder until image worship shall be overthrown and God shall be Lord of all.   Again, it is written, "Thou shalt not take the name of the Lord thy God in vain. Remember the Sabbath day, to keep it holy. Six days shalt thou labour and do all thy work, but the seventh day is the Sabbath of the Lord thy God; in it thou shalt not do any work—thou nor thy son, nor thy daughter, thy manservant, nor thy maidservant, nor thy cattle, nor thy stranger that is within thy gates. For in six days the Lord made heaven and earth, the sea, and all that in them is, and rested the seventh day, wherefore the Lord blessed the seventh day and hallowed it."

No pope, no legislation, no nation can interfere with these commands without taking out of the grasp of the individual, the community, and the nation a blessing which impoverishes them. The other commands are quite as binding, and yet popery makes light of them all. "Honour thy father and thy mother. Thou shalt not kill; thou shalt not commit adultery; thou shalt not steal; thou shalt not bear false witness against thy neighbour." The Romanist has a way of making lying no lying, by saying, "*I only made this up in my head;*" and so on, to the end of the chapter.

The Confessional,

as revealed in the light of instructions given to priests, who act as confessors, is a dangerous weapon to be placed in the hands of anybody, and especially of godless men. Here are some extracts from Liguori's Moral Theology: "The confessor is cautioned to be extremely careful how he hears confessions of women, and should not hear them after dark or before twilight " Then words point to scenes which need not be described. Recently much was said because it was charged that nuns in nunneries and sisters of charity were exposed to peculiar temptations, and a leading priest said the only answer which ought to be made to such a suggestion is a *bludgeon*. Well, here is what St. Liguori says: "In hearing the confessions of spiritual women the priest is advised to be brief and rigid; neither are they to be less guarded against, on account of their being holy, for the more holy they are the more they attract. And he adds "that such persons are not aware that the devil does not at first level his poisoned arrows, but those only which touch but lightly and thereby increase the affection. Hence it happens that such persons do not conduct themselves as they did at first, like angels, but as if clothed with flesh. But, on the contrary, they mutually eye one another, and their minds are captivated with the soft and tender expressions which drop between them, and which still seem, to them, to proceed from the first fervors of their devotion; hence they soon begin to long for each other's company, and thus the spiritual devotion is turned into carnal. And, indeed, how many priests there are who before were innocent, have on account of these attractions, which began in the spirit, lost both God and their soul."

Moreover, the Saint proceeds: "The confessor ought not to be so fond of hearing the confessions of women as to be induced thereby to refuse to hear the confessions of men. O! how wretched it is to see so many confessors who spend the greater part of the day in hearing the confessions of certain religious women who are called Bizocas" (a kind of secular nuns), and when they afterwards see men or married women coming to confession overwhelmed in the cares and troubles of life, and who can hardly spare time to leave their homes or business; how wretched it is to see these confessors dismiss them, saying, 'I have something else to attend to, go to some other confessor;' hence it happens, that not finding any other confessor to whom to confess, they live during months and years without their sacraments—without God." This is one side. Let us turn to the other. One who fled from the convent as from an earthly hell, says: "Sisters go to confession every Friday to the parish priest, and every three months they make an extra confession to a Jesuit or a Passionist Father. The rite of confession affords the Fathers great freedom to accomplish the purpose they may entertain; seated in the confessional, priests are empowered to propound questions, which, from the lips of others, would be deemed flagrant insults. Kneeling before him, a sister must listen to and answer questions which fill a pure sou. with indignation, and are calculated to destroy every feeling of modesty which is the handmaid of chastity. Auricular confession in the Roman Catholic Church is the underlying element which gravitates to the priest as its center. The confessional is a spiritual court of justice; the priest is God's legate; he hears the accusation of the soul in its own condemnation; he is minister plenipotentiary to the Omnipotent. Confession produces deleterious effects upon the soul of woman, through the undue persuasion of priests working upon her sensitive scrupulosity, and the excessive intensity of her virtues. After her mental strength has been drawn to the proper point, she is irrevocably in his priestly toils. Oh, how much of this is carried on and buried in the cesspool of the confessional! Sisters are obliged to regard the voice of their confessor with as much credence as if Christ himself addressed them; therefore, no limit is placed to their confidence until they are victimized by the black-hearted betrayer."

Come back again to authorities in the Romish Church. In the "Garden of the Soul," published with the approbation of Bishop John Hughes, New York, are these words: "Those who have deflowered a virgin must pay six gros."

Rev. W. Hogan, in his book on auricular confession, makes statements so damaging to the priesthood that we do not wonder that he was excommunicated, and that the prayer, "*May he, William Hogan, be damned!*," was uttered by pope, bishop and priest. In "Dens' Theology" we find abundant evidence not only that confessors have seduced women who have confessed to them, but

that the priest is screened by priest, by bishop and by pope, and
that to a certain extent incontinence is counted on, and is treated
as a matter of course. It would be indelicate to quote at length,
or, indeed, at all; and yet, could we do so, we could show how
the priest is hedged about with protection, and how the widest
door to prostituting the virtues of his people is opened before
him. In the case of the priest in Brooklyn, now in possession of
his church, who took undue liberties with his servant girl, nothing
has been done with him, though his guilt and his drunkenness
was proven. Here is a specimen statement appearing in the papers
almost daily, and unnoticed because the guilty parties are Romish
priests:

TWO INDIGNANT PRIESTS.

"Milwaukee, Wis., Sept. 30.—A sensation was created at a
late hour last night on the arrest of Isabella Pavulski and her ad-
mirer, Antone Pavulski, an ex-priest. It appears Father Pavulski
was assistant pastor of the Polish church, five years ago, when he
became enamored of the woman, and she has been living with him
since as his housekeeper in defiance of public opinion. A child
appeared later, and Father Pavulski was deposed from his office.
He and the woman went to Father Gorski and accused him of
improper intimacy with the woman, and then to Father Gulski
and accused him of being the father of the child. They threatened exposure unless money was paid. Hence the two good
priests became indignant, and had the bad priest arrested. At the
examination which followed the woman threatened to disclose terrible secrets involving some of the well-known people of the city."

In Boston, a Protestant minister charged gross impropriety upon
a Roman Catholic functionary. He was sued for it. He proved
that his statement was based on facts, incontrovertible facts, and
this so-called representative of Romanism was covered with shame,
but he still holds his place in the church. Is a religion that tolerates such infamies good enough for any one, be they Romanists or
Protestants? Is it not possible that the truth will melt away the
fetters of superstition, and give Romanists freedom?

Dissimulation is Lawful,

according to Liguori; so is gambling. "Laymen, or even the
clergy, do not sin if they play cards, principally for the sake of
recreation, or for a moderate sum of money." Hence gambling
among the priests is extensively practiced.

Drunkenness Not a Sin.

It is lawful to administer the sacraments to drunkards, if they
are in danger of death, and had previously expressed a desire of
receiving them." Hence the murderer executed in the Tombs,
October 18th, 1883, cried for whiskey at the last, though he had
partaken of the Eucharist. He was assured of absolution by the
priest, and went to his death in almost besotted condition, and
Romanism proclaims that he is saved. Another murderer, surrounded by friends while in his coffin and in a drunken bacchanalial

called a wake—they claim to light his soul through purgatory, though death came to him in the midst of his crimes. Is such a religion worthy of the name?

Priests are known to drink to excess. One, in a country town, rode home drunk almost every Sabbath evening after performing vespers in the chapel ; all knew it, and it was tolerated because the guilty debauchee was a priest. It was Liguori who said, "*Among the priests who live in the world it is rare, and very rare, to find any that are good.*" Alexander Campbell, in his discussion with Archbishop Purcell, of Cincinnati, read from Liguori the permission for priests to keep "nieces" or concubines. Archbishop Purcell denied that Liguori ever taught anything so abominable, and that all who say so are guilty of a most flagrant violation of the commandment which says, "Thou shalt not bear false witness against thy neighbour." The book was brought in, and another read therefrom these words: "A bishop, however poor he may be, cannot appropriate to himself pecuniary fines without the license of the Apostolical See. But he ought to apply them to pious uses, which the Council of Trent has laid upon non-resident clergymen, or *upon those clergymen who keep concubines.*"

Did the placing of the Archbishop in this terrible position injure him in the estimation of Roman Catholics ? Not more than the fact that he took $4,000,000 from the pockets of the poor to build churches and convents, and died in their debt, injured him with the principalities of Rome.

Whatever hurts Rome is denied. Whatever helps Rome is affirmed. "What answer ought a confessor give when questioned concerning a truth which he knows from sacramental confession only ? *He ought to answer that he does not know it, and, if it be necessary to confirm the same with an oath.* Is it lawful then to tell a lie ? A. He is questioned as a man, and answers as a man. As a man he does not know truth, though he knows it as God."

"What if a confessor were directly asked, whether he knows it through sacramental confession." "In this case he ought to give no answer, but reject the question as impious, or he could even say absolutely not relatively to the question : 'I know nothing, because the word *I* restricts to his human knowledge." Dens, volume vi., p. 228.

Is such a religion good enough for Romanists ? We see that the Roman Catholic rule sets aside the plain and positive teachings of the Word of God, and annuls at pleasure every law and institution of Heaven. Is it strange that our jails and prisons overflow with Roman Catholics, while in strictly Roman Catholic countries thieving is a trade, and there is no safety for life or property? The teachings of God's Word are essential to the life of the world. Rome rejects them, and substitutes tradition, and proves itself unworthy of trust and confidence. Let these truths persuade Christians to redouble their diligence in carrying the gospel to Romanists, without which they will be lost.

5. *The cruelties tolerated by Romanists* make it imperative that we seek to emancipate this people from its degrading and debas-

ing methods. We are not now to bring a picture from the Spanish Inquisition but from the protectorates for orphan children, to which Americans pay their money, that the helpless may be fed and cared for. Remember that these institutions, like convents, are under the control of Romanists, and that Americans, by acts of the Legislature, have left them in the hands of Romanists, where their terrible cruelties can be practised, and from which no cry goes to the outer world. In Germany these institutions are examined by the authorities of the nation. In free America we deliver over the helpless to the merciless cruelties of soulless women dead to the feelings of motherhood and with no pity for children in their weakness and distress.

Cut a man loose from the Lord, and the devil not only gets him but uses him. Romanism has been the terror of the past. It is as merciless as ever at this hour.

St. Elizabeth's convent is delightfully situated*on the Morris & Essex Railroad, nearly midway between the stations of Madison and Morristown, and commands a beautiful view of the surrounding country. To this institution a beautiful girl goes to join the sisterhood. She left a loving home. She was tenderly reared. For a week she remained a visitor, and was treated with great kindness by the mother and the sisters. At the end of the week she was stripped of her worldly clothes and attired in the plain black dress and white muslin cap of candidates entered upon a probation of three months. It is a custom in all convents to employ freely candidates and novices in every species of labor, and the more repugnant and distasteful any kind of occupation is perceived to be to particular individuals, the more certainly are they chosen to perform it. Accordingly the candidate known to have been most delicately nurtured is chosen to perform the most menial services. Therefore she was chosen to perform the most distasteful and laborious work in the convent. The manner of the sisters changed from the sweet and gentle beings they at first seemed, to harsh, unkind, tyrannical task-masters. She says: "I was one day commanded to scrub with a brush and sand on my knees the large study hall. Great pain was the result. When the task was nearly finished, the novice mistress appeared and in a furious manner chided me for my laziness, snatched the brush from me with such violence as to tear the skin from the palms of my hands, at the same time throwing a pail of water over the hall and thereby compelling me to rescrub the floor with hands torn and bleeding. On another occasion, I was obliged to wash all the pots and kettles and scour all knives and forks in the establishment. My hands, which were naturally soft and white, began to look soiled and dirty. Having remarked in my simplicity to Sister Margaret, the housekeeper, 'Indeed sister, I am now ashamed of my hands,' she sharply retorted, 'Well then, I'll be after making you more ashamed of 'em.' Accordingly she called me to another room where a sister was whitewashing the walls, and commanded me to dip my hands into a pot of hot lime. I hesitated a moment, thinking certainly she could not mean it. However I was soon con-

---

* My authority for the facts on this and the two succeeding pages is Edith O'Gorman, the Escaped Nun, in "Convent Life Unveiled."

vinced of her earnestness by her harsh tone. 'None of yer airs now,
but do as I bid ye, or I'll tell the mother of ye.' I put my hands
down into the hot lime, and she held them there some minutes.
For several weeks my hands were in a pitiable plight. The skin
would crack and bleed at every movement, causing me to suffer
the most excruciating pains, and yet I was forced to wash and
hang out clothes in the frost and cold of December, the skin from
my bleeding hands often peeling off and adhering to the frozen
garments."

Trying one day to reach from the top of the step-ladder to the
summit of the wardrobe, her foot slipped, precipitating her to the
floor. The step-ladder was broken. Tremblingly she gathered
up the fragments and carried them to Sister Mary Joseph, at whose
feet she knelt and asked for a penance. The angelic sister replied:
" *You great, clumsy, wallowing, floundering flat-fish, it is just like
you to destroy everything you touch,* and as a penance you will put
your lazy back to work and make another pair just like them."
Working in a garden, a large earthworm flew up into her face and
made her scream. Being reported, the sister ordered that she eat
the worm. It was impossible. The sister took the worm and
crowded it into her mouth! This is not of Spain we write, but of
St. Elizabeth Convent in New Jersey.

In Paterson, N. J., is the St. Joseph's Orphan Asylum. Enter
there. It is a cold, cheerless morning. Behold the children
without fire, in January, without shoes, bare shoulders and bare
arms, crying and shivering with the cold. They rise at 6 o'clock,
hastily dress and repair to the bath room, the older orphans always
assisting the younger, because the Sisters are forbid touching them.
After they are washed and combed, they proceed to a class room
for morning prayers; then a scanty and unpalatable break-
fast, which, without any change, always consists of dry bread and
coffee without milk or sugar, made from the refuse coffee of the
Sisters' table. The orphans' table is covered with a black, greasy
oil-cloth; to each child is thrown a piece of bread, which is eaten
from the table without a plate; the coffee is served in tin cups.
They do all the work of the refectory, scrub the halls, dormitories,
class rooms, make beds, sweep, and wash dishes, &c. At half-past
eight, A. M., those who are permitted to attend school assemble in
the clothes room, where they divest themselves of their old and
tattered clothes and don the red or green plaid uniform, with
which they appear in public. At 12 M. they go to dinner, if it can
be so called, made of infected meat, thickened with the waxy
remnants of the unleavened wafer and crusts of mouldy bread,
portioned out to them in cups, from which they eat with discolored
pewter spoons. At one o'clock they again go to school, and
remain there until three, when school is dismissed. After school
the uniform is replaced by their old comfortless rags. At five
o'clock they have supper, consisting of mush and molasses, and at
times of mush and buttermilk. Sometimes a child's stomach refuses
this food. He is then whipped or starved until he is glad to eat
anything.

"The children, on the second day of my arrival were compelled by Sister Ann Joseph to run with bare feet in the snow for one half hour, and she applied the cat-o'-nine-tails vigorously on the bare shoulders of those who stopped or hesitated. When asked a reason for such conduct, the reply was, 'to make them tough and hardy,' as she did 'not believe in making hot-house plants of orphans.' Children were left until their heads were covered with vermin and with sores and scabs. For the least digression they were cruelly beaten, sometimes until the blood would flow, and all in the name of religion." *This in America.* PERHAPS IN EVERY PART OF AMERICA, and will continue so until America shall declare Romanism is not good enough for anybody, and it shall be treated as it deserves to be treated, as the mystery of iniquity which must be resisted and overthrown.

It is a foreign plant, and will not be domesticated. Space will not permit us to give the bishops, the priests, and the laymen's oaths. All bind to Rome. The Council of Trent decreed, "that the oral traditions of the Catholic Church are to be received with equal piety and reverence as the books of the Old and New Testament." Then she asserts, "It belongs to the Church to judge of the true sense and interpretations of Scripture, and that no person shall dare to interpret it in matters relating to faith and manners in any sense contrary to that which the Church has held or contrary to the unanimous consent of the fathers." Here, then, we have the essential elements of mental slavery, for if no person dare to interpret the Scriptures contrary to what the Church has already held, or to the unanimous consent of the fathers, there can be no liberty of thought, speech, or action on the most important of all subjects, our moral and religious relations, without which liberty is without meaning, and mental independence without a name.

Romanism is an Oath-bound System,

the most solemn and binding that religion can suggest or human ingenuity can devise. She governs by her bishops. They hold the property of the Church, and do with it what they will. In their oaths all say this in every part of the world, "Heretics, schismatics and rebels to our said Lord or his foresaid successors, I will to the utmost power *persecute and oppose.*"

Every Jesuit has sworn and declares that the pope is Christ's Vicar-General, and the only head of the universal Church throughout the earth, and that by virtue of the keys given him by the Saviour Jesus Christ he hath power to depose heretical kings, princes, governments and what not, all being illegal without his sacred confirmation, and that they may be safely destroyed." Because of this oath they have been banished from every kingdom of Europe as enemies of the public order, and yet they are welcomed to the United States, though all know them to be enemies to our liberties and the trained life-guards of the Papacy. Their cardinal principle is "that the end justifies the means." Their system of lax and pliant morality, justifying every vice and authorizing every atrocity, has left deep and lasting ravages on the face of the moral world, causing their cry everywhere to be,— *Extirpate Christianity.* Burned Bibles, martyr fires, the torn and mangled victims of their hate, mark their track through the centuries. The Inquisition has been their ally, and truth, for which Jesus died, their foe. Is such a doctrine good enough to be domesticated and sheltered beneath our free institutions?

Romanism is Anti-American.

Over and over again have priests declared, let Romanism gain the ascendancy in this land, and religious freedom comes to an end. Romanism is doing something with our American institutions. What will Americans do with Romanism is the question in order. The chains of error dissolve in the radiance of the cross of Christ. Preach truth, and Romanism will disappear. The Bible and the Bible only is our hope. Here there is liberty, truth, progress, sunshine. Let us make of the Bible. "In Romanism," said Chillingworth, "there are popes against popes, councils against councils, some fathers against others, the same fathers against themselves, the church of one age against the church of another age." The Bible is the same for every age. We must not add to it; we must not take from it. It is complete in itself; the voice of God to man. Let us hear and heed it. Romanism cannot be reformed. Romanists may be redeemed. The only reason why lovers of Romanism praise the liberties of America is because here they are permitted undisturbed to lay the foundations of a despotism which is the curse of Europe, whose paralyzing touch puts shackles on the limb, hatred in the heart for God's Word and those who proclaim it, and deliver over to superstitious practices a people who might have glorified God and built up man in virtue, in morality, and in the knowledge of the saving truth of revelation.

Let it be ours to cause Romanists to love America for a better reason. Here let them be taught the truth as it is in Jesus. Let them, by the constraining power of the gospel, be drawn away from image worship, Mariolatry, and the forms and usages of ancient paganism towards the better life, the ennobling thought found in the teachings and examples of our Lord Jesus Christ, and then shall they come into the freedom which truth gives, into the light which flashes from the throne, and they with all who enjoy the blessings that enrich and that add no sorrow will enter a path that grows brighter and brighter unto the time when faith shall change into fruition, and the shadow of the evening into the light of an eternal day.

GOD'S WORD AGAINST ROMANISM.

LUKE 11 : 28.

"Blessed are they that hear the Word of God and keep it."

If the Word of God is against Romanism, its doom is written, and its overthrow and extinction approach.

When the king of Babylon saw the handwriting on the wall, the king's countenance was changed, and his thoughts troubled him, so that the joints of his loins were loosed, and his knees smote one against another.

" What does it mean?" cried the king. " Bring in the astrologers, the Chaldeans, and the soothsayers." They came. And the king said to the wise men of Babylon : " Whosoever shall read this writing, and shew me the interpretation thereof, shall be clothed with scarlet, and have a chain of gold about his neck, and shall be the third ruler of the kingdom." God had spoken ; the king felt that it meant something to him and to his people. He must find out the meaning of the mystical characters. The wise men could not read the writing. This troubled the king.

The queen thought of Daniel, and he was brought forth. A man that could interpret God's Word was of value then. He is of value now. Though the words *mene, mene, tekel, upharsin,* told that God had numbered the kingdom and finished it, that the king had been weighed in the balances and found wanting, and that his kingdom was divided, he commanded that Daniel be rewarded for his exposition of the Word of God ; and so he clothed him with scarlet, and put a chain of gold about his neck, and made a proclamation concerning him, that he should be the third ruler of the kingdom.

Is it of less consequence that we study the teachings of the Word of God concerning Romanism ? We know that the Old World was destroyed by the flood, which was foretold of Noah, that Sodom and Gomorrah were burned, in accordance with the warning of the angel ; that the mightiest kingdoms have been overthrown, and the most magnificent cities have gone down before an edict of God. Nothing can withstand or successfully head against an Almighty " shall." This history declares.

The Word of God is more than a book. It is God's embattled host, always on the field, ever on the alert, ready to be wheeled into action at a moment's notice. There is no break in the line ; no weakness in the column. Death has not thinned its ranks.

Abraham, Isaac, and Jacob, though relieved from their watch here, are still doing yeoman service, though on another part of the field. They did not die. They simply passed into the visible presence of the Commander-in-Chief. The dead are with the Lord and us. The Lord is with the living and the dead. The man with the Bible enjoys the society of patriarchs, prophets, and Apostles. Paul is still with us. His voice rolls out louder, clearer than when he declared, " I am ready to preach the Gospel to you that are at Rome also, for I am not ashamed of the Gospel of Christ, for it is the power of God unto salvation to every one that believeth, to the Jew first, and also the Gentile. For therein is the righteousness of God revealed, from faith to faith, as it is written, The just shall live by faith." The words of the Apostle seem as if written for us. They are as brave, and more defiant than when he wore the chain at Rome. Peter is still here, not wearing a mitre and a cope, for he never saw such mummery, except among the Pagans, to whom he preached the Gospel. He is no longer even with the fisherman's cloak, but clothed upon with the vesture of salvation. We see him, redeemed and disenthralled, converted to Christ, and striding forth as a champion of the cross. On the day of Pentecost he so holds forth the Word of Life that thousands cast their deadly doing down, and obey gladly and eagerly the divine command.

John is here, on whose breast Jesus leaned when in the flesh ; and in the Spirit he is unchanged. The Paulicians, the Waldensians, the followers of Luther and of Calvin, the supporters of William the Silent in the Netherlands, the Puritans of England, the lovers of God in Wales, are all encamped on the green banks of deliverance, whether the believer touches this shore or that. " Blessed are they that hear the Word of God and keep it." Joseph heard it, so did Joshua, and Samuel, and David, and Daniel, and Matthew, and Mark, and Barnabas, and Cornelius, and an innumerable company, all with us now, resembling the army the prophet saw, visible to the eye of faith, as wheeling in the air, with horses and chariots and soldiers led by the great Captain of our salvation, striking blows where they are deserved, giving succor where required, and doing here and everywhere what the Lord commanded. It is a blessed truth. Our God is nigh us, even in the Word, which is in our mouth and heart—the word of faith we preach, commissioning us to say to each and every individual with whom we come in contact that " If thou shalt confess with thy mouth the Lord Jesus, and believe in thine heart that God raised Him from the dead, thou shalt be saved." The Bible is then a living fact. It is the life and support of every believer. It belonged to the first century no more than it belongs to this or will belong to the one hundred and nineteenth century, if Christ shall still keep His Church encamped on the earth, to do battle with the enemies of truth.

It is because the theory prevails that Romanism builds on the Word of God that it holds a place in the world. Mohammedanism, Mormonism, and Romanism, each and all, make much of the "Thus saith the Lord," which they do warp and bend to their purpose. Romanism claims that the Word of God is the foundation-stone of the building, to which is added the decrees of the Church and the teachings of the fathers. Here is where the battle is joined. To the true believer in Christ, the decrees of the Church of Rome and the teachings of the fathers are without authority ; their appeal is to the Bible. There stood Luther. There stand all who see in the divine revelation the standard of authority.

1. God's Word is against Romanism because it builds on Peter rather than on Christ. The Apostles heard Christ's words to Peter about " the rock" on which He was to build the Church. Not one of them ever dreamed that Peter was referred to. Paul, in his letter to the church at Rome, whose faith then was spoken of throughout the world, had no reference or allusion to the claim now made for Peter, and in the letters written there he made no mention of his being in Rome or of his having been exalted to a place of primacy among the Apostles.

Peter was equally silent on the subject, and was in his estimation no more than any other disciple, while Christ to him, after his conversion, was all and in all. The mistakes of Peter were many. They were grievous and sad. Christ rebuked him because of them. He assumed too much. He was too forward. His self-assertion offended his Master. The contrast between Christ and Peter is very great. Yonder was Christ alone. Judas had betrayed Him. The disciples had deserted Him. There He stood in the judgment hall alone, and of the people none were with Him. He was without even a friend at court. There stood Peter by the fire—not in the cold, but in the glare of comfort—warming himself. A maiden saw him, and earnestly looked upon him. There is nothing more terrible at such a time than a woman's eye. It searches through and through. Turning to some one, she said : " This man was also with Him." And he denied, saying, " Woman, I know Him not." And after a little while another saw him, and said : " Thou art also of them." Peter said : " Man, I am not." Christ was right. He is always right. What He said came true. The words of Christ always will come true. If God could have a choice on whom to build His Church, is it presumable that He would reject His Son and confer the honor upon Peter? Behold the Son of God, as, unbroken and unbent, clothed with majesty as with a garment, He stands in the presence of His enemies in such a way that He commands the admiration of His judges, and bears Himself in such a way that though the gaze of centuries has been directed toward Him, the judgment of Pilate has become the judgment of mankind, and all have been compelled to say, " I find no fault in Him."

Peter, on the other hand, despite his boasting, fled like a coward, and then, perhaps lured on by curiosity, crept into the place of trial, only that he might deny his Lord, and so in the presence of his Master, of the judges, and of the multitude, he turned traitor.

There he was, dwarfed and withered, despicable in his own esteem and utterly set aside, when his great-hearted Master looked on him in love and pity. Peter saw it as it flashed from Christ's eye beneath the crown of thorns and surrounded by the lines of agony and cruelty. That look went like an arrow to Peter's soul. It tore through all his hypocrisy, laid bare his selfishness, and revealed the man on whom the Romanists claim, Christ declared, " I will build My Church." Monstrous assumption ! Satan had sifted him. He was exposed and deposed. His soul was smitten. He yielded to conviction. He repented with weeping. He gave himself to Christ and was converted, and was coward no more.

Ever after he strengthened his brethren. None from this time was more resolute. The man who by the fire said with an oath " I know not the man," after his conversion, on the day of Pentecost, when the battle was formed, when the swirl of human opinion struck Jerusalem, when it was to be known and decided that Christ, who had been crucified and buried had risen, stood forth no longer alone and apart, but with the eleven, and raised his voice and said to them, " Ye men of Judea and all ye who inhabit Jerusalem, be this known to you, and hearken to my words, This Jesus hath God raised up, whereof we are all witnesses. Being then exalted by the right hand of God, and having received of the Father the promise of the Holy Spirit, He both poured forth that which ye see and hear. Therefore, let all know assuredly that God hath made this same Jesus whom ye have crucified both Lord and Christ." Not a word from God concerning Peter, not a word from Peter concerning himself. Not a word for a Pope ; not a thought of a Pope. All was for Christ. Every crown was cast at His feet. The people heard the Word of God and yielded to its claims. Three thousand bowed their knee to Jesus and obeyed His mandate by enrolling themselves in the army of the Lord.

Again, when it pleased God to visit the Gentiles, in the family of Cornelius, a Roman centurion, an angel sent from heaven commanded Him to send for Peter to Joppa to come, and tell him and his relations words by which himself and friends might be saved. He did so. He sent for the Apostle. Peter came. Why call for Peter ? Because Christ's gifts are without repentance. He had given him the key (Matt. 16 : 19). He therefore must open the two-leaved gate, and introduce both Jews and Gentiles into the kingdom. This being once done need not be repeated. The gates of heaven have not since been closed or locked. There is no more use for the keys. " Peter," said Alexander Campbell, " has them yet ; he took them to heaven with him ; he did not will them to any heir or successor. The Popes are fighting but shadows. Heaven never trusted such gentry with the keys. They might take it into their heads to lock the heretics out. I thank God he gave them to Peter ; that Peter opened the gates of the kingdom of heaven to us all, and that as the Popes cannot shut, we do not need them a second time. Peter will guard them till he who has the key of David, who opens and none can shut, will appear the second time."

Rome claims that Peter had not only a primacy of orders, but also a primacy of dominion ; so says Bellarmine.

As to primacy of orders, nothing is more certain than that Peter did not receive such an assignment at the hand of Christ. Christ promised that the twelve Apostles should have thrones "When the Son of Man shall sit on the throne of his glory, these shall also sit upon twelve thrones judging the twelve tribes of Israel." (Matt. 19 : 28.) In Matt. 23 : 8, it is written, "Be not ye called Rabbi (or master), for one is your Master even Christ, and all ye are brethren." There is no primacy of orders here.

As to primacy of jurisdiction, it is quite as clear, for the promise made to Peter in Matt. 16 : 19, "Whatsoever thou shalt bind on earth shall be bound in heaven," belonged not only to the Apostles, but to the Church of Christ in all ages.

The acts of God's children on earth are recognized in heaven. This is shown by the feeling that comes to an individual when received into the Church of Christ. He feels that he comes into a kingdom at the head of which is God. He inherits blessings prepared for him from before the foundation of the world.

The same is shown by what he suffers when excluded from the Church. The heavens above were as iron and the earth beneath was as brass. It seemed impossible to reach the ear of God. Descriptions have been written of the gloom and utter desolation that come to men anathematized by the Church of Rome. Descriptions as sad might be written of men and women who have been excluded from the Church of Christ. The mark is on them. The people that love God have withdrawn the right hand of fellowship. It is a terrible withdrawal. Terrible for the withholding on earth and from the portentous dread which comes from the thought that what is done on earth is ratified in heaven. The power conferred on Peter, in Matt. 16 : 19, is given to all the Apostles in Matt. 18 : 18, by Christ before His crucifixion, and to all the disciples after His resurrection, in John 20 : 23, where it is written : "Receive ye the Holy Spirit ; whose soever sins ye remit, they are remitted to them, and whose soever sins ye retain, they are retained."

The Church is built upon the foundation of the Apostles and prophets, Jesus Christ Himself being the chief corner-stone (Eph. 2 : 20). The Apostles and prophets have the same rank, the pre-eminence is given to Jesus Christ alone. It is not even true that Peter was always named first, as Romanists claim. In John 1 : 44, Andrew has the primacy. In 1 Cor. 1 : 12 Paul and Apollos precede him. In Gal. 8 : 9 James is first. In Acts 15 : 7 all spoke before Peter, and James presided at the council and pronounced the decision. In Acts 8 : 14 Peter is sent to Samaria. In Acts 11 : 2, 3 he is complained of ; and in Gal. 2 : 11 he is rebuked by Paul, for he was to be blamed.

2. God's Word is against Romanism, because it substitutes the name of Mary for Jesus Christ. The Scripture saith : "This is

the stone which was set at naught of you builders, which is
become the head of the corner. Neither is there salvation in any
other ; for there is none other name under heaven given among
men whereby we must be saved."

If ever woman had reason to say, " My spirit hath rejoiced in
God my Saviour," it was Mary, the Virgin Mother of Jesus. God
recognized her as a helper in restoring men from the ruins of sin.
Notwithstanding this, Satan seeks to use her as an ally to lead
millions away. But Christ withstood the tendency as it cropped
out at the marriage supper of Cana of Galilee, and whenever and
wherever it flamed up in His path.

What a contrast between the first and the second Adam ; the
first went all down, without remonstrance, and apparently without
a thought of what he surrendered and of what he might have retained, and yielded to Eve, who had worshipped the creature
rather than the Creator, and thus paved the way for the introduc-
tion of idolatry. She gave the devil welcome to her heart, and he
employed her to break down the kingdom of God.

The second Adam is before us. Again Satan, through a woman,
tries to turn the current of an Almighty purpose. The devil saw
Mariolatry in its true light, Christ saw it also and withstood the
tendency and trampled upon the very germ. " Woman, what
have I to do with thee?" (John 2 : 4). Suppose Christ had
wavered a hair's breadth? Suppose He had given to Mary at the
marriage feast the recognition which nature may have prompted,
and which Romanists contend belonged to her ; how the Church
would have been bound hand and foot ! It was not to be. Christ
guarded His position with sacred and prescient care. So when
He turned to His brethren, when it was said, " Thy mother and thy
brethren are without, desiring to speak with Thee," Christ, stretching out His hands to His disciples, said : " Behold my mother and
my brethren, for whosoever shall do the will of my Father who is
in heaven, the same is my brother and sister and mother ;" and
again, when the multitudes thronged Him and over the crowd went
the womanly cry, " Blessed is the womb that bare Thee and the
paps which thou hast sucked," Christ replied : " Rather blessed
are they that hear the Word of God and keep it." These three
verses are as if blended into chain-shot and hurled at this image
of Mariolatry, shattering and shivering it to atoms. At the cross
Jesus calls Mary not the " Mother of God," as Rome impiously
names her, but " Woman," and pointing to John says, " Behold
your son," and then tells John to give Mary welcome as to a
mother. Mary's name is mentioned in Acts 1 : 14, for she was
with the disciples as a worshipper of the risen Christ on the day
of Pentecost, not as the Queen of Heaven or the intermediate
between the disciples and Christ, but as a sister beloved. She
holds in the Bible a woman's place, and holds no other place. Let
us give to her and to Peter a place in our hearts. They belong to
the household of faith. Satan would gladly estrange us from
them. It must not be done. Mary is beloved and honored.
With her, God's true children will assemble before the throne and

shall worship their and her Christ with Peter and all the blood-washed throng.

This is seen in the images they wear, and in the images before which they bow. The Second Commandment is left out of their collections, and is eliminated from their faith. The devout Psalmist cried, " Not unto us, O Lord, not unto us! but unto Thy name give glory, for Thy mercy, and for Thy truth's sake. Wherefore should the heathen say, Where is now their God?" But our God is in the heavens ; He hath done whatsoever He hath pleased. Their idols are silver and gold, the work of men's hands. They that make them are like unto them. Here is the curse of idol worship. We resemble what we worship. The godlike worship the Most High ; hence their cry is, " O Israel, trust thou in the Lord ; He is their help and their shield. Ye that fear the Lord, trust in the Lord ; He is their help and their shield."

As men turned from God, Paganism came back, image worship spread. It went on until in the sixteenth century the revolt came. How it rebuked the transgression, and declared in thunder-tones, God's law against images shall be recognized ! See the iconoclasts in Antwerp. They enter the great cathedral. They fly upon the image of the Virgin. They drag it down and bear it forth to the street, stripped of its tawdry tinsel and lace. They break the images into a thousand fragments and scatter them upon the floor. A wild shout is heard. The multitude cry, " Down with images." They crowd about, armed with axes, bludgeons, and sledge-hammers ; others bring ladders, pulleys, ropes, and levers. Every statue is hurled from its niche, every picture torn from the wall, every wonderfully-painted window shivered to atoms, every ancient monument shattered, every sculptured decoration, however insensible in appearance, hurled to the ground. A colossal and magnificent group of the Saviour crucified between two thieves adorned the principal altar ; the statue of Christ is wrenched from its place with ropes and pulleys and the thieves are left as if in mockery.

A very beautiful piece of architecture decorated the choir—the repository, as it was called, in which the body of Christ was figuratively enshrined. This much-admired work rested upon a simple column, but rose arch upon arch, and pillar upon pillar, to the height of three hundred feet, till quite lost in the vault above. It was now shattered into a million pieces. And into the city went the iconoclasts, smiting every image of the Virgin, every crucifix, every sculptured saint, every Catholic symbol which they could find. " Thirty churches," says Motley, " were sacked." Monasteries were entered, and their libraries of monkish legends burned. Nunneries were swept clean, and the occupants were set at liberty. Through it all no life was sacrificed, no insults offered to priest or monk or nun, and not a farthing of the immense amount of property destroyed was appropriated. They heard God's voice, and they broke down the idols, and destroyed the altars and burnt the graven images of false gods with fire, believing that they were an abomination unto the Lord. The time is coming when Romanists shall awake from their sleep ; they shall see the glory of the Lord ; they shall break in pieces their images ; repent of their sins, and turn unto the Lord their God with a full heart. " Therefore, saith the Lord, the Lord of hosts, the mighty One of Israel. Ah, I will ease Me of Mine adversaries, and avenge Me of Mine enemies. And I will turn My hand upon thee ; and," according to pureness, " purely purge away thy dross, and take away all thy tin ; and I will restore thy judges as at the first, and thy counsellors as at the beginning ; afterward thou shalt be called the city of righteousness, the faithful city." " Zion shall be redeemed with judgment, and her converts with righteousness." (Isa. 1 : 24-27.) "And the loftiness of man shall be bowed down, and the haughtiness of men shall be made low ; and the Lord above shall be exalted in that day. In that day a man shall cast his idols of silver and his idols of gold, which they made each one for himself to worship, to the moles and to the bats ; to go unto the clefts of the rocks, and unto the tops of the ragged rocks, for fear of the Lord, and for the glory of His majesty, when He ariseth to shake terribly the earth." Why not believe in the fulfilment of this prophecy? Pagans, who were like Romanists in faith and morality, were converted in vast numbers under the preaching of the Apostles. They are being left at the present time unthought of and unprayed for. In the name of our God and of His Christ, let us rear again the old banner of the cross, and preach to them a crucified Christ, the power of God unto salvation to every one that believeth.

3. God's Word is against the worship of the host. Romanists claim that the host, under the form of bread, contains the Mediator's total and identical body, soul, and Deity. " Nothing of the bread and wine remains after consecration. All except the accidents is transformed into the Messiah, in His Godhead, with all its perfections, and in His manhood, with all its component parts, soul, body, blood, bones, flesh, nerves, muscles, veins, and sinews. Our Lord, according to this Romish claim, is not only whole in the whole, but whole in every part. The whole God and man is comprehended in every crumb of the bread, and in every drop of the wine." In reading such a horrible statement, one hardly knows whether to weep over the imbecility of his own species, or to vent his bursting indignation against the impostors who, lost to all sense of shame, obtruded this mass of contradictions on man. As Edgar, in his " Variations of Popery," truly says : " History, in all its ample folios, displays, in the deceiving and the deceived, no equal instance of assurance and credulity."

In Luke 22 : 19 we read that at the close of the Passover feast Jesus took bread, and when He had given thanks, He brake it and gave it to them, saying, " This is My body which is given for you, this do in remembrance of Me," and the cup in like manner after supper, saying, " This cup is the new covenant in My blood, even that which is poured out for you." That was all. It was a supper. Matt. 26 : 26 says, " And as they were eating, Jesus took

bread and blessed and brake it, and He gave to the disciples and
said, Take, eat, this is My body. And He took a cup and gave
thanks and gave to them, saying, Drink ye all of it, for this is
My blood of the covenant, which is shed for many unto remission
of sins. But I say unto you I shall not drink henceforth of this
fruit of the vine until that day when I drink it new with you in
My Father's kingdom. And when they had sung a hymn they
went out unto the Mount of Olives." That is the simple record.
How blessed the communion has been to the soul! In this
broken bread we behold a type of the broken body, and in this
wine we see a type of the poured-out blood shed for us, and so
with full heart we sing :

> "There is a fountain filled with blood
> Drawn from Immanuel's veins,
> And sinners, plunged beneath that flood,
> Lose all their guilty stains."

4. God's Word is against the cardinal doctrines of Romanism.
Rome says the Holy Scripture doth not contain all that is necessary to salvation. Paul, in 2 Timothy 3 : 15, says, "The Holy
Scriptures are able to make thee wise unto salvation, through
faith, which is in Christ Jesus." "The law of the Lord is perfect, converting the soul." (Ps. 19 : 7.) Rome says the Holy
Scripture is dark and obscure. The Word of God says, "The
commandment of the Lord is pure, enlightening the eyes." (Ps.
19 : 8.) "Thy word is a lamp unto my feet, a light unto my
path." (Ps. 119 : 105.)
Rome says it is not for the people to read the Holy Scriptures.
God says, "Search the Scriptures." "These are they that bear
witness of Me." (John 5 : 39.) "These words which I command
thee this day shall be in thine heart, and thou shalt teach them
diligently unto thy children." (Deut. 6 : 6, 7.) "Blessed are
they that hear the Word of God and keep it." (Luke 11 : 28.)
Rome says, "To enter a cloister, it is permitted to break the
bonds of marriage." Christ says, "What therefore God hath
joined together, let not man put asunder." (Matt. 19 : 6.)
Rome says : "The monks do well to swear to their superiors a
blind obedience."
God's Word says : "Ye are bought with a price, be not ye the
servants of men." (1 Cor. 7 : 23.) "Be ye followers of Me, even
as I also am of Christ." (1 Cor. 11 : 1.) "Whether it be right in
the sight of God to hearken unto you more than unto God, judge
ye." (Acts 4 : 19.)
Rome says : "Concupiscence is no sin." God's Word says :
"Thou shalt not covet."
Rome says that "we may satisfy the justice of God by our
sufferings." (Council of Trent.) The Word of God answers the
question : "Who are these which are arrayed in white robes?"
by saying, "These are they which came out of great tribulation,
and have washed their robes and made them white in the blood
of the Lamb." (Rev. 7 : 14.)
Rome claims "that ministers of the Gospel pardon sins, not as

ambassadors of Jesus Christ and heralds of His grace, but as judges, and by way of jurisdiction." (Council of Trent.)

In our Bible it is written : " Who can forgive sins but God alone?" (Mark 2 : 7.) " I, even I, am He that blotteth out thy transgressions for Mine own sake, and will not remember thy sins." (Isa. 43 : 25.) " It behooved Christ to suffer and to rise from the dead the third day, and that repentance and remission of sins should be preached in His name among all nations." (Luke 24 : 46.)

Purgatory is a doctrine of Romanism, which claims that our Lord Jesus hath not delivered us from all punishment that was due our sins. (Council of Trent.) God's Word says : " There is therefore now no condemnation to them which are in Christ Jesus." (Rom. 8 : 1.) " Verily, verily, I say unto you, he that heareth My Word, and believeth on Him that sent Me, hath ever-lasting life ; and shall not come into condemnation, but is passed from death unto life." (John 5 : 24.) This one passage opens the gates of hell to all who have had friends die in the faith of Christ : " Christ hath redeemed us from the curse of the law, being made a curse for us." (Gal. 3 : 13.) " Surely He hath borne our griefs and carried our sorrows. . . . He was bruised for our iniquities, the chastisement of our peace was upon Him, and with His stripes we are healed." (Isa. 53 : 4, 5.)

Rome says " that besides the blood of Jesus Christ there is a purgatory for the expiation of our sins, and that he who does not believe it, will be damned." (Bellarmine.)

God's Word says : " If we walk in the light as He is in the light, we have fellowship one with another, and the blood of Jesus Christ His Son cleanseth us from all sin." (1 John 1 : 7.) For this let us glorify God.

So we might go on and refute with Scripture, position after position taken by Rome.

Romanism is what it is because it rejects the Word of God. Bring Romanists to the light of the truth, by Bible readers, by public discussion, by private conversation, and their eyes will be opened and they shall come to the light, and with us they will walk in the light. If Romanists now living are to be saved, we must preach to them the Gospel. In this night of error they are going down the broad road to death. Pray for them, work with them, and the mists of error will roll away, and Romanists will accept the Word of God, which uproots the foundation of error and permits Christ to be the corner-stone of hope.

INDEX OF NAMES AND SUBJECTS.